T0026600

ALSO BY H. M. LONG
AND AVAILABLE FROM TITAN BOOKS

Hall of Smoke
Temple of No God
Barrow of Winter
Pillar of Ash

DARK
WATER
DAUGHTER

H. M. LONG

TITAN BOOKS

Dark Water Daughter
Print edition ISBN: 9781803362601
E-book edition ISBN: 9781803362618

Published by Titan Books
A division of Titan Publishing Group Ltd
144 Southwark Street, London SE1 0UP
www.titanbooks.com

First edition: July 2023
10 9 8 7 6 5 4

A CIP catalogue record for this title is available
from the British Library.

Printed and bound by
CPI Group (UK) Ltd, Croydon, CR0 4YY.

For Mum, who read every iteration of
Dark Water Daughter—from a child's excited
scribbles to this final, long-awaited form.

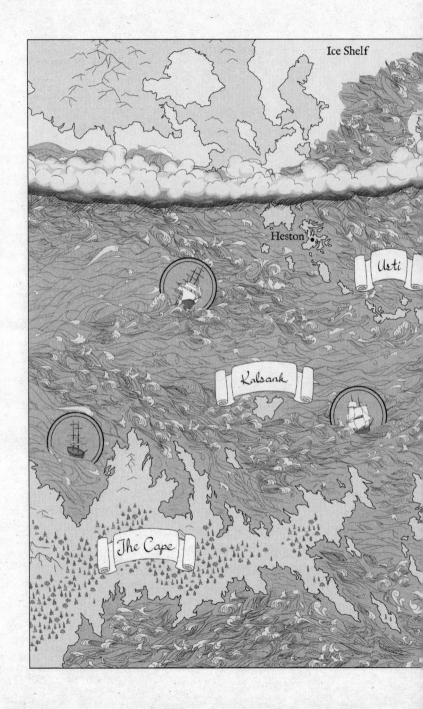

Ice Shelf

Heston

Usti

Kalsank

The Cape

Northern Mereish Isles

The Storm Wall

Aeadine

Tithe

Ghistwold

Whallum

Aeadine Anchorage

Mere

-PART ONE-

GHISTING [gih-sting]—*A non-corporeal creature from that world which is Other. Grown within Ghistwolds, they inhabit wood of various forms, and are predominantly utilized in the figureheads of ships. Once merged with the vessel, their task becomes one of maintenance and guardianship, protecting their new host from the rigors and threats of the Winter Sea. See also* STRANGERS, WOOD-WIGHT.

—FROM THE WORDBOOK ALPHABETICA: A NEW
WORDBOOK OF THE AEADINES

ONE

A Song for the Noose

MARY

The first rain I called was misty and fine, billowing down the slate hills east of the Ghistwold. It crept over the roof of the inn, the steeple of the little stone church, and the jumbled roofs and chimneys along the river. It muffled the violet-gold morning as it came, diffusing beams of sunlight into an otherworldly haze.

I remember how that rain felt, heady and sweet, bold and bracing. I remember how it collected on my cheeks and the leaves of the yew above my head.

That rain was my quickening—the moment my sorcery awoke in a lilting, child's song.

My mother found me beneath the yew, brushed dirt from my frock and took my face between her hands. Her wrists, mottled with scars, funneled my gaze into wide-set blue eyes, each iris rimmed with wisps of grey.

"Never do that again, child," she told me, her voice cool and level. Over our heads, the yew rustled, and water fell from its narrow leaves in an innocuous drip. "They'll take you away if you sing like that. Do you want to go away?"

I shook my head, unsure and unsettled. What I wanted to do was speak—I was dying to, with the wind curling in my lungs. I wanted to sing, to soothe the ache of it. But when my mother used this tone, I dared not disobey.

"Then hush." She put a work-worn thumb over my lips. Every inch of her was rugged, from her fraying brown braid to the muscles of her upper arms, taut beneath the sleeves of my father's jacket. "You don't want to end up like your mama now, do you?"

That was the day she returned to sea. The summons had come, and there was no escape. She murmured in my father's ear, kissed his cheek, and stroked my hair. Then she perched on her sea-chest, strapped to the back of a mud-splattered coach, and trundled out of sight down the long road between the Ghistwold and the slate hills. She watched me as she went, her gaze at once a farewell, a warning, and a reminder of what she had said.

She did not return. War had sparked again, a great war in a line of greater wars, and my mother's place was with the Queen's Fleet and the tens of thousands of men and women who protected Aeadine's shores. But even in her absence, I heeded her warning. I did not sing again, not in the way that might command the wind and the clouds and, some said, water itself. I did not sing again for another sixteen years.

By that time, I had already begun to follow in my mother's footsteps, footsteps that led me to the gallows and a rough hempen noose. There, my descent into depravity would soon come to a sudden, swinging stop.

"Abetha Bonning," a justice in a trim white wig and black tricorn hat declared from beside the gallows, backed by the thick stone walls of Fort Almsworth and a single, pacing redcoat.

The redcoat glanced down but continued his route, the barrel of his musket resting against his shoulder, muzzle pointing towards the sky.

"That's not my name," I mumbled under my breath, though my heart hammered so loud I could barely hear myself. My skirts and bodice were soiled with dirt, and my shift and stays soaked with sweat despite the cool autumn day. I quaked against the noose, weak and disheveled and wishing for all the world that I'd never left the Wold.

The justice began to read a list of my crimes, his breath misting before him, but I stopped listening. The chill wind whispered to me, as it always did. It whisked over the heads of the thirty or so other prisoners in the courtyard, all clad in the same spoiled garments they'd been arrested in months or years ago. Men and women, sullen and scowling, desperate and sick. Shivering children, all bones and big eyes.

I closed my eyes and leaned into the wind, even now taunted by the urge to sing. Wouldn't that be a fitting last act, to sing down the rain at my execution? Neither the infamous Navy nor murderous pirates could drag me to sea if I were dead.

Except I would not be dead. My heart clawed up into my throat. If I sang, this execution would stop. I would go back to a cell until the Navy—or someone worse—came for me, like they'd come for my mother.

There are fates worse than death, child. My mother's voice drifted through my memory. But here, staring death in the face? I wasn't so sure I believed her.

I wished I could have seen her again. I wished that, as soon as I'd been set adrift in the world five weeks ago, I'd gone to find her. I wished I'd tried, even if it was a hopeless task.

But I hadn't had the courage, or the strength. Now I would die, never knowing what happened to the woman who bore me.

"If you're not Abetha, who are you?"

It took me a moment to realize that the speaker was not the justice in the tricorn hat, but the criminal at my side. My companion in condemnation had a bag over his head but sounded young, with a refined accent to match his fine teal frock coat, buckskin breeches and high boots. To my further surprise, his clothes were clean. Except for his shoes, which were splattered with fresh mud from the trek across the courtyard.

"They let you dress for… this?" I asked, ignoring his question. My real name had fallen on deaf ears for weeks, so I saw no point in telling him. Even now the justice droned on, listing the many crimes of Abetha Bonning—who, as I stated previously, I am not. Nor were they my crimes.

At least, not all of them. Some of them were. Accidentally.

Saint, I truly was going to die today.

The other prisoner shifted his bound wrists against his coat, making silver buttons flash in the meager sunlight. "The clothes are a small grace."

"Yet you've a bag over your head."

"Yet I do. My identity is something of a liability. Come, tell me your name before we stand before the Saint and he spoils the surprise."

"I doubt we'll be standing before the Saint," I murmured. I pressed my bound fists to my stays, trying to hold my watery stomach in place. Could he hear my heart pounding? I was sure he could. "I'd think this hatch would drop us straight to Hell."

"Speak for yourself…" He left the sentence open-ended, waiting for my name. "Elizabeth?"

"Mary," I admitted, though I was not sure why I bothered. I glanced at the justice, who was now reading an extensive prayer for mercy upon the damned.

I realized the justice had not named the man at my side, nor listed his crimes.

"Good day to you, Mary," my companion said pleasantly, as if we were at a dinner party. "I am Charles."

"Good day to you, Charles." I laughed a little, a hysterical sound that was more of a choke. I blinked hard. The world felt less and less real with each passing moment. The wind was so cold—my skin pinched and muscles clenched. The other prisoners were so quiet, their despondent eyes fixed on my face.

Surely this was a dream. Surely there wasn't a noose around my neck, or a black-coated figure waiting next to the gallows with his hand on a long, iron lever.

My eyes dragged down to the hatch beneath my battered boots and Charles's buckled shoes.

"Mary," Charles repeated, hesitantly this time. Looking up, I saw his knuckles were white and knotted together in the buttons of his coat. The only other part of his skin I could see was a thin strip between bag, noose and cravat, which was flushed red with cold and anxiety. "Could you... cause a distraction?"

Suddenly terrified the guards would notice us conversing, I stared over the courtyard.

"Pardon me?" I hissed.

"I've some... small details of an escape plan. But I'm short a distraction," Charles informed me, his voice still pleasant, if tight. "You see, I've a great deal of debt, to a great many individuals in this city, including several soldiers at this fort, all of whom will lose money if I die today. Hence the bag to dispose of me anonymously. Still, word has gotten out and the soldiers have agreed to open the riverside gate if I can get myself there. I will bring you along, if you can cause a distraction."

The wind tugged strands of brown hair into my eyelashes. I drank it in, letting it open my lungs with a spark of... was that hope? No, hope had no place here.

Regardless, the wind and the spark began to form something I hadn't let myself feel since that day under the yew when I was a child. It was arresting and reckless, visceral and instinctual.

Sorcery.

"I can," I said, a little hoarsely. "But why would you take me with you?"

"Because you are not Abetha Bonning, notorious highwaywoman, murderess, and mistress of Lady Adale Debeaux. And, criminal I may be, but I cannot abide you dying in her place." Charles spoke faster now, racing the justice to the end of his prayer. "So, if you could please scream and confess to be quick with child, I would be greatly indebted."

Declaring that I was pregnant might provide a distraction and even gain me a temporary stay of execution, but the wind was inside me now, and I could do much better than that. It meant breaking my promise to my mother, risking a fate supposedly worse than the noose. But the will to live burned hot in my chest.

"Then make yourself ready." I filled my lungs, right down to the bowl of my belly, and began to sing. *"With her pistols loaded she went aboard. And by her side hung a glittering sword."*

The wind whisked the justice's papers into a suddenly stormy sky. Grey clouds billowed like an underground spring, layering and darkening with each passing second. The wind turned arctic and the prisoners scattered with startled cries, while the justice clutched his hat to his head and shouted at the stunned guards around the yard.

I barely heard Charles choke, "You're a bloody damn Storm—"

I kept singing, *"In her belt two daggers: well armed for war."*

Out of the corner of my eye, I saw the redcoat on the wall point his musket at me—just as he was joined by half a dozen other soldiers, their double-breasted uniforms blotches of scarlet against the darkening sky.

A warning bell began to ring, but I barely heard it. The frigid wind rocked me, snapping my skirts and tearing my hair loose from its knot. *"From her throat a soulless cry, 'But by my voice you all shall die, but by my voice you all shall die.'"*

Sleet hit with hurricane force, battering my face and turning to snow. Darkness came with it, thick and eerie, but I grinned a wild grin. This was power. This was what I'd been denied all these years, rushing across my skin and turning my thoughts clean and sharp.

All too soon the wind stole my breath and my song died, but it didn't matter now. The storm was here, and it raged.

A voice shouted in my ear, "With me!"

Charles. Right, it was time to run.

My hands were still bound but I grabbed the noose, jerked it over my head, and seized Charles's arm. We stumbled together towards the edge of the gallows, hunkering against the rain and potential musket balls. He leapt to the muddy ground, then his hands—miraculously free—were at my waist. I jumped.

My feet crunched into freezing mud and we bolted. Other bodies shoved past us, faceless in the chaos, but I clasped Charles's hand in mine. I would not be left behind.

A soldier snapped into sight, his red coat leached of color in the snow and the shadow of the courtyard wall. I cried out, staggering like a newborn colt in mud, but the soldier only fell into stride and waved at one of his comrades, who opened a hefty outer door.

Mud turned to cobblestones. We barely slipped through the door before it slammed shut again. A cacophony of echoes harried us through a stone passageway, our footsteps and ragged breaths filling the empty space.

Charles hit another door with a grunt. It held and I panicked, terrified that it was locked, that soldiers would come, muskets would fire and—

The door crashed open. Charles ducked through and the storm swallowed us again with whirls of wind and sleet.

A stone quay lined the fort here, with the river and the outskirts of the port city of Whallum beyond. Four squat, fully enclosed riverboats rocked at their moorings, one with a lantern lit, two dozen oars pointed skyward and an open door. Charles sprinted towards it and I followed.

Right before we reached the boat, Charles shouted through the tempest, "You can keep running, or come with me!"

My skirts stuck to my legs, threatening to trip me with every step, and cold crept into my bones. I clenched chattering teeth and squinted at him. "What?"

He turned to me. "I cannot promise you will be safe in that boat!" I could barely see his unfamiliar face in the storm, even inches away from my own. But I heard the tension in his voice.

I turned my gaze to the boat, then past it. A path laced away around the fort walls, slick with mud, slush, and rivulets of water. I could take it, but I'd no idea where it went. I also had no idea what lay inside that boat, except the morally dubious people to whom Charles, a stranger, was indebted to.

Lightning flashed. I glimpsed Charles clearly for the first time, disheveled blond hair plastered across the large, almost feminine eyes of a man in his mid-twenties, with soft cheeks and a smooth jawline. Not an unappealing face, but one far too gentle for a criminal. Fine snowflakes whisked behind him and snagged in his hair.

The temperature dropped with each passing moment. By now, everyone in the city would know there was a weather witch on the loose.

"Mary! Answer me!" Charles shouted. "We haven't much time!"

I could have run. I should have run. But before I knew it, my choice was gone.

Two men lurched out of the boat's hatch and dragged us inside.

STORMSINGER—*An individual, most commonly a woman, who can control the wind and weather with her voice. A Stormsingers' Guild was founded in 1221 and abolished in 1693 by Queen Maud II after the loss of the Aeadine Anchorage in the War of Unhallowed Saints, a naval conflict in which the Stormsingers refused to participate. Sentenced to indentured servitude for treason to the Crown, all members of the guild were officially absorbed into Her Majesty's Royal Navy, though many subsequently fell victim to villainy. See also* WEATHER WITCH, WEATHER MAGE, WINDWIFE.

—*FROM* THE WORDBOOK ALPHABETICA: A NEW WORDBOOK OF THE AEADINES

TWO

Her Mother's Name

MARY

Charles's protests grew suddenly loud as we toppled into the riverboat's belly. I hit the deck hard and glimpsed rows of trousers, shoes and benches before Charles staggered after me.

He grabbed an overhead beam just before he tripped over my legs. I scrambled back with my hands still bound, wiping wet hair from my eyes and fumbling to fix my skirts. The men on the bench nearest to me, two of them with one long oar between them, watched without a word.

I found my feet and braced myself on a stack of crates. At the same time, a bull of a man flung Charles into the bulkhead with a casual palm to the chest. He followed this with a single-handed choke, lifting my companion until the toes of his wet, finely buckled shoes tapped frantically on the deck.

"Charles Grant," the man growled. He had the complexion of most southern Aeadines, milky-pale skin prone to redness at the slightest variance in mood or temperature—particularly anger. And he was, at this moment, very, very red. "Now it's triple due, and another two for the girl, whoever the hell she is."

The riverboat began to move, propelled by the wordless oarsmen. Wood groaned, oars ground in their cradles, and someone near the front began to call time above the howl of the storm. Beneath us, the rocking of the deck steadied somewhat.

"It doesn't matter who the girl is," another voice drawled. "All that matters is that you pay me."

A more reasonably proportioned man with black hair and a bladed nose stood nearby, pipe in one hand and his coat open to reveal a knife and two flintlock pistols. A pair of oil lanterns swung from the ceiling, casting him in oscillating, orange light. Combined with the rhythm of the oars, the misting of breaths and the backdrop of the storm, the scene took on a hypnotic quality.

I shifted farther into the crates, dripping as I went. I was afraid—quite properly afraid—but fear was a part of me now. It had been since the day I left the Wold, disgraced and alone. It knotted in my chest as I studied the men and cursed myself for not taking my chances on the path. As soon as the boat docked, I would run.

Charles's heels dropped back to the deck as the brute loosened his grip, just enough for the younger man to wheeze, "I can. I can pay, Kaspin. I've a stash, in the Lesterwold—"

Kaspin, the smaller man, raised his brows and tapped the bit of his pipe to his chin. "The one in the pilgrim's shrine to Pious Leonardus?"

Shock emptied Charles's face.

That seemed like a bad sign. Surreptitiously, I tugged at my bindings. They were still as tight as they'd been when the soldiers dragged me to the gallows. Whatever Grant had used to free his own bindings, he hadn't used it on me. Perhaps he'd lost it in the chaos. Perhaps...

An unwelcome premonition prickled across my skin.

"Well." Kaspin puffed out a breath. "That *is* unfortunate. Your stash has been found and confiscated by the Crown to fund the war effort. Quite publicly. Don't tell me that's all you have?"

Charles's eyes flicked from me to Kaspin, then to the man whose hand still rested around his throat like a meaty collar.

"Of course not," Charles bluffed, badly. "There's always more."

"More already in your possession?" Kaspin inquired. He sauntered closer, free hand fiddling with the knife at his belt. A curved thing, it screamed *gutting*. It was well-made too, as was his silver-buttoned, knee-length coat. Whoever Kaspin was, he had money. "I haven't time to wait for you to steal it. The Queen's Guns are hunting your kind like dogs."

The Queen's Guns. Yes, I knew for a fact that the Queen's Guns were currently hunting brigands in the Lesterwold, because they had arrested me there two weeks ago. Kaspin was implying that Charles was a highwayman, like I was supposed to be. Not just a gambler, then, down on his luck. A proper criminal.

I shifted my wrists again in my bindings, but they still didn't budge.

Waiting for Charles's reply, Kaspin slowly drew on his pipe and exhaled a stream of smoke.

Charles stared at him, unable or unwilling to answer.

"Because if you do not have the money," Kaspin continued, "I will open your throat right now and take your head back to the fort tomorrow. There will be a reward, no doubt, and that will alleviate my losses. Speck, did you bring a saw?"

"Just a hatchet," his bruiser replied. "Bit blunt. Sorry, boss."

Kaspin frowned, but nodded. "All right, go fetch it."

"Saint's blood—I can pay!" Charles shouted, cutting through the rhythm of the oars, the shush of sleet on the roof and the slamming of my heart. His frantic eyes fixed on Kaspin and my dread redoubled.

Charles would not look at me. That tilt of the chin, the tension in his shoulders—it was the same way my father had held himself when his new wife bundled me onto a coach with nothing but a satchel and the clothes on my back.

I was right. Unfortunately.

"The woman is your payment," Charles Grant said. "Enough for all my debts."

Speck and Kaspin both looked my way, and even some of the nearby oarsmen cast a sideways glance.

I, for my part, could only stare at Charles. Betrayal gouged through me, irrational though it was. I'd known this man for mere moments, but we'd faced death together. I'd saved his life. He'd saved mine. And now...

"Her?" Kaspin repeated. "She's not even pretty, man."

From the way the big man Speck considered me, he disagreed with Kaspin on that point; I wanted to crawl out of my skin.

"She is a Stormsinger." Charles delivered me into servitude without falter. "A powerful one too. She called up this storm herself, Kaspin."

Kaspin considered me fully. He advanced, head tilting in consideration, pipe smoldering. "A Stormsinger. Is that right, woman?"

I raked in a breath, willing time to slow so I could order my thoughts. But all I could think of were my mother's scarred wrists and her warning blue eyes.

Six years in chains, that's what these are, love, my mother's voice said. *Chained to a bulkhead. Chained to a mast. I sung fleets into battle. Sung good men and women to the bottom of the sea. That, Mary, is a fate worse than death.*

Now I faced the same fate, wrists scraped raw by rough rope, surrounded by strangers in the swinging lantern light. What if she *was* right? I would be passed from crew to crew, each more disreputable than the next. Furthermore, with the war still raging across the Winter Sea, I might end up in the hands of the Mereish or the Cape. I might be used against my own countryfolk, perhaps even my mother, if she still lived and sailed somewhere out there.

But was that a fate worse than death? I'd looked death in the eyes today, felt her noose around my neck, and I couldn't bear to face her again. Not tonight. My will to live still burned, hot and ready to blaze.

As a Stormsinger, I had value. I'd be kept alive. I'd suffer, but I'd live. And while I lived, I could escape—I couldn't say what I'd escape to, not yet, but that would come.

I met Kaspin's eyes and thought of my mother, of her strength and the hard line of her jaw. And so, I gave them her name instead of my father's, together with all its promises and destiny.

"Yes," I said. "My name is Mary Firth, and I am a Stormsinger."

SOOTH—*Being a mage with an unnatural ability to conjure visions and trespass into the Other, whether by striding the border between worlds, where future, past, and present can be glimpsed, or by sinking fully into that other realm, where they may sight and track the souls of other, unwary mages. See also* SEER, EDGE-WALKER, MEREISH SUMMONER.

—*FROM* THE WORDBOOK ALPHABETICA: A NEW
WORDBOOK OF THE AEADINES

THREE

The Fourth Man

SAMUEL

"This is despicable and I will have no part of it." I glared out of the windows at the back of the great cabin. Through their frost-latticed glass, Whallum's assemblage of narrow houses, shops and warehouses leaned on one another like drunkards, capped with snow and skirted by sailors, dockworkers, hawkers and townsfolk. More snow dusted from the sky, early even for this corner of the Winter Sea, summoned by the meddling of the very woman I now found myself defending. "We cannot bring a Stormsinger aboard. Not like this. Not against her will. We should wait for a proper indenture from the Crown."

"An indenture will never come, Mr. Rosser." Captain Slader laid down the pistol he had been polishing and took up its pair. A retired naval captain and as shrewd as they came, he was small-eyed and bore the disposition of an aged cat.

He picked up a turnscrew, removed the pistol's lock and handed the rest of the weapon to Ms. Helena Fisher: ship's master, first officer, and my rival. "We're privateers—hardly priority."

"I will have no part," I repeated.

Fisher gave a soft snort. She cocked one eyebrow, fine and black against light brown skin, and fit a swath of flax wool to the end of a ramrod. Vulpine to Slader's feline, she had keen brown eyes and an artist's fine fingers.

Twisting the wool into place, she commented, "There is no chance of capturing Lirr without a Stormsinger. Surely you understand how these things work."

I kept my gaze flat. Fisher was not wrong. Silvanus Lirr, pirate, warlord, and our sole commission, had a weather mage aboard. Without one ourselves, we risked the Winter Sea battering our ship to pieces in the pursuit, or Lirr's mage sinking us with an ensorcelled wind. We would be handing him every advantage, and our chances of catching him would be slim.

But it was not impossible.

Captain Slader began to clean the pistol's lock with a cloth. "Ms. Fisher is correct. This auction is an unsavory business, I agree. But this Charles Grant fellow seemed respectable enough. I assume the woman will be well treated."

I stared at him in indignation. "Well treated? You know how they find singers, sir, and what they do to them if they are not powerful enough."

"We need the witch." Fisher dampened the flax. She emphasized her next words by plunging the rod down the barrel of the pistol. "If our methods are so distasteful, perhaps you should return to the Navy, *Lieutenant*."

Slader measured my response as he smeared tallow and beeswax about the mechanism. A beat of silence stretched as both he and Fisher waited for me to erupt, but I took my anger in an iron fist, focusing on the sounds of snow shushing off the window and the cleaning of dismembered pistols. The scent of old gunpower, fat and wax soured my nose.

Disappointed by her failure to provoke me, Fisher removed the blackened flax and spun on a new portion to dry the barrel.

"If the auction is our only option, I will go," I grudgingly conceded.

"Good." Slader glanced over the newly oiled lock and set it aside. "But for now, you are dismissed, Ms. Fisher. Mr. Rosser, stay here."

Fisher looked as though she wanted to protest but relinquished the pistol and rod to Slader. Then, burgundy hem of her frock coat brushing the doorframe in an elegant swirl, she left the cabin.

The door closed and the captain looked me over, from the buckles of my worn black shoes to my neatly tied hair, now disheveled by an agitated hand. "I've said it before, but I shall say it again, Mr. Rosser. Your past will never leave you, nor will those like Fisher. You must reconcile yourself to your circumstances, or you'll lose your place on this vessel. As you did on your last."

I forced my gaze out the stern windows again, and nodded.

"As to this Stormsinger," Slader said as he began to reassemble the flintlock, "I understand your principles. I know you want to redeem yourself in the eyes of the world, and bringing down Lirr is certainly a good opportunity to do that. But we need the Stormsinger to succeed. She will be much happier in our company than others, in any case. Or would you rather she's taken on by pirates? Saint, there are captains of the Fleet with less scruples than you or I. You know that as well as I do. Now, you've three thousand solems to bid—use them well."

The last of my anger wavered, then released into weary resignation. This was the way of the world, the nature of life on the Winter Sea.

One day I would rise above it. One day I would scrape the mud from my name and face my family without shame. But for now, I would do Slader's bidding.

"I will, sir."

∞

Fisher waited for me on the snowy dock as I descended the gangplank, her hands shoved deep into the pockets of her coat and her tricorn hat already christened with snow. She gave me a prompting look and started walking before I had stepped onto the dock.

I, in turn, made no effort to catch up. Instead, I popped the collar of my coat and fastened the top button as I glanced back at *Hart*. He was a solid vessel, his forty-two guns quiet behind their white-painted hatches, three masts standing tall with each sail neatly furled. Formerly a fifth-rate Aeadine warship, he had been decommissioned and sold to Slader some twenty years ago after single-handedly sinking three Mereish sloops. *Hart* had barely survived the encounter, worth little more than the ghisting who inhabited his figurehead.

During the ship's restoration, Slader had removed many of the hallmarks of Aeadine warships, including the decorative paint that once adorned the circumference of his quarterdeck—blue or red or white, depending on the fleet, with quotes from the Saint in illegible gilt letters. All that remained now were *Hart*'s black hull, white hatches, and the figurehead.

The great hart for which the ship was named reared up beneath the bowsprit, head thrown back in a soundless bay. His coat was painted a muted red-brown, while his white antlers enclosed the entire beakhead, ghistenwood twining together with lesser, standard material.

"Are you well, Mr. Rosser?" Fisher called back to me.

I looked away from the ship and lengthened my strides to catch up. "Do not pretend you care, Fisher."

"And you wonder why we're not friends." She *tsk*ed, dropping down onto the quayside, both heels landing at once. "Really, Sam."

"I have never wondered that."

"Not once?"

"Not at all."

I joined her and we left *Hart* behind, weaving through stacks of goods to the main street. Scents of cooking food and hot mulled wine wafted from taverns, where locals mingled with sailors and travelers under smoke-heavy beams. Music wafted from windows too, strings and drums and fifes, as I followed Fisher through the premature winter.

Cold nipped at my skin. I shoved my hands into my pockets, where my fingers brushed across the smooth, long face of an oval coin. I fingered it, letting its worn surface steady me. A soft hum, ever present at the back of my mind, quietened.

Our destination was a tall inn, some distance down the docks. The Bell and Barrow was one of the better establishments in Whallum, its plaster intact and painted a pleasant, sea-foam green. Cream moldings surrounded each window and separated its four levels, depicting various aspects of port life—eccentric hawkers, ships, fish, farewelling lovers.

The inn wife opened the front door, her wispy grey hair tucked under a neat cap, and she gestured us up to the second floor.

At the top of the stairs, Fisher and I found ourselves facing an open door. Beyond was a private room, graced by a roaring hearth, a table for six, and two windows looking out over the harbor.

"Lieutenants Fisher and Rosser." A slim man with black hair and small teeth gestured us into the room. "I am Kaspin. Come in, please."

I slowed my steps, letting Fisher, the senior officer, lead. She shook Kaspin's hand, delivering pleasantries as I eyed our host.

Kaspin was one of Whallum's most powerful criminal lords. Any pirate docking in port, any highwayman worth their powder or madam who wanted to keep her whores knew Kaspin, paid homage to him, and respected him well.

I despised him. But pirate hunters were not much higher than pirates in the eyes of the world, and so Captain Slader—and myself— came to the sharp-eyed bastard like everyone else.

There were four others gathered in the room, aside from Kaspin. One was a wiry fellow with an exaggerated grey wig, sitting with his back to the roaring hearth. He peered at me in open hostility over pinched, flushed cheeks—a native of Whallum if I ever saw one. The second was Whallish, too, and obviously Kaspin's muscle, a man built for pulling plows and wrestling bears. He stood next to a young woman in a chair, and I knew without asking that she was the Stormsinger we had come for.

The young woman's clothes were worn, with skirts that might once have been yellow and white calico half covered by a long, men's coat. Her dark brown hair was bound up under a white cap and what I could see of her face was pretty. The rest was locked into a device commonly used upon Stormsingers, a mask that contained the jaw and covered half her face.

My gut twisted, and I looked away. No, not a mask. A gag. A Stormsinger's power was her voice, and without it? She was just a battered young woman with hollowed, wrathful eyes.

I felt those eyes on me as I examined the last man. He was familiar, though it took me a moment to place him. He stood next to the door in a knee-length coat of rich plum, open to show a pistol and a cutlass. His hands were latticed with scars and he wore his sun-bleached brown hair in a short tail. He had no beard and his eyes were somewhere between grey and green, his skin the same mild brown as Fisher's, meaning he doubtless hailed from the islets off the northern coast—descended from the conquerors who'd once swept Aeadine with worship of the Saint, and sent the local ghisting-worshiping pagans, like my own ancestors, skittering into the forests and to the southern shores.

His smile, when he spotted me, was calm. We did not know one another personally, but I supposed he had been a pirate long enough to recognize a Navy man when he saw one. Disgraced or not.

I had seen his likeness on enough bulletins to know him too.

"What are you doing in port?" I asked notorious pirate James Elijah Demery. I moved to stand next to him while Fisher took a seat at the table and greeted the other guests on our behalf. Fisher might taunt me when we were aboard ship, but in situations like this she was all professionalism and reserve.

James Demery mimicked my posture, clasping one wrist at the

small of his back. His voice was low and pleasant as he intoned, "The same reason as you, I'd imagine."

He did not look at the Stormsinger as he spoke. Instead, he glanced at the open door.

The hum at the back of my mind, the one that had haunted me on the street, coalesced into a presentient whisper. There was more to this moment, to this man, than met the eye. He was no mage, not that anyone knew, but he had been in business for decades. No pirate lived so long without gathering rumors and lore, usually from terrified victims—daring battles and escapes under mysterious circumstances, powerful connections and a cool, calculating demeanor.

The hairs on the back of my neck stood on end, but I kept my shoulders level. As companionable as he seemed, Demery could be a very dangerous man.

"We're waiting on one more guest," Kaspin said, filling a glass with whiskey and passing it to his brutish companion, who drank half in a shallow, savory sip, then downed the rest.

There were more glasses set out for Demery and me at empty chairs, but neither of us took them. I eyed the pirate askance, trying to suss out what it was about him and this meeting that had so unsettled me, beyond his reputation.

Demery caught my eye again. "Not long now," the pirate murmured. "I do hope your armsmen are nearby."

My tongue felt suddenly dry. Armsmen? Why would I have brought armsmen? Unless Demery was expecting conflict—but conflict connected to him, the results of this meeting, or the last guest?

The whisper at the back of my mind turned to a hiss, and with it came a dreamer's rootless certainty. The feeling was a familiar one, as common to me as anger or sadness, and it took all my strength to resist reaching into my pocket for the worn old coin.

Stuffing my wits into a façade of self-possessed impatience, I gave Demery a thin smile and asked Kaspin, "I trust we will not be waiting long?"

Kaspin shook his head and glanced at a ticking clock on the mantle. "I doubt so."

Accepting this with a nod, I stepped forward and tapped Fisher's shoulder. She shot me a censorious glance, but paused when she saw my expression.

She rose and we moved to the door.

"Something is not right. We need to warn Slader," I murmured. There was no use pretending that our conversation was not conspiratorial—everyone in the room watched us, even the Stormsinger over her gag. "That man is James Elijah Demery."

"Is he a mage?" Fisher pointedly did not look at the man. "Is he conspiring?"

I shook my head. "Not a mage—not that I have sensed. But he did imply we ought to be better armed and there is something disquieting about this last guest."

"Then go." Fisher nodded to the door. "Right away."

"You ought to," I returned. "Let me stay here."

"I am the senior officer," Fisher reminded me coolly.

"Of course," I acknowledged with a nod. "But I am the Sooth."

Fisher's expression stilled, and for a heartbeat I thought she would overrule me. Then she nodded and said, loud enough for our eavesdroppers to 'accidentally' hear, "Fine, how much more?"

Relief trickled down my spine. She had been convinced, and had the wit to cover our tracks. Fisher did have her moments.

"As much as the captain will give us," I answered with equal faux subtlety.

Fisher looked at Kaspin and produced a polite smile. "Pardon me for a few moments," she said, bowed and left the room.

Kaspin looked pleased. He exchanged a highbrowed look with his muscled companion and raised his glass to us. "To a lively auction," he said.

Five minutes crawled past. Demery sat in a chair and lit a pipe, tilting his head back to watch the smoke rise as he made conversation with Kaspin and the wiry man, called Randalf, about mundane port business.

I sat next to Demery and half listened, alert for any hints of who the last guest might be. The rest of my focus oscillated between the stairs and the Stormsinger, who stared out the window with a dull gaze.

That was, until Kaspin's bodyguard patted her cheek on his way to the window, and her leg lashed out in a sharp, straight kick to his knee.

The big man went down like a sack of grain, if a sack of grain could be bearded and issue obscenities—first in a croak, then a shout, then a roar. The captive snarled something defiantly after him, her words completely distorted by the gagging device.

A laugh lodged in my throat, chased by dread. The man unfurled back to his full height, glaring at the Stormsinger in a way that made me reach for my cutlass.

Demery looked blithely at Kaspin and raised his brows.

"Mr. Speck," Kaspin warned.

Mr. Speck's jaw worked, his head twisted to one side and his fists clenched in fury. He grabbed the nearest chair with a scrape and clatter and situated it next to the window, making himself the closest to the Stormsinger.

"The moment she makes a move," he growled, rubbing his knee with a huge hand.

"You'll carefully ensure she sits back down?" Demery offered.

"What do you care? You're a pirate," the wigged man, Randalf, suddenly accused.

Demery's eyes tracked to him, still amiable. If being outed so publicly perturbed him, he did not show it. One did not go to Whallum without expecting to brush elbows with criminals of all distinctions.

"I've been called as much, yes," he affirmed.

"He's seventh on Her Majesty's contract list," I heard myself commenting. My hand was still on my cutlass, but I loosened my grip, palming it absently.

The Stormsinger noticed my movement and considered me for a narrow second, then looked at Demery.

"Pray, seventh?" The pirate frowned. "Last I heard I was fifth."

"You've lost your touch, old man." Randalf chuckled. "There's a pirate *hunter* in this room, but has he interest in you? No."

I shot him a look. How did he know what I was?

Reading my expression, Randalf flapped a dismissive hand at me. "I've eyes in my skull, boy. I can see *Hart* in the harbor, same as everyone else."

"I've not lost my touch. Rather, I've been preoccupied," Demery said in a way that made my dreamer's sense prickle. "It's hard to steal enough tobacco and molasses to stay on the Queen's List, even in peacetime. Besides, any position higher than four and there's already a noose strung for you at Fort Almsworth. Hardly something I aspire to."

The Stormsinger flinched at that, and my curiosity strayed back towards her. Her eyes met mine, still edged with the anger that she had unleashed on Mr. Speck. They were the deep grey of summer storms, infiltrated with shocks of equally dark blue. The combination was odd, but even odder on a Stormsinger. Her kind usually had pale blue eyes, many to the point that they were blind.

Or, in the worst cases, intentionally blinded in an ill-informed attempt to increase a singer's power. It rarely worked and occasionally had the opposite effect, but that did not dissuade avaricious slavers from the attempt.

Gooseflesh prickled up my arms.

Demery's voice pulled me back to the rest of the room. "At least Mr. Rosser knew me on sight, did he not?"

I tore my eyes from the young woman's and gave him a nod. "Yes, sir."

"Good." Demery looked back at Randalf. "You, you're a smuggler?"

He pursed his lips. "A merchant. *Juliette* is my ship."

Demery leaned back in his chair and stacked his heels under the table. "Oh?"

Randalf rolled his eyes. "Merchant and occasional purveyor of tax-free goods."

The Stormsinger looked between the two of them, her eyes losing even more of their light. Had she just realized how bleak her options were?

The sight made my guilt triple. I could not drag this woman aboard *Hart*. I had been a fool to agree to this errand, a fool to think there was any world where I could stomach exchanging money for another's freedom, let alone dragging a village girl—which, from her clothes and manner, she certainly was—onto a warship with a contract as dangerous as ours.

Everyone looked up as footsteps sounded on the stairs. Demery's hand drifted beneath his coat and every muscle in my body went taut. Silently, I prayed Fisher and the armsmen were not far off.

I leaned back slightly in my chair, angling myself so I could see the top of the stairs.

A young gentleman came into sight, his blond hair swept back into a fine red ribbon and his cheeks flushed with cold. There was more than a little snow on his clothes, and he brushed it off as he topped the stairs and came through the door.

"He is not coming," Charles Grant, the man who had brought us our invitation to Kaspin's auction, announced. He took an unclaimed glass of whiskey from the table and retreated to a corner, close to the fire but far from the light of the window.

Irritation flickered across Kaspin's face. "Not coming at all? Or is there another day he'd prefer?"

"He is not coming." Grant nursed the whiskey, the cup brushing his bottom lip and distorting his voice as he added, "He was also very rude."

"Well, then." Kaspin was clearly put out, but rallied. "Let's introduce our witch."

I stole a quick look at Demery as Kaspin removed the Stormsinger's gag. The pirate's expression was inscrutable except for a few lines around his eyes—not irritation or disappointment. Perhaps... preoccupation.

The gag came off and the Stormsinger coughed. Kaspin stepped back, proceeding to load a pistol as he said, "This is Mary. Mary, sing for us, something... subtle." He cocked the pistol and pointed it at her head. "A simple demonstration will suffice."

Half the woman's face was rubbed red from the gag. She noted the muzzle of the pistol then surveyed the room, taking in each one of us in a way that made me overly aware of how I must appear, here among criminals. As if I were one of them.

There was fear beneath her resentment, and I reminded myself what Slader had said. She would be safest with us. Demery was a pirate. Randalf was just a smuggler, but from the way he leered, his company would be little better.

"*One for sorrow, two for mirth*," Mary began to sing. Her voice was low and soft, not forceful, but cajoling. Outside the windows, the wind snuffed like a candle, and the falling snow became impossibly still. Beyond it the sun flashed through the clouds and bold, iridescent beams struck the water between snow-dusted ships.

Awe washed through me. Her voice did not just still the wind. It stilled my dreamer's sense and left me feeling unexpectedly... whole. Awake and grounded in a way I had not felt for many years.

Logic told me this was simply my imagination, but for now, I ignored that cynical voice. I watched white flakes drift, caught outside of time, and let myself be captured too.

The Stormsinger sang, "*Three for a death, and four for birth*."

Kaspin looked around with obvious satisfaction as Mary's voice faded and Mr. Speck refitted her gag. The wind picked back up and the sun disappeared, but there was no doubt as to her power.

And I? An irrational yearning wove through my ribs, smothering my breath as surely as Mary had smothered the wind outside. I wanted, more than anything, to hear her voice again. To see the sun break through the clouds and the snowflakes drift to her unnatural song. That power. That peace—imagined, or real.

Kaspin's voice broke the silence. "Mr. Rosser, need we wait for your companion to begin?"

"Begin?" I repeated, still disoriented. "No, no."

Kaspin eyed me, then ducked his chin. "Then let's open with one thousand five hundred solems."

"Five hundred," Randalf said, turning up his nose. "She strikes me as untrained. Stilling a breeze and calling a storm are one thing. *Dispersing* a storm and maintaining a fair wind for a voyage? Those are another."

Kaspin looked to Demery.

The pirate laced his arms loosely over his chest. "One thousand five hundred," he affirmed.

Now, Kaspin turned his eyes to me.

My throat felt thick, the number poisonous on my tongue. I forced myself to look at Randalf again, at Speck and Kaspin and Demery, and reminded myself again that the singer would be better off with us.

That was not my only motivation, though. That voice. That song, and the way it had affected me. I wanted to help her. I needed to—even if my only means was contemptible.

"My captain is prepared to offer two thousand," I said.

"I'll raise to two thousand five hundred," Demery countered calmly.

Silence overtook the table. Randalf sucked at his teeth, obviously unhappy with the price. Kaspin refilled his cup with a soft clink and sat back, expectant.

As to Mary herself, she paled even more. She blinked hard and her face locked into an expressionless façade.

Demery noticed. "You'll be well treated on my vessel, Mary. I run a clean ship, no drinking, no fighting, no gambling. A cabin of your own."

"Puritan pirates," Grant muttered from his gloomy corner, though I could not say if anyone else heard him. "Laud them."

"The witch isn't here to be wooed," Kaspin said. "Three thousand, anyone?"

"Four thousand," Randalf burst out, spitting the words as if they were broken teeth. "Four thousand bedamned solems."

My heart hit the floor beneath my boots. Kaspin's hand froze on his cup and Demery slowly twisted to regard the smuggler.

"What exactly, Mr. Randalf, do you smuggle?" the pirate asked. His tone was benign, but I saw the frustration behind his eyes. My guess? He could not afford to outbid that.

I could not, either. I fingered the worn coin in my pocket to calm myself, running the numbers in my head. Slader could not pay more than three thousand. One could buy an entire ship for four thousand solem weight.

"I deal in pineapples, for the most part," Randalf said, still looking disgusted, but our shock had soothed him. A touch of arrogance tugged at the corner of his mouth. "You wouldn't believe what the rich sots on Jurry will pay to carry around a pineapple at their parties, or just how fond Her Majesty is of pineapple syrup in the mornings. But they do not keep, which is why I need a weather witch, and my last one drowned herself. Fair winds, fresh cargo, good business."

The Stormsinger stared at him in abject horror. I felt much the same.

Kaspin chuckled. His cheeks warmed now, greed and glee glinting in his eyes. "Well, well. Demery? Rosser? Any final offers?"

Demery emptied his cup and set it down with a hollow thunk. His expression was contained, but there was a glimmer of murder in the way he looked at Randalf. "No, sir."

My dreamer's sense roared, and this time there was no stopping it. It buffeted and pulled at me, threatening to drag me out of the room entirely and into that Other place—the one where dreams walked, ghisten spirits ruled, and my soul was irreparably tethered.

I saw the Stormsinger's face in a winter wold of ice and snow, windburned and desperate. Then she was not one, but two—her living, breathing human image mirrored in spectral shadow.

I grasped the worn coin in my pocket so tightly that my palm nearly split and the embossing on its face, three serpents biting one another's tails, stamped into my skin. The roar dampened to a hushed moan, then faded altogether.

Relief coursed through me, though it was a sour thing. I had just glimpsed the Stormsinger's future, and whatever it meant, I could not change it.

"Any more offers?" Kaspin prompted again, looking to me. When no one spoke, he leaned over to top up Randalf's cup with a soft clink and a stream of amber liquor. The deal was done.

I stood up with a scrape of my chair and started for the door, ripping my eyes off the Stormsinger. I had lost her, and that bothered me more than anticipated. Empathy, guilt, and a touch of longing coiled through my chest. But none of it mattered. I could not change what happened in this room, any more than I could change my own past.

"Mr. Rosser," Kaspin called, "I do have other assets which might interest your captain. Perhaps you would stay and take a drink with me?"

"I will be going," I replied with a tight smile. My eyes alighted one last time on James Demery, who watched me with an inscrutable expression, and my dreamer's sense coiled again. I ignored it. "Good day to you all."

With that, I left. And I did not look back.

The Girl from the Wold

The girl from the village between the Wold and the slate hills knows that the ghisten trees have souls. She has grown up in their shade, and sees them for more than their twisted, gnarled trunks and spreading canopies, which refuse to bow to the seasons as normal wolds do. She has marked the way their shadows sometimes stretch from unseen suns, and how, every so often, their leaves stir without wind.

The girl's summers, short though they are on the edge of the Winter Sea, are full of birdsong and bare feet in moss. Long winters bring the hush and creak of snow-laden boughs, the burble of buried streams, and here and there the rustle of leaves from a rebellious ghisten birch, green in defiance of the cold. She breaks the ice and drinks from those hidden streams, nourished by the same water that nourishes the forest, and eats the berries that grow between twisted roots. She belongs in the Wold.

And when she puts her small palm to the trunk of the yew, behind the inn where her family lives, she thinks she can hear a whisper. The tree has a soul, she knows, a soul drawn up through the dirt and clay and stone. It is a soul from another world, with other suns and seasons. A soul now housed within oak and elm and yew.

That soul is called a ghisting.

∞

FOUR

The Company of Smugglers

MARY

After a fortnight locked in a room, being in the company of Kaspin, Speck, and their guests had tattered my nerves.

My only forays consisted of two ill-fated escapes. One ended in Speck tripping me before I reached the stairs, then carrying me back to my room like a screeching child. The other ended in a lush parlor, where, distracted by a gaudy portrait of Kaspin over the fireplace, I hadn't managed to pry open the frozen window before the inn wife strode in and punched me in the stomach.

Finally, as I sat at Kaspin's meeting, gagged and beset by appraising gazes, tension spread across my shoulders like cracks in ice.

I tried to ignore the men. It did not matter who they were or what they said. It didn't matter that the one called Randalf struck me as slimy and despicable, that James Elijah Demery seemed oddly familiar, or that the young pirate hunter looked at me with what might have been sympathy. I did not have a choice in who took me, and they would all bring their own kind of hell.

Randalf came to fetch me that night with an escort of a dozen toughs. He set a chest down at Kaspin's feet with a thud and opened it to reveal more solems than I'd seen in my life.

Meanwhile, Speck wrapped a cloak around my shoulders and patted me on the cheek—or rather, on the Stormsinger's mask, which was still locked over my jaw.

"Mayhap we'll see one another again, dove," Speck murmured as he pulled the hood over my head, casting my face into shadow. "Don't miss me too much."

I kicked his shin.

"Bitch!" He hopped backwards, but before he could retaliate, Randalf tugged me out into the winter night. I flashed Speck a smug, slit-eyed look as I went, but there was no heart to it.

Cool wind rushed into my nostrils. I raked in a desperate, fragile breath, careless of the cold. For an instant, I imagined this was freedom—snowflakes melting on my forehead and clear, salty wind in my face. But it wasn't. My mouth was dry and sour beneath the mask, Randalf's hand was iron on my arm, and our escort of burly sailors loomed all around.

"Right," Randalf said to his men. "To the ship."

Randalf's ship was a sleek, two-masted affair, painted with broad stripes of red and yellow. That was all I saw before he hustled me down a steep set of stairs, across a small gun deck, and down a short passage at the stern of the ship. Then, he locked me in a cupboard.

"Sleep well," the smuggler commanded through the hatch and slammed it shut.

Blackness surrounded me. I held still as my other senses pressed to the surface—the slight bob of the ship in the harbor waters, the creak of wood, and the scent of damp and salt and hemp. The last came from the coils of rope and bundles of canvas which dug into my backside. They, apparently, were my bed.

Holding despair at bay, I found a position that passed as comfortable and wrapped my arms across my chest. My cloak was thick—and musty—but cold seeped through the wood all around. I was going to have to make myself a proper nest in the canvas, or else I'd freeze overnight.

A nest, like a rat. Desolation came at me in a sudden gust and I clenched my eyes shut—though, dark as it was, the act made little difference.

I should have run back at the fort. This was what one moment's hesitation had won me—a cupboard on a smuggler's ship, a Stormsinger's mask locked about my head, and a future of suffering, pain, and constant anxiety.

The urge to wallow battered me, but I fought back with anger and determination. Next time I had the chance to flee, I would not hesitate. I'd run, I'd hide, and then I'd find my mother. Somehow.

Eventually I drifted into an exhausted fugue. Dreams came. I saw the Wold and the ghisten yew behind my family's inn, its branches full of sunlight on an autumn morning. In the dream, I spun a basket of black wool into yarn. The spindle whirled, the thread tightened, and from within the yew, a spirit spoke. Not every tree in the Ghistwold had a soul, but I'd always known that this one did.

Sister.

I awoke to the creak of timber. Rope dug into me from every side, and I groaned into my mask as a thousand aches and pains leapt to my attention.

Sister?

I blinked, disoriented. The light from my dream, filtering through the leaves of the yew, was still here. But it had changed from golden and warm to pale and cool blue, and it radiated from… a person.

A woman crouched before me, tucked between the bulkhead and the hatch. She wore full skirts, flowing past her feet and pooling on the ropes around me. She stared from a heart-shaped face, with pale green eyes the consistency of sea-glass. They had no pupils, no depth of soul, but there was emotion in them—fleeting curiosity, appraisal, and compassion.

She shifted and her skirts disintegrated into a swirl of uncoordinated, octopuslike limbs. Not a person. Not a woman. A ghisting.

I stifled the urge to cry out. I knew ghistings. I'd grown up in a Ghistwold. But this creature was not peacefully at rest in her tree, curious but detached from the world. She was captive on the ship, like me, and I'd never been so close to one of her kind while manifested. Why was she here? What did she want?

The ghisting surged forward and I cringed, expecting to feel a chill gust as her specter passed through me. That, after all, was what happened in stories.

Instead, I felt a gentle, solid hand on my face. It wasn't cold, but unremarkably tepid.

Sister?

I screamed into my mask. The woman's—the creature's—eyes flared wide with shock and her visage thinned. Her touch dropped away, she merged with the wood of the ship and her blue aura extinguished.

I was plunged back into darkness, then slapped with a wash of new light as the cupboard door opened. A shadow filled the hatchway—one of Randalf's crew, presumably set to guard me— along with a swinging lantern.

The crewman hauled me into the passageway. He was gruff and far too handsy, but for one blank-minded second, I was too shocked to react. Was I being rescued from the ghisting with tentacles for legs—*tentacles!*—or was I bound for something worse?

I found my feet, but the handsy hands didn't let go. Instead, they gripped my arms and shook me.

"What's wrong with you, witch?"

Obviously, he wasn't very bright—with the mask locked around my jaw, I could hardly answer him.

I squinted in the light of his lantern, its glass belly filled with half a dozen pulsing dragonflies. Their light was purple or amber, depending on the gender of the flies, and they were currently in a blinding frenzy.

The crewman pushed me aside and bent down to peer into my nest of canvas and rope. "Nothin' in here, woman. What—"

It was at this point that I realized there was nothing between me and the short passage to the gun deck. Slowly, I turned my head. I could feel a draft from that direction and see a shaft of gentle, natural light, coming from one side.

Had they left a hatch open?

I grabbed the crewman's lantern as he stood up, smashed it across his face, and bolted down a short passageway. Glass hit the deck, the man screamed, and dragonflies burst into freedom.

I stumbled down a short set of stairs. Sure enough, moonlight and cold air poured through an open gunport. Randalf's ship, *Juliette*, had eight guns in total, all docile and lashed in their cradles. Normally, the deck would also be populated by swinging hammocks and sleeping crew, but apparently they were all on watch or ashore.

Except, of course, for the crewman who was currently bellowing like a wounded bear and barreling after me. Footsteps thundered across the deck above us too. Other sailors had noticed the disturbance.

Three glowing dragonflies zipped past me and out the open gunport. I darted after them and craned to look out. The line of a jetty wasn't far below.

A hand seized my forearm. The smuggler I'd attacked jerked me around and slammed me into the bulkhead between the hatches.

"You little bitch," he snarled, his face covered with scrapes and blood.

The Stormsinger's mask smothered any reply, which was likely for the best. My vocabulary was degrading by the second.

Sister. A rootless voice wafted past me. My skin started to crawl, even as I fought to escape the sailor's hold.

The creature from my cupboard peeled out of the wood beside me. The smuggler reared back, letting out a choking shout. Back by the stairs, the hatch to the upper deck crashed open and boots flooded down towards us.

Breath wedged in my throat, I turned to find the ghisting's nose so close to mine I felt the tips brush. Her huge sea-glass eyes crinkled in concern, her octopoid legs once more contained in a rippling skirt.

Sister, why won't you speak to me?

Speak? Ghistings and humans could not speak, just like ghistings didn't have flesh. I couldn't be hearing this right now, couldn't have felt her hand on my cheek or her nose brushing mine. This was madness. This was...

Whatever it was, my wild thoughts occupied what remained of my opportunity to escape. Randalf's crew surrounded us.

"What's the creature doing?" I heard one whisper.

"Juliette?" another murmured.

"Don't go talkin' to it, you idiot!"

The ghisting ignored them. She drifted backwards and looked me over as her 'skirt' rippled in an unseen current. Her eyes were still soulless, matte and featureless, but there was something in them I recognized as she noted my mask and bound hands: solidarity.

Then, between one blink and the next, the creature vanished.

"What happened?" Randalf's voice cut through the deck. He spun me to face him and I recoiled, but all he did was hold up a small, delicate key. The key to my mask.

I relented. The gag fell away into his hands with a click and I coughed, spitting and wiping at my lips with my bound hands.

"What happened?" the smuggler demanded.

My mind churned, excuses piling up. I could beg, claim the crewman had mistreated me—he hadn't exactly been gentle—but what I wanted to say, what I *needed* to say, came out instead.

"Your crewman hauled me out of my cupboard, so I smashed his lantern over his head and tried to escape," I stated, lifting my chin a fraction.

"Escape?" Randalf looked at the open gunport, then at the crewman with the bloodied face. "You left that open?"

The bloodied man suddenly looked more cautious than angry. "For the handoff with Merrow, Cap'n."

"That was at first bell!" Randalf made an admirable attempt to loom, even though he was shorter than the sailor and considerably leaner. But from the way the entire crew reacted, there was viable threat to his displeasure.

"They're late," the crewman protested.

Randalf edged closer. "So you left it open *and* let the Stormsinger loose?"

The crewman paled. "Cap'n, I—"

Randalf abruptly turned to me and held up my gag. "Ms. Firth, here is your first lesson about life aboard my ship. You do something good, I reward you. You do something bad, I punish you. It's a simple arrangement, is it not? One simple enough system for any lack-witted Barrowside dullard to understand?"

The captain's eyes dragged back to the crewman, identifying the dullard in question. That look was so cold and so cruel, I suddenly understood the crew's fear.

The urge to sneer, to curse my captor and strike out, died. As angry and frustrated as I was, I had to be logical. I had to protect myself.

"I understand," I said lowly.

"Wonderful." Randalf spun on his crew. "See this man tied to the grating above and fetch my lash. Then make this ship ready for open sea. I want us leaving Whallum by tomorrow night."

"Sir?" another sailor asked. "We're not set to depart for three days—"

"No matter." Randalf's smile remained intact, but it turned distinctly nastier as he began to fit my gag back in place. It took all my strength not to fight back. "As soon as we're in open sea? Tie our new Stormsinger to the mast."

GHISTWOLD—*Being forests of most ancient and uncommon origins, Ghistwolds, more commonly referred to simply as Wolds, are to be distinguished from the common wold as places where the two realms—that which is human and that which is Other—intersect. In such places, Ghisten Trees rooted in the Other grow into the human plane and manifest in a variety of common trees, though these trees frequently reject the laws of nature in terms of seasonal shifts or the directions of their shadows. These trees are then harvested for shipbuilding, most frequently the figurehead. The spirit of the Ghisting within the Ghisten Tree then merges with the ship, to remain there until it is moved, or the last of its figurehead is burned away, or taken by the degradation of time. The spirit of the Ghisting, then, will roam free until it eventually returns to the Other—a process that may take days or centuries. In Aeadine, the Ghistwold cuts across the center of the main island, intersecting with various common wolds (that is, wolds without Ghistings) such as the Lesterwold, to form a vast wilderness. See also* GHISTWOOD, SPIRITWOLD.

—FROM THE WORDBOOK ALPHABETICA: A NEW
WORDBOOK OF THE AEADINES

FIVE

Antiphony Cove

SAMUEL

Fisher squinted at me over the top of a small, green and gilt book. "Slader is still furious with you."

I sat down on the other end of the bench and pulled off my knitted cap, toppling unkempt hair into my eyes. We were in the cabin we both called home. There was a single canvas curtain strung down its center, pulled back during the day, and Fisher's hammock swung from the beams on her side of the divide. Mine was rolled and stowed in my sea-chest against the bulkhead, as I had been on watch all night—repercussions for losing the Stormsinger, Mary Firth. Slader was convinced I had intentionally thwarted our chances, and my sending Fisher away had not helped.

Our cabin had no other furnishings save a hanging dragonfly lantern, a fortified iron woodstove, and a narrow table with a bench, where we sat. The lantern was a luxury, as it posed no risk of fire and could be used during the worst of storms. The dragonflies themselves were as immortal as any other creature from the Other, requiring no food or water or even air. They simply pulsed gentle purples and golds in their sleep and lit to a bright, shining frenzy when they awoke.

Fisher wore a striped blanket over her shirt, stays visible in a line across her breasts, breeches but no shoes, and appeared to have stolen a pair of my socks to wear over her own. Normally, I would return from a night watch to find her dressed and gone, already above decks taking command. But this morning there was no need for her to leave the cabin so early. I would be taking her watches today. And tomorrow.

I shook the snow off my hat and pushed my hair back from my face. I could feel Fisher eyeing me, prying answers from the tired lines of my face.

"Something was not right," I repeated. "With Demery and that last guest. Not calling up the armsmen would have been foolish."

Fisher lowered her book to the table. "Oh, I've little doubt of that. But there's no way a smuggler like John Randalf outbid you with four thousand solem. Tell Slader the truth. You intentionally lost the bid."

"I am not lying." I glowered momentarily and tossed my cap onto the table. "He had the money. I ought to have warned Slader, not you."

Fisher put down her book and shifted to straddle the bench. "Perhaps. What of your… inklings? Any further notion what they meant?"

"None." I stared past her at the door. My curse was the last thing I wanted to talk about with her. "Is there still breakfast in the galley?"

"Yes. Hammond saved you some."

"Good man."

"Because I asked him to."

I frowned at her. "Why would you do that?"

She produced a distinctly knifelike smile. "Consider it my thanks for pissing Slader off. Now I've two days to sleep late, go ashore at leisure and spend two years' worth of petty cash on good wine and fine company. I might even put on a dress."

"As if you own a dress," I retorted, rising and starting for the door.

"I do." She sounded genuinely irritated. "I am a woman, Samuel Rosser. Whatever else I am too."

"Really? The way you pass wind in your sleep, I thought—"

Fisher lunged, clipping me on the back of the head with her book as I skittered into the passageway. I tumbled into the far wall

and she came after, cuffing me with the book a second time before
I made my escape.

"You are a boor, Samuel Rosser," she hissed after me.

I fled for the galley, trying and failing not to grin. Slader might
be furious with me, and my dreamer's sense might be a constant,
nerve-tearing hum in the back of my mind, but riling Fisher always
put me in a better mood.

That condition, however, did not outlive breakfast. I was halfway
through a bowl of beans, sausage and rare fresh bread when the
captain's steward Willoughby came to fetch me.

"I've learned something," Slader said as I entered the cabin, still
trying to smooth my hair and look presentable. The man barely
looked at me, handing over a note and returning to the window to
squint at the docks. "Read that."

I scanned the note. "'*Man-of-War in Antiphony Cove. No Name.*'
Where did this come from?"

"A woman I pay to keep her ear to the ground in the city," Slader
said, batting the matter aside with a casual hand. "It's based on
rumor. Perhaps it's true. Perhaps it's a ploy to get us to leave port—
word of us has spread and there are any number of vessels here who
do not want us in sight when they leave protected waters."

Whallum was an Aeadine port, but criminals like Kaspin
paid good money to keep the port neutral in the battle between
lawkeeper and lawbreaker. Beyond the harbor, however? That
protection ended.

Slader crossed his arms over his chest and said, "Take five
crewmen who can ride and go investigate. Over land—discretion
is of the utmost importance. Antiphony is an hour south. I've sent
a boy to arrange for horses at the edge of the city."

My weariness evaporated like smoke. Not only was this a chance
to redeem myself, but if the ship we hoped for was in that cove—we
could fulfill our commission here and now, without even leaving
Aeadine. Without needing a Stormsinger.

"Yes, sir," I said, hard-pressed to control my elation.

Slader held my gaze. "Do not disappoint me, Mr. Rosser."

"I will not, sir."

∞

Roots and twigs dug into my ribs as I bellied through the snow to the edge of a cliff. The spruces we sheltered under caught at my cap—I was out of uniform, bundled into the wool breeches and quilted overcoat of a landsman. I tugged the cap back down over my forehead and rested a musket at my side, gesturing for the men to stop before we sent snow toppling over the cliff.

Antiphony Cove lay below us. A rim of trees, snow and ice decorated her cliffs, which dropped all the way down to a small beach and a girding of deadly, icy rocks. The cove's mouth was equally high and sheer, framing a glimpse of a sunlit Winter Sea.

A sleek man-of-war was preparing to depart. A quick count marked at least sixty guns. The wood of the vessel was weathered to a dull, pale grey, and there was no paint anywhere in sight, no ornate name across her stern or other signature decoration—a lack of features that made my heart beat faster and my resolve tighten. This could be Lirr, just as we hoped. But I could not be sure without seeing the figurehead, and it was obscured at this angle.

A whistle piped, amplified by the cliffs, and crew ferried goods from the beach to the ship by boat. Their every call reverberated with uncanny clarity, along with the clack and grind of block and rope as goods were lowered through open gratings.

"Three bits, boss," one of my men said, crawling up. His name was Penn, and he was a quick, reliable fellow, always my first choice of companion on a mission. A cudgel hung from his hip, dragging at the snow, and his knitted cap had slipped up on his bald, pale head into an impish point.

He propped himself up on his elbows and raised a pinky finger.

"First one, that ship's got no name on her, true, and her figurehead no face, just a shroud, real eerie like. She's Lirr's, no mistake."

I nodded as calmly as I could manage. "Very good, Mr. Penn. And?"

"Second bit," Penn raised his ring finger, "I found the head of the trail, leadin' down there, 'long with half a dozen pirates—I left Kit watchin'." Penn brushed a clot of snow off his forehead and held up a third finger too. "Last, there's a wagon comin' up the road from town as we speak."

More wagons meant the ship was unlikely to depart for several hours yet. But with all we needed to do to intercept it, that was not much time.

"To the trailhead, quickly then, and we will see what we can." I gestured to two of the men to stay put, then crawled back from the ledge until I was far enough away to stand. Snow dislodged from the spruce boughs tumbled uncomfortably down my neck. Swiping at it, I nodded to Penn. "Lead the way."

The trailhead was well hidden among the trees, but the sound of voices and Penn's sure steps drew us onward. We sighted Kit, the watchman, and settled in beside him as wagon wheels trundled into sight.

"Fitch, boy! Run and tell the cap'n *Juliette*'s still in harbor, but not for long," a woman said. I saw her boots as she dropped off the wagon, landing softly in the layers of snow-covered needles. From this angle her face was obscured, but she was Aeadine and wore men's clothes.

At her words, a smaller pair of boots took off at a run towards the cliffs.

"Randalf got the singer, then?" a male voice inquired, his boots sidling up to the woman's. She reset the distance between them with a pointed step, but the man only edged closer again, saying, "Good fortune for us, then. Wouldn't fancy takin' her from *Hart* now, eh?"

"Mind your distance, Deans."

The man snorted. "Why, I seen you eyein' me, I have, and I'm here to say I'm not opposed."

"Opposed to me stuffing your bits down your throat?" The woman delivered these words in a voice so flat, so emotionless and frank, that Deans's sidling step abruptly switched direction.

I looked quickly down, trying to stifle a snort of laughter.

Beside me, Penn pinned his lips closed and gave a strangled hiccup.

"Meant nothin' by it," Deans hastily amended.

"Be sure you didn't."

My amusement faded as the reality of the situation sank in. Lirr's crew knew we were in port—but of course they knew. We had made no attempt to hide. And the singer they referenced; did they mean Mary Firth? What did Lirr want with her?

The answer, naturally, was already there. Lirr had been Kaspin's final guest, the fourth man who had declined his invitation. Perhaps he had done so because he heard Slader was in port. Or perhaps he had simply decided kidnapping the woman would cost less.

But why would a man like Lirr need to buy a Stormsinger? Everyone knew he had a singer aboard and something of a cache of them back in the Mereish Southern Isles, where he lived like a king. Had his current singer unexpectedly died, perhaps, leaving him stuck in Aeadine in an early winter?

I stirred. If Lirr was short a Stormsinger, our chances of capturing him had vastly increased.

The woman spoke again. "We'll have her before they leave free waters," she said in a tone that forbade further discussion, then turned away to supervise the unloading of the cart.

I looked at Penn and saw my own urgency reflected in his eyes.

"Mr. Penn, please recall all the scouts and return to the horses." I spoke in a low voice, already retreating across the forest floor. "Then make for the ship with all haste. Warn Captain Slader that our quarry is here, preparing to depart, and intends to attack John Randalf's *Juliette*."

"Yessir. And you, sir?" Penn whispered.

"I will warn Captain Randalf myself."

My coat snapped around me as a storm descended upon the docks. It came from the heavens in a great waterfall of snow and grey cloud, striking the waves and billowing out in tumbling swirls. These clawed towards Whallum's huddled houses and bobbing ships, and walled off the entirety of the harbor mouth in a deafening, muffling roar.

Breathless, I skidded to a halt on the end of the dock where Randalf's schooner ought to have been. Snow swallowed me in a whirl of bone-cracking cold, peppering my face with ice and freezing the sweat on my skin.

I threw up an arm to shield my eyes and squinted through the tempest. The ship was gone. I realized that at the same time as I heard a voice on the wind, low and sweet and sad. I lowered my arm, staring as if I could make out Mary Firth singing down the storm and bearing Randalf's vessel out of Whallum.

The smuggler must have already learned Lirr was coming for her. Relief, trepidation, and a spark of disappointment turned in my stomach. The Stormsinger was gone. All that was left was her voice on the wind, her indistinct words teasing the edges of my hearing.

Slowly the wind lessened, and a form materialized beside me. He was hatless, the wind tossing his blond hair as he squinted through the snow. But there was satisfaction around his eyes, the grim contentment of a man who has both won and lost.

"I heard the rumors and warned Randalf," Charles Grant informed me, clearing his throat and shoving his hands into his pockets. "Sorry to spoil your heroics. You look quite dashing, if that's any consolation."

I opened my mouth to say something curt, but caught myself. The Stormsinger was safe from Lirr, if not from Randalf. They had been warned. That was all that mattered, and now I needed to get back to my ship.

There was no way *Hart* could navigate that storm, not without its own Stormsinger, but neither could Lirr. As soon as the weather cleared, we would be ready to meet him. We would ensure that he never threatened anyone again, and my name would be associated with something good, something honorable.

"Why?" I asked Grant as I turned away. "Why warn her?"

Grant shrugged. "Mary Firth saved my life. I figured I should begin repaying my debts."

The Girl from the Wold

The Girl from the Wold decides that the trees love music as much as she. There is no magic in her voice yet, only a child's innocent exuberance, and she sings every song she knows in the mossy shade and tall ferns. She is sure the boughs of a hemlock dip a little lower at her voice, and that a ghisting in the form of a doe watches her from beyond a willow veil. The doe trails her for a time but eventually fades, at the end of her roots' reach.

One day, in the very heart of the Wold, the girl discovers a new tree. Its branches rise above the rest and its roots stretch so far over the ground the girl cannot find where they end. She sits herself down in a cradle of those roots and sorts through a pocket full of forest treasures—acorns and feathers, a fine bone and carefully plucked wildflowers.

As she sorts, she sings softly to herself. A voice responds in perfect harmony. But though the girl looks around, she is alone in the forest.

Her eyes rise to the great tree above her. She sings again, and the voice responds again.

She is still staring at the tree when her mother emerges from the forest. She scolds the girl for staying out so long, but when the girl tells her that the tree can sing, her mother goes quiet.

"Can't the tree sing, Mama?" the girl asks. "Is it special?"

"It is special," her mother replies. Her pale grey eyes are guarded as she looks up at the grand tree. "This tree is the heart of the forest. The Mother Tree. But she cannot sing, Mary. Ghistings and humans do not talk to one another. You're being foolish, and you shouldn't stray so deep into the Wold. Come home and leave her be."

Mary does. And as she ages, her waist narrows and her skirts lengthen, she decides she must have been mistaken. The Mother Tree could not have joined her song—it was just the creak of branches, or the wind in the trees.

But sometimes when she wanders the Wold, singing to herself, she still swears a voice replies.

∞

SIX

The Elusive Art of Stormsinging

MARY

The shadows of the sails crept across the deck as our second day out of Whallum closed. The sun neared the horizon in a cloudless sky, bleached and crisp and sparkling with cold. The wind was frigid on my cheeks, but not as bad as it could have been.

The Winter Sea was poised on the edge of true winter, the long season—eight months of the year—where only ships with ghistings and Stormsingers dared to challenge the waves. It was a season for covert warfare and risk-taking, a time of terrific storms where an enterprising smuggler like Randalf could make a fortune in one fortuitous venture.

I sat by the mainmast on a stool, dull-eyed and wrapped in my musty cloak. Whatever courage and stupidity had fueled my escape back in Whallum was long gone, stolen by a day tied to the foremast in the wind and salt and cold. Now, simply sitting on a stool felt like luxury.

Freeing me hadn't been a kindness or a reward, however. It was purely practicality—if Randalf left me there any longer, I'd have died.

So he had given me a blanket and allowed me to spend a night near the stove in the galley. My gag had vanished and my hands were freed, but I was no less a prisoner. The waves were my shackles now, stretching to the horizon. Even the tips of Aeadine's ragged peninsulas were gone from sight, swallowed by sea fog and distance.

The only way off this ship was into the waves.

My last Stormsinger drowned herself.

I remembered what Randalf had said back at Kaspin's and shivered. But part of me took the idea and tucked it away, grim and abyssal though it was.

Around me, Randalf's crew went about their work. They watched me, constantly. I slept in fragments at night, terrified that I'd wake up to a shadow creeping into my closet, or the ghisting's unearthly face. To make matters worse, I was barely fed—I'd earn better food, Randalf said, when I proved my value.

The storm I'd conjured to cover our departure from Whallum hadn't been enough to do that. Apparently calling a storm was a lot easier than dispersing one or maintaining a good wind and, as Randalf had speculated to Kaspin, I was untrained. The Navy's Stormsingers were apprenticed and instructed from a young age, but I'd been hidden in the Wold, voiceless, for my entire life.

It had taken a mere hour for me and everyone aboard ship to realize I had no idea what I was doing. Now I hummed to the winds by luck alone, and every time the sails luffed my hunger gnawed deeper.

A blond-haired sailor strode by, cracking a cake of hardtack between his teeth. I stared at the food, eyelids flickering with want. I knew I shouldn't look at him, shouldn't do anything to attract attention, but I was so hungry.

He noticed my interest. Circling back, he scratched crumbs out of his scraggly beard and squinted down at me. He still held half the cake in his hand. It was plain, a little charred, and desperately enticing.

"Hungry, love?" he asked.

My humming died, and with it, the wind I'd been currying. The sails began to sag, changing the pattern of shadows on the deck from full to rippling. Woodsmoke from the ship's stovepipes wafted past us.

I forced myself to look away from him. "No," I said, and began to hum again.

He crouched, forcing his face into my line of sight. There was frost on the brim of his hat and the whiskers around his mouth. "I could make sure you were fed right well," he said contemplatively, biting off another chunk of the hardtack. Crumbs rained down into his beard and onto the deck, and I could have cried at the waste. The sailor cocked a grin, looking at my lips as he added, "Take care of you, I would. Keep that mouth of yours full."

Above us, the sails luffed again with a thunder of canvas.

"Witch!" the helmsman shouted.

Before I could respond, another shout went up from a lookout at the fore of the ship. "Sails! Sails on the horizon!"

The man before me shot upright, looking to the helmsman in sudden attention. Across the deck his companions did the same and foreboding slithered through me.

"What colors?" the helmsman called to the lookout. "Who is she?"

"No colors, sir," was the response.

I stared in the direction of the mysterious vessel, the cold of the wind biting to my bones.

"What does that mean?" I asked the sailor with the hardtack.

He still stood over me, gazing in the same direction as the lookout. All his crudeness and smirking had fled. "She's flying no flag, so she's hiding who she is. If we're lucky? She'll be a merchant trying to nip the last run of the season and stealin' your witch wind. If we're not… Mereish? Cape? Navy? Pirates? Everyone out here's our enemy."

His gaze flicked, not leering this time, but noting the darkness under my eyes and the paleness of my face. Then he held out the hardtack and reached into his pocket, producing another. Making sure no one was watching us, he shoved them both into my hands.

"Keep us alive, witch," he said, then jogged away across the deck.

Another ship. *Rescue*. The word whispered through the back of my mind as I hid the food into my pockets for later. I couldn't be seen eating, not with Randalf's current orders to starve me, and 'rescue' had little meaning here. Even if that sail belonged to a Navy ship, I'd just end up serving them instead of Randalf. Just because a ship sailed on the right side of the law didn't mean I'd be better treated. My mother had spoken of serving pirates and the Navy with the same empty eyes.

There are fates worse than death, Mary.

∽

Randalf called me to his cabin that night. I'd covertly consumed the hardtack earlier, but it had done me little good. When my eyes fell on the food-laden table before Randalf, desperate hunger consumed me.

There was a loaf of bread, a bowl of fish that smelled of dill and butter, and a hearty topping of pickled beans. Not the most appetizing combination in my opinion, but by that point I'd have eaten a salted shoe.

"Go on," the smuggler said, waving a hand and sitting back in his chair. "You need your strength."

That was the same reason the sailor had given for feeding me earlier, and it did not bode well. Still, I wasn't about to question him. I sat down and dug in, tearing a piece of bread with my teeth and shoveling fish into my mouth in the same breath.

Randalf watched me a moment, grimaced in distaste, and turned back to his plate. Beyond him, out the window, a distant bow lantern hung like a glistening star between the night sea and clouded sky.

"Who is she? Mereish? Cape?" I cited our nation's enemies around a mouthful. "The crew said she's big enough to be a warship."

Randalf shook his head and reached for a mug on the table. Tea, but darker, with a smell of rum. "Nay. If they'd a mind to board us, they'd have closed by now. They're just stealing a wind on the way west. It's common enough, especially this late in the season."

He and his crew seemed to be preparing me for a challenge, though. I kept eating, not risking another question until my belly began to cramp. I sat back, taking a cup of water and sipping it with one hand on my stays.

"What about that pirate?" I asked. "James Demery?"

Randalf sucked his teeth thoughtfully and frowned. "James Demery is not the kind of man to waste time on us. Stormsingers like you aren't common, but there *are* enough Mereish and Cape skulking in these seas to make unnecessary journeys inadvisable."

I eyed him. "Pineapples are necessary?"

Randalf leveled a glare at me. "Profit is necessary, and the war and the winter make my venture very profitable. Most free merchants like myself, and pirates like Demery, stay around the coast at this time of year. Hiding. Keeping their heads down in their villages. But me? The Winter Sea is mine."

His claim was grandiose, but he was right about pirates lying low during the winter. In a world of constant warfare and the chaos it brought, small fishing villages would strike deals with lesser pirates for protection, hiding them and providing places to stow families and loved ones. After all, my father had told me, most pirates were little more than common sailors, down on their luck or hiding from the Navy's press gangs.

Only the most enterprising pirates caused a proper stir, ravaging coastal settlements and threatening lives. I suspected Demery was one of these. He was on the Queen's List and had enough coin to weigh in at Kaspin's. I found it hard to imagine him sitting the winter out in a seaside village, mending nets with a cheery wife and half a dozen children.

"Girl. Girl!" Randalf leaned across the table to snap his fingers in front of my face.

I recoiled. Indignation bloomed so fast I almost insulted him, but I caught myself.

"Listen to me," my captain growled. "*I'm* not afraid of those sails. Whoever they are, they've no Stormsinger of their own, or else they wouldn't need our wind. So long as you do your job, we'll breeze into Tithe in three days."

I took another sip instead of replying. From my limited tutoring on the wider world and snatches of overheard conversations, I knew that Tithe was a free port not far west of Aeadine. There was a small Ghistwold there, and Tithe was a shortening of the poetical name, *The Tithe to the Sea*.

Randalf continued, "We pick up as much wool, fur and tobacco as this ship will take, then head to warmer waters as planned, down the south channel."

"Where you'll claim your pineapples and begin the journey back north?" I clarified, vastly uneasy about the whole affair. My food sat heavy in my stomach.

He nodded. "Precisely. Back in Whallum within a month and a half, and Her Majesty will have pineapple syrup for Festus."

Her Majesty? I had a hard time believing that a man like Randalf supplied our monarch with anything. I drank a little more to cover my skepticism.

Whallum wasn't a place that had ever sparked hope in me—or anyone else, I suspected—but now it did. Our return would be the ideal time to make an escape and try to find my way somewhere safe.

Safe. I turned the word over, trying to see if it would shape itself into something substantial. I envisioned sunlit windows and rustling green leaves. A harpsichord, under my fingers. A home.

My mother, standing at the back door.

My heart dropped. Where *was* she? She was all I had left in the world now, and I didn't even know if she was alive.

I had to find her, but I'd need to earn Randalf's trust before that could happen. And I'd need to survive.

"I'll get us there," I said, trying to sound confident, and gave him a vague smile. I set down my cup and reached for the bread again.

Randalf seized my wrist. He jerked me towards him, and I barely stifled a scream. The tabletop dug into my ribs.

"Don't you look at me like that. Like you think I'm a fool." His breath gusted across my face, thick with rum and vinegar. His nails, chewed to the quick, still bit into the tender flesh of my wrist. "Have some respect. I paid a lot of money for you, and I'll earn it back one way or another."

"You're hurting me." I knew the words sounded pathetic, but they leaked out, anyway. I tugged back, wishing there weren't tears in my eyes, wishing I weren't so frightened and exhausted. Where was my anger? Where was my rage? Lost to hunger and the winter wind.

"I'll do it," I assured him, breath thin in my lungs. "I swear."

Randalf glared at me, preparing some new threat behind his narrow eyes.

The ship's ghisting, Juliette, materialized behind him. Tentacle skirt flowing and eyes wide, she hovered in absolute silence beside the windows. Randalf didn't even notice, though the quality of light in the room tinted a subtle blue.

"If you fail," Randalf started to warn, "you'll beg me for a night tied to the mast, just to escape the—"

Behind him, the ghisting pointed out the window. Where our pursuer's lantern had hung like a distant star not long ago, now there was nothing at all.

And I heard a song. Someone sang, distantly, boldly, and I knew that melody in the marrow of my bones. There was another Stormsinger out in the night.

Randalf followed my gaze and stood suddenly, dropping my wrist. "Saint of—"

Thunder cracked over the waves, barely muffled by the hull. I froze, poised over the carnage of my meal as the sound merged into an ominous whistle. That had to be—

Randalf's hands went limp at his sides. He stared, helpless, as the ghisting vanished in a swirl of spectral light, and the cabin exploded.

∞

Hands held me upright. My head was a blur of pain, thoughts stuttering between instinctual terror and dreamy haze. The latter was far more welcoming, curling through my thoughts like smoke from my father's pipe. I leaned towards it.

Water hit my face. I staggered back into consciousness with a shrieking gasp, the sound drowned by a chorus of laughter.

My back hit something solid. A mast? The hands holding me loosened and I sagged, gasping in lung-rattling shock.

I blinked away water and saw a wall of strangers, alternately shadowed and outlined by a blazing fire at their backs. Beyond them knots of men and women spread across a broad deck, laughing and moving and clustering and bearing crates, bundles and barrels. I saw prisoners here and there—on their bellies, on their knees, being interrogated. Bled.

A rope sung, a noose went taut, and a gargling man swung above my head with a weighty squeak of hemp. His cries suddenly cut off, leaving only the frantic scrabbling of nails against the noose as he swung.

I didn't scream. I was too stunned, too deep in my horror.

Nearby, another of Randalf's crew was pinned to the deck. I recognized the cuts on his face from where I'd smashed the lantern across it—the fool who'd left the hatch open, and nearly let me escape. More figures, new figures, crowded around him. A pirate with dark hair assessed the lash marks on his back, sticking his fingers callously into the wounds as the sailor howled. Then his tormentor casually flipped his victim onto his back and slit open his belly with a short, curved sword.

I saw the coils of the man's insides bulge out of the wound and begin to spill, accompanied by a wash of blood. I saw him shriek and spasm, his eyes glassy in shock. I saw those coils trail behind him like rope as strangers hauled him to the side of the ship and tossed him overboard.

With his departure into the waves, the pirates dispersed. Light glinted off their weapons—a random assortment of cutlasses, machetes, pistols and muskets, all held or slung with a victorious nonchalance. Their skin colors and clothing choices reflected no specific people or nation. Not Northern or Southern, no Mereish or Cape, or Aeadine or Usti.

Pirates. The word slapped my wits back to life and I wavered forward, ready to run, but my feet refused to coordinate. I staggered right into a waiting pair of arms. More figures converged, slinking in behind me and circling like wolves.

The woman that had caught me murmured in my ear, "That's no way to greet a lord. Stand tall and mind your manners, now."

She thrust me upright and this time, I found my feet. My captors—the pirates—parted to allow a man through. He was of medium height, dark-haired with a short beard and an athletic form beneath buckskin breeches and an open coat. He wore a cravat but no waistcoat over his shirt, exposing a handsbreadth of tanned chest. He carried a cutlass, slick with blood, which he passed off to a nearby pirate.

I'd just seen that weapon slit open the beaten man's belly, and the realization made my throat clot with bile. Off to the side I heard a steady drip, and looked up to see the man they'd strung from the yard had ceased his twitching. The smell of piss and blood wafted to me.

I bent over and retched on the deck, spilling half-digested beans, fish and bread before my captors' boots.

The man who'd held the cutlass neatly stepped out of the way and paused, waiting for me to stop heaving. I coughed and spat and choked on a sob, blinking up at him through tear-filled eyes and shanks of messy hair.

"The ghisting escaped, Cap'n," the pirate who'd taken the man's sword murmured, though the words didn't root in my mind right away. I was still spitting bile and trying to find my balance.

The newcomer looked displeased. Firelight still cast his face into shadow, but this close I could make out his features—steel-grey eyes, a man in his mid-thirties with a fine jaw and a face that wasn't so much handsome as demanding.

Power. I recognized his unnaturalness on an instinctual level. It was like what I felt when near Randalf's ghisting, or in the Ghistwold. But this was rawer and sharper, tainted with iron—human and hateful.

He saw the recognition in my eyes and held my gaze. My thoughts scattered like ants as he closed the remaining space between us.

"It's you." His voice was a summer wind, cutting through the cold and brushing across my cheeks.

He knew me? Impossible. Shivers skittered from the back of my neck to the tips of my fingers. Away. I had to get away. But where? I was on a ship, still at sea. And those flames...

"Where is Randalf's ship?" I asked.

"Hm?" His eyebrows lifted slightly. "Speak up."

"The *Juliette*, where is she?"

He glanced over his shoulder to the fire. It was far enough out that, as the pirates parted, I could see the shape of the entire ship—*Juliette*, burning upon the waves. A few shapes dangled from her yard arms, and it took me a moment to realize that they were more people, hung from ankles, throats or hands. As I stared, mesmerized, I saw some of them were still moving. Convulsing. Roasting alive.

The horror of it lashed me like waves. I couldn't rejoice at the demise of Randalf and his crew, not like this. So many lives ended in agony, before my very eyes.

Why would the pirates burn their prize? Randalf's ship wasn't large and the hole the pirates had blasted in it was certainly a flaw, but it was worth money, especially with a ghisting aboard.

A ghisting who had escaped, I now pieced together. A ghisting who'd looked at me with solidarity. She'd been freed by the fire, as ghistings often were.

The thought of her escape comforted me, in a distant, melancholy way. But that consolation was fleeting. I caught a waft of crisping fat on the wind, and the scream of a dying crewman aboard *Juliette* shrilled over the roar of the flames.

Above me, the hanging man swung with the roll of the ship, still dripping piss and blood.

"Are you going to ask who I am?" The pirate pulled my attention back to him. "Or perhaps you remember me?"

I found my voice. "Why would I remember you?"

His eyes dropped, lingering in the center of my chest in a way that made my skin crawl. It wasn't a lustful look, but a prying one— as if he expected to see something on my dirty, cold-pinched skin. He reached out, pushing my collar aside an inch, and his finger brushed across my flesh.

Run. The impulse struck me again like an arrow in the dark. It was directionless, futile and irrational, but I couldn't stop it. I inched back, coming up against the mainmast again. This time I didn't stop. I twisted, ducking around the trunk and shoving through the crowd.

I burst out onto open deck. Pirates backed off and their captain— the man I should know but did not—trailed in my wake.

"There's nowhere to go," he called. There was no taunting to his voice, just statement of fact. "You're safe here, with me. No need to run. No more need to hide."

I hit the ship's rail and stared over it, an animal in a trap. Dark water. *Juliette*, burning. Bodies, writhing. I locked the back of one hand over my mouth to keep from screaming and stared at the waves below.

The pirate was right. There was no escape. I was no ghisting, to slip between worlds or off through the sea, immortal and deathless. I was just a woman in a world of sudden brutality, and I had only one way out.

There are fates worse than death.

"Who are you?" I called the question over my shoulder on a cold wind. "Who are you and how do you know me?"

"Lirr," was his simple response. I sensed he'd stopped a few paces behind me, and there was no other sound save the wind and the roar of the flames. He added, almost an appeal, "Remember me."

I waited for him to go on, to answer my second question. When he didn't I looked back, again glimpsing the fire over his shoulder. His expression was nearly inscrutable, but there was a tightness around his shadowed eyes, something that might have been hurt— if everything else about him hadn't emanated danger and death.

I began to sing, urgently and softly. Within a few words I caught the scent of snow, and the patter of my heart against my ribs turned into thunder.

"You will remember," he said quietly. He noted the snow, now a thick white veil between us and reached out, fingers parted. "Come."

The need to flee still burned through me, but my thoughts thinned with every passing second. My vision was full of his face— his eyes, his compulsive draw. I felt like I was back on the gallows again, slipping prematurely from my own skin.

My ears began to ring. In that void, someone else took over—a feral, reckless side of myself that knew no fear or logic.

I hurled myself over the side of the ship.

OTHER, THE—*Being that second plane of existence, which is outside the experience of common men. The Other is the birthplace of an array of creatures, including ghistings, morgories, implings, dittama and huden. It remains inaccessible to all humans save the preternatural: mages and their ilk, who may even walk its ethereal paths.* See also DARK WATER, SECOND PLANE, WINDWARD REALM.

—*FROM* THE WORDBOOK ALPHABETICA: A NEW
WORDBOOK OF THE AEADINES

SEVEN

The Mereish Coin

SAMUEL

*H*art nosed down the coast of Aeadine, tense and quiet. Half a dozen hands equipped with spyglasses were positioned all about the ship, from bow to maintop, with Fisher at the stern.

I scanned the horizon, all grey storm clouds and docile waves. We had found Antiphony Cove empty several hours before and commenced cruising the shoreline, but there was no sign of Lirr. The only vessels in sight belonged to fisherfolk, small and single-masted. Many of them were hauling in torn and tangled nets, yesterday's storm having caught them unawares. Gulls wheeled over us all and converged on shit-streaked cliffs.

Lirr was gone. I felt the truth like I felt the cold wind biting my cheeks, freezing my breath in my beard and the fine hairs inside my nose.

I lowered my spyglass and fiddled with the oval coin in my pocket, trying to disperse the sense. But though it dulled, it stayed.

"Mr. Rosser." I looked up as Slader joined me at the rail, hands clasped behind his back in his usual stance. He was not dressed for the cold—I wore a large overcoat atop my usual coat, along with scarf and a cap, but he wore only his frock coat and waistcoat. His cheeks were flushed though, and I caught drink on his breath as he ordered, "Find him."

"Sir?" I released the coin, tension wending up the back of my neck.

"You're a Sooth," Slader stated, dropping his chin to glare at me. We were of a height, he and I. "He's a mage. You told me you could track creatures like him in the Other."

"If I had met the man, yes," I protested. We had had this discussion before. "But without having touched him, I cannot just… find him. Sir, we ought to set course for Tithe. He had an interest in Randalf and the Stormsinger, that much was clear—"

"I'll decide our course, Mr. Rosser," Slader cut me off, loudly enough to earn glances from several nearby hands. The wind eased at the same time, and the scent of rum wafted off the captain as he leaned forward, offering his next words to me alone. "You've only one use to me, boy. So, prove your worth, or get the hell off my ship."

I locked my expression down before my frustration—and worry—could show. "Sir," I grunted, folded my spyglass, and went below.

The stove in Fisher's and my cabin was cold when I entered, but I did not stoke it. The dragonflies in our lantern pulsed gently in their sleep, giving me barely enough light to see, but I did not wake them. Cold and discomfort would serve me far better than light and heat.

I methodically divested myself of my outer clothing. I unbuttoned my frock coat and waistcoat with fingers that trembled with anxiety. I pulled off my cap and unwound my scarf—it felt too much like a noose, anyway—and sat on the deck on my side of the canvas divide.

I toyed with the worn coin, trying to sap some last thread of comfort from the talisman. The peace of it, the way my senses settled, reminded me of Mary's song. My concern for the Stormsinger redoubled.

I slipped the coin back into my pocket, closed my eyes, and opened my mind.

The Other's dark waters rushed into my head as if through a fractured hull. It came with a roar and a hiss and a deeper, more profound cold—the cold of midwinter nights and forgotten tombs.

The human world dissipated until all but the walls of the ship vanished. The ghisting-saturated wood retained some of its solidity, but allowed me to see through it to the endless, black sea and twisted, upside-down forests of the Other. The dragonflies in their lantern remained too, dozing and pulsing with the same soft glow as they had in the waking world.

Anyone entering my cabin right now would see nothing amiss. I would still be sitting there on the floor, fully clothed and breathing steadily. But my mind, my *self*, was in the Other.

I was visible on the Other side too, though my clothing was not. I was left naked, clad only by a Sooth's earthy green light; I was stripped bare in a world where I did not belong. A world of monsters and visions, where past and future had little meaning.

A world where, without the coin in my pocket, I could easily become trapped.

Lights began to appear, visible through the transparent wood of the ship. Some were in the water, dark and gently shifting. Some were in the murk of a starless night sky. Some clung to the huge, twisted trunks and branches of a distant forest, a forest with no leaves or boughs, just knotted roots where they ought to have been. I was too far away to see the details of that Wold, but I had visited ones like it before. I knew how the Dark Water perpetually washed around their roots, and how they sheltered an endless array of monsters.

One of the lights in that flat, endless sea was myself—my deep, woodland green. Another was the Hart himself, our ship's ghisting. He was at rest, ensconced within the stag figurehead and radiating soft blue. Many of the other lights were a similar color: the gentle indigo of ships' ghistings, trapped in the human world, and the sapphire blue of free ghistings roaming the Dark Water.

Other lights were amber, teal, burnt orange, white or grey. Most of them were distant, in or beyond the forest.

I forced my breath out in a long, settling gust. A clock began to tick in the back of my mind, and I went to work.

Lirr. I pictured him as I imagined him to be: middle-aged and plain, with the sunbaked, weathered skin of every Aeadine sailor and the coiled muscles of the violent and bloodthirsty. I conjured his victims in my mind's eye too—burned ships, bloated bodies shredded by torture as much as sharks and morgories. Seaside towns in flames. Mutilated prisoners set adrift as warnings to the rest of the world.

My internal clock chimed and I scanned the lights on the horizon to make sure none were closing in. They danced impassively, the waves of the Other slapped against the hull, and I was undisturbed.

Good. I changed my imagining of Lirr, trying to find the combination of vision and feeling that would connect the pirate and I. But as I had told Slader, it was impossible. In theory, I could locate any mage with connection to the Other—and Lirr was a mage, we knew—but not without touching them first.

Prove your worth or get the hell off my ship.

Panic and cold prickled into my flesh. I ran my mind over my limbs back in the waking world, reassuring myself of my connection to them, and sunk deeper into the Other.

The lights grew brighter. My limbs grew lighter. I made a soft sound of dread—half groan, half grunt—and refocused. Lirr. Fire. Blood.

Snaking, orange light.

I spun, coming halfway to my feet and bracing myself on the insubstantial deck. Inside the lantern, the dragonflies awoke with a start. Their light tripled and their wings made a hushed, rattling drone.

Something surged through the dark water towards me, quick as a snake in the grass, though far bulkier and many-limbed. It was the fodder of my every childhood nightmare, reflections of days spent trapped in this realm as a sick, frightened young boy. Only the coin in my pocket had saved me then, and only it could save me now.

I shoved my hand into my pocket. But there was no pocket here, just cold, ethereal flesh. I was too far into the Other, my connection to my true body too thin.

I forced myself back into the real world one breath at a time, ears roaring, heart thundering. Finally, the Other faded. In my last glimpse of that world I saw the orange light slow, disoriented, and drift east.

I slipped into my own bones, only to immediately lose grip again. I clung to the divide between worlds, the edge where time had no meaning and Sooths like myself could see the future, the past and present. I tried to lurch past it, tried to get free before the visions came, but I was not fast enough.

Images assaulted me, fragmented and stark: Mary Firth holding a pistol to a man's head on a dusky road; Charles Grant with a bloodied face; and myself in a summer Wold of lording ghisten trees.

I fumbled the coin out of my pocket and locked it into my palm. The visions cleared, the world righted, and my back hit the deck with a thud. I lay as still as I could, panting up at the ceiling.

I blinked the visions away, sending the one of Mary and the pistol last. That was odd, to be sure. But I saw dozens like them every day, about anyone and anything around me, and interpreting them was routinely futile.

I cannot find Lirr. The words rang through my head, as true as they had ever been. Maybe a better Sooth could have done it, even without having met the pirate. Maybe a better Sooth could slip to and from the Other with ease, without fear of being trapped. A better Sooth could make peace with their premonitions, living a step ahead of the rest of the world, unstoppable and immeasurably valuable. But I was only myself, fractured, and imperfect.

And stuck. If I came back to Slader without results, by tomorrow I would be abandoned on Whallum's docks, alone and freshly disgraced. I would lose my best chance to redeem myself in the eyes of the world, my family, and myself.

Anger burned away some of my anxiety and cold, replacing it with smoldering indignation. I pressed my fist into my aching chest and closed my eyes.

Well, then. If Slader threatened me and asked for impossible results, I would give him the next best thing—even if my conscience roiled at the idea.

A lie.

∽

"You're sure he was bound for Tithe?" the captain asked, watching me from his seat at the table in his cabin. A view of the snowy coastline stretched beyond him, partially blocked by a half-drawn curtain.

"I cannot speak with absolute certainty," I cautioned, "but there is nothing else like him in this region of the sea."

"Good enough," the older man said with a nod, and I could tell that he was pleased—not necessarily with me, but with this change in fortune. "See the ship readied for departure, then get some rest, Mr. Rosser."

The Girl from the Wold

The Girl from the Wold is drowning. She flails and panics, naked beneath her shift in the black water of the midnight millpond.

Her mother's arms come around her, lifting her above the surface. The girl struggles for breath and hangs at her mother's neck. Her small arms shake.

"You're fine, Mary," the mother says, prying her daughter's hands away and letting her bob back into the water.

The girl flounders. Her toes barely touch the muddy bottom of the pond and she battles to keep her mouth above water, head tilted back. "Mama! I can't—"

"You can. Hush." Her mother steps back, increasing the space between them. "Don't want to wake the miller now, do we? What would he say, finding us half naked in his pond?"

The girl starts to laugh, but she's still afraid. Rallying, she grabs hold of her fear and lifts her toes from the mud, beginning to pump her legs and move her arms in the rhythm her mother taught her.

Her chin leaves the water. She breathes easier, her muscles warm, and her mother smiles.

The girl begins to smile back, but her eyes catch on the collar of her mother's shirt. It has come unlaced in the water, showing a slice of ribs and breast and belly. But the girl doesn't notice those things. Instead, she looks at the deep, knotted scar over her mother's heart. It's the size of a coin, a swirl of tight, opalescent skin in the moonlight.

"It looks like the moon," the girl says, legs and arms still churning.

Her mother smiles and adjusts her wet clothing, covering the scar again. "That it does, little one. Now, race me to the shore."

The Girl from the Wold is drowning again, many years and miles distant. Frigid water punches the air from her lungs and her lungs demand it back in the same, screaming instant. Her world is one of shadows, lit only by the distant light of a burning ship atop the waves. Her world is solitary, save the figure of a woman with drifts of spectral hair, a childlike face and sea-glass eyes filled with bereaved compassion. Her skin is ghostly, and her skirts are a ripple of tentacles.

A ghisting. The girl has glimpsed these beings before, in the shadows of the Wold, and in the little cupboard where she sleeps. She has even seen this one herself, perhaps.

The creature reaches out in the deeps, places her hands on the girl's cheeks, and speaks.

Sister. Breathe.

∞

EIGHT

Pirates

MARY

Something bumped my head. I flailed, grasping it and hauling until I broke the surface of the water. I raked in air and coughed, clutching my salvation for a trembling moment before I squinted at it.

A rope? Why was I holding a rope? Why was I in the water?

Because I'd jumped off a pirate's ship.

I cried out in shock, whatever insanity that had led me to jump shattered by the cold water.

A salty wave broke over me. I clawed back up into the free air, spluttering and panicking. I could swim—my mother had ensured that—but my skirts were so heavy, the water so cold. My lungs burned between fits of coughing and—

I reclaimed the end of the rope and clutched it fiercely.

"Ahoy there," called a voice I didn't know, female and quizzical. Squinting up through wet eyelashes, I could just make out her form at the rail of a ship, lantern light spilling down one side of a hard, olive-skinned face. "Hold fast and we'll lower a ladder."

"No!" I shouted, despite myself, the need to live and the need to stay away from Lirr colliding like waves against the hull beside me. "I'm not— You will not have me!"

"I'm trying to save you," the woman chided. She had a light accent, something warm and lilting. "Would you prefer to drown?"

"No! Yes!" I shrieked. Some rational part of my mind informed me that I was hysterical, but if there'd ever been a situation that warranted hysteria, this was it. "That's why I jumped off the bloody damn ship!"

More heads appeared down the rail. Dozens of sailors looked on, conferring and pointing.

"She wants to drown," the woman informed one of the figures, who drew up beside her in a tricorn hat. "Jumped off Lirr's ship, she says."

Lirr's ship? So, this ship was... someone else's? How many ships were out here?

"Ms. Firth," the newcomer called. It wasn't the pirate, Lirr. This was James Demery, from Kaspin's auction. "There's no need to die tonight."

Confusion overwhelmed me.

"Where are the pirates?" I shouted, voice cracking. How long had I been in the water? Where was the light of the burning *Juliette*? And her newly freed ghisting with her sea-glass eyes and the floating hair... She was gone too.

Gone. They were all gone. The sea around me was devoid of light save the glow of this vessel's lanterns. There was no wreckage, either, no tangles of rope or charred wood.

New panic spiked through me, along with a healthy dose of bewilderment. My eyes stung—emotion and cold, stinging seawater. What had happened to me?

"Where are the pirates?!" One of the bystanders mimicked my question, and a laugh rippled down the deck. "We're all pirates, lass."

I'd gone from one ship full of criminals to another. I clutched the rope and murmured a weepy, "Damn."

"Come aboard and I'll answer all your questions." Demery gestured and a rope ladder toppled over the side of the ship, quickly occupied by two men. They started to descend with the surety of acrobats.

I hadn't the strength to swim away. The rope was the only thing between me and drowning, though the cold was so deep in my flesh now, I could hardly feel myself holding it.

"Ms. Firth," Demery's voice became cooler, "Silvanus Lirr is gone, likely believing you dead. And if that is the end you desire, so be it. But you can make that decision tomorrow, once this night and its terrors have passed."

Something inside of me, knotted and frantic with tension, loosened. He meant those words, or at least, I thought he did. And if he didn't? I couldn't afford to care.

The last of my will faded and when the pirates reached the end of their ladder, I held my hands towards them. One dropped into the water and pulled me in, locking a strong arm around my waist and helping me onto the first rung. I didn't even care when he shook my sodden skirts out of the way. The second pirate watched, hanging above us with a mop of dark, curly hair in his eyes. Then the three of us, painstakingly, began to climb.

I collapsed onto the deck in a shivering, dripping mess. The crew gathered in, curious as hounds. Demery crouched down beside me and the woman I'd seen earlier hovered at his shoulder in men's trousers and a thick winter coat.

"My name is James Elijah Demery, and this ship is the *Harpy*," the captain said. "This is my first, Athe Kohlan. You're safe here."

The woman nodded, her eyes flinty. She was in her thirties, easily six feet tall with broad hips, broad shoulders, and a mismatched collection of men's clothes. But there was no mistaking her femininity; her features were striking, with high cheekbones, a smooth jawline and honey-dark eyes, twined with grey and lined with thick black lashes. Her hair was black too, and showed a hint of stubborn curl despite the severity of the braid she'd bound it in. Those features, combined with her darker skin, made me suspect she had Sunjani in her blood, at least by one parent.

"Safe? That's what *he* said," I chattered, devoting the last spark of my energy to vehemence. My breath curled in the air before me. "You're the same as him—a pirate, a Saint-damned pirate."

Something flicked across Demery's features at the accusation, but he didn't respond. He just stood up and nodded to the woman, Athe, who hauled me to my feet. When I staggered, her iron arm kept me upright.

"Right, Ms. Firth," Athe said, leading me towards the quarterdeck and its waiting doors. She thumped and rubbed my upper arms like a mother with a fussing toddler. "Let's thaw you out."

∽

I lay in my cocoon of blankets, head resting on the creaking hammock's edge. I watched firelight dance through the murky glass of the cabin's woodstove, trying to imagine I was anywhere but here. The bulkhead and decking around the stove were covered in standard iron plating and the stove's belly was small enough to go out if it wasn't tended every few hours.

It was burning low, again, and cold seeped in through the walls. Someone had come to feed it at least once since my arrival aboard Demery's ship, but time was a slippery thing, and I had no window in my cabin to judge the light.

I was alone. Alone and so far unharmed, ensconced in blankets that smelled of salt and lavender and lye.

My thoughts drifted back to Kaspin's auction, to the promise Demery had made that aboard his ship, I'd be treated fairly. Was that proving true? Did it matter if it was? I was still a prisoner.

I buried myself deeper in my blankets, hair poofing up around my head. My thoughts swerved away from my current troubles and back to Lirr.

Do you remember who I am?

No, I couldn't bear to think of him, either, or of the ghisting who'd called me sister. She was the last thing I remembered before Demery's appearance... But how had he found me? And where had the wreckage of *Juliette* gone? Had the ghisting carried me away?

The thought was absurd, but less absurd than other possibilities. I certainly hadn't swum away from Lirr, and he must have searched for me. He wouldn't have simply sailed away, even in the storm I'd conjured with my last breaths. His singer could have dispersed that if she wanted to, whoever that poor soul was.

I didn't want to think of her, either. Instead, I chose to remember my childhood room at the inn, high on the third floor under the eaves. I imagined opening the shutters to a sunny view of the Wold. I recalled the smells of earth and green, manure and woodsmoke and baking bread that always permeated our side of the village.

In that memory, I played the harpsichord and practiced the flute. While I did, the washerwoman and her daughter hung the laundry out back, sheets billowing in the breeze. The women would sing a call-and-response song as they splashed and scrubbed and wrung out the weekly washing. My father, Joseph Grey, would wander through the nearby garden within its short fence, a pipe between his teeth, eyes scanning the rows for weeds and pests. Chickens and ducks would scatter from his ambling, bare feet.

I didn't think beyond that image, fixed in that restful time before my father's eyes had strayed beyond the garden, the washerwoman's daughter had fallen with child and she'd become his new wife. Before he'd given up on my mother, and our world of predictable days and quiet hope had become... something else.

A knock sounded on the door. I cracked an eye.

The knock came again and when I didn't reply, the door opened. Daylight cut across the deck and revealed a woman, not Athe but an older person with leathery, wrinkled porcelain skin and a black dress with a ruffed collar, fifty years out of fashion. She was one of the Ismani peoples, her hooded eyes lined with white lashes and her equally white hair swept up with a long, carnelian hairpin. Only a few strands of her former, youthful hair color remained—dashes of glossy, chocolate brown.

"Little mage," the woman said, squinting at me with her arms full of cloth. Despite her obvious heritage, her accent was an ambiguous one, reminding me of some of the travelers we'd see at the inn when I was a child. Her pronunciation was clear, patient—one used to speaking to those who didn't share a native tongue. "I have clothes for you, and a bucket of hot water on the way. Are you fit to ready yourself?"

I found my voice. "Who are you?"

"My name is my own, but you may call me Widderow," the woman replied. "Ship's steward. The captain needs to speak with you."

"I don't have a choice," I observed.

Widderow smiled flatly. "No, child, you do not. Get up."

Twenty minutes later, I stepped out into the grand cabin to find the old woman gone. I'd barely seen my surroundings when I came aboard last night, but my small cabin attached to this larger one. Together, they took up most of the quarterdeck. The galley was here too, judging by the magnificent scents drifting through an open door to a passageway. There was a bigger woodstove in its iron nest at the stern, along with windows on either side of a door to a sheltered balcony. It was snowing outside, flakes drifting down and disappearing into mild waves.

"Ms. Firth." Demery entered, followed by Widderow and a girl of about fifteen.

Widderow carried a pot and several mugs, while the girl had a tray stacked haphazardly with toasted bread, buttery eggs, thick bacon and cheeses. The scent of it all hit me like a mallet and my stomach growled. My appetite, it seemed, was unaffected by my volatile circumstances, and seasickness had yet to bother me.

The meal was left on a large table in the center of the room. The girl vanished and Widderow sat, pouring herself a stream of dark coffee. Seeing the look on my face, she pointedly set out a second cup and filled it halfway, leaving room for it to slosh with the tilt of the deck.

"Stop gawking like a fool," she scolded. "Come and drink it. And eat. You are making me uncomfortable."

"It takes a lot to make the Old Crow uncomfortable." Demery cast me a distracted half-smile as he sat at the table across from the steward. He pulled out a plate and began to fill it.

"She has a touch of the blood fugue," Widderow informed him without looking at me. She patted her carefully pinned hair with one hand and smoothed a stray piece. "Less than I expected, but more than is practical. She may not be much use for a time."

I didn't like being discussed like this, but her words gave me pause. I gathered my scattered wits and sat slowly. Blood fugue. Shock. Was that why I couldn't remember what had happened to me after I hit the water?

Demery pushed a plate in front of me and Widderow nodded to the coffee. "Do not let that get cold or slide onto the floor."

I obligingly took the mug in hand. I wanted to drink it. I wanted to seize everything on the table and consume it like a feral dog. But the attitude of my captors unnerved me.

"Why are you doing this?" I asked, holding the warm mug between my hands. "Why are you treating me… like this?"

"I told you you'd be treated well aboard my ship," Demery said, pouring his own coffee and adding lumps of brown sugar.

"But I'm a prisoner," I reminded him. "Prisoners aren't served coffee and bacon."

Demery stirred his coffee, eyes quiet. "Randalf was a bastard."

Was. That word usurped my former question, and I distantly recalled the sight of bodies hanging from the yards of a burning ship. "He's really dead?"

"Most likely. Lirr will have taken the most valuable members of his crew and left the rest to burn with the ship. That's his way."

He hadn't just left them to burn, though. I blocked out images of blood and violence and trailing guts and lifted the coffee to my lips, letting the warmth and scent anchor me. The faces of Randalf's crew flickered through my mind, alive and whole. They'd not been good men by any stretch, but not purely evil, either. Did they deserve their fate?

"Who is he?" I asked. "Lirr? I think... I know there was a pirate by that name, but that was a long time ago."

Demery nodded, elbows planted on the table to either side of his plate. He'd started to eat and gave no sign that he intended to answer my question.

Widderow spoke up instead, leaning back in her chair. "He *was* a pirate, yes, up until a decade ago. That's when he bought himself a Mereish title and set himself up in their southern islands, took a few wives and slipped out of Her Majesty's sight. But he's back now."

"Why?" I asked.

Widderow exchanged a look with Demery, the kind of silent communication that passed between siblings and old soldiers.

"You," Demery said. "Or rather, your mother."

My mug connected to the tabletop with a clatter. Hot coffee spilled over my fingers, but I barely felt it. "What?"

"Your mother is his Stormsinger," the captain said without feeling. His eyes dropped to the spilled coffee on the table, then up to my eyes. "I assume she convinced him to acquire you, or he intends to use you against her. He would have done so in Whallum, if I hadn't showed up—we're not on speaking terms, he and I—or if Randalf hadn't left prematurely."

My world became a muffled, distant roar. My mother. I'd heard a Stormsinger before the attack, I recalled that—a distant, bold song that I instinctively recognized as sorcerous. But that could not have been my mother, could it?

"She was there—" My own words were almost lost to my ears. "—on his ship?"

It was too much. I sat perfectly still, blood roaring in my ears, heart slamming in great, unwieldy beats. I wasn't breathing. Wasn't thinking.

"It's too soon." Widderow's voice drifted to me from a vast distance, flattened and dull in my haze. "She needs more time, Eli."

Demery's response was equally flat. "Then tell Athe to set course directly for Tithe."

TITHE—*Whimsically called The Tithe to the Sea, this small cluster of Usti-controlled islands is situated near the center of the Winter Sea. It has been a place of rest for seafarers for millennia, with the current settlement established by Usti, who allied with the Ghistings of their ships and utilized them in the building of their homes. The Ghisten Trees of Tithe thereafter appeared, though this growth is not yet considered a full Wold. See also* USTI TERRITORIES.

—FROM THE WORDBOOK ALPHABETICA: A NEW
WORDBOOK OF THE AEADINES

NINE

Tithe

MARY

I passed the remaining four days to Tithe in the privacy of my cabin. Demery didn't require me to sing, even when the weather worsened, and the moaning of the wind kept me awake. I was lost inside myself, in my shock and my unrest, and neither he nor Widderow tried to pry me out of it.

I slept as much as I could and saw no one other than the captain, the steward and the cook's girl. Then on the fourth day, the sound of the ship changed. I felt the vessel slow, heard shouts and chanting and the clatter of the anchor chain, then Athe's voice sounded through my cabin door.

"—ashore in an hour."

Shore. We'd reached Tithe. I slipped from my hammock, aching from inactivity, and pressed an ear to the crack between door and frame. The deck was frigid beneath my stocking-clad feet, but relatively still.

"I'll visit the port mistress and pay the tithe." Demery sounded distracted.

"What about the Stormsinger?" Athe lowered her voice, and I sensed a change in its direction—she was looking at my door.

I stilled. The woman couldn't see me, but I felt her eyes on the other side of the barrier.

"She'll come ashore with me," Demery replied.

There was a strained silence, into which Athe finally asked, "You're willing to risk that?"

"Course I am," the captain returned tartly. "She's hardly in any condition to run off."

I felt a flush of indignation. Running away would be a challenge, but that wouldn't stop me from doing it. Tithe was a busy port. There would be ships back to Aeadine. There might even be word of my mother—proper word, not the lies Demery had spouted to me.

My mother was not aboard Lirr's ship. Surely, I would have known. Surely, she would have screamed the ship apart to get to me, to protect me.

Athe's voice came again. "That was not what I meant."

"Lirr won't come for her in Tithe. Between the storm she called and the ghistings, we've enough time to get ourselves sorted."

I recoiled from the door, staring at the crack in bafflement. Lirr coming for me again? Ghistings buying us time?

The questions that had been moldering in the back of my head for days shook themselves into wakefulness. I would have to pry answers from Demery. But I couldn't be rash, and I couldn't take his word for anything, especially when it came to my mother.

Another silence, then Athe spoke again. "And if he saw us tailing him?"

"Then we wouldn't be having this conversation," Demery said with finality. His footsteps approached my door and I beat a hasty retreat.

He rapped. "Ms. Firth?"

My back bumped into my hammock. I didn't want him to realize I'd been eavesdropping, so I pushed the bundle of canvas and blankets to make it creak, as if I were waking up.

"Ms. Firth," the captain began again. "We're in Tithe, and I'd like you to come to shore with me. We'll pay our dues then see you set up at an inn. I've several days' business here, and there's no need for you to remain aboard ship."

"An inn?" I repeated. "Why would you do that?"

"You'll be more comfortable there."

Incredulity crept into my voice. "Why would you care about my comfort?"

"I want you on my crew," Demery said bluntly. "I need a Stormsinger. I was willing to pay to get you here, though that was a regrettable way to meet. Now I've plucked you from the waves and I'd like to start fresh."

"Start fresh?" My voice cracked, too high. "With a slave?"

"With an ally. I've no use for slaves or any relationship built on fear. Loyalty goes much further. And I so enjoy being loved."

I bit my tongue, not just because I didn't dare believe him. Athe was right—if Demery took me to shore, my chances of escaping went up considerably. I wasn't foolish enough to think I'd be left at an inn unwatched—my freedom would certainly be a façade—but there were far more variables on land than ship.

On the other side of the door, the captain took my silence for agreement.

"Get dressed and put yourself together," he said, turning away from the door. "I'll be waiting in the boat."

I stared warily at the dock beneath my feet as I waited for some of Demery's crew to disembark. The captain sent most of them off on individual errands while three big men trailed after Widderow like oversized goslings. The old woman wore a hefty black cloak lined with white fur, worn but well kept, and I swore I saw a white crow fly over her head as she reached the shore.

She glared at me from beneath her hood before she merged with the crowd. She did not speak, but her warning was clear enough.

Don't you run off, girl.

Well, I would, once I'd found my legs again. Neither Widderow nor the sailors appeared to have much trouble adjusting to the steadiness of land, besides sauntering with broad stances between stacks of crates, trundling carts and laboring dockworkers. But my world still tipped and tottered.

I gave up trying to stand on my own and put a hand on one of the mooring posts, using the time to examine Tithe. I'd imagined it would be like Whallum, with tall wooden buildings, clustered and jumbled. But this settlement looked more like the village I'd grown up in, with stone houses and slate roofs. I supposed it was much older, though—several huge standing stones protruded from the water, bedecked with snow, skirted with ice and carved with strange runes. Ruined fortifications also stood high on a forested hill to the east, melancholy and mysterious beyond a veil of smoke, steam and low cloud.

"Why is that castle abandoned?" I asked Demery as he paused beside me, tugging the collar of his coat against the cold. "Don't they need it for defense?"

"Tithe needs no defenses," the captain said, gesturing up the dock for me to precede him.

I lifted my hand from the post and tested my feet again. I didn't fall over, so I took a cautious step, and we started for shore. "How is that possible?"

"It's Tithe," he said simply. "The Tithe to the Sea. It belongs to no nation—save the Usti, in a roundabout way, but that's rather complicated."

"I know all that," I protested, offended. "But that doesn't mean anything. It can't just sit here, undefended. Someone will try to take it eventually."

"Ah." Demery sunk his hands deep into his pockets. His eyelashes were bleached by the sun, I noticed, but long and thick around his grey eyes. "Then you've been misinformed. Follow me and watch your pockets. Tithe is a good deal cleaner than Whallum, but there's greedy fingers in every port."

"I've nothing to steal," I muttered. I sidestepped a pile of steaming manure as we turned onto the main street.

A flash caught my eye, and I looked up just in time to catch a coin singing through the air. I stared at it, flat and nearly filling my bare palm. A solem. A whole solem, silver and embossed with a relief of Aeadine's matronly Queen Edith. The only other time I'd held one of these was the day I'd become betrothed, and my father had presented me with the single solem he'd put away for my wedding dress and other wifely provisioning.

I'd never gotten a chance to wear that dress. I imagined it was still packed away in the attic of the inn, along with everything else that might be called mine.

"You'll need to buy new clothes," Demery said, by way of explanation. He tucked his hands back into his pockets and started through the town. "I'll not have my Stormsinger looking like an urchin."

"I'm not your Stormsinger," I grumbled, but I was distracted by the coin. I slipped it into the pocket of the short sailor's coat Widderow had given me and held it there. A solem should be enough to buy passage back to Aeadine if I played my hand correctly.

But the word 'Stormsinger' dredged up a host of questions, the foremost of which slipped from my lips. "Does Lirr truly have my mother, Captain?"

Demery looked at me, his gaze level and without a hint of falseness. "Yes. But the street is not the place to speak of such things. Tomorrow, or tonight if your mind is fit for it, I'll answer all your questions. But not now. There are some things that shouldn't be spoken under an open sky."

I pressed my lips shut. My questions still burned, but I kept my head down as we pushed through the crowd.

Scents wafted past me. Pastries, mulling wine. Woodsmoke and tobacco. Coffee too, along with the ever-present crispness of the Winter Sea, the musk of horses, manure and mud. They were the scents of early winter and the approach to Festus season, the month of celebration that marked the beginning of the long, hard winter. They were scents tied to a host of pleasant feelings and childhood nostalgia.

But as we wandered, a newer, stranger feeling overtook me. Vague and warning, it crept up from the ground, from the wood of lintels and beams, and it grew stronger as we went.

The people and buildings gave way to a churchyard on the northern side of town. The feeling was strongest here, where tombstones and statues were arrayed on a sweeping hill beside the sea, each sad monolith bastioned by snow and harried by wind. The abandoned fort rose on the forested hill beyond it, but only a few trees dared to grow in the graveyard itself: all huge, ancient, and unmistakably ghisten.

The central one was an ash, its unseasonably lush canopy covering half the churchyard and weighted with snow. Even without the greenness of its leaves, there was no questioning the tree's nature—I felt its draw and I picked up my pace, edging ahead of Demery. He let me go, falling in behind on a narrow, well-worn path between banks of snow.

I paused under the branches and raked cool air into my lungs, relishing the familiar energy of a ghisten tree. It was an intangible thing, like the quiet of an empty chapel, or the hush of the graves all around. But the ash was more... alive, more insistent. It was fingers around my ribs, tugging me forward. It was the strongest pull I'd ever felt to a ghisten tree.

Then I noticed the coins. There were hundreds of them—no, thousands, tens of thousands—wedged and stuck and grown into the thick bark. They'd become part of the tree itself, like scales of a hundred different sizes and metals and origins. I scuffed snow away from the roots to find they, too, had been armored with coins, and when I looked up, even the highest branches bore the same.

"What is this?" I breathed as Demery drew up.

"The Tithe," he said, offering me a small copper coin between two fingers. "Find a spot to stick it."

"Why?" I took the coin, warm from his pocket, and held it as the cold sea wind blew around us.

"Because if you spend a night in Tithe without making an offering, this island will try to kill you." Demery took his own coin, then circled the tree until he found a hammer hanging from a leather tie. He took it up and circled more, squinting. At length, he spied a spot where the bark had grown up around previous coins. Flipping the hammer around, he used a spike on one side to break the exterior of the bark, then set the coin in on its edge, and flipped the hammer back around.

Tapping rang out in the quiet churchyard. The coin sank in and Demery stood back, holding the tool out to me.

"Try to kill me, how?" I asked, taking the hammer. Its haft was cool and smooth. "Why?"

"A few hundred years ago, Usti settlers used ghisten wood from their ships to build homes." Demery nodded back to the jumbled roofs and rising hearth smoke of the town. "A dangerous decision, true, one that went ill for many others in the past. But here, the humans and the ghistings found an accord. The ghistings vowed to protect the island in exchange for not being sent back to sea—and a ghisting's vow can never be broken, not unless the other party breaks it first. The humans kept their end of their bargain, and eventually new ghisten trees started to grow. Here, ghistings and humans live in harmony."

I looked up at the sweep of the ghisten ash's branches over my head.

"Ghistwolds like this sprout where many ghistings converge," Demery continued, looking at the tree instead of me. "If there's a Mother Tree's seed among them, anyway. So now, all who'd visit Tithe must pay their respects to the island's rulers: the port mistress, and the ghistings."

"All who visit? Will your entire crew come here?"

"If they intend to stay a night on shore," Demery said with a nod. He turned, indicating the other trees in the graveyard, and the glint of coins told me they'd undergone the same tradition. "I told you, Tithe needs no forts, no castles. The ghistings guard this place. It is The Tithe to the Sea—both our Winter Sea, and the Dark Water."

The Dark Water. That was what sailors called the Other, the realm where ghistings, morgories, implings and even lantern dragonflies originated. It was also where Stormsingers, like me, sourced their power.

I ran my fingers across the coin-mottled bark of the ash. Branches clacked and the sound of the sea rushed past my ears, but as I began to sing under my breath, the wind, for once, subsided.

Demery watched me keenly, noting the change in the wind as I began to circle the ash, trailing my hand as I went.

The bite of the cold faded. I found a narrow spot of unbroken bark between a Mereish dette and an unrecognizable tin piece, then tapped my offering into place.

When I finished, I passed the hammer back to the pirate and he hung it on an iron hook. Then, desperate to recapture the feeling of the Wold, I pressed both palms into the bark of the tree.

I closed my eyes and instinctively reached. The impulse might have unnerved me, but before I could acknowledge it, I saw something with my mind's eye—a trumpeting angel with bladed wings, his face forever frozen in a pious, heavenward gaze. The tree's ghisting. A guardian. A herald. A warrior.

My hands pressed harder into the bark and ridges of coins, palms and fingers spread. The pull that had drawn me to the tree now dragged me deeper, reaching out with ethereal lines of communication—a mixture of emotion, thought and memory.

The angel's eyes abruptly clapped onto my face.

Sister.

All the breath left my lungs.

With impossible grace, the angel reached through the wood to place a palm against mine.

Images slammed into my mind, so rapid and vivid that I gasped. In one moment, I saw centuries of memories. I saw dragon-headed longboats, junks and great hundred-gun Capesh warships. I saw gun smoke and blood. I saw a younger, sparser Tithe growing along the shore. I saw saplings with roots that went not into soil, but through the fabric of one world and into the Other. The Dark Water.

Sister.

My knees wavered, but my fingers dug into the coin-laden bark. More images came, but I sensed that they did not originate from the tree. They came from me, images of fire and Lirr's fingers upon my chin.

"Ms. Firth." A hand closed on my upper arm and I squinted into Demery's face. "What's wrong with you?"

"Just… dizzy," I said, though in truth I couldn't describe what had happened. I'd sensed ghistings before, but this had felt like a conversation of images and feelings, along with that single word, *Sister.*

"Do ghistings speak?" I asked suddenly. "Everyone in the Wold… my Wold… says they don't. My mother said so too."

I expected the captain to laugh, or worse look at me with pity over my ignorance of the world. But instead, he inquired in a voice that suggested he already knew the answer, "The ash spoke to you?"

I shook the snow from my skirts. There was no hiding it, given my reaction to touching the tree. "Yes."

Demery did smile then, a nearly invisible crinkle in the corner of his mouth. His hand, still on my arm, released. "It's more common than one might think, if one knows how to listen. You're a child of the Wold, a Stormsinger tied to the Dark Water."

That wasn't far off my own reasoning. I still didn't trust the pirate, but I saw little reason for him to lie about this. Relieved, my breath came a little easier. "Do you hear your ship's ghisting?"

"Harpy?" Demery shoved his hand back into his pocket. "Sometimes."

That was enough to satisfy me for the time being. Despite my claim to dizziness, my thoughts came quicker now. "You promised I could stay at an inn, Captain…"

The wind I'd ensorcelled tugged stray hair into his grey eyes as he waited for me to go on, backed by the windswept graveyard and the snow-laden roofs of the town, with its piping chimneys and bustling inhabitants. I noticed for the first time that the grey of Demery's irises was not solid—rather a rim of grey with a warm green heart. They reminded me of my mother's eyes, and of my own. It was an odd similarity, but I'd only just stepped out into the world beyond my Wold. There was much that struck me as strange.

"Then take me there now," I said, blinking my observations away, "and I'll consider your proposal."

MAGNI, MAGNUS—*A mage with an unnatural ability to incur loyalty and desire from those around them. It is considered one of the most subtle of the human giftings, and, debatably, the most dangerous. A notable Magni was Sir William Caston of Merrifolk, who, in a fit of madness, ordered five thousand soldiers to their doom in the White Desert of Ambia during the Second Mereish War. Every soldier, it is said, perished without complaint.*

—FROM THE WORDBOOK ALPHABETICA: A NEW
WORDBOOK OF THE AEADINES

TEN

The Edge of the Other

SAMUEL

Exhausted from another day on watch, I languished in my hammock, eyes closed, hands resting on my stomach. Gradually, my consciousness drifted out from the arc of my ribs, beyond the tips of my fingers towards the Other.

I twitched, realizing I had left the worn coin in the pocket of my coat, on my trunk. I ought to retrieve it before the Dark Water swelled, or visions started in full. But my tired body refused to move.

A vision flickered across my eyes—a glimpse of Mary Firth on the deck of a ship, singing under her breath.

"Slow is the knell of summer's end…"

Then I was a child. I sat next to my brother Benedict on a bench in a wood-paneled study, his bloodied hand—my aunt's work—hidden under his opposite arm. The scents of coffee, aged wood, wax and wig powder filled my nose, sigils of my uncle, Admiral John Rosser.

I heard the admiral's voice: *You are his elder brother, even if that be only by a few moments. He is your responsibility. He and his darkness. My name can only protect you two for so long.*

I heard my father next, older, fainter. One hand on my cheek, one hand on Ben's as he looked down at us with pride. *Take care of one another, my boys.*

My mother's voice came last, candlelight on her face and her back to a moonless night. *My boys, my sweet boys. How powerful you will be. How proud your father, when he comes home.*

I clenched my eyes shut, trying to smother the memory. Back then, I had not seen the madness in her eyes. Back then, I did not know that my father was already dead, and she living in denial—her mind shattered by grief.

But when that spring night had come, moonless and dark, I had foreseen the danger. I had had a chance to save Ben and myself. Yet I had been too afraid, too trusting, too—

"Reconciled, her bended knee." Mary's voice wafted to me, sweet and low, and I saw her on a ship—Randalf's yellow and red schooner. She wore a cloak with the hood pulled back, and a dark braid fell down the length of her spine, frayed by the constant wind.

I followed her hollow gaze to the horizon, shedding memories of my mother and Ben like ash. A tower of sails rose from the waves in three sun-bleached tiers. Behind it, snow clouds loosed a cascade of thick flakes, veiling the pink and gold of a setting sun.

Something moved in the water, creeping towards me in a sickly orange haze of light. It was a creature with a horse's shrunken head and the body of an emaciated dog, prowling the waves on its back two feet. The long claws of its bony forepaws dragged across the surface of the water in frothing rivulets, but it did not sink—it moved as if the water were no more than a few inches deep.

This was not part of the vision. This was real, in the Dark Water.

A huden. As my eyes met the swirling, light-filled hollows of its eyes, its jaw unhinged with a moist clatter, and it howled.

The vision shattered. I cried out and flailed, toppling out of my hammock in a tumble of elbows, knees and blankets. Between curses and my bones cracking off the deck, I almost missed the ping of a coin rolling away.

I sat up, bruised and panting, and pushed hair back from my face. No huden here. Just sweat coating my forehead and the cool impression left by a coin, right between my eyes.

"Does Slader know?" Fisher's voice curled out of the darkness.

I gave a strangled shout and staggered to my feet, clutching a bruised elbow. "Damn you, Fisher! Do not skulk!"

"Does Slader know?" Fisher repeated. I just made her out in the thin light from our woodstove and hooded lantern. She wore a shift to the knee and no stays, with loose trousers beneath and bare feet. "About that coin?"

Still half drugged by the Other, I struggled to catch up. "Pardon me?"

Fisher bent, picked up the small, glinting piece from the deck, and approached me. "Does Slader know about this coin?" She enunciated clearly, holding it out between two fingers.

"Why would he? It's nothing," I countered lamely. Memory of the huden still lingered with me, unsettling and sharp. It took conscious will not to snatch the coin back. I did not like to see it in her hand. It was my sanity, and Fisher... she knew?

"It's a talisman. You're using Mereish magic to suppress your gift—the very gift he keeps you aboard for." Fisher dropped the coin in my palm. "No wonder you're such a shoddy Sooth."

I had no time to be offended. As soon as the coin touched my skin my disorientation fled and air rushed into my lungs in clean, full gasps. With that came the realization that the coin could not have found its own way onto my forehead. Fisher had put it there, like a priest put pennies on the eyes of the dead.

"Why?" she asked.

I startled at the question and squinted at her. "Pardon?"

"Why are you doing this to yourself?"

I was grateful Fisher had intervened in my visions, but could not tell her more. She had already discovered the coin and its purpose. If I told her anything else, all my secrets would begin to unravel.

"It's hard to sleep," I finally admitted. "Visions can feel a lot like nightmares."

Fisher twisted her lips into a frown, and I sensed she was deciding whether to believe me. "You have 'nightmares' a lot more than you used to."

I flinched. She was not wrong. The more I used the coin to anchor myself to the human world, the more I needed it. It was a crutch, and the longer I leaned on it, the more my muscles atrophied.

It had been twenty years since my uncle slipped the coin into my fingers and saved me from my wanderings in the Dark Water. Twenty more, and I was not sure how much of my sanity would remain.

But for now, I had the coin. For now, I had my mind. And I would use every bit of my strength and wit to ensure my legacy was something that I, and my uncle, could be proud of.

I needed to distract Fisher. "I dreamed of Mary Firth," I admitted. I felt like if I voiced what I had seen, it would make sense. "The Stormsinger."

Fisher winced, even the darkness unable to hide her disdain. "How pleasant for you. Please *do not* share."

"I saw her ship, being trailed by a man-of-war," I clarified, ignoring Fisher's implication.

My counterpart paused. "Was it real? Your visions aren't always… well…"

Now that I was awake and clearheaded, I had to admit that the vision had not felt quite right, though I had been suppressing my abilities for so long I hardly remembered what 'right' was.

When I thought back on tonight's ramblings, only two things demanded my attention—the way the light fell on Mary's face, and the sound of my uncle's voice.

He is your responsibility.

Both of those seemed far more like my warped subconscious than true visions.

"I am not certain," I admitted.

Fisher held out her hand. "Then would you like me to hold that while you chase her back to the Dark Water?"

"No," I barely kept myself from snapping. "It was nothing."

"As you please, Mr. Rosser." Fisher slapped her thighs in a gesture of finality and stood to vanish behind the curtain between our hammocks. "If you wake me up again, I will smother you."

Tithe adorned the shores of a long, natural harbor, backed by gentle hills and distant forest. Everything, from the houses to the town's heavy walls and the pier, was built of grey weathered stone with heavy wooden lintels. Green-copper steeples glinted under a weight of icicle-girded snow, and a series of ancient runestones protruded from the water down the quay. The streets themselves were clean, the crowd of cloaks and skirts punctuated by maroon-coated soldiers. It was an orderly, calm place, steeped in years and assured of its position in the world. It suited and steadied me.

I watched from the deck of *Hart* as our longboats ferried men and goods to and from shore, the steward and his mates orchestrating the provisioning of the ship while fortunate sailors took shore leave.

Fisher returned on one of the boats. Catching my eye as she stepped off the ladder, she approached with one hand under her coat and a sly grin on her face.

"Fisher," I greeted her dubiously. Memory of our conversation in the dark surged back to me, and with it a niggling fear. Would she tell Slader about the coin?

"Mr. Rosser." She pulled out her hand with a flourish and presented me with a flaky pastry wrapped in soft brown paper.

My suspicion deepened. "Did you spit on it?"

"No! Never."

I took the pastry and folded the paper away. There was a noticeable bite out of the back.

"Best you'll get." She clapped me on the shoulder and strode away to take command of the anchor watch. "It's delicious."

I scowled down at the cinnamon-dusted reminder of my disfavor, until Slader's shadow fell across the rail.

"Go ashore, Mr. Rosser," he said, without looking at me. "Next boat."

I scanned his face for some sign of compassion or deception. I found neither. His expression was one of mild disinterest beneath greying eyebrows and black bicorn hat.

"Sir?" I asked. Fisher, now standing on the quarterdeck, was squinting at the crates of chickens the steward had brought aboard that morning. The chickens' clucking increased to an accusatory clamor as Fisher leaned in. My counterpart kicked the cage lightly, and the birds, chastened, fell silent.

Slader turned to face me, lowering his voice. "James Demery just dropped anchor."

I recalled the blithe man from Kaspin's auction and the unsettled feeling he had left me with. Then, more slowly, I recalled the ship I had seen trailing Mary in my vision—or dream, or whatever it had been. Could that ship have been Demery's?

My skin prickled with unease. "Why would he be here?" I asked.

"You tell me," Slader said. "Are you on good terms with the man?"

I nodded, choosing not to tell Slader how troubled I had been by the pirate. "We are acquainted and there were no outward hostilities."

"Good. Then go find out what he's doing here." Slader's smile settled into a grim, subtle twist of the lips. "And for Saint's sake, have a hot bath and a good night's sleep ashore. You're taut as a fiddle."

I opened my mouth to defend myself, but swallowed my words and took the victory. "Yes, sir. Demery's ship, what is she?"

"A modified brigantine, I believe." Slader clasped one wrist behind his back and noted the expression on my face. "No more than twenty guns. If we need to take her, the matter will be well in hand."

Demery's vessel was too small to be the one in my vision, then, but my dreamer's sense itched. Could Mary's pursuer have been Lirr? Could I have ignored a critical vision and jeopardized our whole mission?

I dragged my gaze to Slader, imagining what fury he would unleash if I admitted the possibility. More eager than ever to get ashore, I touched my hat and gave the captain a short bow. "Very good, sir."

ELEVEN

Gentlemen and Pirates

SAMUEL

James Demery's *Harpy* was an economic vessel, unassuming and clean. She rested beside the dock as the Winter Sea's early evening came on, the sails of her two masts neatly furled, a few hands visible on deck. Her stovepipes, one fore and two aft, trickled smoke into the sky, and dusky blue paint highlighted her lintels, gunports and rails. On her stern, blue met with silver to trace out her name, while her figurehead—a stoic, flint-eyed harpy with bare breasts and spreading wings—was painted in startlingly lifelike hues.

Between the vessel and I, wagons trundled, dockhands dispersed, and fishmongers lowered their prices, dispensing increasingly pungent wares as night approached.

I occupied a bench outside a coffee house on the quay, thawing my fingers on my second cup, when Demery appeared from the crowd and made for the gangplank of *Harpy*. I sat a little straighter. He paused at the rail, caught a word from one of his crew, then looked straight at me.

I raised an empty hand in greeting, and told myself that the buzz of my nerves was simply from too much coffee.

As I had hoped, the captain came over. He unbuttoned his coat as he did and let it fall open to show that he was armed with two gleaming pistols.

I shifted on my bench, making my cutlass equally obvious—as gentlemen and pirates did.

Demery sat, rested one ankle across his opposite knee and cast me a half-smile. "Have you paid your Tithe, Mr. Rosser?"

"Of course." I nodded and tapped my mug. "Something to drink?"

"Not with the smell of fouled fish in the air." Demery sniffed in displeasure and looked back through the bustle of dockhands and townsfolk, carts and wagons, sailors and darting children. "But thank you. May I ask why you've been watching my ship for the last hour?"

"I hoped to speak to you, but assumed your crew would shoot first."

Demery's head bobbed in a contemplative nod. "A fair assumption. Me and mine have little cause to trust when you and yours come kicking at our hatches. So, what is it, Lieutenant?"

"My captain wants to know why you are in Tithe."

Demery looked me full in the face, eyebrows arched. "You're not subtle now, are you?"

"It is cold, I need to piss, and I have no desire to spend my whole evening teasing the truth out of you."

Demery's grin crept up into his eyes. "Well, I appreciate someone who doesn't waste my time. I'm here for the very same reason you are."

I glanced at him, eyes narrowing. "Oh?"

"Lirr sailed southwest out of Whallum a week ago." Demery's voice dropped, all amusement fading away. "Chasing John Randalf into a storm. It's well known Tithe is Randalf's first port of call. So, anyone looking for Lirr would do well to sail the same route as Randalf and wait. For sails on the horizon. For rumors."

Sails on the horizon. Again, my vision of Mary reared.

"You are waiting for Lirr?" I clarified.

Demery shrugged. "We have personal business to attend to, but he's disinclined to meet with me, so here we are."

James Demery had personal business with Silvanus Lirr? I shifted deeper into my coat and made a considering sound. "What kind of business?"

The older man looked at me levelly. It was not a hostile expression, but it was clear he had no intention of explaining. "Randalf is late," he stated instead.

I drained my coffee to the grounds and balanced the mug on my thigh, glancing back out to sea. My mind turned over possible connections between Lirr and Demery—old scores and grudges? Shared history in the piratical sphere? Whatever they were, it could seriously complicate *Hart's* commission.

"Perhaps his new Stormsinger has yet to learn her verses?"

Demery huffed ambiguously, but there was a weight to his gaze. "Or Lirr's already found him, and you and I wait in vain."

That thought made my pulse quicken. "How would Lirr catch Randalf without a Stormsinger? He obviously does not have one, otherwise he has no reason to pursue the man to begin with. It is a miracle he even made it out of the storm in Whallum."

Demery stood up and began buttoning his overcoat. "Well, lad, that's where you're wrong."

I stood up too, setting my mug on the sill of the coffeehouse window. "How?"

"Lirr has the best Stormsinger on the Winter Sea and she's been with him for years," the other man said as he popped up his collar against the chill.

I was hard-pressed to hide my shock. "Then why would he be interested in Mary Firth?"

Demery tugged at his scarf, letting it bunch under his chin like a cravat. "Damned if I know."

I shoved my hands into my pockets and glanced down at the slush-covered stone beneath our boots. My vision of Mary must have been real. But I had been so disused to proper visions, so reliant upon the Mereish coin, that I had not known it.

"You believe Lirr caught up with Randalf at sea, then?" I asked. The question felt like a fist in my gut—a fist of guilt, frustration and something more. "And took Mary Firth?"

Demery shook his head. "I cannot say anything for sure. But either Randalf will show up in port soon, hurt or hale, or Lirr will."

I locked gazes with the older man and dared to press, "Captain Demery, why are you hunting Lirr?"

He did not speak right away. I watched him for any change in expression, any hint at the truth. I saw a tightness around his grey eyes and a flicker of his lips, but could not decipher it.

"As I said before, we've personal business to discuss. But I would have both you and your captain know, Mr. Rosser, that our interests are not exclusive of one another. Our paths may cross again. Give me no trouble, and I'll give you none in return—scratch my back, and I may scratch yours."

With that, Demery stepped back out into the street and crossed, boarding *Harpy* without a backwards glance.

As the Winter Sea's early evening drew in and the cloud-choked western horizon turned violet, I wandered. My head felt sharp and clean, but my nerves ground as I pieced the mystery together.

Demery was after Lirr for personal reasons. As I had pondered before, that was not too hard to believe—they had both been sailing long enough to have shared history. Whatever the specific reason was, Demery was right to say our paths would likely cross again, and depending on how Slader took Demery's offer, that meeting would either be to our advantage or peril.

Mary Firth's connection to it all was growing more undeniable, though the nature of that connection was another unknown. If Lirr already had a Stormsinger, he had no need of her. Unless she was more than she seemed. An elusive lover? A missing daughter?

My dreamer's sense ignited, rushing over my ears like a gust of smoke. I did not have the answer, but I intended to find out.

AEADINE—*The term Aeadine encompasses both the peoples of Aeadine (also called Aead, by foreign tongues) and the island which they inhabit. One of the largest landmasses within the Winter Sea, the island is graced with various natural resources including the infamous Aeadine Ghistwold. Aeadine is well-situated for trade with Tithe, and its coast supports a profitable fishing industry. The Aeadine Anchorage, southwest of the main island, provides a natural blockade to the Mereish and their many invasions, as well as a port of departure for trade in the southern seas. The Aeadine officially worship the singular Saint, and are ruled by the Aeadine Monarchy—may they forever wear his scarlet crown. See also* AEADINE ANCHORAGE, AEADINE MONARCHS, GHISTWOLD.

—FROM THE WORDBOOK ALPHABETICA: A NEW
WORDBOOK OF THE AEADINES

TWELVE

Dangerous Men

MARY

I stood in a room with a blazing hearth, a small bed and a steaming wooden bath. Though I was sure spies from Demery's crew wouldn't be far away, I was alone for the first time since I'd been arrested as Abetha Bonning.

The inn was a nice one, with a clean common room, middle-class guests, and unstained sheets. The presence of ghistings soaked its wood, lending me a sense of security, and the maid—who spoke Aeadine with a light Usti accent—filled a steaming bath, right in my chambers.

My board could not have been cheap. Demery seemed determined to woo me onto his crew—though 'wooing' implied I had a real choice.

All the same, habit took over at the sight of the tub. I stripped. The smell of my clothes, all brine and sweat, nearly toppled me as I tugged and untied and unpinned. I screwed up my nose and tossed them all into a wicker basket, then stuck the basket into the hallway and rang the service bell.

The departure of my clothes left me naked and vulnerable, but they needed to be washed as badly as I did.

I scuttled back to the tub, where the sight of my reflection on the firelit surface brought me up short. Lanky, tangled hair fell beside a face filled with hollow eyes, dark shanks obscuring collarbones and ribs that were a good deal more visible than when I'd left home.

I looked unwell. Dirty, hungry and weak. Not my mother's daughter. Not a Stormsinger. Just a desperate woman who should have both hanged and drowned.

No, no more thoughts, no more memories. I had a night to myself on dry land and a chance to escape—once I had my clothes back, at least.

I stepped into the tub, sinking down until the water hovered just under my nose. After a few breaths, I submerged my head. Ensconced in a womblike hush, the drumming of my heart slowed to a steady, measurable beat. Somewhere distant, through the floor, I picked out the hum of patrons. But in the water, my solitude was complete.

My mind wandered, leaving behind cloying thoughts of my mother and Lirr's fixed gaze. Instead of my fears and misfortunes, I thought of the sea. I thought of the *Juliette*'s ghisting in the water before me, with her mane of drifting hair and tentacle skirt.

She had been freed when her ship burned, but Demery implied she'd done something to help me before she disappeared. Where was she now? Free and swimming through the deep? On her way back to a Wold—perhaps even my Wold—as I so longed to be?

I was vaguely aware that I should come up for air but felt no urgency at the thought. My heart beat on and my lungs were at ease. My hair billowed around my face, brushing my cheeks.

When I came back to myself, I was still lying on the bottom of the tub. But the hum of activity from the common room below had died—which was odd, considering it was still lunchtime. It was also odd that my feet, hanging in the air beyond the end of the tub, were completely dry. And the water around me was… freezing cold.

My eyes snapped open. No firelight flickered across the surface of the water and the daylight in the room was dim.

The surface of the water. I was still underwater?

I came out of the tub in a bubbling, shrieking lunge. I landed in a clatter on the floor, flailing and dripping like a newborn calf. On my knees, I raked air into my lungs and stared at the coals of what should still be a roaring hearth fire.

I gaped at the window, only to see the sky darkening. I lifted my palms to find my fingers wrinkled like dried berries.

I'd been in the tub for no more than a few moments, surely. It wasn't possible for so much time to have passed. Then I'd be drowned, dead in a bath in Tithe.

Shock. I pushed wet hair back from my face and pressed my palms into my cheeks, trying to settle my nerves. I'd lost hours. I wasn't myself, and I perhaps shouldn't have expected to be for a while.

I needed answers. Still dripping and cold and trying not to think about my lapse, I strode over to the service bell and tugged it hard.

∞

The smell of food and the clink of glasses drew me down a creaking staircase to the warm, low-ceilinged common room. Clad in clean clothes that smelled of lavender and lemons, I braced myself and wove through a press of patrons to the bar.

"Excuse me," I called to the inn wife as she set plates of steaming food onto the worn surface and a maid swept them into the crowd. I hesitated, unsure whether the woman would understand my Aeadine. "I'm—"

"I know who you are, girl," the inn wife said brusquely. Like the maid earlier, she spoke my language with a light accent, and I began to wonder—mildly embarrassed at my own lack of Usti—if everyone in Tithe spoke Aeadine. "Go have a seat and I will have something sent over. Your sir should be along any minute."

I opened my mouth to ask who she meant by my 'sir,' but the woman vanished back into the kitchen. The answer was apparent, anyway, if uncomfortable. She meant Demery, and assumed I was his mistress.

A pirate's mistress. Well, that was safer than being a Stormsinger—though the positions often overlapped.

I turned, scanning the company for an empty table. There was one near a window, drafty but unoccupied. I tugged my short coat tighter around my shoulders and made my way over.

I settled in. The chatter and hum of the room seeped into my bones, drawing me unexpectedly back across the sea, to the inn where I'd spent my childhood. There, the patrons had been villagers, shepherds and foresters and road-weary coachmen, rather than wealthy merchants and petty officers from various ships. The rumbling babble had been Aeadine, rather than the strange mix of tongues I heard now. But it still felt like home.

I eased back in my chair, hardly minding the curl of wind that seeped in around the shutters. Just for a moment, I could imagine that I was back in the village, between the Wold and the hills.

That, naturally, was when James Elijah Demery sat down before me with two cups and a bottle of very dark, fine wine. "Ms. Firth."

"Captain Demery," I returned. I was cautious but unafraid of him, surrounded as we were by the honest folk of Tithe and the whisper of the ghisting-riddled island.

"You seem much recovered," he commented. I noted the pistols at his waist as he opened his coat. "That's good to see. You've not been bothered by anyone, I take it?"

"No one," I returned smoothly, but something in his posture made me glance around. I realized the occupants of the next table had their chairs and boots positioned to block my path to the door—or anyone's path to us.

One of them, a stocky sailor stuffed into a fine frock coat and wig, waved daintily and grinned a gap-toothed grin.

"There's a Mereish warship in port." Demery noted the direction of my gaze and leaned across the table on his elbows. "I thought it best to increase your security."

"Or to make sure I didn't run?"

"Are you going to run?"

The question, and the reality that I was surrounded, left me unexpectedly exhausted. "I want to be left alone," I mumbled. *And I want to find my mother, though I still can't believe she's with Lirr.*

"I could never forgive myself if I left you alone, Ms. Firth." Demery's voice was soft, carrying just between the two of us. "It'd be as good as killing you. Abandoning you in a foreign port, hunted by Silvanus Lirr?"

"Hunted because he supposedly has my mother?" I shook my head. "If I'm going to believe you, I need to know more than that."

Demery examined the bottle of wine and popped out the cork. "Well, I'm unsure how to convince you, but she is with him. You saw the man with your own eyes?"

"He said nothing of my mother," I replied, my voice much steadier than I felt with memories of Lirr's attack and butchery so close. Did I dare tell Demery what Lirr had said about knowing me? Would he be able to explain it?

"Well, whatever transpired between the two of you doesn't change these facts: he has your mother and he'll come for you again." The pirate poured two cups of wine and slid one towards me. There was no amusement in his eyes, no taunting or toying. "His interest in her—and subsequently you—is old, stretching back to our youths. We used to sail together, you see. Back when we all crewed for a man called Bretton."

My mouth fell open. I no longer heard the inn, the chatter and the footsteps and the clink of glasses. I barely noticed the curl of the wind through the shutters beside me, wafting over my throat and cheek in consolation. All I saw was Demery, and all I heard were his words.

"Bretton?" I repeated. I'd heard the name before, though the memories attached to it were vague—overheard conversations between my parents, perhaps. "Who was he?"

Demery tapped the side of my cup. "Have a drink and settle in, Ms. Firth. I'll make this as short as I can, but you're pale as bone."

I took the proffered wine and pulled it close. "Tell me."

"Bretton was a pirate from the Cape," Demery began, the low rumble of his voice making up the edges of my world. "He docked in Kalsank some twenty-five years ago, fitting out a crew. Kalsank was the port to do that, in those days, and to find place on a free ship, being far enough from the eyes of all the navies—Capesh, Cape being the closest to Kalsank, Mere and Aead. That brought sailors like me to the island too."

"What about my mother?" I asked.

"Bretton already had her aboard, along with Lirr." Demery's lips tightened into a thin, crack of a smile. "She, naturally, was his singer. Lirr was his Sooth—to warn of the storms that Anne was to dispel and so on, working in concert, as was the way. Anne was young, barely sixteen. Bretton wasn't a kind man, but your mother was fierce, and it was her that began to stir the crew to mutiny. Bretton had an endeavor in mind, one with a grand prize at the end. He, your mother and Lirr had seen it before. The wreck of a Mereish treasure fleet. It was agreed that we'd see the venture through before slitting Bretton's throat."

I watched the rings on Demery's fingers glint as he continued. "Bretton never found his great riches again. He went too far with your mother one night. She killed him, on the edge of the Stormwall."

Gooseflesh rippled down my arms. My mother had killed a man, at sixteen? That was a grim thought.

"Why was Bretton near the Stormwall?" I pressed. The Stormwall was a region of the Winter Sea shrouded in legends and myth—a great storm that stretched across the far north without beginning or end. The stories said summer never came beyond the Stormwall, and the world was forever locked in ice.

Not that there were many stories, since most who ventured into the tempest never came out again.

"Because his hoard was on the other side, and it's still there." The pirate held my gaze. "We took Bretton's ship. Lirr saved your mother's life during the confrontation, and she was finally free of her chains. He took command and declared we would continue Bretton's mission and claim his prize, but the ship was too damaged. The war was heating up again as well, what with Aeadine trying to take the Mereish North Isles and fleets in every direction. So we sailed for quieter waters to lie low and recoup."

At the table next to us, Demery's crew dealt out a game of cards.

"No one knew where Bretton's prize was except your mother. Lirr had seen it, of course, but couldn't find the way alone. The Winter Sea is, as you know, a volatile place, but as the Stormsinger, your mother was privy to all the navigational details." Demery held my gaze, both gentle and forceful, and I knew whatever he would say next would be personal. "But your mother fell in with one of the crew, a tar, a nobody called Joseph Grey, and decided she wanted a quiet place to birth and raise their child. Lirr was jealous. Furious. Refused to let her go and put her back in chains."

My mouth tasted dry. Slowly, I raised the cup to my lips and drank. I'd known my parents met aboard ship, but I'd always assumed it was in the Navy. My father, who always smelled of cigars and coffee, had been a pirate? A common pirate in love with his ship's Stormsinger?

"Of course, your mother refused to help Lirr, and swore to take the secret of Bretton's prize to the grave. She and Grey escaped—to this day, I've no idea how—and vanished. Completely."

They went to the Navy, and then the Wold. I'd long known my mother sang for the Navy for protection, and scant freedom in peacetime. But until now, I'd never understood just what she'd run from. *Who* she'd run from.

"Her departure broke Lirr, somehow," Demery continued. "He became wild and reckless. Half the crew left, including myself. I heard that he tried to sail the Stormwall without a singer and failed. So he set his mind to conquest, pillaging his way into something like lordship in the South Mereish Islands—most of their rulers down there are pirates of one form or another. But all the while he looked for your mother, and with her the location of Bretton's Hoard. Finally, he found her."

Quiet fell between us while I struggled to process it all. It was a mad tale, but it wasn't impossible. Still. Demery's claims didn't explain the way Lirr had spoken as if he knew me personally, and I should recall him. And unless Demery was lying, all this had taken place before my birth. Lirr would have only been a boy.

"Lirr is too young," I countered, suspicion creeping up my spine. "Or… I'm not sure. It was hard to tell. He looked younger than you, in any case."

Demery tapped his rings against the side of his cup in absent rhythm. "How kind of you to say. I assure you, he's older than he looks. I can't tell you why—a kindness from his parents? An effect of his magecraft? He is a mage, Mary, and an unusual one."

"What kind?"

"A Sooth, as I said before, but also a Magni," Demery said. "It's a dangerous combination. He has a Sooth's foresight and connection with the Other, but also a Magni's influence over others. What else, I can't say. The unnatural was never an area of particular interest for me."

I narrowed my eyes. "What is your area of interest?"

"I enjoy cards, military memoirs and complicated women," Demery returned. "But at this time, I'm interested in Bretton's lost prize. I'm tired of this life. I want to retire somewhere warm, where there's no noose waiting for me. So I plan to rescue your mother, convince her to take me to Bretton's lost prize, and then hang my hat."

My breath lodged in my throat. "You intend to rescue my mother?"

"Yes, and it would go a lot better if I delivered her daughter to her, safe and sound. Which is possibly why Lirr is after you, though he could also intend to use you against Anne. I can't be sure, and I won't pretend to be. Their relationship was always unpredictable." Demery lifted his cup to his lips, adding along the way, "In any case I need a Stormsinger, and you need protection from Lirr, so we both win if you come with me. I have a vested interest in your health and happiness, for your mother's sake."

"I don't believe you."

Demery looked dour. "That's foolish of you."

"You're a *pirate*," I shot back, my cheeks beginning to flush with anger—anger at my confusion, anger at him and at the world, which had left me so alone and uprooted. "I can't trust— It doesn't matter, does it? Are you going to drag me back to your ship now?"

Demery considered his wine. "Maybe. Though as I'm trying to endear myself to your mother, I'd prefer not to abduct you. And like I said, I want your loyalty, Mary."

"I don't believe you." I spat the words this time, cold and disgusted. They were not a lie, but they weren't entirely true, either. My heart wanted to believe him; my mind knew better. Even if he'd shown me relative kindness up until now, who knew what the coming months would bring—particularly once he realized I was untrained.

Thrusting myself back from the table, I stood and glared down at Demery. "We're done here."

"I'll be here all night, and back tomorrow," he said, ignoring me. "Drinking quietly and awaiting your response."

"This is my response," I stated and stormed away into the crowd.

I went back up to my room, but the walls felt too close, and I had no desire to be in a place Demery had paid for. It was time to go, to find space—and from there, sort out my thoughts and make my own decisions.

Checking to ensure no one saw me, I followed a second stair I'd seen the maids use earlier in the day, skittered past kitchens full of clinking and calling, and out a back door.

I shouldered past a pissing man and out into the snowy brightness of the street. I let the press of townsfolk sweep me away from the inn, from Demery, and all that he'd tried to tell me.

"Miss?" A figure materialized from the crowd, clad in a worn brown overcoat, a cloak, and a clumsily tied scarf. He had dark hair, ineffectively constrained by a tricorn hat and a short braid, and brown eyes rimmed by dark lashes in a pleasant, if currently ominous, face.

I knew him. The memory was thin, but I'd seen this man before. One of Lirr's men? No. One of Demery's?

"Miss, are you well? Do you need help?"

I kept walking for a few steps, rage boiling up in my stomach. Of course, Demery would have the doors watched. Of course, I wouldn't be able to slip away unmolested.

Well, I'd had enough of Demery and captivity. I'd had enough of hiding from punches, of trying to keep myself alive in a situation beyond my control. I'd take what scraps of power I could and run with them.

If Demery and his pirates wanted to keep me locked up? They'd just have to catch me.

I bolted into the night.

THIRTEEN

The Man in the Shadows

SAMUEL

Mary Firth lunged into a passage between two houses, skirts rippling in her wake. I skittered to a stop at the end of the alleyway, peering after her into the shadows.

"Ms. Firth!" I panted. "I am not your enemy!"

There was no response. The alley ended in something of a courtyard, but it was blocked by a fence. I doubted the woman had managed to scale that in skirts. So where was she?

There. Movement behind the bulk of a chimney, its warm stone steaming softly in the gloom.

I glanced back into the street. A pair of men walked towards us on the other side, deep in discussion and more than a little merry. Still, I hardly wanted to catch their attention. Having to bail me out of prison for chasing a woman through the streets might just be my last straw with Slader, even if that woman was Mary Firth.

I slipped into the alleyway, letting the shadows hide me. "Ms. Firth? Please, I have no intention of hurting you. I—"

She stepped out from behind the chimney, shoulders hunched in fear—no, rage. There was no mistaking the woman's glare, her grey eyes glittering in the night.

She was taller than I expected, her forehead level with my eyes, and she was beautiful—in a vengeful kind of way, with a full bottom lip and flushed, pale cheeks.

Startled, I took a half step backwards. Her breath drifted between us, white in the frigid air. She looked at me as if I were... as if I were a criminal, a monster.

As if I were a man stalking her through a darkened city in the middle of the night.

I raised my hands, realizing too late that it was the same gesture cart drivers used to calm anxious horses. I also recognized that I had completely blocked off the mouth of the alleyway, which could do nothing to soothe the situation. Yet she would bolt if I moved, and though I could certainly stop her, I did not want to.

"Mary Firth," I began. "Allow me to apologize—"

She cut me off. "Tell your captain I'm not coming back. Chasing me like a dog? Expecting me to swallow his lies? I shouldn't expect any better from the likes of him, from the likes of *you*."

The words hit me like a slap. "I—"

"How dare you follow me!" She cut me off again. Her accent was stronger than mine, a rural Aeadine lilt typically sported by shepherds and woodcutters. It was distractingly endearing, even if it was currently scolding me. Perhaps even more because it was scolding me.

"You terrified me," she snapped. "And I do not react well to being terrified."

I glanced anxiously over my shoulder. Those drunken men had to be close now, and I needed her to quiet down.

I took a small step forward and she fell silent. Nervousness flashed through her anger. I took no pride in it, but she was listening now.

"Hold up, Ms. Firth, please," I started, praying she saw my sincerity. "You looked unwell and I was startled to see you. I ought to have declared myself. My deepest apologies. I'm Samuel Rosser, of *Hart*—"

"You were in Whallum," she interrupted me, her face an iron mask.

I nodded. "The same. I am a pirate hunter under Her Majesty's Commission."

Mary let out a derisive, tired laugh. "Pirate hunters don't normally sound like such prigs."

So, she had identified my accent too. She was right—most of my kind did not sound like they had just walked out of the Royal Academy.

I tried not to rankle. "Have you met many pirate hunters?"

"What do you want?"

I glanced back at the darkening street and lowered my voice. "How did you get here? Have you escaped Randalf?"

"Why are you here?" Mary returned obstinately.

"I am hunting Silvanus Lirr." I lowered my hands. Back in the street, the drunken men passed by, bawling a lewd song. "He was last seen chasing John Randalf out of Whallum, bound for Tithe."

Her eyes flicked to the singing men. "You're hunting Lirr?"

"You know of him?"

Her face paled in a way that made my stomach curdle. "I... I met him. At sea."

A horrible, thick silence fell between us, and the queasy feeling in my stomach grew. "Did he take your ship?" I asked.

She looked away. The flintiness had faded from her eyes and, despite her height, she looked smaller. That was answer enough.

"How did you survive?" I wondered aloud, my head conjuring up dozens of horrific images. Lirr was not a common pirate, striking and running with loud guns and threats. He took his time. He tortured, killed and burned. If he had taken Randalf's ship...

"Ms. Firth, is he here? Are you running from him?"

"No." Her answer was quick, insistent, but her tone dulled as she went on, "No, I jumped overboard. A... merchant ship picked me up."

I gaped at her. "You jumped ship? In the middle of the ocean? You had to know you would..."

"Drown?" she supplied. "Yes, I assumed I would. There are fates worse than death, Mr. Rosser."

"Indeed." Mary had chosen the waves over capture by Lirr, and she spoke those words as if they were a common mantra. *This* was why I had signed on to hunt the pirate down, why I had staked my redemption on him. I could do nothing greater for the world than stop a man so violent and vile. "How did you survive?"

She did not speak for a heartbeat, then, "I clung to some wreckage, until the merchant came along. I remember little of it."

That seemed inordinately lucky, but here she was. I hesitated. "Does Lirr know you survived? Did he follow you?"

She laced her arms over her chest, and I noticed for the first time that she was wearing no more than a sailor's short coat—no scarf, no hat or even a woman's cap. Saint, I was cold in my full weather gear. She had to be freezing, and here I was interrogating her.

"Since he didn't find me, I'm sure he thinks I've drowned," she said.

Some of the tension ebbed from my shoulders. She might be right. Though, since Lirr was a Sooth like me, there was a chance he would realize she was alive. Perhaps she was not worth the trouble? I still had no clue why he had wanted her and Randalf to begin with.

"Ms. Firth." I cleared my throat, beset with the sudden urge to get us off the street. "Will you have dinner with me?"

"What?" she asked, her rural accent sounding particularly strong.

"You are freezing." I gestured to her. "And there is an inn around the corner. We can sit, you can warm up. I will buy us the best hot food and wine this port has to offer, and we can figure out what to do."

"Why would you do that?"

I opened my mouth to reply, but could not find the words. To get her next to a fire, so she would stop shivering? To convince her I was no monster in the dark?

Or to keep her away from Demery? If the pirate discovered she was here, he would waste no time in snatching her up. That last option struck me broadside, giving me renewed urgency. I resisted the impulse to step closer, shifting my weight into my heels instead.

"I want to convince you to join my crew," I said, simplifying. "*Hart*."

Amusement flicked across her face, then it was gone. "Just convince?"

"Yes."

"What if someone sees us together, from your crew?"

"Only Ms. Fisher knows who you are." I shrugged, trying to appear nonchalant. "And she is on watch. Anyone who sees us will think I am sharing a meal with a local woman."

"Do you do that often?" She crooked an eyebrow. That look was almost coy, despite the cold and all we had discussed.

An answering smile tugged at my lips. "Not often, no."

Wind gusted through the alley. She visibly gritted her teeth and forced her chin down in a nod. "All right. What did you say your name was?"

"Rosser. Samuel Rosser."

"Well, then, Mr. Rosser. You may take me to dinner."

SAINT, THE—*The Saint is that most revered being whom the Aeadine serve, and whom their rulers represent to the populace. In contrast to the myriad Mereish and Usti 'Saints,' Aeadine's singular Saint is the Bringer of Order, who gave feral humanity logic and reason and sealed the boundaries with the Other, before retreating to the Far Seas. Before the establishment of the Aeadine monarchy and the acknowledgement of the Saint, the people of Aeadine's mainland devoted themselves to local deities, degrading the Unified Mind and turning humanity to barbarism, including the worship of Ghistings. However, after the conquest of 463, in which the Blessed Kings of Aeadine's northern coast scourged the mainland, worship of the Saint became the formal faith of a newly unified Aeadine. It remains the most prominent religion in Aeadine and the only one sanctioned by the queen, who to this day wears the Saint's Own Crown and guards the nation against various heretical foreign factions, who in their err promote worship of gods and innumerable fictitious 'Saints.' See also* AEADINE: WORSHIP, CHURCH OF THE SAINT.

—*FROM* THE WORDBOOK ALPHABETICA: A NEW WORDBOOK OF THE AEADINES

FOURTEEN

Dinner with Mr. Rosser

MARY

The common room of the inn Rosser chose was narrow, stretching into a firelit, low-beamed den of irresistible smells and aching warmth. Rosser escorted me to the very back of the establishment, turning sideways to wade between a smooth, dark-wood bar, smiling serving girls and clusters of patrons. The latter's snowy coats, hats and cloaks hung on overwrought coatracks like festive trees.

I eyed the coats, wondering what a set of light fingers might find in their pockets. But my hands were frozen, and just the thought sent guilt curling through me. I still had Demery's solem. That was enough to get me a ship back to Aeadine. If I didn't freeze before I found one.

In a quiet corner, Rosser shrugged off his outer cloak and nodded to a tiny table next to a hearth. There was no one else back here, the only other table occupied with a regiment of empty, froth-streaked glasses.

"Is this acceptable?" he asked.

I was already throwing my coat across the back of a chair and crouching next to the fire, holding my snow-damp skirts just out of reach of the flames. I couldn't feel my fingers yet, but heat prickled over my cheeks.

"Yes, it's wonderful," I replied distractedly. My gaze caught his as I looked up, and for a moment we watched one another, appraising, hesitant and a little too long. I'd been around enough young men to know what that exchange usually meant—both to him and to my own, fluttering breath. He was attractive, with his dark hair and strong shoulders.

His appearance wasn't why I was here, though. I was here because Rosser seemed to know a great deal about Lirr, and though he'd yet to mention my mother, perhaps he knew something about her.

I was taking a gamble—both with trusting him and lingering in town. Demery would be looking for me by now. I'd won a chance at freedom, but I might be throwing that away, staring into the large, dark eyes of Samuel Rosser. It was cold, though, it was night, and the answers Rosser had might just keep me alive.

A serving maid with curly blonde hair appeared as Rosser hung up his cloak and outer coat. A steaming jug and two mugs in one hand, she glanced between him and me, and settled on him.

She bobbed a short curtsy and set the jug and cups down on our table, speaking in Usti. I couldn't understand, but straightened in anticipation of a meal and the scent of hot, spiced wine. My stomach rumbled. I didn't regret storming out on Demery, but I did regret not eating first.

Rosser replied to the maid in the same language, casting her a distracted glance—uninterested, which I found oddly satisfying. He sat in the back chair, the one with the best angle on the door and added something I suspected was thanks.

The maid vanished and Rosser poured our wine. I tucked myself into the chair opposite to him, back to the fire, and rested my fingers on the sides of the mug. Heat returned to my flesh in painful, stinging waves.

"You speak Usti?" I observed.

He nodded. "I learned at school."

"Ah," I acknowledged, uncertain how far I wanted to pry into his past—and how familiar I should let us become.

He was either of a similar mind or had nothing to say just then, so we fell quiet and looked to our wine. The space around us filled of muffled chatter, the clink of earthenware mugs and plates, and the crackle of the fire. Like the inn where I'd been staying, this place sounded like home. That familiarity, the shelter and the warmth seeped into me, slowing my heart even though I sat across from a man who could, quite easily, become a dire enemy.

Our food arrived. The maid served Rosser first, and it was all I could do not to immediately steal a slice of steaming bread from his plate and drown it in butter. Instead, I sipped my wine and waited until my own plate appeared.

We ate. At some point, our hands brushed. It was a simple touch, accidental, but it nudged every thought from my mind. Another time, Rosser wordlessly put a slice of his bread on my plate. His motives probably weren't charitable, but I didn't care—or rather, I couldn't. I was not about to repeat my experience with Charles Grant, trusting a stranger's goodwill. I'd take what I could from Rosser and move on before the noose tightened.

The maid brought us more wine and butter. My head already felt light with the drink, washing down bites of stew thick with venison, carrots, potato and turnip.

Only when my stomach was full did I feel like myself again, the fog of hunger clearing and my nerves settled by the wine.

I sat back and asked him, "What do you know about Silvanus Lirr?"

He took up his knife and cut into a piece of chicken in one slow slice. "He's a murderous pirate, and I intend to deliver him to justice."

He sounded so sure, so prim and pompous about it, that I almost laughed. I'd already learned that people didn't talk like that out here in the world, not unless they were fools or liars.

Rosser must have sensed my skepticism. His eyebrows twitched up. "Pray, do I amuse you?"

There wasn't an ounce of deceit in his expression and, for a moment, I almost forgot who he was and where we were. He was just a handsome, slightly ridiculous man, sitting across from me over dinner.

"No," I decided. "How do you intend to catch him?"

"With your help," Rosser said immediately.

Yes, that was why he was here, wasn't it? To convince me to join his crew. Something flickered through me, and it felt an awful lot like disappointment.

"Of course," I returned. "What are you willing to do to convince me?"

He pointed to the bowls and plates before us. "I hoped this was a good start. Is it succeeding?"

"It's not doing any harm," I admitted. But I knew that if I stepped aboard his ship, I'd never leave again. Though Demery had told me a lot of unbelievable things, I did trust him when he said he wanted to retire. That didn't mean he wouldn't sell me to another ship before he did, but it was something.

The pirate hunter kept speaking. "What else do you want? Your own cabin? You'll have that. Protection? I'll give it myself." He leaned his elbows on the table and ducked his head to my height. There was no boasting to his words now, no pomp or fluff or gravitas. Just a hard undercurrent to a soft voice.

For a moment, words evaded me. Then my wine-softened tongue produced the most honest, and most impossible, answer. "I want to go home."

I want to find my mother and take her home with me.

He did not reply. Then his eyes dropped to my lips and my heart gave an uncertain, warning twist. I had to tread carefully.

"I think you know that is impossible," Rosser said. His gaze was back on mine, as if it had never strayed. "To all appearances, Lirr is searching for you. You understand what he is?"

"Of course," I returned, not liking his tone. Heat crept into my cheeks, from the wine and frustration, but also his attention. "He's a mage. A Sooth and a Magni."

"Yes." Rosser's tone became flatter and more guarded. "It's the Sooth part that concerns me. He will have premonition, visions, access to the Other. As a Stormsinger, you have a reflection in the Dark Water. Did he get close to you?"

Despite the heat of the fire, I felt the warmth leach from my cheeks. "Yes."

"How close?"

My discomfort tripled. "As close as we are now."

Rosser was silent for a moment, then asked, "Did he touch you?"

I remembered the brush of Lirr's finger across my skin as he pushed my collar aside. I reached compulsively for my wine and emptied the cup. "Yes."

"Then he can track you, in the Other."

I shook my head, fighting down a swell of panic. "Maybe. But someone will catch him eventually," I insisted. "I'll lie low until then."

"He will not be caught." Rosser paused for two overwrought thumps of my heart. "Not unless *Hart* has a Stormsinger."

This again. "Then find someone else," I challenged.

"There is no one else," he said, his voice becoming more emphatic as he went on. "Lirr is looking for *you*. Why?"

"I don't know," I told him. *Except that he claims to know me. Except that my mother might be his prisoner.*

Rosser paused for a moment, evidently deciding whether to believe me, then went on. "Whatever the reason, the fact remains. He can, and will, find you. So why hide? Why wait for him to come for you again? Take the fight to him. With us."

Just then, the option struck me as tempting. If Lirr did have my mother, I could rescue her as readily with Rosser as I could with Demery. But: "And after it's over, your captain would let me leave?"

Rosser's arms remained crossed over his chest, unmoving. "It is not impossible."

"But it's not guaranteed."

He frowned. "Nothing in life is guaranteed."

"Well, aren't you the sage," I muttered.

The maid reappeared to clear away our plates, her eyes assessing our body language and stubborn silence without a word. She left again, whispering something to one of the other maids. They both giggled and looked at me with something between jealousy and pity.

"Ms. Firth, Lirr will find you." Rosser lowered his voice, and a dark kind of certainty threaded through his eyes. His hand moved compulsively, as if to reach into his pocket, but his coat was hung on the rack nearby. He rested it on his thigh instead, forefinger tapping. "If he found you once, he can do it again. Any Sooth can."

I couldn't think of anything to say, so I did not speak.

"He will find you," Rosser repeated. "So, lead him right to us. Right to the noose. Then, and only then, you will be safe."

I smiled tightly. "Safe from Lirr, maybe, but not from men like you. If I step foot on your ship, I'll be trapped. Or can you honestly tell me your captain is a good, trustworthy man?"

He pushed the question aside. "I will ask the inn wife if there are any rooms available."

"What?"

"If you are not coming back to *Hart*, you will need somewhere safe to sleep." He stood up, brushing past his hanging coat and cloak on the way to the bar. "So I will arrange for a room, here. For you. And return at breakfast for your answer."

He left before I could say anything else, let alone admit I already had a place for the night, if I dared to go back to it. I watched him go, my heart thundering in my throat.

My eyes dragged to his coat pocket, heavy with unseen contents, and the door beyond. I could accept his proposal and risk losing my freedom again, or take what I'd been handed and leave right now.

I stood and went to the rack where Rosser's outer garments hung. Up ahead in the press of bodies, I could see the young man leaning over the bar, speaking with a burly woman in an apron and black cap. She nodded to the side, and the two of them vanished up a staircase.

Rosser's gaze glanced off me as he went and I offered a small, instinctual smile. Something about that expression must have startled him, because the way he smiled in return was almost relieved.

Then he was gone. I shrugged on my coat, walled out a stab of guilt and took his too. The garment was heavy and warm and smelled pleasantly masculine, like coffee and sweat and musky soap, all twined with sea salt. It was too big but I pulled it tight, threw his cloak over the top and started for the door.

Bodies pressed. Men threw good-hearted jests at one another and boots stomped. A snow-caked dog shoved past my leg and two women leaned onto one another's shoulders at a corner table, whispering and laughing.

On my way past the bar, I scooped a loaf of bread off an unwatched plate and shoved it into my pocket. I was already a thief. Why stop now?

Cold wind struck my face as I stepped into the street. The door closed with one last waft of stew and beer and warmth, and I started to walk.

I strode quickly, sure Rosser's enraged shouts would echo after me at any moment, or Demery's pirates would peel from the darkness. But fortune was with me, and I was alone.

I made for what I assumed would be the edge of town, cobbling together a loose plan as I went. The forest beyond the graveyard would shelter me, I thought. I knew how to survive in the woods, and I was sure there'd be some summer cottage or woodcutter's shack I could hide away in until Demery and Rosser gave up and left in pursuit of Lirr. I'd be hungry, but I'd survive. I'd be cold, but Rosser's coat and cloak were warm.

I could do it. But should I?

Snow reflected starlight as I reached the graveyard. I darted across the open space and tucked myself into the shelter of one of the tithe trees, laboring for breath. I leaned against the trunk, taking solace from the familiar hum of ghisten life as I untangled my hands from my new cloak and brushed stray hair away from my face.

I steadied my breathing as the quiet of the night swelled. The ghisting in the tree did not greet me but I sensed its intelligence all the same, watching.

The wind gusted in off the sea, so cold that I shuddered. Some of the wine cleared from my head and I had a moment of hard reflection.

Even if I ran and Demery or Rosser didn't find me, even if nothing went wrong and I survived however many days it took them to give up, Lirr could still track me, and my mother was still beyond my reach. Rosser had been nothing but sincere about Lirr's abilities, and I believed him.

The pirate hunter was right. If I went on the offensive, I might be able to help bring down Lirr and save both my mother and myself. That was what I wanted, wasn't it?

I sat down at the foot of the tree. Snow cushioned me and the coin-scaled trunk, when I leaned my head against it, almost felt warm.

"Mother," I murmured. I felt the shape of the word on my lips, listened to my voice form its sounds. I thought of her, and all that I'd felt as I watched her carriage trundle away down the road between the Wold and the hills.

Tears seeped into my eyes, my throat clotted and I pulled my knees into my chest. If I went into that forest now and turned my back on her, on this chance—even if it was a lie—I would never forgive myself.

I shoved my beleaguered courage into line, pushed myself to my feet, and started back towards the town.

FIFTEEN

Negotiations

MARY

Demery met my eyes through a haze of pipe smoke. He sat in the far corner of my inn's common room, beyond the late-night crowd of patrons, serving staff, and light and shadow.

I wove my way towards him. A table away, a long leg stretched out into my path. I managed not to jump—again, thanks to the wine in my veins—and looked over at the appendage's owner. It was Athe.

"Ah, so that's what you were at," she mused, eyeing me. "Did you leave him his britches?"

I blinked. "What?"

She pointed to my overlarge coat and cloak. "The fellow you robbed. I'm assuming he was in a state of some… vulnerability, given you running off with his coat and like."

Color rushed to my cheeks.

"Let her through." Demery beckoned to me. He leaned forward, resting one forearm on his knee as he reached across the table and tapped the contents of his pipe into a bowl. Then, leaving the pipe hooked over the brim, he pushed out the chair across from him. "Ms. Firth, you changed your mind? I've had my crew scouring the port for you for the last hour."

Athe's leg retracted from my path. I gave the taller woman a bracing smile, as if that could make up for the redness of my cheeks, and stepped past her.

"Captain Demery." I sat, a little stiffly. "I've a proposal for you."

"Let's have it."

"I want my own cabin, with a lock on the inside and none on the outside," I said, holding his gaze. In my lap, my fingers laced together to hide a lingering tremor. A small voice at the back of my mind screamed that I was mad, that this plan was suicide, but I ignored it. "You'll teach me to shoot and use a knife. I'll have privacy and security. Absolute protection from your crew and anyone else that might do me harm. Still, I require my freedom, freedom to leave the ship and do as I please. And I will have a cut of all your... profits."

Up until the last sentence, the pirate had been nodding in consideration, but at the last his eyebrows shot up. "Pardon me? Are you turning rogue, Ms. Firth?"

"No. As soon as Lirr has been..." I almost chose softer words, but vagueness wouldn't serve me. "As soon as he is dead and my mother secured—though I still hardly believe you on that front— I'll be on my way, with my mother and enough money to start a new life. I'll also need a daily pension while I'm with you, to provide for my needs."

Demery's smile was gone, but his eyes glimmered. Amusement? No. This was cooler than that. It was the glisten of an impassive winter sun, clouded and distant and without heat.

My determination hardened, my conscience and qualms obscured, and I leaned forward across the table.

"String up Lirr and help me rescue my mother, and I'll sing you through every storm of the Winter Sea—even beyond the Stormwall itself." Never mind that I was a terrible Stormsinger— I'd figure that out later. "You'll have your treasure, your retirement, and Silvanus Lirr."

Demery's hand leveled across the table. No questions. No negotiation. "You have yourself a deal, Ms. Firth."

His fingers were warm and rough as they closed around mine.

"Captain." Athe raised her voice. I glanced over my shoulder to see her watching the door, which had opened to admit a gust of cold wind and a dozen newcomers. Armed newcomers, led by Samuel Rosser in his shirt and waistcoat.

He scanned the inn, posture etched with anger and cold, and his chest heaving. He had a cutlass in one hand and a pistol in the other.

Fear cracked through my determination and guilt punched clean through. Not twenty minutes ago this man had looked at me kindly and honestly, in a world where few ever did.

I'd thrown that away. I'd done it for good reason, but I still felt a stab of regret.

Athe stood, draining her cup and placing herself directly between Rosser's gaze and my frozen form.

"So you did leave him his britches," she commented, making a show of shrugging on her coat. It widened her already broad silhouette, completely concealing Demery and me from the doorway. "Captain? Shall we?"

Demery's gaze flicked from my stolen coat, to Rosser, and back to me. His bottom lip pinched in a frown and his hand, still around mine, tightened in warning.

"He tried to recruit me," I explained hastily.

"So you robbed him?" Demery asked.

"I did."

"Clearly you chose the right crew." The captain released me and stood, throwing his own coat over one shoulder and nodding towards a side door. "Mary, stay close. Mr. Howell? If you could cause a disturbance?"

A dark-skinned man at a nearby table saluted and sniffed, flexing his hand and giving the fellow across from him a wan smile. "Right. Jack? Fancy a dance?"

The Jack in question looked around the inn, one hand lingering on the embroidered tablecloth. "Here? But it's so fine—"

"Lads, please," Demery persisted.

Jack drained his cup and pushed his chair back. "Right."

Demery nodded towards the side door again and we started off slowly, Athe stalking beside us and blocking me from view.

A shout rang out, followed by the crash of a table and a howl of pain. A few patrons screamed in shock, others in outrage, then madness took the room.

Demery opened the side door. I stole one last glance at Rosser's handsome, brooding face, barely visible through the chaos of men and women standing to their feet. I couldn't say what made me look, but the knot in my stomach felt a whole lot like shame.

My resolve, however, was harder than ever. It had to be.

A few hours later, I watched Tithe vanish into a veil of snow. My gaze drifted from ship to ship, the turmoil of my thoughts as muffled as the lights of the port.

I leaned against the windows in Demery's cabin and slipped a hand into the pocket of Rosser's coat. Cool metal touched my fingers. I withdrew a single coin, long and thin and oval, worn smooth on one side. I didn't recognize the stamp on the other, which depicted three knotted serpents, each biting one another's tails. The text around its circumference looked Mereish, though— all swirls and slashes.

Toying with it, I watched the anchored ships as we passed. Spars and yards, decks and lines were coated with sticky snow, and stovepipes trailed smoke into the night. One of those vessels was *Hart*, I knew. Would Rosser be back aboard, or was he still searching the town? How long would it take for him to realize I'd vanished at the same time as James Demery's ship?

I turned the coin over in my palm—once, twice—then slipped it back into my pocket.

~PART TWO~

BLACK TIDE, THE—*A variant of the original cultus of the Aeadine Mainland, which worshiped pagan deities and revered mages. With sympathies towards heretical Mereish magics, cultists are most widely known for their claims to amplify the magic of mages who undergo their rituals. Magni and Stormsingers are frequently subjected to various forms of physical torture, meant to expand the sorcerous mind through suffering or loss of senses. Sooths are often drugged until their connection with the Other is irreparably broadened, and they can no longer reside fully in the human world. All these rituals, according to their beliefs, must take place during the moonless nights and high tides of spring, hence the title of THE BLACK TIDE. The efficacy of their rituals is highly debated, and their practices formally outlawed under King Edmund in 1655. See also* MOON WORSHIPERS, AEADINE CULTS.

—FROM THE WORDBOOK ALPHABETICA: A NEW
WORDBOOK OF THE AEADINES

SIXTEEN

Defiance

SAMUEL

I sat on the deck in my cabin, eyes closed, skin prickling through my shirt. The woodstove had long burned down. Cold wrapped its fingers across my arms and made the fine hairs inside my nose tickle, but it kept me rooted in my flesh as the Other welled.

I needed the cold as an anchor, now more than ever. The Mereish coin was no longer in my pocket, ready to soothe my nerves, dispel my curse and keep me in the human world. It was gone. So was Mary Firth, and with her our only lead to Lirr.

What I told her had been the truth. Lirr was a Sooth, and he would be able to track her in the Other now that he had touched her.

So could I. One brush of our hands when she reached for her wine, and we were irreparably bound.

I stretched my neck one way, then the other, pushing out my frustration in a long, misting breath. My thoughts of the Stormsinger were insidious, and not in the way I needed them to be. I had to find her, not dwell on whether she'd gone to Demery willingly, or the way the firelight played down the curve of her cheek. She was a task, a goal, and a thief.

Anger stirred, along with an irrational feeling of betrayal. I had been kind to her, genuinely tried to do the right thing, and she had stolen from me. I had failed Slader again, and my position on *Hart* was more tenuous than ever.

Off in the town, a church bell began to ring. With each peal I barreled my emotions away, narrowing my focus to my breath, the cold and the Other.

That second world rushed in, preceded by a vanguard of thin, fragmentary visions and the sensation of falling asleep—my consciousness waxing and waning with every heartbeat. Then, between one breath and the next, an invisible tether snapped and the Other swallowed me like a whale from the deep.

I opened my eyes. Just like last time, *Hart*'s bulwarks and deck thinned to transparency, and I was alone save for the lantern with its sleeping dragonflies. The Dark Water surrounded me, its surface occasionally punctuated by swaths of moving, shifting light. But this time, I could see the land surrounding the harbor—if anything in the Other could be called land.

Smooth sandbanks and stretches of flooded forest reached as far as the eye could see. There was no ocean at my back anymore, just more shoulders of opalescent sand and tufts of copper-black grasses, pulsating with the light of the free dragonflies that converged there. In the other direction—what would have been the mainland, in the human world—the ghisten trees of Tithe reached into the Other's bruised sky. Three muted suns cast light and shadow across the Wold. But those shadows were gnarled, twisted things, dancing across the surface of the water, and the trees here had no leafy canopies or rustling boughs.

This was the Dark Water, the Other, where ghisten trees' true roots spread, ancient, tangled, and full of sapphire ghisting spirits. The creatures lingered and swirled, separated and entwined, weaving the patterns of a daily life I could not fathom, while dragonflies skimmed across the water around them in streams of gold and purple.

The dragonflies in my own lantern stirred and fluttered, perhaps sensing their free cousins through the barrier between worlds. I considered releasing them—the sight of the creatures behind glass had always saddened me—but Slader would just buy more.

I suppressed a shiver and glanced up through the deck, sails and rigging to the sky above *Hart*. There, the lights of more strange beings drifted through the muted sky like fingers through oil.

There were many more creatures in Tithe than I was used to. They stirred memories of a childhood before I had the coin, when I had spent days lost in a forest just like this, hiding from glowing monsters. After *she* had let them take my brother and I. After they made us what we... became.

But my coin was gone, and every moment I spent in the Other was a risk. If I was careful, if I was quiet, my presence might go unnoticed. And if I was calm, my tether to my body would remain firm.

I hoped.

I looked back to the sea around me. At the same time, I pulled up a memory of Mary Firth at Kaspin's, singing the snow to stillness. I recalled sitting across the table from her at the inn last night, her cheeks flushed with cold, lips red with wine. The way she had smiled softly at me through the crowd, before she robbed me of the only thing that kept me sane.

My consciousness fluttered in my skull like the dragonflies in their lantern. I closed my eyes, but the feeling only worsened. My dreamer's senses converged like a summer storm.

"Mary Firth." I stated her name and pulled at the memories again. Unwelcome feelings came with them—longing, unease—but I embraced them, letting them blossom and pull my eyes out over the Winter Sea.

A new light appeared on the horizon, vaguely teal-grey against the blackness of the sea. It was faint, a candle's reflection in a frosted window, but it was there. It sang, an unearthly song at the edge of my hearing. Her.

At the same time, movement caught my attention. I looked down through the deck of *Hart* and into the sea below. We were just offshore of the Wold and sandbanks, but the Dark Water was deep just below the ship. So murky. So endless.

White light surged through the depths towards me.

I pushed out of the Other and into my flesh. The cabin solidified, walls folding into place as I staggered to my feet. In the dragonfly lantern on the wall, the creatures churned in a chaotic, panicked swirl. For an instant all I could hear was the shushing ping of their bodies against the glass, then the ship's bell began to ring.

I lunged out of my cabin and hit the bulkhead on the other side of the passage, clawing towards the companionway in the dark.

I came above to a chorus of shouts and a blast of cold wind. The anchor watch ran for the rails and, on the quarterdeck, Fisher grasped at a line and leaned over the water. White light flooded her face, but it did not come from the ship's lantern.

It came from the sea.

"Mr. Rosser!" Penn called from the forecastle, where he stood precariously close to the rail. His knitted cap, as usual, threatened to pop off his bald head. "What is this?"

"Back from the rail!" I panted, sprinting up the quarterdeck stairs. "Something is trying to follow me back from the Other!"

Fisher did not flinch. Her eyes raked me, taking in my untucked shirt and wild hair. "The kind of thing that *can* follow you back?"

I shook my head, breathless. "I have no clue. Where is Slader?"

"Still ashore with the harbor master, along with Mr. Keo and Ms. Skarrow." Fisher named the bosun and gun captain, respectively. Her eyes strayed over the expanse of harbor between us and the docks. The light in the water was constant now, giving her eyes a bleached hue. "Tell me what it is."

The instinct to flee felt like a thousand ants rushing up my spine, but I quashed it and joined her. Below, light swelled beneath the lightly chopping waves. "I am not sure."

On the deck of every other ship in port, sailors ran to the rails. On the docks, the small figures of soldiers on patrol stopped to watch, rifles and lanterns in hand, and townsfolk on late-night errands clustered.

Without warning, the light beneath the waves shattered across our hull into hundreds of glowing creatures, each one the size of a cat—sleek, equine and unmistakable.

"Morgories," I said, dread turning my guts to water. Like myself, morgories were flesh-and-blood creatures that had one foot in the Other world and one foot in ours. They would consume anything and everything in their path—even a ship.

"Quiet!" Fisher called across the deck, raising her voice just enough to be heard by the sailors. She pointed to Penn. "You, Mr. Penn, get below and keep everyone in their hammocks. We wait."

Penn left at a stealthy jog and silence fell, horrified understanding spreading across *Hart* and the rest of the harbor. The hush was eerie, interrupted only by the swirl of morgories beneath the water, the creak of ships and the soft intake of Fisher's bated breath.

The ship rocked on the glowing tide. Fisher grabbed a line and I seized the rail with frozen, aching hands.

"Lieutenants!" a nearby sailor choked. "Sirs, should we make for shore? If we—"

"Hush!" Fisher commanded, but she looked to me, her eyes round with a fear her calm exterior masked. "They'll eat the boats to splinters before you get a dozen yards. Our only hope is for them to lose interest or Hart to intervene, so shut up."

Silence clapped over the deck. A hiss rose in its place, a slithering grate of rough morgory hide on the hull of the ship. Or teeth. It was a sound few of the crew would have ever heard before—and quite possibly would never hear again.

I was transfixed. This was a waking nightmare, boyhood terrors made flesh. I wanted to run or arm myself, to do anything except stand here praying I would not die tonight. But there was nothing I could do.

"Come now, Hart," Fisher murmured to the ship, resting her hands heavily on the rail beside mine. "Wake."

I felt something shift in the wood beneath our palms. It was a breath, a sigh, and in the next instant the form of a great stag materialized atop the waves beside the ship.

Hart's ghisting raised his head and looked up at Fisher and I for one glassy-eyed instant. He was over twenty hands high, with antlers broader than I was tall and a ruff of thick hair about his throat and chest.

More ghistings materialized on shore. They formed between the houses, glowing threads connecting them to lintels, doorframes and ancient ornamentation. Some were human in form, mirroring the staring townsfolk in the street around them. Some appeared as animals or strange beasts, and others as formless entities. All were still. All were silent.

They were Tithe's ghistings, come out to watch, to wait, and to protect the town.

On the waves beneath me, Hart huffed, stomped, and ducked his head to the water.

The morgories scattered into a broadening swirl about him, taking their illumination with them. Fisher and I fell into shadow as the swarm finally dove in a comet of light towards the mouth of the bay and vanished into the Winter Sea.

As they went, the ghistings on shore extinguished one by one. Finally, only the ghisting Hart remained, standing atop the waves and watching the other morgories leave with a steady, unmoving gaze. Then he slipped out of existence, returning to his home within the figurehead.

"Well." Fisher turned to lean against the lattice of the shrouds, giving me an arch look. "You were in the Other again? Pray, was what you found worth nearly killing our ship and everyone aboard?"

I nodded, using the movement to cover a swallow, and shot the woman a humorless smile. "It was. I found the trail of Mary Firth."

∞

The open sea felt like forgiveness. I stood watch, calm and rested after a night relatively undisturbed by visions. Though I knew the peace would not last, I relished the clarity of mind and strength of will that came with real sleep.

"Sails on the horizon!" a pale-haired woman called from the stern. "A warship, sir."

I left my post beside the wheel and took her spyglass, directing it in the direction of her pointing finger. Sure enough, a tower of sails appeared with a long, deep indigo banner streaming from her maintop. I did not need to see the colors of Aeadine at her mizzenmast to know precisely who and what she was.

The shape of the pennant meant Navy, the color of it, the North Fleet. The fleet under command of Lord Admiral Rosser Howe, my uncle. And the lines of that ship? The arrangements of her sails, the indigo paint and gold lettering along her quarterdeck and the number of their guns? I knew her.

"Sir?" The watchwoman's voice pressed into my thoughts. Her accent was Midland Aeadine, likely from the Wolds. She almost sounded like Mary. "All's well? Who is she?"

"Her Majesty's *Defiance*," I said, giving her a polite nod and handing the spyglass back. "We are sharing these waters with honorable company. Let me know if they signal, Ms. Fitz."

"Aye, that." She peered at the vessel again, an awed smile touching her lips.

I returned to my post by the wheel, gloved hands clasped firmly behind my back, expression clear of all disruption. I had known the Navy sailed these waters, including my brother's ship. There was no reason to let sighting them perturb me.

Fisher materialized, greatcoat wrapped about herself and breath misting from her nostrils in draconian swirls.

"Old friends?" she asked mildly.

"Yes," I said, making sure my tone and expression gave nothing away.

"Which ones?"

"*Defiance*."

Fisher looked back at me in surprise. "*Defiance*? Isn't that your brother's? Mr. Rosser, we can signal. I know you left your post in some... well. But your brother—"

"No." The word snapped out of me before I could temper it. "Benedict and I have not spoken in some time."

"Ah." Fisher fell quiet. After a moment she produced a flask from beneath her cloak and held it out to me.

I hesitated. There was no mocking in Fisher's manner, no hint of our usual conflict. I was wary of pity too, but there was none of that. Just a flask.

I accepted and uncapped it, taking a cautious swig.

The helmsman eyed our exchange, and Fisher gave him a wan look. "It's coffee, crewman. Nothing proper."

"Could still share," he muttered, his huge, mittened hands wrapped around the spokes of the wheel.

I passed the flask on, and over the next few moments, the three of us drank in silence. Then Fisher tapped the empty flask on my arm in farewell and vanished across the deck.

"She's not all bad," the helmsman commented, then added hastily, "an' I mean no offense by that."

I glanced at the man sideways and grinned. "Still, be careful not to say that in her hearing, crewman."

"I wouldn't dream of it," he said with all seriousness.

Fisher had already slipped from my mind, though, as my eyes strayed back to the speck that was *Defiance*. It was true. My brother Benedict and I had not spoken in years, not since I had resigned my commission. The words we had exchanged on that day were not easily forgiven.

With any luck, this was the closest I would ever come to my brother again.

SEVENTEEN

On the Account

MARY

I awoke to singing through the deck above my hammock, rumbling baritones accompanied by the steady beat of a drum. Disoriented, I squinted around my dark little chamber, trying to recall what ship I was on and how I'd gotten here.

Lighter female voices joined in and feet stomped right above my head. I heard what sounded like a clap of thunder—a sail filling?—and the whole cabin creaked, tipping to one side. My hammock swung, ropes strained, and I braced my hands in a beam above.

Demery. What had I done?

I'd joined a damn pirate crew, that's what I'd done.

The urge to stay in my hammock indefinitely assailed me, but my bladder was full, my stomach empty and the cold chamber stank of wood and damp and sweat. Besides, hiding wasn't an option. I had a job to do, and that job was the only leverage I had.

I grasped the beam above my head, slipped my legs out of the hammock, and dropped with a *whump* of blankets and skirts. I hadn't fully undressed the night before, just removing my bodice and loosening my stays enough to sleep. I tightened my stays again with a few tugs as I picked my way over to the lidded bucket hung on one wall and saw to my necessities. Then I dressed, fixed my braid, and stepped out into the main cabin.

It was empty, its table clean, chairs lashed and trunks closed. The windows and balcony door filtered bright sunlight through murky, bottle-bottom panes. Each had a small section that could be opened, and one of these was carefully fastened back.

Salty wind gusted through on a shaft of cool light. I made for it, closing my eyes and letting the clean air fill my lungs. The songs of the crew drifted to me more clearly, the drumbeat steady and punctuated with laughter.

"Ah, you are awake."

I froze. The voice was familiar, tugging me back to the gallows and rough hempen noose.

Footsteps approached, two cautious paces, and I turned to see Charles Grant standing on the other side of the table, between me and the cabin's main door. Our eyes met and for a heartbeat he looked appropriately chagrined, then his expression locked into a pleasant smile. The handsomeness of the look was marred only by two bold cuts down one cheek, still crusted with scabs and edged with fresh, puffy, pink flesh.

"What happened to your face?" I asked, stunned. "Why are you here?"

The man's smile twitched and he rubbed a thumb along his jaw. He ignored my second question. "Speck did. Or rather, he held me down while Kaspin took his due."

A shard of pity wedged into my heart, but it was easy to ignore after what he'd done.

"Why would he do that?" I asked hotly. "I thought you'd settled your debt by selling me into a life of servitude."

"A warning. He's a killer, Mary, and he would have butchered both of us if I had not… did what I did." He took another step forward, and my eyes dropped to the cutlass at his hip. "I saved your life."

"And I saved yours from the noose. How are you here?" Fury rippled through me. If he hadn't sold me out, if I'd have run off into the snow instead of lingering beside that riverboat... My path would have been so different.

Or would it? Inexplicable as his motives were, Lirr would still be hunting me. And I would be alone, on the run, with no idea what was happening or where to find my mother.

But I'd just awoken on a ship full of pirates, far from home, and come face-to-face with the man who had set that series of events into motion. I was in no mood for fortitude.

"I did what I had to do," he insisted. "Life is full of difficult decisions, Mary."

Mary. He tossed out my name as if we were friends.

I snorted. "What are you doing here, Mr. Grant?" I demanded for a third time.

He plastered a smile back on his face and gave a sweeping bow. "I've gone on the account."

"What?"

"I've become a pirate."

"You joined Demery's crew?"

He nodded and rested a hand on his cutlass, one foot forward and slightly turned to the side in a dandy's pose. "I have. It was time to start a new life, and I figured—hoi, pirates are the highwaymen of the seas, so my skillset ought to transition well. Provided I don't have to sail anything. Luckily, Demery said he's in need of a man like me."

"You really want that noose, don't you?" I trembled, a bone-deep shudder of tension and anger.

"What's life without the threat of death?"

"Pleasant?"

"Insufferable."

I stewed for an instant before another question struck me. "How long have you been aboard? Not since Whallum, surely?"

His response was a smile that reminded me of a dog caught chewing a shoe. He shrugged. "Well, you were rather unsociable after we picked you up."

"You've been here the whole time?"

"Ah, I see you two have been reunited." Demery strode into the room with a large ledger under one arm. Passing us, he stepped up to the table and set the book down. "Mary, if you wouldn't mind?"

I was about to demand why Demery had taken Grant aboard, but self-preservation stayed my words. Besides, between my frayed nerves and trembling hands, I felt wearier with every passing moment. I should have stayed in my hammock.

I shot Grant one last look and joined Demery at the table. He opened the ledger and fetched quill, ink and drying powder from a trunk, then set them out.

"These are the ship's articles. Her accord," the captain informed me, tapping the open page. "See here, *'Every One shall obey civil Command. The Captain shall have two full shares of all Prizes.'*—that's me—*'They who are found Guilty of Cowardice in the Time of Engagement, or should Murder Another, shall suffer Death.'* So on and so forth. You see how it is. Everyone aboard this ship signs. Everyone aboard this ship is held to account. That includes you. Do you understand?"

I was privately shocked that pirates would have such a code of conduct but didn't comment. Instead, I wanted to know, "Did *Charles* sign?"

Demery flipped farther into the book and stopped on a page that was only half full. Both it and the one before it was scrawled with dozens of names and dates, interspersed with signs for those who could not write and occasional sums in the margins. More than a few names were crossed out with single, black strokes. But the last one stood out clean and sharp, its flowery scrawl taking up twice as much room than any other.

'Charles Addison Grant, on the 14th Day of the First Turning of the Bountiful Moons, in the 20th year of the reign of Her Majesty Queen Edith. Ambassador.'

"Ambassador?" I looked between the two men.

"A man of good education who I can send ashore to parley with various powers over the course of our journey," Demery returned, uncorking the ink and passing me the quill.

"I am educated, charming, persuasive, and willing to do bad things." Grant sat in a chair across the table and glanced at my hand, hovering, quill poised. "Are you going to sign?"

I couldn't help thinking that the scars on Grant's cheek would likely hinder his reputability in the future, but brushed the thought aside. Demery was looking at me with expectation too.

I flipped back to the articles and read them slowly. But despite my efforts, half the words fluttered away. If Demery and his crew were captured, this ledger might send me right back to prison, if not the noose. Sure, I could plead innocence as the ship's Stormsinger, but there could still be unpredictable repercussions.

I dipped the quill in the bottle of ink, holding it there a heartbeat longer than was necessary, then signed. I signed as large as Grant had, my mother's maiden name sealing my fate within its graceful letters.

'Mary Firth, on the 24th Day of the First Turning of the Bountiful Moons, in the 20th year of the reign of Her Majesty Queen Edith. Stormsinger.'

Demery sprinkled drying powder over the page and blew it away in a swirling gust, then closed the ledger and smiled at me. "Welcome, Ms. Firth. Now, let's find you something to eat, and I'll tell you what's next."

I ate a breakfast of hot oats and dried berries as Athe arrived, along with a grey-haired, narrow-eyed man Demery addressed as Bailey, and the old woman Widderow. The latter sat without an ounce of formality, took me in with one long look, then set to tapping a stylus on a bottle of ink.

Athe settled in beside Demery. They began to converse about daily matters, and I finally understood that she must be the ship's master. First mate, as it were. Bailey was the bosun, whatever that meant, and Widderow, as she told me previously, was the steward and purser.

Grant situated himself next to me with a thin smile. "Enjoying your breakfast?"

I turned to Demery.

"Now," the captain said, taking a seat of his own. "To business. Our goal? Locate Silvanus Lirr and rescue Anne Firth, preferably leaving Lirr dead in our wake. Then Anne will guide us to the location of Bretton's Hoard."

"No crossing the Stormwall without a Sooth." Widderow stopped tapping the ink with her stylus and ran it across the tiny vessel's smooth surface with the barest, gentle rasp. "Too many ships wrecked in those waters, and too many ghistings trapped in them. We need someone to manage the Other. And we need an Usti Voyager."

"A Voyager?" Athe gave the older woman a long-suffering look. "We've sailed the Winter Sea for decades, Crow. No need of a Voyager."

"And I've sailed it for half a century," Widderow returned with a tight-lipped, thoroughly unnerving smile. "Because we always kept a Voyager in the pocket when I was anywhere near the North Line." Her smile turned even slyer. "What of… the Uknaras?"

I must have looked lost, because Grant leaned in. "A Voyager is a survivalist, of a sort," he murmured. "From one of the Usti tribes that live near the Stormwall, or the North Line, as our elders may call it. Occasionally, Voyagers live on the other side of the wall too."

"No one can live over the Stormwall," I countered.

"Voyagers can. In specific areas," he informed me. "Or so the Usti say. They're as private about the north as the Mereish are about their magics."

"Old Crow is right." Demery overrode the discussion. "We'll pick up the Uknaras in Hesten."

Whoever the Uknaras were, everyone appeared to believe they were a good choice, and nodded in acquiescence.

Demery went on, "We'll have to move quickly to keep ahead of Lirr, but with any luck he won't realize Mary's survived for some time."

"How is that, exactly?" Grant asked curiously.

"Randalf's ghisting carried her off quite swiftly, as I understand it," Demery said, unruffled by the bizarre nature of what he was saying. "Ghisting light can confuse the sight of Sooths, particularly a newly freed ghisting who is already skirting the divide between realms. I've been told it can be blinding."

"Juliette wanted to hide me," I observed, pondering the implications of this information.

Demery shrugged. "She saw in you a kindred spirit, perhaps."

"You were both Randalf's captives," Athe put in dismissively. "Ghistings are complicated creatures."

Widderow *tsk*ed, irritated by the conversation. She reached across the table and took a piece of paper from in front of Demery, uncorked her ink, dipped the stylus, and began to write.

"We'll need a good deal of gear beyond the Line, young man," she informed the captain. "I hope you're prepared for that and have some private funds *not* in my books, which are looking quite spare. This is only a preliminary list of goods, however—"

"We'll also need investors," Demery cut in. His smile, I noticed, had an edge to it. "I'm well aware, and I've a story prepared to lure them in."

Widderow paused at her writing, stylus poised over ink. "Oh?"

"Yes. So, while I convince the Uknaras to join our ignoble cause, our ambassador will secure investors around Hesten."

Hesten was the Usti capital, and my imagination sparked at the thought of seeing it myself—a sight that few of my childhood friends could ever hope to glimpse. Never mind that it would be with Grant. I decided I was willing to put up with him for a chance to see a foreign port.

"Let me go with him," I put forward impulsively. "A good Stormsinger is key to your success, so let your investors see me."

Grant looked dubious. "Will it not be dangerous, touting a Stormsinger around Hesten?"

"Not overly so. My name has sway there." Demery looked ponderous. "Mary, do you have any experience in society's higher echelons?"

"My father wanted me to marry up," I answered, unsure of just how high he meant, "so I had a governess for a time."

"Did you spend any seasons in Jurry?" the captain pressed. "Do you speak Usti?"

I shook my head, ashamed. "I've… I'd never left the Wold until a few months ago. And I only speak Aeadine."

Grant gave me a sideways look at that, brows knitting. "You've spent your entire life in a Ghistwold? You never left? Truly?"

I nodded, leveling my shoulders. "Never. But I had a governess, as I said. I learned my histories and poetry, and I can dance and play several instruments. Be polite and such. Things ladies know."

Demery surveyed me silently, an inscrutable calculation passing behind his eyes. Grant nearly looked pitying.

"I want to do this," I asserted, indignation rising. "I'll be helpful."

"Follow Mr. Grant's lead, then," the captain decided, turning back to his books.

I smiled in relief and glanced at Grant. He seemed concerned, but at my look he arched his brows suggestively.

"This ought to be entertaining," he observed.

Widderow spoke over him, asking me, "How are your numbers, girl?"

"Fair."

"She's mine." The old woman pointed at me with her ink-bloodied stylus. "Eli, your crew cannot count beyond their fingers, and Saint save me, I could use an assistant at my age."

"You? An assistant?" the bosun, Bailey, spoke up for the first time. "I was under the impression devils had 'minions.'"

Demery cleared his throat. "Mary, when you're not tending the weather, you'll assist Widderow."

It didn't sound as though I had a choice, so I nodded. The old woman gave me a narrow-eyed smile, a cat to a trapped mouse, and went back to writing her list.

"What's your plan for cornering Lirr?" Athe asked.

"I've a location in mind where we can lure him," Demery said. "Once we're ready, supplied and crewed, we'll head there and make our stand."

"And rescue my mother," I said.

"Then head over the Stormwall," Athe added.

"To riches." Bailey rocked his chair back onto two legs and crossed his arms over his chest.

"Precisely," Demery finished.

"So, we go to a graveyard of our predecessors, locked in ice and haunted by unimaginable quantities of Other-born beasts," Widderow said lightly, stoppered her ink, and stood to present her list to Demery with a flick of paper. She nodded to me. "You do realize that no matter what you say to the crew, there will be trouble with this one. She may not be Lady Abwery but she is no sack of potatoes, and that is all these boys care about."

Caught between offense and a spike of panic, I looked at the captain. "What is she saying?"

"I'm aware," Demery said to Widderow without feeling.

"Trouble?" I repeated, looking at the old woman, but she was on her way out of the cabin with a rustle of dark skirts. "You promised me protection, Mr. Demery. If your crew can't be trusted, our arrangement—"

Across the table, Bailey rolled his eyes and stood. "Didn't know we had a princess aboard."

"I'm nothing of the sort," I snapped, brazen in my indignation.

"No doubt of that," Grant muttered. "You ought to have seen her the day we met."

"I worked an inn for ten years—I can handle myself." My mind tracked back to a dark forest, the open door of the coach, scraped palms, and heavy boots stalking through the autumn deadfall. I added, "And enough to know that sometimes a slap isn't enough."

"That's why I'm assigning a crewmember as your guardian," Demery stated.

Athe caught his eye over the table and relief sunk into my muscles. The woman wasn't overly kind, but I felt safe in her shadow.

"Gods, no, not me," she said, slapped a palm on the table in farewell, and strode out the door. "I have a proper job to do."

Bailey followed her, turning on his way out the door to tug his forelock at the captain.

That left me with Grant, suddenly quiet, and Demery, who cocked his head at the highwayman.

Grant looked as though he'd swallowed a fly.

"Well," the captain said, "there's only one other person here who can't sail and has nothing else to do with their time. You two can get better acquainted before your time in Hesten. Keep her out of trouble, Mr. Grant."

Bonny, Bonny Grant was He,
He was, or so they said,
Handsome as a Devil be,
With Gold upon his Head

Lace he wore about his Throat,
His Breeches, Buckskin fine,
His Eyes they danced a-merrily
His Coat was darkest Wine

A Road, a Coach, a fine Lady,
He'd offer out his Hand
He'd rob her blind a-while she swooned
And pluck her Wedding Band

The Girl from the Wold

The Girl from the Wold is in shock. She sits in a rattling carriage with half a dozen strangers, staring out the window and trying not to think, not to feel. There is a bag in her lap, stuffed to bursting with her most treasured possessions. Her father and stepmother are sending her away, to an aunt who can find her a suitable husband.

She is twenty-two years old. Her last fiancé went to war, and he had no house to leave her in. So the marriage was called off. The girl and her fiancé did not love one another, but their fondness had been growing, and the girl is devastated.

The girl sees something out the carriage window, among the trees—a shadow, too dense for a waning autumn wood. They are not in her Wold, but they are in a normal wold—the Lesterwold, which cloaks the road west in fallen leaves and reaches spindly, clacking fingers up into a grey sky. These trees have all obeyed the change of seasons, and their shadows stretch obediently away from the meager sunlight.

Instead of soothing the girl, the predictability of this common wold doubles the ache in her chest.

There is movement again, among the trunks and branches and bobbing conifer boughs. It does not scare the girl, though she leans forward and squints through the shutters. She is used to forests and their creatures. This is their place, not hers, and she understands her position as guest in a wild realm.

But soon after, the horses whinny and the carriage

stops. The girl hears raised voices and the other travelers glance at one another.

The carriage door bangs open. Another passenger shrieks in surprise, then terror. Hands grab the travelers closest to the door and haul them out like screaming chickens from a coop.

When the hands come for her, she lashes out with a boot. She hears a curse. But another set of fingers digs into her skirts.

Then the girl is in the leaves beside the road, terrified and clawing to her feet. Running away.

And a highwayman with a pistol stalks behind her.

∽

EIGHTEEN

Lanterns in the Snow

MARY

"The key to learning how to fight is not maiming your instructor, even if you happen to resent them for wholly valid reasons." Grant passed me a stick roughly the length of a dagger. He kept its twin in his own hand. "So use this, please. I will ask Demery to find you something more suitable later, but for now... Take it. Mary?"

I grudgingly took the stick. Demery had given us the cabin for an hour to begin my lessons, but even with only Grant's eyes to see me, I still felt absurd in trousers and a hitched-up petticoat, with loosened stays and a man's shirt belted over the top.

"Fingers like this to start." Grant showed me how to grip the hilt of the knife. "Yes, good."

I slowly complied. I knew I was being petty, but it didn't change how I felt. Every time I looked at Grant, I remembered the feel of the Stormsinger's gag in my mouth. The madness of isolation. The helplessness of locked doors. Not knowing what fresh threat the next day would bring.

But his scarred cheeks reminded me that he hadn't come out of that unmarred, either. His movements were a touch stiff, too, as if he'd injuries beneath his loose shirt and waistcoat.

I reined myself in and imitated his grip. "What's next?"

An hour later, I was bored, of all things. We'd spent the entire time shifting grips and stances, over and over until I wanted to lunge at Grant, just to make him move more quickly. But my hands grew accustomed to moving about my fake dagger, and my strained muscles affirmed my need for training.

"Good," Grant said. "Very good. Tomorrow we'll do the same and I'll arrange for some pistols."

I nodded, shoving my 'knife' into my pocket and raking frayed hair back into its simple knot at the back of my head. "Then I've winds to summon."

"And I've..." Grant looked around the cabin, frowned when he saw nothing distracting. "Well, your back to watch."

I sang Demery a rather feisty southerly and spent the rest of the day trying to keep it under control with a simple, repetitive song. We were nearly into the second turning of the Bountiful Moons now, and the rough waves and sudden squalls made it clear that, as far as weather went, I'd been spoiled aboard Randalf's ship. The three Bitter Moons of deep winter were coming. The world would shed her sheltering leaves and cede us to a baleful wind and driving snow and ravenous sky.

Despite my bravado and promises to Demery, I wasn't fit to face that turbulent season on the water. Yet.

The waves rose, choppy and capped with white. Snow clouds hemmed us in as the sun dipped towards an early slumber, and even the southerly wind brought a bitter, lung-cracking cold.

I turned my song to dismissing the clouds, but my throat ached. I accepted a flask of hot, honey-laced coffee from Grant, so tired that I felt only dull gratitude as I clutched it between my mittened hands and let steam tickle the fine, frozen hairs inside my nose.

"Not going well?" Grant inquired.

"No." My eyes drifted to the rail, where Demery, Athe and Bailey conferred. The wind tore most of their words away, but the glares Bailey kept shooting me were clear enough. "From the look on *his* face I'm going to get dumped on the nearest cay."

"You brought winter down on Whallum a month early," Grant said, mystified. His disbelief consoled me, somehow. "You are very powerful."

"My mother forbade me to sing," I admitted, though I immediately regretted it. Was my situation so dire that I was confiding in the highwayman? But there was no taking the admission back. "She forbade me to sing so I wouldn't get carried off and sold by brigands."

Grant smiled humorlessly. "Ah, you are subtle. Are you sure you were not kept quiet because of Lirr? Sooths can track Unnaturals in the Other, can they not? Perhaps never singing made you harder to find. Lirr only reappeared after you sang in Whallum."

I frowned, perturbed by the thought. "I doubt that. Besides, I thought Sooths needed to touch a person to track them?"

Grant shrugged. "I haven't a clue."

Despite his dismissiveness, we were both quiet for an instant. The wind blew, hot coffee cooled on my tongue, and Demery and the others still conversed.

"Out of curiosity, where was Lirr before Whallum?" I asked.

"South Mereish Isles, they say."

"That's what, a month's journey?" I eyed the horizon without really seeing it.

Grant calculated for a moment. "Give or take, depending on which island you're coming from. Let us say an average of five weeks."

Five weeks. Five weeks before Lirr appeared in Whallum was not when I sang at the gallows, but when I left the Wold. When my stepmother banished me from the shelter of my home and forest, and I'd stepped out into the world for the first time.

Could it be coincidence that that was precisely when Lirr would have departed the Mereish Isles? Presuming he hadn't been somewhere else, first.

My stomach fluttered with unease, and I took another sip of coffee. Lirr's words drifted back to me, somehow both more meaningful and more opaque now.

Do you not remember who you are?

Remember what? I was Mary Firth, born Mary Grey and occasionally mistaken as Abetha Bonning. I was a Stormsinger, if an unreliable one. I should have been nothing to Lirr save the key to manipulating my mother. But the way he'd looked at me said otherwise.

My mother. My belly sank, filling with hope and unease. I still barely believed that she was aboard Lirr's ship, much less that, if Demery's plan succeeded, I'd see her again within a couple months.

I batted the thought aside and downed half the coffee in one gulp, burning my throat.

Grant abruptly asked, "Lirr isn't your father, is he?"

I choked on the coffee and descended into a fit of hacking and spitting. "What?"

Grant tried to thump me on the back, which I warded off with a flailing hand. "Well— Ouch! Considering their past…"

"Lirr is *not* my father," I spluttered. "I look just like my father and the way Lirr… He didn't treat me like that."

The former highwayman's eyebrows went up again, something colder inching into his gaze. "How did he treat you?"

"Sail!" The cry went up from somewhere in the rigging. "Three sails!"

Demery, Athe and Bailey splintered, all three of them snapping to attention.

"Colors?" Demery shouted.

"Dark purple, flying war pennants! And they're making for us, Cap'n."

"Running us down with a storm blowing in," Bailey snarled. "Craven Mereish bastards."

Mereish. Of course, our world was at war. It wasn't just pirates and pirate hunters who plowed these seas.

"Pray, Mereish?" Grant repeated, loud enough for the pirates to hear. "We're in neutral waters, barely out of Tithe! The Usti are supposed to—"

"That storm's pushing them south out of the passage," Demery decided. He pushed up the brim of his hat, scratching at his forehead. "They may not attack."

"To the crows with that. We should beat to quarters." Athe sucked her teeth, unfocused eyes cast towards the danger. "Show our spines and keep them at a distance."

"Nay," Bailey countered. "Three Mereish? We keep our heads down and pray for mercy."

Demery followed the direction of Athe's gaze for an indecisive moment, then nodded. "Beat to quarters."

Bailey scowled, but Athe leapt into motion. She strode off, issuing a string of orders that left both Grant and I baffled. Bailey followed her, separating midships and heading below to bellow more orders to the pirates off watch.

Demery approached Grant and I, lowering his chin. "Both of you, below."

"I can help," I protested, half out of a need to do something, and half out of the desire to prove myself. "I can turn the wind against them."

"Or you'll sink us," Demery said, flat and mild and without ire. "Besides, the last thing we want is the Mereish realizing we've a Stormsinger, even if you're unseasoned. Go below, get some rest. Grant, stay a moment."

I flushed, chastened, and left without looking back at him or Grant. In the main cabin, I pulled my mittens off beside the woodstove. I drained the flask of coffee, knowing I'd hardly be able to sleep, anyway, and returned to my cabin.

Grant strode in. "Hoi," he protested, wedging his boot in the door of my cabin before I could close it. "You're truly going to lock yourself away? In circumstances like this?"

"What else am I to do?" I inquired.

He nodded to the table. "Play a hand of cards with me."

"You want to play cards while we're chased by Mereish warships?"

Grant's smile was wan. "It calms my nerves. Besides, you're going to have to learn how to gamble if you intend to be part of this crew."

I had no intention of fitting in with Demery's crew, but that was beside the point. "I already know how to gamble," I returned archly. "I grew up in a tavern, Mr. Grant."

"Ah, yes, you have alluded to that before." He leaned into the doorframe, boot still lodged in place. "Where? Maybe I passed through."

I tried to close the door again.

"Well, then, I don't believe you. You've probably never even held cards before."

My pride rankled, ridiculous and wholly inappropriate.

Grant saw my expression change and pounced. "Prove it," he teased, leaning into my room.

I opened the door wide, shouldered past him, and sat down at Demery's big table.

We played late into the night, slapping down cards and gambling away odds and ends from our pockets. I lost the solem Demery had gifted me, but consoled myself there would be more on the way.

Around us, the ship groaned, feet passed across the deck and the sky beyond the gallery windows was swallowed by snow. We had no chance to see the Mereish ships with our naked eyes; the storm was fully upon us.

The wait was strained. Tension ate at my stomach, but I channeled it into the game, feet braced wide beneath the table so I wouldn't slide off my chair with each beleaguered roll of the ship. Grant did the same, his focus narrowing as time passed. We raided the galley for bread and cheese and uncut carrots, and wrapped ourselves in piles of blankets against the cold when Bailey ordered the stoves put out. We discreetly lit a candle lantern—Demery had no dragonflies—and hung it in the center of the cabin, both knowing it was probably unwise, but neither taking the step to care.

We discussed the games we played, taunted and teased, but neither of our hearts were in it.

"How did you become a highwayman?" I finally asked, half because the question had been bothering me, and half to distract him. He'd won two games in a row.

Grant laid down a card. "Debt. Many of my stories hinge on debt."

I laid a card of my own, eyeing him promptingly.

"My father's a count," Grant confessed. "But I've five older brothers, no responsibility and no real inheritance. Father intended to send me into the army at seventeen, which was a terrible idea by all accounts. Luckily for me, a week before I was to head off to some Saint-forsaken fort on the north coast, I met a beautiful woman who was unreasonably good at dice. I found myself rather destitute, but she offered to wave my debt if I joined her in a certain venture, which may have included waylaying travelers."

My stomach turned, and it had nothing to do with the rolling ship. I thought it unlikely that Grant had been connected to the highwaymen who'd attacked my own carriage in the Lesterwold, but I couldn't know for sure.

I laid down Rosser's Mereish coin as my wager and eyed my hand. Its three coiled serpents glistened in the lanternlight. "Is this Mereish?" I asked, off-topic, and pointed to the coin.

"Mm. I'd say." Grant laid down two pieces of his own and resumed his tale. "That woman was Abetha Bonning."

My mouth fell open. So much for distracting Grant—now I was the one completely preoccupied. "You knew Abetha Bonning?"

"I did! Lovely woman. Terrifying woman. You two really do look alike—honestly, it's a bit bizarre—but she's ten years your senior and not nearly so prudish."

I was growing so used to his jibes that I only flicked him a glance. "Then what happened?"

"Abetha never works in concert for long, so after I paid off my debt I struck out on my own. That was six years ago."

My suspicion abated. If Grant worked solo, he hadn't been involved in my carriage's capture. "And eventually you were arrested?"

"Queen's Guns dragged me out of my favorite tavern." Grant laid down his hand. "You won."

I glanced at the cards in surprise and grinned widely. "Well, would you look at that."

It wasn't until near midnight when we heard the rumble of the cannons being run out, the coordinated shouts of gun crews. Grant left the table, opened one of the hatches in the stern windows and peered through.

I crowded close behind him, a heavy blanket clutched like a cloak. "What do you see?"

"Ships' lanterns." Grant stepped aside, holding the hatch for me to look through.

Sure enough, two lanterns glowed out through the veil of snow, rising and falling with the rhythm of the waves. They were eerie things, diffused and faint, but the threat of them made supper spoil in my stomach.

"Where's the third ship?" I asked.

"Already passed us, drawing up for a full broadside?" Grant suggested.

I tried to find a witty retort, but I'd lost the will. I stared out at the Mereish ships, anxiety deadening my tongue, then returned to the table.

I sat, hard, and Grant returned to perch across from me, tense on the edge of his chair. Our cards lay forgotten on the tabletop for a silent minute, sliding to and fro with the rocking of the ship.

"What was it like, where you grew up?" the former highwayman suddenly asked. "The inn? The forest?"

I looked at him for a moment, numb and battling not to think of the Mereish ships. Then I sunk back in my chair and looked past him, past our pursuers, over the sea and back to the Wold. "Safe."

∽

Soon after, all lanterns passed beyond sight of the stern window. Grant and I crept out the quarterdeck doors and peered across the ship, past the snowy forms of pirates at the long guns.

Demery and Athe stood at the rail, shoulder to shoulder, hats and coats dusted with snow, and watched the great warships sail beyond them. The Mereish sailed close enough that I could make out the shadowed shapes of crewmen on their decks, hear the rush of their bows and the snap of war banners in the wind.

I saw *Harpy*'s ghisting too. She slipped from the wood of the mainmast, a faint blue glow and feminine shape. In the snow it was hard to see her clearly, but she glowed with an ethereal blue light. She, too, watched the Mereish, her head slowly turning as they passed.

Finally, the warships vanished into the night. The ghisting disappeared and the crew relaxed, coughing and clearing their throats, thumping one another on the back and saluting Athe and Demery.

I retreated into the passageway and offered Grant a weak smile.

"We're not dead," I pointed out, all hostility forgotten. "Or captives of the Mereish."

Grant returned my smile with one equally as tired. "Yes, thank the Saint. And thank you for the distraction, tonight. I'll admit, you're a fine hand at cards."

"It was my pleasure." I retreated to the door of the cabin, hiding a smile in the shadows. I tapped the doorframe with a few absent fingers, feeling as though I should say more, but unable to put the words together. "Good night, Mr. Grant."

He touched his hat, his face equally hidden in the darkness. "Good night, Ms. Firth."

NINETEEN

Daughter of the Fleetbreaker

MARY

"Did no one train you to stormsing, girl?" the old woman asked. She shut a crate of grenados, packed in straw. "Good thing I have a use for you, or we might feed you to the chickens. Fourteen. Girl? Do not make me regret—"

"I'm writing!" I gestured to the ledger I'd wedged between my elbow and a crooked wrist, inkpot perilously cradled in my fingers above. Unable to sleep and with Grant comatose in his hammock, I'd reported to Widderow for numbers duty. A decision I was beginning to regret. "I wrote it, see. And as to the singing, no. No one trained me, but I'll learn. All I need is practice."

"As you say, as you say." The older woman sniffed, surveying the goods stacked around us. We were in the small, ironclad hold that served as magazine, surrounded by kegs and barrels of powder, racks of shot and crates of various other deadly things. Widderow barely seemed conscious of the nature of the items. All morning she'd been pinching gunpowder as if it were flour and assessing grenados like a grocer might apples, complaining at our lack of provisioning and lamenting Demery's strained finances. I'd little concept of what a stocked armory should look like, but I could see the empty racks for shot and half-empty kegs of powder.

Demery's lack of preparedness made my nerves hum. I'd seen Lirr's crew, armed to the teeth and at ease in their gruesome victory. I could only pray that we'd find willing investors in Usti.

Usti. I'd never in my life considered visiting such a place, let alone leaving the Wold. I missed it, the leaves and the sun and the hush. For a moment I let myself drift back there, quill in hand. Widderow's muttering and shuffling faded away.

"Old Crow." A man stepped into the corner of my eye, snapping me back to reality.

"Away!" Widderow threw out an arm, banishing him. "Boots outside that doorframe, sailor."

The crewman retreated into the passageway. He scowled, glanced at me self-consciously, then looked back at Widderow. "Captain wants to speak to you."

"About what?"

"Hesten Port."

Widderow frowned, jowls draping over her collar. "Fine. Ms. Firth, do the last two crates yourself and bring me the ledger. Do not smudge those numbers. Understood?"

I nodded, setting down the book, inkpot and quill on a barrel. Widderow left. Footsteps faded as I moved to one of the crates the woman had indicated, unlatched it, and carefully leaned the lid against the bulkhead. Grenados packed in straw lay before me, just waiting to be filled with powder and hurled at enemies.

I stared at them, remembering the attack on Randalf's ship. A man swinging from the rigging, piss and blood dripping from his twitching toes. Then I imagined lobbing a grenado into Lirr's face and felt marginally better.

I released my breath and stared across the chamber, holding ill memories at bay. I would not live in fear. I finished taking down Widderow's numbers and passed back through the ship quickly. Down a passageway, up a steep stair, and onto the gun deck.

Harpy's dozen guns were stowed after last night's show of force and the space had reverted to living quarters, home to some fourscore pirates. A quarter were at work somewhere about the ship but the rest were at their leisure, asleep in hammocks, lounging between the guns, talking and mending and whittling and singing and all the other things men and women did to pass the time. I passed one particular hammock, swinging and bracketed by a pair of naked, hairy, female legs. I fixed panicked eyes on the deck and hurried on before I could see—or hear—anything else.

Closer to the fore of the ship, I saw Grant's coat slung over the lines of a full hammock. Bundling Widderow's book and inkpot under one arm, I poked at the canvas cocoon.

"Mr. Grant," I said, poking him again. "Grant. Charles!"

A nearby pirate caught my eye, sitting on top of a lashed gun. She squinted at me over the sock she was darning, the overly domestic image juxtaposed by the cannon, her worn men's clothes and the shaved sides of her head. What remained of her hair was braided from the nape of her neck up to her forehead, and there it was folded over itself and pinned with two long wooden hairpins behind her skull.

"Slap 'im," she urged. She indicated a rounded portion of the hammock, roughly where Grant's legs connected with his body.

Heat spread across my cheeks, though I couldn't decide whether it was from the woman's suggestion or the continued memory of dangling legs.

I shoved at the hammock. Its steady swinging disrupted. "Charles Grant!"

Still nothing.

"That one sleeps like the dead. Slap 'im, I said," the pirate insisted, her face lit with a wicked grin. "Do it, witch."

I shook my head sharply. "I will not."

"Fine." Before I could protest the woman stood and shouldered past me. She gave Grant's backside a firm, full-palmed slap.

Grant came awake with a flail and smacked his head off a beam. "Fucking shit-bucket boat!" He wilted back into his hammock, clutching his forehead.

I stifled a snort with the back of one hand and several nearby pirates laughed uproariously.

My amusement died when Grant's squinting eyes fell not on the offending pirate, but on me. The other woman was already back at her darning, a look of startled innocence plastered across her face.

She winked at me.

"Saint, Mary!" Grant half fell out of the hammock, shirt askew and trousers—thank that same Saint—intact. I'd seen entirely enough legs for one day. "What do you want?"

"That wasn't me!" I protested.

"Oh, it was," the sock-darning pirate said sagely. She waved a knitting needle at me. "This one's predatory, Bonny Grant."

Grant stared at me again, flabbergasted.

"It wasn't me," I started to protest again, but half a dozen nearby pirates contradicted me. I gave up, blushing furiously, and raised my chin. "It's past noon. It's time for my lessons."

"What you need," Grant growled, shuffling around me and shoving his shirt into his breeches. "Is a lesson in manners."

"Says the half-dressed man who slept past noon," I quipped.

Grant eyed me, brows rising. "What's gotten into you?"

"Lessons," I reminded him, still crimson, and strode away down the deck.

Over the next ten days, I battled the wind. Occasionally I made headway—the weather shifted as I willed it and *Harpy* flew over the waves as pirates cheered and the wind lashed my cheeks. But my control was inconsistent, and when the skies darkened with oncoming storms, Demery banished me back to the cabin. It was safer, he claimed, for the pirates to manage natural weather than rely on my unpredictable magic.

Storms upon the Winter Seas, however, were long and frequent. My stomach, which up until now had been unperturbed by the sea, finally gave in to the increasing severity of the tempests. I had two choices as to how to pass the time—sit in my little cabin, worrying away the hours and throwing up the contents of my unsettled stomach, or spend them with Grant, gambling and throwing up the contents of my unsettled stomach.

When I was alone in the darkness, my thoughts turned to Lirr and my mother and the future. So I chose Grant more and more. It was not that I'd forgiven him, but I had no other choice. There was camaraderie in our misery and general uselessness, and when I returned from another bout of retching, he'd crack a resigned smile and pass me a flask of water to wash out my mouth.

We continued our lessons when the seas were calmer. My muscles ached less and began to recall the stances and movements Grant had taught me. I learned to manage a pistol and took to it well. We began to properly spar too, and in the brief spaces when I managed to stop laughing or mocking myself, I found a new confidence in that skill. I was by no means proficient, and I knew I'd be trounced by a trained opponent—but it was the confidence I needed most.

I was no longer defenseless.

On the eleventh day, another tempest wrapped around us. Grant and I tried to play cards, but staying in our chairs was impossible. Eventually Grant staggered back to the gun deck and I retired to my cabin, taking one last look at the eerie stormlit windows and clinging snow before I closed the door.

Darkness stifled me. The quiet was loud, riddled with creaking and moaning, howling and roaring. It blended in my skull as I braced myself in a corner, choking down familiar anxiety and praying that this wouldn't be the night *Harpy* joined the graveyard of ships on the bottom of the Winter Sea. But that night, the silence and fear felt different.

Perhaps it was the closeness of death. Perhaps it was the keen, piercing sense of my own fragile life, of each misting breath and every beleaguered heartbeat. Perhaps it was my recent successes with Grant's lessons.

Whatever it was, I felt a shift within myself. Apprehension retreated, and a blind, dire courage took its place.

I was a Stormsinger, after my mother. I might have been silenced for sixteen long years, but I had my voice and the power to calm this storm, somewhere inside me. I simply had to do it—before it killed me, *Harpy* and her crew.

I opened the door and staggered across the cabin, climbing uphill as the ship lurched forward. By the time it tilted back, I braced my hands on the frigid windows. The wind seeped in, finding the barest cracks and edges, and through the frosted glass I saw the ice-caked balcony and menacing, dark waves.

I pulled those threads of wind into my nose and searched for the right notes, the right words. Instead of commanding the storm like an unruly hound, I thought to appeal to it—one power to another.

My song was a lullaby, simple and sweet. My emotion went with it—the same desire for freedom, peace and security that had fueled my voice as a child under the yew, at the gallows, and Kaspin's auction. There was no questioning in that longing, only honesty.

> *"Oh, hush thee, my baby, the night is behind us,*
> *And black are the waters that sparkled so green.*
> *The storm shall not wake thee, nor shark overtake thee,*
> *Asleep in the arms of the slow-swinging seas."*

The tendrils of wind whistling through the window eased. I held my breath for an instant, senses straining, hardly daring to believe I'd succeeded. The ship still rolled and complained, but the wind had lessened.

I sang again, and again. On the third round, I became aware of a new presence in the cabin but didn't tear my focus off the window. It was likely just Grant.

The last of the wind retreated in a slow exhale.

"I can do nothing for the waves—at least, not yet." I glanced over my shoulder. "But—"

It was not Grant who looked back at me, but a ghisting. She was small, translucent and smooth, hovering just beyond the wood of the bulkhead. Unlike Randalf's Juliette, this ghisting—Harpy— had no face, simply a blank space between falls of straight, ghostly hair. She wore smooth skirts that I immediately feared might be tentacles, but as she swayed with the movement of the ship, I saw legs press against the fabric.

She was beautiful, I realized, in an abstract way, her only distinct features being the fall of her hair and the belt at her waist, from which hung an array of closed fans.

As I watched, awestruck, she picked up one fan and unfurled it with a deft twist of her fingers. She raised it to her face and watched me for a moment, even though she had no eyes. But the fan did. It had a full painted face with a secretive smile, a sharp nose and eyes the color of a spring sunrise.

She lifted the fan fully in front of her. It vanished but the face remained, now imprinted on the ghisting's own head. She smiled at me, gave a graceful, liquid bow, and murmured. No sound came from her bowed lips, but a single word thrummed in my chest.

Sister?

I held my breath.

Harpy spoke again, and this time there was no question to it. *Tane.*

"Tane?" I repeated, confused.

Her smile slipped into a passive, blank expression. I couldn't tell if my lack of understanding had caused it, or the ghisting simply couldn't maintain any expression for long.

"What does Tane mean? Is it a name?" I asked. The ship still rocked, and I braced myself against the window frame. "Or a word? Do ghistings have their own words? I…" I trailed off, realizing how ignorant I must be of the creatures I'd grown up beside.

We do, Harpy said. She slipped forward, beginning to circle me with no regard for the tilting of the deck. She passed through the wood of the table and chairs, smoky wisps of her flesh clinging to their surfaces in her wake. *We have our own words, our own thoughts, our own desires. Do you not know that?*

I shook my head.

What do you know of us?

I felt as though this was an odd time to broach such a topic, given the ship was still in jeopardy and the ghisting should be attending to its hull and such—whatever ghistings did. But Harpy's gaze was so intense, I had to reply.

"I know you begin as trees in the Wold," I said. "Or a Wold, not necessarily Aeadine's. You grow first in the Other, and sometimes your branches reach through the barrier between worlds and become our ghisten trees. Not always, but sometimes. If a Mother Tree is present."

Harpy nodded slowly, liquidly. *That is true. I myself entered this world through Aeadine's Wold.*

This admission, this similarity between us, struck me. I struggled to stand straighter, but the tilting of the deck didn't allow it. "That's where I'm from."

I glimpsed Harpy's smile again, quick and fleeting. *In a way,* she hedged. *I grew there long before your arrival. Very long. A hundred years or more.*

"Do you miss it?" I asked, because the question felt natural.

I do. Do you?

"Always."

Harpy made a sympathetic sound and slipped closer. *As do I. We're both far from home.*

"Do you wish you could go back?" I worried that the question was insensitive, given how she was bound to the ship, but I truly wanted to know the answer.

Harpy didn't reply for a long moment, full of the creaking of timbers. I wondered if her attention was somewhere else entirely, then she said, *No. And yes. I was never content in the forest—I wanted the world. When the Foresters came, searching for a ghisting to harvest, I drew them to myself.*

That shocked me. "I thought…"

Ghistings are always prisoners, like you? Harpy finished for me. *There was a time when the people of Aeadine remembered that we were allies instead of servants. But now… perhaps most have simply forgotten.*

The hair on the back of my neck prickled. I didn't speak, sensing she had more to say.

She selected another fan with absent fingers. *Much has been forgotten.*

"Like what?" I asked.

She lifted the new fan to her face and opened it. Before I could see what was on it she transformed from coy beauty to a twisted, bent woman with pointed teeth and a cavernous smile.

It was so grotesque, so unexpected, that I gave a startled shout.

Harpy vanished back into the bulkhead. I slapped a hand over my mouth, stifling myself before someone heard and came running.

Too late. A sodden, ice-rimed Demery opened the door, looming in the half-light, stance broad and hands braced to either side of the frame. The ship rocked again, and I just managed to keep my feet.

The captain surveyed me with haggard eyes. "What is it? Why are you screaming?"

"The ghisting." I pushed loose hair from my eyes. "She startled me."

"She likes to do that. Don't encourage her." Demery spoke the words in an off-handed way, as if his thoughts were already past the topic. "Did you still the wind?"

"Yes," I replied, loosening the tension in my shoulders.

The captain's stance also eased, but his scrutiny did not. "Good," he decided. "We'd have lost more than a sail or two if you hadn't come through."

I almost grinned. "Thank you."

Demery glanced upwards as the ship rolled again, then stuck a hand towards me. "Come above, Stormsinger. The night's not over yet."

TWENTY

Brothers

SAMUEL

In the midst of the storm, I foresaw Fisher's death. The vision punched into my skull, leaving my inner eye filled with her motionless body, drifting into oppressive silence below roiling waves.

The bosun's whistle shrilled, tugging me back into the moment—the wind and the waves and the tossing ship. Above me, sailors battled to lash the thundering foresail as their comrades hauled, yells and chanting almost drowned by the storm.

Then, as I had known it would, a shadow toppled from the rigging. I could not hear their shout, but I felt their ribs crack on a yard. I would have felt the crack of their skull hitting the rail too, but one leg snagged in the braces. Stunned and limp, they swung high above the deck.

I bolted, blood roaring in my ears, and stopped just under the limp figure. "Helena!"

There was no reply and I stared, open-mouthed, into the snow. A young man's face blurred over me, short hair frozen to his cap, arms dangling. He was unconscious, and he was not Fisher.

My thoughts skipped wildly. I had to find the woman, *now*, but I could not leave this man to die. The sailors around him had already scattered, fighting to keep themselves aloft in the tempest. Perhaps they had not even seen their comrade fall.

"Man in peril!" I bellowed to them, pushing my hat back and

pointing to the injured crewman. The wind stole my words away but I kept shouting. "Secure him, now!"

There was no time to see if anyone heard me. I staggered as a rogue swell struck *Hart*. Screams rose above the howl of the wind and the whole ship moaned a timber-cracking, gut-melting lament. Ghisting light skittered across the hull as Hart labored to right the vessel. Everywhere sailors clung to whatever they could, while the dangling crewman swung like a pendulum above them all.

I found my balance and struck out for the ratlines. The sooner I got the fallen sailor to safety, the sooner I could find Fisher and stop my vision from coming to pass.

But my feet found no purchase on the wave-washed deck. My body went one way, my feet the other. I fell hard and scrambled for an anchor, but I was already sliding towards the opposite rail and an abyss of black, roiling sea.

Forget Fisher drifting alone into the depths of the Winter Sea. I would be right there with her.

A hand seized my sleeve. I instinctively twisted, grabbing whoever had caught me—a slim wrist, and a forearm like iron.

Fisher hauled with all her strength. I scrambled along with her and seized the forecastle rail just as the deck leveled out.

I fell upwards, onto my knees and into the rail. Pain cracked through my shoulder and head.

"Fuck," I groaned into a sudden, brief hush.

"You all right?" Fisher panted, still clutching my wrist. Her voice sounded overloud, despite the pain in my head. The wind had suddenly, completely quieted.

I gripped her arm in return—probably hard enough to bruise, but she held on with the same ferocity. She had lost her hat and her black hair had come loose, hanging past her jaw in frozen shanks. Her cheeks were scalded with cold, her lips dry.

"Samuel?"

My earlier vision flashed back to me, drowning her words.

"You must go below." Ignoring a badly bruised shoulder, I kept a grip on her forearm and staggered upright. I pulled her with me, my eyes straying to the injured sailor, still hanging from the yard. "Mr. Keo and I will manage."

Fisher found her feet and flashed me a perplexed look. "I will not. Oh, Saint!" Halfway through her rebuttal, she saw the man suspended from the rigging. She tore away, sprinting past me to the shrouds and swinging up into the lines.

I shouted after her and began to follow, but the Other welled close, paralyzing me on the edge between worlds.

The vision came again, quick and fast. A storm and howling wind, Fisher's body hitting the waves like a cadaver landing in a gravedigger's cart.

But she did not fall. The Other came to me in fits and starts, and in my brief moments of lucidity I glimpsed her straddling the yard, joined by two topmen—the most skilled sailors. Together, they hauled the injured man to the shrouds. There they began to descend, all while the Other roared through me.

When the wave came, I could not discern which world it was in— the mortal or the Other. Huge and unfathomable, it loomed over our larboard as Fisher and her comrades scrambled down.

I tried to shout a warning, but my mouth would not open. My fingers scrambled uselessly in my pocket and I screamed at my muscles to loosen, to *move*—

The Other retreated. Relief made me stagger and gasp, but the reprieve was fractional.

The great wave remained, real and ravenous and looming. It frothed over the heads of Fisher and the three sailors as they hastened for the deck.

I hit the shrouds and grabbed Fisher's wrist just as the sea swallowed us in a rush of frigid, brutal force. Salt burned in my nostrils, my eyes, inside my screaming mouth. Up and down lost all meaning. Sailors clutching the ratlines with desperate fingers, their bodies swinging out, then floating. Rope gouged into my shoulder, my cheek, my chest, but I hauled Fisher close and did not let go. I felt one of her arms lace through the shrouds before me, clinging right back.

I could not breathe. All I knew was icy water, Fisher's grasp and the rough ropes. I braced, willing my body to stone as the water raged, the ship trembled and the Other tugged.

Then the wall of water vanished. Horizontal sailors dropped back against the shrouds, drenched and choking. Some quarter of my consciousness not occupied with coughing counted them—one, two, three, and Fisher, still locked in my grasp. Not one had been lost, even the injured man, protected by his fellows.

Suddenly the deck rocked in the opposite direction, lifting Fisher from the sea. I hauled, shouting, blood hammering behind my eyes with the strain. Her free hand seized a line, her boot found the rail, and she toppled into me.

We hit the deck, all elbows and obscenities. Sailors dropped around us, frigid water splattering around their boots and shoes and knees.

I forced myself upright. Fisher started to follow, but sagged back to the deck. A sailor rushed to help her and she fended him off.

"Hold up!" she croaked, windburned face caked with freezing hair. She clutched an arm to her chest. "Gently, you fool! My arm—I landed on my arm."

The hammering of my heart slowed another degree. Just an arm. Just an injured arm. She was alive.

"Here." I offered her a hand, hoping the seawater excused the hoarseness of my voice. "Let me."

She glanced at the proffered fingers, then pressed her good hand into them. I helped her carefully to her feet and gathered my wits to say something, to try to express my relief that my vision had not come to pass.

"The wind's gone," Fisher said.

I looked up, startled. Yes, the sea roiled and the ship moaned and cold made every inch of my flesh ache, but the wind had vanished.

Stormsinger.

I grabbed the nearest sailor, Penn, who had lost his customary hat. "Help Lieutenant Fisher below, quickly now."

"As you say, Mr. Rosser."

Fisher shook her head at Penn's offered shoulder and something in her eyes struck me. Hurt? No. Terror. A haunted, empty fear that I recognized well. The Winter Sea had nearly taken her, and she had just realized how close to death she had come.

The vision passed through my mind a third time—silence, distant waves, drifting hair. A fresh ache lodged in my chest. I had stopped the vision from happening. The danger was over. Why, then, did it still feel so potent? Was there more to be seen, another threat in the near future?

Of course there was, I chided myself. We sailed the Winter Sea. The feeling was just another symptom of my brokenness, and perhaps an overattachment to Fisher. One she would not welcome. We were not, after all, friends.

"I'm quite all right, Mr. Penn," Fisher said to the sailor in question, straightened and pointed to the injured crewman. "Help him. I'll manage."

I gave her a short smile, hoping she could not see the lingering anxiety behind it. She gave me an exhausted nod, her gaze glancing off my face, then turned away and started issuing orders.

Pushing the last of the vision aside, I made my way to the very fore of the ship. *Hart* became steadier with each step and Slader joined me, emerging from the quarterdeck with sleepless eyes—he had taken charge for the first watch of the storm, Fisher and I the second. But there was no sleeping through something like this.

"The Stormsinger can't be far," Slader observed without greeting me or mentioning Fisher, though I knew he had seen her heading below. "Where is she?"

I grasped the rail to hide the shaking of my hands and let my senses slip. The transition was too easy, and I saw Mary's grey-edged light just over the border.

"Nor-nor-west," I said, blinking away the starless sky and black-bellied sea. But it lingered at the edges of my vision, quiet and waiting. "She is closer than before."

Slader nodded. "Then go take your rest, Mr. Rosser."

A hasty knock on my cabin door jarred me from a fitful sleep.

"A shroud on all you hack-faced shitlings," Fisher growled from the other side of the curtain, proceeding to mutter further obscenities which may have included my name.

I dropped from my hammock and answered the knock quickly, stepping out into the hall and closing the door to keep the heat of the woodstove in.

"Hush, Ms. Fisher is sleeping," I chided the boy on the other side. My shoulder ached from striking the rail, and I rolled it carefully.

He nodded, eyes wide and voice low. "Aye, sir. Sorry, sir. Those Navymen we sighted the other day, they've come upon us an' you've been asked for."

My awareness slipped to the movement of the ship beneath me. The seas were calm, and we had slowed. Significantly.

"Are they aboard?" I asked the boy.

He nodded. "Rowing over now."

Anxiety welled like bile in my throat. I fought the feeling as I dressed and rammed my hat onto my head.

By the time I joined Slader on deck, I had regained my composure. I stood tall, stance set against the roll of the ship as the sailors formed up to greet our guests with doffed hats and lopsided salutes. Behind them, sunlight broke through storm clouds and a less-than-arctic breeze tossed fringes and hems.

The sight of my own reflection climbing over the ship's rail almost cracked my veneer. Backed by the towering masts of *Defiance*, a second-rate man-of-war of the North Fleet, Benedict Rosser straightened to his full height. His eyes glassed over me before he stepped left, clasped his hands behind his back, and stood to attention.

His captain, Amory Ellas, came aboard. She was a weathered, serious woman, with greying hair and a practical demeanor. She had a peppering of scars across one tanned cheek, perhaps from shrapnel or powder burns, which only made her more intimidating.

Slader strode forward to clasp her hand.

"Captain Slader," she said, releasing the man's hand. "I hoped we might have a word in private."

Slader nodded and gestured towards the quarterdeck doors. The two of them left without pleasantries, though Ellas gave Benedict a meaningful nod before she disappeared.

Around us, sailors resumed their tasks—casting not a few startled glances between Benedict and I. But my focus remained on my brother alone.

I had not seen my twin in two years. Looking at him now was like glimpsing a past version of myself—the practical naval uniform, dark blue with deep black cuffs and stiff collar, his straight chin clean-shaven and his brown hair bound in a short tuft. We stood the exact same height, had the same breadth to our shoulders and narrowness about the eyes from a decade of squinting into the sun. But where my stance was stiff, his eased now that his captain was out of sight—the stance of a man with no conscience and no regrets.

I decided to be the better brother and strode forward. I felt the eyes of the crew follow me and heard their whispers, but I had no desire to seek privacy. Away from watching eyes, this meeting would degrade rapidly.

"Sam," Benedict said.

"Ben," I returned, stopping close enough for the mist of our breaths to mingle.

"You are looking piratical today." My brother tilted his head to one side, noting my short beard and the quality of my coat. "It suits you."

I snorted. "Yes, I am the rogue here."

Benedict's smile was humorless, but something flickered behind his eyes. A glimpse of an old, tired emotion—a boy sitting on a bench with beaten hands.

Weight settled in my stomach and my façade suddenly felt foolish. I stuck out my hand.

Benedict stared at it, then slowly took it in his own—so much larger and more scarred than it had been, back when we were children. His skin was warm and his grip loose. The touch sent an ache through my chest, an ache that made me want to forget all our grievances, all the lies and strife and simply be... brothers. Family.

Benedict let go and shoved the hand into his pocket. I saw it clench inside, knuckles stretching the fabric. "Shall we take a turn about the deck?"

I nodded. Together, we ascended to the forecastle, passing staring sailors on our way to the bow. There, by unspoken agreement, we stopped over the spreading antlers of *Hart*'s figurehead.

"The girl is healthy and well." Benedict spoke just loud enough to hear over the waves and bustle on deck. Behind him, *Defiance* continued to rock in all her glory, gunports closed, sails furled, deck and ropes immaculate. "She looks like... you."

"Of course she does," I said dully.

"Has..." Benedict hesitated, long enough for me to wonder if he actually cared when he asked, "Alice, has she written you?"

"No."

My brother fidgeted, running his tongue along his teeth behind closed lips. "You would not tell me if she did," he decided.

"Alice does not matter to you." I sidestepped the question. "She never did."

"She never mattered to you, either," Benedict retorted, then caught himself. He looked away, over the sea before the ship. "Or her husband. The child, though. I am glad she's well. I assumed you would be too."

I tried to read him as I had done when we were boys. Benedict's range of emotions were stunted, usually vacillating between aloof, coy and enraged. But now I saw something almost like regret behind his eyes. Our eyes.

He looked at me, his expression softening even further. "I'm sorry, Sam."

My heart became uncomfortable in my chest. Was that sincerity? Had his condition… improved?

"Do not look at me like that." Benedict visibly swallowed and collected himself. "Years have passed. I have changed. I have seen the girl and…"

Hope. It lit a far corner of my heart, tremulous and dangerous. "And?"

"She looks like us," he said again and blinked hard. Twice. It was such a studied, subtle motion that I would have fallen for it, if I had not known him so well.

My hope died. Benedict had not gotten better. He had simply become better at pretending.

He lowered his voice. "She is a piece of us, brother. I cannot have her and do not want her. But it… changed me, knowing she is in the world. It makes me want to be someone she can respect, when she's grown."

I was caught between desire to believe him and the knowledge that I could not.

He saw the strain in my face. He leaned forward, smelling of salt and coffee and latent magic. If I had slipped into the Other then, I would have seen it all around him—the soft, reddish hue of a Magni. But where the average Magni might exert a gentle influence over those around them, manifesting in charm or charisma, Benedict's was sullied. Broken. Twisted.

Benedict's magic turned the mind itself, transforming lies to truth and poisoning himself further in the process. He was trying to turn my own thoughts, right now.

And it was all my fault. His degradation, his condition. I had seen it before it came to pass, but unlike Fisher's death, I had not had the courage to thwart Benedict's unraveling. Or my own.

"You are ill, Benedict," I said softly. "You will only make it worse. Do not let… do not let what she did to us destroy you."

"Mother did not make us," Benedict bit out, breaking my gaze and glaring off over the sea. "You and I are Black Tide Sons. They took advantage of her."

I started to correct him, but bit my tongue.

My brother scoured my face for a moment, eyes narrowed. Then he leaned closer and dropped his voice to a whisper.

"How is your head, big brother?" he asked with more snideness than concern. "How are the visions?"

My throat clogged. I started walking, continuing our turn of the deck.

He caught up in two strides. "Well?"

"I manage," I returned.

"What do you see now?" Benedict ducked past me as we descended the forecastle stairs. He glanced back as he began to saunter across the waist of the ship, throwing out his arms. "Tell me my future."

Benedict's words were laced with magic. They snatched at me, threatening to plunge me into the already pressing Other.

I dug my fingernails into my palms. Fresh pain made my eyes spark but it kept me rooted.

"I do not look into your future." I stopped walking. "You know that."

Not since that day.

He fell back in at my side as I started up the stairs to the quarterdeck. "Fine. Then tell me—and I ask this with genuine, familial concern—how are you?"

Familial concern meant something quite different to him than it did me, but I took what I could get. "Well. I am Slader's second. We have been commissioned to hunt down Silvanus Lirr."

"Second!" Benedict clapped me on the back, startling me. "Good for you."

I shot him a sideways glare.

"As to Lirr, there is a challenge. Slippery bastard." He glanced over at *Defiance*. "I am jealous, I admit. Captain Ellas will be too… This cruising about, shaking our shields at the Mereish has got her terribly restless. Who would have expected we would meet like this, you the pirate hunter, practically a brigand yourself, and I the respected Navyman?"

"Yes, who would have thought?" I repeated bitterly.

"Let us trade places." Benedict grinned at me, bringing us to a stop at the stern of the ship. "Like when we were boys."

My patience broke. Of all the things for him to suggest.

"Like when you got a child on my captain's wife?" I hissed. "Pretending to be me?"

He ignored me, smiling up into the cold wind. I recognized the glint in his eyes, and I did not like it at all. It was the one he got before he slipped down into a place where the Navy's rules and regulations could not protect him.

"I will paint the decks red with pirate blood," Benedict said, tasting each word, "and you can go back to the Navy. You would love that, I know. And I could… Ah, all I could do if—"

I turned and punched him in the stomach. Nearby sailors shouted, but no one intervened.

Benedict doubled over, wheezing and gasping. He sat down hard on his backside and squinted up at me, his arms clasped over his stomach. But the glint in his eyes was gone.

"Did I deserve that?" he croaked.

I rolled my aching shoulder. "You did."

"All right." He took a second to catch his breath, then climbed to his feet, one hand still pressed over his stomach. At the same time, I heard the quarterdeck door open.

Our captains reappeared. Benedict recovered himself with practiced stiffness and we descended the stairs as our captains said their goodbyes and Ellas returned to the rail, where she would descend to their waiting longboat. Benedict surreptitiously adjusted his hat, looking a little ill but otherwise giving no sign of what I had done.

Behind us, the sailors resumed their work, wide-eyed and muttering.

"Good day, then, Captain Slader," Ellas said and beckoned to Benedict. "Mr. Rosser?"

Benedict looked at me. He remained pale but smiled a flawless, melancholy smile for the sake of watching eyes and pulled me into a fraternal embrace. I endured the gesture stiffly, my shoulder aching, and my instincts both yearning to hug him back and punch him again.

Then he was gone. The longboat rowed back to *Defiance*, and Slader beckoned me.

"Your brother seemed well," he commented.

"He is," I replied tonelessly. "May I ask what Captain Ellas wanted?"

"A private matter," Slader said, though there was no rebuke in his voice. "But we've a good ally in *Defiance*—in Ellas and your brother. The Winter Sea is unforgiving, and our quarry dangerous. Perhaps there will come a day when we need such allies, Mr. Rosser."

MERE—*The title Mere encompasses both the chief island of the Mereish peoples, south of Aeadine and east of the Cape, as well as the various other islands within their control: the Mereish North Isles and the Mereish South Isles, though rule of the latter has degraded in recent centuries and now resides primarily in the hands of pirates. The Mereish are well known for dabbling in strange magics, the secrets and traditions of which they guard with religious fervor. They possess one of the greatest naval forces upon the Winter Sea and are close allies with the Cape, leading these more peaceful neighbors into frequent war with Aeadine. See also* MEREISH, MEREISH NORTHERN ISLES, MEREISH SOUTHERN ISLES, MEREISH-CAPESH ALLIANCE.

—*FROM* THE WORDBOOK ALPHABETICA: A NEW WORDBOOK OF THE AEADINES

TWENTY-ONE

Pirates in Name

MARY

Two days after I calmed the storm and spoke with Harpy, I sat by the window in Demery's cabin, quietly humming as I hemmed Rosser's cloak for my smaller frame. I felt laughably domestic, plying stitches into fine wool on a pirate ship, but the sun was warm, the glass cool, and the roll of the ship more familiar with each day. Even Grant was absent, freed from his duties so long as I remained in the cabin.

I slipped another stitch into place and examined my work in the sunlight. I still felt a hint of guilt when I looked at the stolen garment, but pragmatism was there to console me. The cloak was mine now, and I might as well make use of it.

I'd gained skill in singing since the storm. Until that night I'd considered using my power a matter of will, of straining against the current weather and compelling it to obey. Now, I understood it was more nuanced than that—a matter of honesty, emotion and need. My song, in the end, was simply how the weather understood me.

As if in mockery of my reflections, an unruly gust whistled through the window. I hastily shifted my chair away from the draft, blinking and frowning. This, here, was my greatest challenge. As soon as my mind wandered or my emotions strayed, the wind resumed its natural course.

I still had a lot to learn.

"As long as Bailey doesn't throw me overboard before we find Mama..." I muttered to myself, then froze at my use of the childish name, and all the trust and familiarity it entailed. I corrected in a softer voice, "Mother."

Footsteps rippled on the deck above my head. The wind gusted again, straining against my already frayed attention. Before I could refocus, I heard shouting both above and below decks.

"Harpy?" I ventured to ask the quiet cabin. I wasn't sure making inquiries of the ghisting was appropriate, but I suspected she would hear.

Come.

The ghisting's glowing presence seeped over the wood beneath me like a flood across a parched field. She passed across the deck, up the far bulkhead and into the deck above.

What remained of my control over the wind disintegrated. Curious, I set my work aside and got to my feet.

A pirate shouldered past me through the doorway as I emerged midships. Other pirates hastened through hatches and out of sight, while still others ascended the lines under the piping of Bailey's whistle.

"Mary." Athe's voice cut in from the quarterdeck above me. "Up here, please. Where's Mr. Grant?"

"He took the morning off." I ascended the stairs as quickly as I could.

Athe frowned at that. The wind tossed my hair and skirts and as I joined her, Captain Demery and Bailey on the quarterdeck. I glanced about for Harpy, sensing her nearby, but she didn't take form.

Winter clouds blanketed the sky in all directions, warning of snow, and above us the sails luffed. Pirates scurried to trim them, darting along yards and hauling lines along the ship's rails.

Bailey, who'd been monitoring the sails, shot me an accusatory look. "What's wrong with this wind?"

"You're distracting me," I shot back. "Running about and shouting."

The bosun *tsk*ed in irritation. "Damn useless woman. Mayhap Randalf had the right of it—"

"Hush, the both of you." Demery shot Bailey a stare so flat the man visibly flinched. The captain was next to the ship's wheel, where one of the huge helmsmen stood with his eyes on the horizon and one ear on our conversation. "We've no time for your bickering today."

"We're pirates, James," Bailey grumbled, but he wouldn't meet the captain's eyes. He directed a veiled half-glare at me instead. "This is what we do. She's battered and loose, just waitin' for us. Hell, we can take her without the Stormsinger!"

The cold wind raised goosebumps on my arms. "Take who?"

No one seemed to hear me.

"I'm not losing an entire day to sack a light merchant," Demery stated. "I understand the crew's restlessness, but it's shortsighted. She doesn't have a Stormsinger, judging by her tack—therefore, she's not wealthy enough to merit our time."

A ship, then? I glanced around at the horizon, but couldn't see anything but distant ice floes, indigo and white against a grey sky.

Demery held out a spyglass to me, indicating a location with his other hand. "We've sighted a Mereish merchant, and we're discussing whether to take her."

"Ah, I see," I said, hiding my unease behind an expression of passive interest. I took the spyglass, warm from his hands and cool from the wind.

Bailey saw through my façade. His upper lip wrinkled beneath his beard, and breath curled from his nostrils in a scornful gust. "What, lass? Forget what ship you're on?"

I ignored him, training the glass on the spot Demery had indicated. The other craft wasn't large, with two masts, a sleek build and a dark purple pennant fluttering.

In a rush, I remembered seeing Lirr's lanterns through the windows of Randalf's cabin. Lanterns on the horizon. Stalking. Hunting.

The merchant might be Mereish, enemies of my people and our queen, but I knew what it was like to be hunted by pirates. That fear was still close, and it made the hair on my neck stand on end.

It made no difference that I was aboard the pirate ship, now— that just gave the fear a stronger, more dangerous flavor. I stood with the predators and had signed my name next to theirs. As soon as we boarded that ship, would these men and women I spent my days with turn to butchery? Would I watch them torture the Mereish as Lirr and his crew had tortured Randalf's crew?

I lowered the spyglass a fraction and glanced at Demery, then Athe. No. Perhaps I was being willfully naive, but I couldn't imagine them gutting prisoners like Lirr had.

Looking through the spyglass again, I saw the set of the Mereish's sails begin to change. Specks that were sailors ascended her lines, a boom swung, and the vessel's profile changed.

"Captain?" I ventured, uncertain.

"Put it to a vote," Athe suggested.

"Aye, a vote," Bailey said.

The Mereish ship began to tack. I hadn't been aboard ship long, but I knew enough to suspect what was happening.

"Captain," I repeated, louder this time. "I think she's trying to come this way."

"What?" Demery pushed the brim of his tricorn hat up with a knuckle and took the spyglass, training it on the other ship. He frowned, flat and resigned. "Damn."

Athe cleared her throat. "You can hardly deny the crew a prize sailing right into our laps."

"Yes, yes." Demery lowered the glass, scratched his forehead, and fit his hat back into place. "Well, we're pirates, so I suppose we should act piratical. Mary, you're looking disarming today, would you mind remaining on deck?"

I frowned at him. "Why?"

"Give us a good wind, smile and wave at the Mereish as we close. Look pleasant."

Nerves fluttered in my stomach. "You want to trick them? But they're already coming towards us."

"So ensure they don't grow wise—let's get this done quickly and cleanly, no delays and no damage to my ship, thank you." Demery looked to Athe. "Run up Mereish colors and the mail flag. They'll assume we've letters to the homeland. You—" He turned back to me. "Go find some pretty Mereish clothes and paint your eyes, then come back and stay here with me. It'll be a few hours until we close, providing they don't run."

"I don't look Mereish," I protested, gesturing to my face. The color of my skin and hair were passable, Mereish and Aeadine coming in the same varieties of pale or dark, or blond or raven-haired. But the structure of my features was classic Middle Aeadine—small nose and mouth, broad cheeks and round face.

"You don't have to look Mereish, just like you belong to them," Demery told me and offered his arm. "Come, I need to change too."

I didn't find that precisely consoling, but I relented.

Together we returned to the main cabin. I locked myself into my smaller room and donned the required clothes, exchanging my short bodice, neckerchief and outer skirt for a Mereish-style wrap overgown with jewel tones, fur trim and thick embroidery from wrist to elbow. I removed my hip pads too, narrowing my silhouette, and located a small jar of black eye paint.

I stared at it. I'd never applied the substance before, and no matter how I wedged my small hand mirror into a stack of books and clothes, it toppled with the sway of the ship.

Finally, I opened the door to the main cabin again. "Captain, the gown is enough. This paint—"

I paused. Demery was securing a broad leather belt over his own wrapped overcoat, knee-length, sapphire and trimmed with heavy silver embroidery. Not only did he cut a dashing figure, but he wore the garb with a suspicious level of confidence and familiarity.

He caught me watching him and grinned crookedly. "Ethnic ambiguity is a useful thing," he observed, then held out his hand. "You must see me in an Usti kaftan, I look like I stepped from a Yustoff painting. Come, I'll help you with that."

I handed over the paint and brush, both his appearance and the thought of him applying the paint giving me hesitation. "Perhaps Widderow could help me?" I suggested.

"Widderow is as useless with paints as Bailey would be." Demery uncapped the little jar and set it on the table, then dipped the brush and gave me a prompting look. "Tilt your chin back and look down."

I complied, and with great care, he drew fine lines from the outer corners of my eyes. I was keenly conscious of our proximity, and strove to breathe quietly.

Demery, for his part, appeared unperturbed. With a nudge of a knuckle, he directed me to turn my head one way, then the other. He applied a few more careful strokes, then stepped back.

"Perfect," he pronounced, brush still poised. "Try not to blink until it dries."

I immediately blinked. His grin deepened and I smiled wryly in return. "Sorry. Where did you learn to do that?"

"No matter, I'm sure it will smudge in the weather anyhow. Where did I learn? I've lived a varied life, and loved varied women."

"Do you have a woman now?" I wanted to know. "Somewhere on shore?"

"No, no." Demery started to shake his head, then his eyes crinkled. "Well, your mother has always struck me. Perhaps she'd be interested in retiring with me? We're still young enough to make a good go of things."

I drew back, scandalized. "If you dare—"

Demery burst out laughing, drowning my indignance. "Your mother is a sister to me, Ms. Firth," he soothed, rubbing at his chin and giving me a look that might have been fond, however brief it lingered. "We've been through too much together for romantic entanglements. Romances born out of such trials? They rarely last."

"Good," I bit back. I could imagine my mother with someone other than my father—my father, after all, had already moved on. But the thought of her with Demery made my cheeks burn.

"I do intend to retire after this, though, and your mother is welcome to come along, if she's in need of a… discreet hideaway," the captain said, picking up an ink cloth from the table and cleaning off the brush on its stained fabric.

My heart sank a little. I watched him work, turning over the thought. I wanted to take my mother home to the Wold, and try to reclaim the happiness we'd once had. But that was impossible.

Someone knocked at the door and Charles Grant stuck his head in. He noted the pair of us, his eye snagging on my face and clothes for a surprised moment before he cleared his throat. "I, ah, was told my services were required?"

"Yes," Demery said, striding to his open trunk and pulling out a second Mereish coat. "Be so kind as to put this on and stay by Ms. Firth. I don't expect any trouble from this prize, but let's be cautious, shall we?"

TWENTY-TWO

Guise and Guile

MARY

The wind blew, guns thundered, and I stood with Charles as the Mereish merchant surrendered. *Harpy* closed upon her with every passing moment, devouring the waves with a roar of water and wind and spray. The weather strained against my song, but it was a hound on a leash—unruly, yet limited in its rebellion. The seas themselves were calm, mirroring my own efforts to contain my anxiety… and a rush of exhilaration.

Guilt and memory threatened to douse that thrill. But the wind and my song fed upon it, growing stronger and steadier.

From across the deck, Athe gave me an appreciative salute, and I warmed at the affirmation.

Finally, when we were close enough to see the petrified faces of the Mereish sailors as they fled below decks, Demery cried out, "Boarding party to the rails!"

Grappling hooks, ropes and long pikes latticed the space between the two ships. Ladders and nets were hauled into place and pirates swarmed from one deck to the other under Demery's ringing command.

The pirates howled. They cheered. They roared and leapt at their victims, or strode with the confidence of seasoned victors, bristling with weapons. But no more than a handful of shots were fired, and those were for show.

There was none of the recklessness of Lirr's attack, the wanton waste of life and resources. I watched in fascination as Demery's pirates shoved their prey to the deck and bound them, chasing the rest below decks. Other pirates loitered like dockworkers, jesting and chattering.

"It's the shock of it that matters," Grant observed in my ear. "The shattering of resolve and summoning of a victim's most base instinct—fear. Pirates or highwaymen, we've the same tactics. We're lazy, the lot of us. Cleaning blood from your clothes is a chore, I tell you."

"Not all of you," I replied distantly. I thought of Lirr, and the highwaymen who'd taken my carriage back in the Lesterwold. I remembered the shock of the door flying open, and the blinding, visceral fear that had sent me fleeing into the wild.

But I also remembered leveling a stolen pistol at a terrified peddler under a noonday sun. I recalled seeing that same fear in his eyes. Fear of me.

The last of my unease abated into a hollow resignation. Was this the world, then? Violence and the threat of violence? Was that all there was outside the inn and the Ghistwold?

Was this who I would—and perhaps, already had—become to survive it?

"Mary?"

I realized Grant had continued speaking, but I hadn't heard. I looked at him sideways and smiled sadly. "Just pondering my descent into depravity."

"Ah. Well, one choice leads to the next," he said with a shrug, and I was surprised to hear a thread of resignation in his voice. "And too often there are no honorable choices to be had. We are our circumstances, are we not?"

I elbowed him. "Don't go philosophical on me. You're supposed to be a dashing rogue, remember?"

"A dashing rogue with an unfortunately broad education and

tendency towards the existential," he admitted, watching as pirates hustled the Mereish captain across the gap between the ships and onto *Harpy*.

Midships, they presented her to Demery. He spoke levelly to the woman, who was grey-haired and lean as a whippet, her fierce eyes lined with black just like mine.

She spat at him.

Grant winced. "Did you see that?"

I nodded, mute, as Demery stepped back from the other captain and looked down at the front of his coat. Back aboard the Mereish ship, the captive crew began to shout and struggle to their captain's defense.

A gun cracked. Demery glanced at the captured ship at the same time as the Mereish captain struggled free of her guards.

Chaos broke out. Pirates surged in to reclaim her but I saw a flash of steel, then lost sight of her altogether.

Grant drew his cutlass and I steeled myself against a flurry of panic. All would be well—Demery and Athe were not fools, their crew seasoned and already prepared for action. This was just a scuffle and soon—

An explosion split the air. I spun and saw the Mereish ship quaking, tackles rattling and lines humming. Smoke began to billow up from her hatches.

Whatever had transpired below decks, it came with screams and shouts and a flood of armed men and women—armed men and women who did not belong to Demery's crew. With a roar they threw themselves at the pirates, driving them back from their captive crewmates and hacking them free.

Grant's shoulder bumped into mine as he moved close. "Stay calm, Mary."

I started to protest that I *was* calm, but cut myself off. My confidence was cracking, and for good reason. The Mereish ship was no merchant, and we were truly under attack.

"We need to get below," I told Grant. I might have a basic understanding of how to defend myself now, but it was foolish to remain where we were.

He nodded. "Let's go."

We barely made it to the stairs before battle overflowed to the quarterdeck. I whirled as feet thumped behind us and shouts filled my ears, all in indecipherable Mereish.

Armed enemy sailors poured over the rails. Just as we'd boarded them, now they used our own nets and ladders to clamber aboard *Harpy*. Some dropped right onto the quarterdeck behind Grant and I, unfurling like wolves from a forest.

They saw me backing towards the stairs and roared in challenge.

I spun to flee—right into someone's embrace. I started to push past, expecting the arms to belong to Grant, but found myself face-to-face with the Mereish captain.

Her fingers gouged into my upper arms and her eyes, a startlingly gentle blue rimmed with black, crinkled in satisfaction. She shoved me backwards, a casual hand on my shoulder, and I toppled into the grasp of her crew.

Warm, slick steel pressed into my throat. My body twitched with Grant's remembered lessons, but I forced them to still. I wasn't armed, and the blade was so close.

Grant was nowhere in sight. All I saw were strangers and the Mereish captain striding to the rail that overlooked the middle of the ship. One of her crew seized the ship's bell and began to ring it.

"I have your mage!" the captain shouted in accented Aeadine. "Lay down your weapons, or she dies!"

Thus I found myself standing at the rail beside a Mereish pirate captain—for a pirate she was, I would later learn—looking down the length of the *Harpy*. Faces turned towards us, one by one and then in droves as Demery's voice bellowed, "Stand down!"

Muskets and cutlasses lowered. Demery's pirates backed away from Mereish ones, cutting a clean divide down the center of the ship. Through that no-man's-land of bloodied, sand-strewn deck, Demery picked his way over staring bodies and a single, severed hand.

My stomach roiled and memories of Lirr's attack on *Juliette* surged. I battled them, funneling all my concentration into looking for Grant.

I finally spotted him pressed against the rail behind a knot of crew, blood on his face. Athe was beside him, close enough that she might have been holding him upright.

Demery spoke as he approached the quarterdeck, holding his pistol and cutlass out to either side. But he spoke in Mereish, and all I caught was his name.

The Mereish captain replied in stubborn Aeadine. "You will surrender, you and your crew. If you do so quietly, I will leave you all on the nearest islet."

"Madam, one Stormsinger is not worth my ship and crew. She can be replaced," Demery said, also switching into Aeadine. He came to a stop directly below us, far enough back that he didn't have to crane his neck. "You've played this whole encounter rather badly. How about you surrender and I'll leave *you* on the nearest islet, grateful for your lives and having learned a valuable lesson?"

My heart jarred against my ribs. Not only was he taunting the Mereish captain, but there wasn't a hint of a lie in his voice. Would he sacrifice me for his crew?

As if sensing my thoughts, the captain's gaze fell into mine. There was meaning there, if I could understand it.

I felt a familiar rush in the deck beneath my feet, and my skin began to crawl.

Sister, Harpy whispered.

Oblivious to the voice, the Mereish captain glanced at one of her crew and held out a hand. They gave her a pistol, which she leveled at my stomach.

"Do you have a surgeon aboard?" she asked me, glancing me over with the practicality of a farmwife choosing a Festus goose. "Or will you die wherever I shoot you?"

A choking sound eked from my throat. I unconsciously sucked my stomach in, as if that inch could save me from a lead ball.

"I…" I heard the fear in my voice, hated it, and fought to pull myself together. I was a Stormsinger. I had value.

And beneath my feet, Harpy stirred.

"Take me with you," I impulsively said to the Mereish pirate. "You need a Stormsinger. Don't waste this opportunity. Run now, take me with you, and I'll call down a storm to secure *our* escape."

She held my gaze for a moment, then sniffed and brushed the mouth of the pistol at the fur lining of my gown. "What I need is this. So pretty." Switching into Mereish, she snapped something at her crew.

Hands grabbed at my belt, jerking it loose, then pulling my overgown away. I fought back but there were too many hands, tugging and pushing and digging into my hair.

Then my gown was gone and my accosters retreated. Cold rushed over my skin and I gritted my teeth, watching as the Mereish pirates bundled my fine clothes away.

Left in my shift, stays and petticoats, I clasped my arms around myself. So many eyes. My knife, absent. Grant, Demery and Athe out of reach. I had my magic, but what would wind or snow do against a point-blank shot?

The Mereish woman smiled in pleasure. "There, now my new dress won't get bloody."

"Captain?" Demery called from midships, no hint of tension in his voice.

"I am deciding," the other captain called back.

"I'll help you get away," I insisted. The bloody knife at my throat was gone, but the pistol was still leveled at me and her finger rested on the trigger. "I'm a prisoner, can't you see that? Save me, and I'll help you."

Her startled smile and the crinkling about her eyes told me that I sounded naive. Good. The less of a threat I was, the more opportunity I'd have to... What? Make a nuisance of myself and get killed? Take advantage of whatever Harpy was up to?

As if in response to my thoughts, I felt something slip into my hand, down at my side and partially hidden in my petticoats against the cold. I felt the brush of something else too—cool, smoky flesh against my fingertips. The pirates around me did not appear to notice.

I tried not to show my confusion.

"Your mage is trying to barter for her freedom," the Mereish captain informed Demery. "Perhaps I'll take her with me, what do you say? You let me and mine return to our ship, with the mage, and we'll be on our way."

"Leave the mage and you can have your lives," Demery answered. "You have my word. We'll pretend this unfortunate incident never occurred."

"Do you have a surgeon?"

"Yes, would you like him?"

"Indeed, I would."

I wrapped my arms across myself, making a show of shivering, and felt at the object in my hands. It was wooden, light, sharp and narrow. A shard of wood.

Movement tugged my eyes to the side of the ship. The glimpse was momentary, but I saw Harpy standing by the ship's rail, her clutch of fans dangling from her belt, and her face... She wore my mother's face, exactly as my childhood memories recalled. I was struck by how alike we looked, my mother then, and I now.

The Mereish captain saw the ghisting too. She whirled, then spun back to me in sudden, blatant panic.

"*Ghiseau!*" she shouted. The Mereish word for ghisting?

No time for thought, fear or second-guessing. I lunged.

She pulled the trigger.

I twisted around the gun. I felt the rush of heat as the spark met the pan and powder ignited. Smoke burst into my eyes.

I knocked her pistol arm aside with the quick, sharp blow Grant had taught me and drove around her. My free hand found her hair, the other put the stake to her throat, and then there was silence.

"Surrender and you'll live," I said, pressing the tip of the stake into the thrumming vein at her throat. My eyes burned with smoke but my heart slammed at my own audacity—I feared it, and I relished it. "Make one more move and you'll die."

She chose to live.

USTI—*The most powerful nation on the Winter Sea, the Usti control the entirety of the Usti Island Chain, the Northern Continent and Tithe. They are a governing force in neutral waters, remaining impartial to all Aeadine–Mereish conflict and ensuring the continuation of trade and growth in the Winter Sea in times of peace and war. Originating from various lands, this people group is both hardy and spiritual, revering the gods of their assorted ancestors and numerous Saints. See also* USTI ISLAND CHAIN, USTI NEUTRALITY.

—FROM THE WORDBOOK ALPHABETICA: A NEW
WORDBOOK OF THE AEADINES

The Girl from the Wold

The Girl from the Wold cannot run any longer. Her legs are weak and her chest burns. She stumbles into a tree and looks back, harrowed eyes scanning the forest.

Sunshine in autumn leaves. The smell of earth. She cannot hear screaming from the carriage anymore, but she can hear the footsteps. Steady. Approaching.

The highwayman reappears, pistol hanging at his thigh from a casual hand. He's unhurried, but she can see in his eyes that he's losing patience. His eyes meet hers and he snarls. He starts to run.

She chokes on a scream and forces herself back into movement, trying to buy a few more seconds of denial, of freedom, before she faces what's next.

The ground gives way. The breath slams out of her lungs. She can't see, but when the world stops whirling, she lies at the bottom of a ravine.

The highwayman lies a few paces away, his pistol just beyond the reach of his fingers. She crawls away, terrified to look at him and terrified to take her eyes from him.

But he does not move. His neck is broken, its angle too sharp and his eyes too blank.

The girl watches him for a long time. Slowly, her gasping breaths start to steady, though her lungs still burn. Sweat and tears dry on her cheeks.

She crawls forward. She picks up his pistol, pulls herself to her feet, and climbs out of the ravine.

∞

TWENTY-THREE

Hesten Port

MARY

The port of Hesten clung to a series of small islands within the extensive Usti Chain, which Grant showed me on Demery's charts as we drew near. Hesten's islands were linked by ancient walls, gates and locks, and capped by a crown of heavy towers, domes and chimneys. Church bells clanged in a glorious cacophony from a hundred spires and steeples. Smoke and steam from tens of thousands of homes, shops and factories blurred the grey sky, while the northern horizon brimmed with the infamous Stormwall.

A shiver crept over my shoulders. The Stormwall might have been mountains from this distance, an indistinct grey-white divide, but I knew what it was: the eternal tempest that we would soon venture into. If all went as planned, my mother would be the one singing us through, but the sight still made my nerves tingle, and I hardened my resolve to master my magic as quickly as possible.

Demery called from the quarterdeck rail, "We'll head to the Knocks and see if there's wet dock for us. Everyone is to be on their best behavior. I don't care if you're in the Knocks or the Shasha—keep your noses clean. Anyone in prison or a gutter when this ship sails, stays there. And there'll be time ashore for all, so spread the word and see Widderow for your purses." He then noticed me.

"Ms. Firth! Go make yourself presentable. You look like a fishwife."

I shot him an arch look up the stairs, but quietly thrilled with anticipation. I couldn't wait to have solid land under my feet, shops and good food at my fingertips, and space from the pirates.

So, I prepared. In the privacy of my cabin I stripped and bathed with warm water from a bucket, then donned as many layers of wool as I could while still looking refined. Athe had dumped a chest full of women's clothes in my cabin not long ago, and though more than half of it was outdated or badly fit, I made do. I could order my own clothes while we were in port.

First came stockings, shift and stays, then hip pads and pockets. Next were two petticoats, the outer heavily quilted, and an overgown of dark mustard wool that buttoned in two lines up the chest. I wrapped a white shawl across the ensemble and fastened it behind my back, then set to pinning my hair about a small form and under a simple, sheer lace cap.

By the time I brushed rouge onto my cheeks and settled Rosser's freshly hemmed cloak around my shoulders, the shouts and thuds of the ship had settled. New sounds seeped in—deep, lofty church bells ringing the hour, backed by the suppressed roar of a living, bustling city. It both delighted and daunted me.

I heard voices in the main cabin. Feeling something between proud and awkward at my appearance, I shook out the cloak and stepped out into the warmth of the larger room.

"Much better," Demery informed me. He sat next to the woodstove, running through a sheaf of papers while Grant stood behind him.

Grant wore a jade frock coat, embroidered with cream and yellow that nearly matched my gown. Beneath that his buckskin breeches were perfectly fitted and his boots were up to the thigh—a style so absurd aboard ship that even I raised an eyebrow. Lace frothed from his collar and cuffs and a saber hung at his hip, hilt dark bronze and pommel inlaid with obsidian.

"Where did that come from?" I asked, focusing on the sword. It was a welcome distraction, given I'd just realized how attractive Charles Grant was. His appeal was prettier than, say, Samuel Rosser's, but the thought of being on his arm wasn't unpleasant. In fact, my heart gave an uncomfortable kick.

Grant took me in too, and raised his brows in appreciation. The short beard and scars he'd gained since we met did nothing but complete his roguish look.

My belly filled with warmth and wariness. I'd do myself no good thinking of Grant in this way, let alone comparing him to Mr. Rosser. Whatever attractiveness each of them possessed had to remain a factual, private observation.

I was here for my mother and the security of my own future. Not men who were, at best, untrustworthy.

"That? A loan," Demery said without looking at the weapon in question. He held out a sheathed knife to me, attention still on the ledger. "Here's one for you. Carry it openly unless you're in polite company. No need to feign demureness in Usti—it'll only endanger you while you're ashore. I've already sent a letter declaring our arrival and intention to one Lady Phira, so you'll be expected within the hour."

I frowned, accepting the knife. It had an obsidian hilt like Grant's saber and was attached to a slim but strong belt, which I slipped around my waist.

"You're not coming?" I asked, pulling the knife partway out of its sheath and glancing at it. It looked quite sharp.

"Phira are I are on good terms, but I would not be seen in her company without direct invitation." Demery removed several papers from the sheaf, folded the rest together and handed them to Grant, who tucked them into an interior pocket of his coat.

My eyes lingered on the former highwayman's hand, the strength and movement of it. Capable hands, I thought. Warm and pleasantly large.

"You are my vanguard," Demery continued, shooting me a narrow-eyed look. He'd seen me watching Grant, and that was enough to cool the heat in my cheeks. "If all goes well, you'll return with the invitation today and negotiations can begin tomorrow."

I nodded slowly, no little pressure settling on my shoulders. I exchanged a look with the former highwayman and was relieved that my heart stayed steady this time, the shock of his new appearance past.

I held out my arm towards him. "I see. Shall we be off, Charles?"

He took up his cloak from the table with a murmur of affirmation, swung it around his shoulders with overdone drama, and took my arm.

TWENTY-FOUR

The Enemy's Magic

SAMUEL

Hart entered Hesten Port several days after my conversation with Benedict. Still, as an Usti pilot guided *Hart* to her dock in the district called the Temweish, the memory of my brother stayed with me. So did the cloying, false sincerity he had plied, and the impact of his words.

You are ill, Benedict. You will only make it worse.

You're just as ruined as I.

Black Tide Sons.

He was correct. My Sooth's magic was tainted. And whether he had intended it or not, Benedict's reminder of that had left me uneven, and my reluctance to enter the Other multiplied. The last time I had gone, Mary's light had been elusive, and it had taken me three attempts to return to my own flesh.

But I sensed Mary's nearness and as Hesten was the closest port, I decided we were most likely to find her there.

I found Slader in his cabin and stood by as he paid the pilot and sent her on her way. Fisher was notably absent, her usual vigor checked by her brush with death, a sprained wrist and numerous torn muscles. Slader had offered her extra time to rest, and she had taken it.

Slader turned his attention to me as the pilot vanished and the door closed. I noticed he was dressed more richly than usual, wearing a fine pale blue frock coat and a lightly embroidered cream cravat. He was freshly shaved and a wig sat on its stand nearby, newly powdered and smelling of citrus.

"Are you going ashore, sir?" I inquired politely.

"I am," Slader returned in a tone that made it clear he had no intention of sharing more. "How close is the Stormsinger?"

"Close," I replied, coming to stand in the middle of the cabin, hands clasped behind my back. "She may be here already."

"You cannot say, precisely?" The captain squinted at me and ran a hand down the buttons of his coat, then checked the froth of lace at his sleeve cuffs.

I remained composed and shook my head. "No, sir. There are many Stormsingers here, and even more ghistings—the shipyards alone have enough to obscure anyone nearby. I would like to speak to the harbormaster concerning Demery's ship and make some discreet inquiries. Perhaps they can be bribed to alert us when he arrives, if he is not already here."

"Very good," Slader affirmed. "But there is more than one harbormaster in Hesten—one in each quarter. The Knocks, Temweish and the Shasha. The military docks we needn't concern ourselves with, however. He'd hardly dock there. But I'll take a wander past there myself, later today. Just to be sure."

I nodded, noting his ensemble again. I was curious as to the rest of his intended outing, but asking would only irritate him, and my dreamer's sense was quiet.

"I will see to the rest," I agreed.

Slader met my gaze, obviously pleased. "Take the day, then."

Greatcoat buttoned against the biting Usti cold, I made my way to the Temweish's harbor master, but the woman was absent. Back in the street, I stood aside as laborers shoveled snow and manure into a cart before endless rows of fine flat-fronted warehouses and shops.

I screwed up my nose against the smell and a vision came, lashing like a whip from the shadows. I saw Benedict and I as boys, waiting for the grooms to finish saddling our horses. I glimpsed Benedict's face on a day not yet come, a noose tightening around a screaming throat—but I could not tell if the throat was his or mine.

My hand shot into my pocket, scrambling for a coin that had not been there since Tithe.

I was in Usti, however, and the crowd that flowed past me now boasted the garb of a dozen nations, all gathered under the Usti flag to live and trade. And the Usti, as a neutral party in the war, would have plenty of Mereish traders.

I set off, scouring the vision from my mind and hiding shaking hands in my pockets.

"Mereish?" A black-skinned trader with a thick Sunjani accent squinted at me half an hour later, the brim of his felt hat sitting low atop thick eyebrows. "Why is an Aead looking for Mereish goods?"

I cleared my throat and gave a bracing smile. "We may be at war, but the Mereish are still the finest jewelers on this side of the world."

"That is fair." The trader considered for a moment, lips pursed, nose flared. "Just remember, your people have no power here, Aead. These are Usti waters. Do not bring your war. Do not bring your grudges. You will be in irons up at the keep before nightfall, and those dungeons flood *every* tide."

I nodded and shoved my hands deeper into my pockets.

"Now, if you are looking for Mereish goods," the trader mused, "try the bridge on the Boulevard of the Divine, south of the bridge in the Knocks. Plenty of Mereish folk there."

"How do I find that?"

The trader leaned over his wares—finely carved pipes of various lengths—and pointed through the market towards a statue of an armored woman riding a great snow bear. "Take a left by Saint Helga—our Helga, Aead, Our Lady of Bears, you see her? Yes? We do not worship your *Saint* here, or his red crown. Keep on for a span past the statue, and you will be on the Boulevard."

I swallowed my brimming offense—I was well aware of the variants of religion outside of Aeadine, and the myriad saints of Usti and Mere—but the merchant had been helpful, in the end. I smiled stiffly and started off, weaving through marketgoers from every imaginable nation—though, considering the varied ancestry of the Usti themselves, it was hard to separate foreigner from local. The Usti were, at their core, a conglomerate of peoples from across the known world, who had banded together and flourished.

I watched a pair of Capesh women with colorful headscarves walk arm in arm past a stall selling dragonflies, the glowing little creatures arrayed in glasses of every size. Men with hooded eyes and long beards—Ismani, from the far, far west—stood beside old Usti men in traditional kaftans, smoking pipes around a brazier. A violinist with prominent Sunjani nose piercings played with an Usti's measured emotion beneath the statue of Saint Helga. The violinist's music was swaying and regal, and ever on the edge of breaking free.

Two round-faced girls in fur hoods darted past me, chasing a dog and followed by a tired father.

"Sorry, sir," the man said in Usti as he ducked around me. "Kat! Iri! Back here right now!"

I watched them go, my Sooth's senses momentarily straying after their footprints in the snow. Another vision trickled around my guard, whispering and full of potential. I saw myself as that man, chasing a little girl who looked back at me, laughing, with my own eyes. Benedict's eyes.

She looks like us.

An ache started in my chest. The violinist's song was no help, tugging the pain along in a medley of regret and sadness, lost possibility and a fierce, burning injustice. For myself, for that girl, and her misled mother.

I started walking again, faster now, following the merchant's instructions until my path emerged onto a broad boulevard and a stone bridge.

The bridge was decorated for an upcoming festival, strung with pine and holly garland. I made for the eclectic sprawl of stalls on the east side, where I caught sight of one in the deep, bruised purple fabric signature of the Mereish.

"*Katash!*" the merchant greeted me, using a traditional Usti honorific. She smiled and touched her heart, then waved a long-fingered hand at the cases of wares on her table. I was in luck, finally. She was a proper jeweler, and the thick saber at her hip attested to her goods' value.

"I'm Aeadine," I said in Mereish. "Not Usti."

She squinted. "Are you and I at war?"

"I am simply a customer," I replied with sincerity. If there was anything I had taken from my time with the Navy, it was that civilians, particularly merchants, were not the enemy.

"A customer who speaks my mother's tongue?"

I had learned it at the Naval Academy in Ismoathe, but she did not need to know that. "I do. I am searching for a charm, the kind only your people can make."

Her chin dropped slightly to the side. Caution slipped into the lines of her plump body, but her smile remained polite. "Mm. What would this charm do?"

"Root a mind in our world," I replied, not bothering to mince my words. "Suppress a connection to the Other. A charm for a troubled Sooth."

The merchant's chin strayed even farther to the side, more of her politeness ebbing into narrow-eyed scrutiny. "That is not possible. A charm for love? I have. For a healthy baby or a good voyage? These are common—not easy, but common. What you seek, you will never find."

"I have had one before."

"Then you had a great treasure." The woman's composure returned. "I wish I had one to sell, *katash*, you may trust me on that."

Anxiety worked its way up my spine, and the ambient noise of the market began to grate on my nerves. "That cannot be true. I... I will pay whatever you want."

A little compassion entered the woman's eyes. "You look weary, Aead. Can you not sleep?"

"No." The word scraped out of me. What could it hurt to tell this woman, with her maternal eyes? I would never see her again. She was not Slader. She was not Fisher. She was not even Aeadine. "Most nights, no."

With a decisive *tsk*, the merchant signaled to someone in the crowd. I stiffened as a man and a woman sauntered over and traded places with the merchant, who offered me a hand. "Follow me, young man."

I hesitated. Admitting a weakness was one thing, but following a Mereish woman off into an unknown city?

"Perhaps I can help you, but not out in the open," the woman chided, beckoning again.

I let her draw me out of the market and down a side street, where I more than expected to be robbed, stabbed and left for dead. But I was desperate enough to take the risk.

Fortunately, the woman did not lead me to my death, but a rose-pink door and hallway that smelled of spices. Down another passage I glimpsed running children, smelled fresh bread and heard the sound of Mereish women discussing daily tasks.

We entered a room with a single, tall window overlooking a canal. I could just see the water and drifts of snow through the foggy glass. It let in little light, but multiple lanterns and a crackling fire ensured the room was well lit.

A black-haired man sat at a desk beneath the window, sipping a short cup of coffee and eyeing a ring on a stand. Other pieces of jewelry were laid about the surface of the desk, along with various tools and a pistol which was already half-cocked.

The jeweler did not reach for the pistol as I entered, but we were both aware of it. "What is this?" he asked in Mereish.

"He needs a talisman, if you can make it," my guide replied, then stepped back out into the hall. "Pay him when you are done, Aead."

That reminded me I had yet to ask how much this would cost, but it seemed late now.

"Thank you," I said to the woman.

She gave a smiling, one-eyed wink, and left me alone with the jeweler. I examined him for a long moment, and he examined me back.

"Well?" the man finally inquired in Aeadine. His skin had an olive undertone like many southern Mereish, and his accent was smooth, all curves and no edges. "What do you want?"

I shoved aside the last of my hesitation and rallied. "I am a Sooth, but I have no control over my visions. I slip into the Other continuously, especially when I sleep."

"Were you born like this?"

"No, my twin and I were… They attempted to amplify us."

Disgust crossed the Mereish man's face. Clicking his tongue, he gestured for me to sit in another chair and took up a battered coffeepot. He poured me a cup and passed it over.

The admission had unsettled me, but I hid my feelings behind a stiff nod. I took the coffee and eased into a chair of dark wood and bright fabric, as out of place in Usti as I was in this shop.

"I can help you," the man said, topping up his own cup. "But I will need a little of your blood, and it will take some time."

The coffee scalded my tongue. "Blood?"

"Yes," the man affirmed. He sipped his cup, oblivious to the heat, and set it aside. Standing, he scrounged a small bronze bowl and a long pin from a wall of overflowing but organized shelves. Turning to me, he held up the needle. "Just a drop. Sooth's blood, for a Sooth's charm."

I thought about leaving, setting aside my cup and striding right out of the room. Bloodletting? That was proper Mereish sorcery, and I knew that Slader would string me from a yard just for being here.

I held out my hand, anyway. The jeweler pricked the end of my finger, waited for a droplet to well, then pinched it into the bowl. It fell in a single crimson droplet, and the man handed me a handkerchief.

I stopped the blood and took a long drink to cover my unrest.

The jeweler began to work. He produced a case of coins, some new and shining, round or oval, with the images on their faces crisp and clear. Others were worn like my coin had been, smoothed by years of worrying.

The jeweler watched my gaze travel over the coins, then selected one that my eyes lingered on—oval and smooth, just like my old one. This one did not have the symbol of entwined serpents, but a stylized owl on the wing.

He dropped it into the bowl with my blood, then began to fetch ingredients. I watched him add pinches of powders and a stream of oil, pungent and amber, then he opened a lantern and lit a long wick. He touched the flame to the oil, which caught in a flare of blue and white before settling into a more normal, orange hue.

"Now," the man said, sitting back across from me, "we wait, soldier."

"Soldier?" I repeated.

He gave me a sly smile. The oil burned steadily, filling the room with a rich, savory scent. I tried not to think about how my blood was in there, burning too.

"I can recognize a man-of-war when I see one, sir. But please, drink your coffee. There is no battle for us."

He seemed sincere. Settling back in my chair I inquired, "How long will this take?"

"Until it burns out." He considered me down his nose. "Your twin, he is like you? Not a soldier, but gifted."

Again, I concealed my hesitation with a long sip of coffee. It was thick and strong, forcing back the fog of fatigue that haunted my steps since Tithe. My nerves calmed, but I sensed that that result came less from the warm liquid than it did from the simple relief of being away from *Hart* and Slader.

This man did not know my name. Neither he nor the merchant had even asked, and there was peace in my anonymity. I could be a new person, here—or rather, I could be myself.

"Yes," I admitted. "A Magni, however."

The jeweler nodded slowly, eyebrows high. "That is a dangerous thing, a broken Magni. And he is broken, I assume?"

I nodded my agreement. "The amplification worked on both of us, but we suffered for it."

"Can I ask who did it to you?"

"Moon worshipers."

"Who?"

I took another sip, trying to think of the Mereish term for the group. "Those who believe moonless nights open a door to the Other. It is a peasants' cult, back in Aeadine. Some call them the Black Tide, as they perform most of their rituals during the spring tides."

"Ah." The jeweler's lips pinched in distaste. "You were a child? Your parents condoned this?"

I stilled for a moment, then admitted, "My mother was a devotee. My father had died by then, and the grief... twisted her. Half the time, she still thought he was alive. She feared to lose my brother and I, and thought that if she was able to amplify our powers, we would be safer. The cult gladly took her money. After the rituals were performed, my uncle discovered the truth and rescued us."

I did not mention that I had foreseen those rituals, and done nothing to stop them. I had been a child, crippled by fear and the need to trust my mother, mad as she was. I had failed to protect Ben, on that first and most vital day, and that failure was one I could never speak of. Even now, the memory sent a tremor through my hands. I tightened them around my cup.

"I see. Is your brother still alive?"

"He is." A thought crossed my mind. "Could you help him? Make a talisman for him?"

"A Magni…" My companion leaned back in his chair, tilting it up onto two legs and rocking thoughtfully. "Perhaps. For the both of you, there might be help. I cannot give it, but possibilities exist in Mere."

I stilled, setting my coffee on the arm of my chair. From his tone, he meant more than talismans. "What do you mean?"

"I mean you can be healed. You said you are twins?"

My throat felt thick. Healed? "Yes."

"Then your conditions are bound," the jeweler determined, frowning. "Even if you are healed, his sickness will unravel you again. You must both be restored together."

I needed a moment to consider that, and he let me have it. The oil continued to burn as I drained my coffee, staring at the desk behind the man. Firelight glistened off gems and precious metals like lights in the Dark Water.

A cure, in Mere. The possibility changed everything, yet nothing at all. It was inaccessible and Benedict had no desire to be healed. He was not like me. I feared my power and lived each day in terror of becoming trapped in the Other, without my coin to save me. But Benedict? He was his darkness now.

"He will never concede," I said at length. "He would not even hear me if I tried to convince him. We have spoken little, in recent years."

"Why?" the jeweler inquired. The front legs of his chair tapped down as he leaned forward to refill my cup.

I started to push the question aside, but I had already broken so many barriers today. What was one more?

"We are identical, he and I," I said. "There was a woman who loved me, a married woman. I refused her. But my brother found the letters she had written to me. He wrote back to her, under my name. He met with her, all the while pretending to be me. They had a child."

The jeweler set the coffeepot down with a start, eyes wide in horror and incredulity. The oil behind him burned lower, bluish flames licking across the belly of the bowl.

"No!" the man exclaimed. "How could a brother do such a thing?"

"He was jealous. He always was, of any woman in my life. And he... He has not the conscience of a normal man, even before the Black Tide broke him." I rubbed my jaw, feeling tension skitter up the back of my skull. "Everyone assumed he was me. The woman believed he was me. Yet if I had tried to prove otherwise, I knew the repercussions would destroy him. So, I took the fall. His... position, the rules, the structure and the respect he is given, they are the only things that keep him from total depravity. I knew I could survive the fall into disgrace. He could not."

At that moment, the light of the oil fire went out. The murky daylight filtering through the window returned to prominence, and the jeweler slowly shook his head.

"That is madness, my friend, and I do not envy you. Here." He picked up the bowl and held it out to me. "Go ahead, it's quite cool."

He was right. I picked up the coin, brushing off bits of ash from its chill surface and settling it in my palm. Warmth spread up my arm and I felt a wash of quiet, like the sun on a summer morning. Thoughts of Benedict and a little girl with his eyes faded. I was at home in my flesh once more, and it made my eyes burn with fatigue and unspent emotion.

"It will weaken as time goes on," the jeweler told me with some regret.

My heart sank. "How long?"

"A month, if you only use it here and there. A week or two, if you use it all the time."

I rubbed my forehead with the back of one hand. A month, at most? Would that be enough time to find Mary and reclaim my old talisman—if she still had it?

It would have to be.

"Thank you," I said to the Mereish man. "How much do I owe you?"

He named a price, which I paid without question. When I asked if I could return for another coin in the future he nodded, but cautioned me, "This will not heal you, and it will make it harder to use your gift."

Curse, I corrected silently. Aloud I said, "I know. And if I was to convince my brother to be healed, where would we go?"

The man shook his head. "I only know that it's possible. A healer-mage could tell you more, but they rarely leave the Mereish Mainland. Perhaps…"

The man turned and made for a shelf on the far wall. There, he rummaged around for a moment before taking down a book, its red cover embossed with Mereish words.

He held it out to me. "I think you should take this."

I accepted it, the soft passage of my fingers over leather loud in the quiet room. So, too, was the rustle of paper as I flipped to the title page. It took me a minute to translate, but when I did, my eyes widened.

A History of Ghistlore and the Blessed; Those Bound to the Second World and the Power Therein.

"I think you will need that more than I," the Mereish man said. "But tell no one where you found it, Aead. My country guards their secrets. Too selfishly, I say. So I am in Usti." At the last, he shrugged, and I glimpsed an unspoken story behind his tight smile. But he said no more, and I did not ask.

My fingers tightened on the tome. I had never held this kind of knowledge before, let alone Mereish knowledge.

I took that with a fortifying breath and pulled another coin from my pocket, then thought better of it. A book like this was worth more than I had.

Awkward, I grimaced. "I haven't enough to pay you."

"It's a gift," the Mereish man said, waving me towards the door. "Go on."

I considered protesting, but the book felt heavy in my hands—heavy and right.

"Thank you," I said.

"Of course." He cast me a smile. "Remember my kindness next time you meet my children at war."

TWENTY-FIVE

Lady Phira's Steward

MARY

I rested my gloved hand on Charles's arm as we strode through the streets of Hesten, following the directions Demery had given us. We traveled west out of the bustling, dingy wood-and-brick tenements of the Knocks and onto a broad thoroughfare called the Boulevard of the Divine. East of a canal between two of Hesten's islands, the boulevard played into its name with a collection of brothels, faux temples and dens of various vices. All were closed at this time of day, but locals passed to and fro, red-cheeked and bundled up to their noses.

My eyes wandered across shuttered windows and doors painted in pastels, snagging on a sign over an alleyway. It had no words but contained a rather lewd and unfortunately educational depiction of several individuals.

"You are blushing," Grant murmured in my ear.

I tore my eyes away from the sign. "And? What's wrong with that?"

He shrugged. "Nothing, I suppose. But I do not suggest looking across the street and up to the second balcony."

I glanced up instinctively and choked. There, through a set of glass doors stood a very naked, muscular man smoking a pipe and watching us pass by.

Charles doffed his hat, and the man raised his pipe in acknowledgement.

I snapped my eyes back to the road. "Charles!"

"Mary!" he repeated, mimicking my tone and fitting his hat back on his blond hair. "Come now, do not pretend you're unfamiliar with the sight of naked men."

I kept my gaze fixed ahead, coaching my expression into blankness.

Charles's eyes widened sightly.

"You *are* familiar," he realized, taken aback. "Ms. Firth, I'm shocked. You do not seem… well. You do not strike me as that kind of young woman."

I stepped over a pile of manure and picked up my pace, forcing him to do the same. The topic was one I wasn't enthusiastic to discuss, particularly given how I'd responded to seeing him that morning, but he irked me. "You must not know very many young women, then."

When he didn't reply immediately, I looked at him sideways. Awkwardness passed through his expression, then he planted a smile on his lips and sauntered on.

The Knocks's half of the Boulevard of the Divine ended at a huge, broad bridge of stone and lanterns, strung with sweet-scented pine garlands for the approaching Winter Festival. Here, both on the banks and on the bridge itself, a lively market of carts and stalls was set up. Patrons clustered around great stone braziers, sipping coffee and hot liqueur while the crowd flowed around them. Laborers cleared snow and manure, women clutched baskets and hawkers of every nationality cried their wares.

Presenting ourselves as we had, well-appointed but obviously visitors, we attracted a good deal of attention. Flowers, fabrics, pastries, candies, fae dragonflies, teaspoons and bottles of foreign air—"Enliven the senses with a breath of the Passara!"—were lauded to us, though at the sight of our weapons, no one dared to come within arm's reach.

I was grateful for that. My nerves were increasingly on edge, my relief at being ashore tempered by something intangible, something

I couldn't quite name. Perhaps it was the foreignness of the port and the volume of its inhabitants—easily more people than I'd ever seen in my life, combined. Perhaps it was the cold, biting at my cheeks and creeping up my sleeves, or the absolute absence of trees. But by the time we passed over the bridge and onto the Shasha's side of the boulevard, something in my chest had hardened.

Daily shops and cafes turned into fine inns and boutiques, the tall face of every building graced by impractically shallow balconies and lavish moldings in Usti style—every arch calculated and every façade a simple variant of pale reds, blues or yellows. Statues of old Usti saints and gods lined the way too, each one stoic and decorated with ice.

"Phirandi House, blue, with odd windows around the door," Grant recited, stopping in the street next to a building of that description. Its double doors were accessed by a broad, fanning staircase and crowned by an array of clear glass windows that reminded me of a morgory's deadly plume. The doors themselves boasted huge, tentacle knockers and the expected notation, *Phirandi House.*

I took one knocker in a gloved hand and dropped it twice. Grant took up station at my side, tugging at his cravat and working his jaw in preparation for a winning smile.

The door opened to reveal a young man with immaculate white brows set atop green eyes and milk-pale skin. He wore a style of clothing I'd noticed on the street, something between a frock coat and a kaftan belted high over the stomach with a broad sash. His breeches were loose at the thigh, narrowing into high dark stockings at the knee, with red garters and fine boots.

Charles unfurled his smile and startled me by speaking in Usti. I'd never heard the language on his tongue before, and shot him a curious glance.

The pale steward surveyed us for a critical moment, then gestured us inside and said in perfect Aeadine, "This way, Mr. Grant, Ms. Firth."

"Does every Usti speak Aeadine?" I whispered to Grant as we slipped inside. I was truly starting to feel my lack of a second language. "And should I have learned Usti?"

"No and yes," Grant hissed back.

Troubled by this, I fell silent as we were seated in a receiving chamber with a hard sofa and too many paintings on the walls. A maid arrived to set out a tray of tea and dry honey shortbread dusted with cinnamon, then she and the steward vanished.

"It seems we are to wait," Grant muttered, wandering over to the fireplace. A huge portrait hung over the mantle, depicting a dark-haired Usti woman in hunting garb with two enormous, barrel-chested hounds I mistook for bears.

"Will you teach me Usti?" I asked. My mind lingered on my embarrassing lack of education and the anticipated arrival of Lady Phira, but I eyed the shortbread longingly. Was it polite to just… eat them all?

"If we've nothing better to do." Grant ran his gaze over the portrait and on to the room's other decorations. "My, Lady Phira does have taste."

I set aside my linguistic concerns and reached for a piece of shortbread. "How does Demery know her?"

The former highwayman trailed a finger along the frame of a painting, which depicted a shipwreck on an icy shore. "No clue. A lover?"

"Maybe." I discreetly shoved the shortbread into my mouth. Powdered cinnamon immediately caught in my throat. "I—ahem— can't imagine anything else."

Startled, Grant turned and smirked as I coughed and choked. I'd just caught my breath and sunk onto the painfully firm sofa when the door opened and a woman breezed in. She was the lady from the portrait, older and harsher in life. Her thick, curling black hair was shot with grey and pinned in looping coils about her ears beneath a structured, circular scarlet cap. She looked as though we'd caught her on the way out the door.

The steward closed the door while his mistress removed her gloves, but not her cloak.

Grant immediately wiped the amusement from his face and bowed. I rose, hastily brushed any traces of cinnamon from my lips and produced a rusty curtsy.

"Ms. Firth and Mr. Grant," she said, her accent light, with each word intentionally arranged and pronounced. She held her gloves in one hand atop heavily embroidered skirts. "I apologize to have kept you waiting, and I hope you will not detain me long. You come from James Demery?"

Grant nodded. "Yes. We have embarked on a profitable venture across the Stormwall and are in Hesten to outfit our vessel and seek investors."

"Investors of the gambling sort?" Phira's hooded eyes traveled over Grant, assessing him like a racehorse and finding him wanting. Her gaze lingered on his cheek, where his new beard failed to hide his scars. "Or the professional?"

I realized there was still cinnamon on my fingers and hid them behind my back.

"Both," Grant returned, unbowed by her scrutiny. "Captain Demery desires to speak to you about this himself, but sent us ahead, as a show of respect."

"As well he should." Phira looked at me with the same assessing gaze. "You are capable of taking a vessel across the Wall, *maugia*?"

Maugia. I might not speak Usti, but I knew that word. Mage. Witch. Either Demery had mentioned my station in his correspondence, or Phira had a very discerning eye.

I nodded, blocking out memories of unruly winds and Bailey's disgust. My mother's rescue was, naturally, not part of the story we would be sharing with investors. So to anyone who asked, I was the one who would sing us across the Wall.

"I am, Lady," I affirmed, hands clenched behind my back.

Phira pursed her lips at me. "Tell your captain he will receive an invitation to my Midwinter Frolick, which is next week. He can plead his case discreetly, with whomever may listen, but I will not otherwise endorse his cause."

"Pray, would there no sooner opportunity?" Charles inquired. "My captain had expressed a desire to speak with you tomorrow."

"No," Phira replied without emotion and began to pull her gloves back on. Sensing our audience was at an end, Charles reluctantly bowed. I curtsied, and Phira left us with a short nod.

The steward reappeared as his mistress's cape and skirts whisked out the door, catching Charles in the middle of giving me a highbrowed 'Well, how do you like *her*?' look. Charles immediately snapped his expression into a polite smile, but the steward had already seen it.

I blanched, imagining all Demery's efforts expiring here and now. But the corners of the steward's mouth turned up conspiratorially.

"I will show you to the door," he said.

We fell into step behind him, leaving our tea to cool and taking our cloaks from a stand by the entryway's hearth.

As the steward put a hand on the outer door, he spoke again. "If your captain seeks investors, allow me to extend a second invitation."

"Oh?" Charles inquired, arranging the lace at his throat with one eye on a nearby mirror.

"I know a group of individuals as… monetarily affluent, but less recognized than those your captain will meet at the Frolick," the steward said, casting his gaze between the two of us.

Criminals, an aloof voice at the back of my mind supplied, as if I hadn't started out this journey on the gallows for highway robbery and subsequently fallen in with pirates.

"We meet for cards and dice and the like," the steward said. "Nearly every evening. Would the pair of you be interested?"

Grant's eyes glinted, and I recalled it was his gambling debts that had put him in Kaspin's hands. My eyes drifted to the scars on my companion's cheeks, and a knot of worry wedged high in my throat. Grant was not my friend, I reminded myself. He was a dubious ally, at best. I should not care what he did with his time.

Still, I jumped in before Grant could speak. "We can bring it to our captain," I said with a smile. "Thank you…?"

"Mallan," the steward supplied. His gloved hand closed on the door handle, and it opened in a rush of cool air and slice of golden evening light. "If you are agreeable, simply join us at The Drowned Prince by ten. Ask for me."

Grant doffed his hat and grinned in a way I instinctively distrusted. "We will be there."

MORGORY—*A small, predatory creature related to a huden, possessed of multiple long fins, a feathered ruff and an equine aspect. Morgories are almost always found to be in ravenous schools and have been known to devour entire ships. First documented in 1624 by their namesake, Captain K.P. Morgory, whose bones were never recovered.*

—FROM THE WORDBOOK ALPHABETICA: A NEW
WORDBOOK OF THE AEADINES

TWENTY-SIX

The Drowned Prince

MARY

A few hours later, another door opened with a wash of rumbling, clinking, perfume-and-cigar-scented lanternlight. Charles strode ahead of me into The Drowned Prince, pulling his gloves off and surveying the establishment through glistening, elated eyes.

"Ah, there's our fellow," he murmured in my ear. His gaze fastened on Mallan, at his ease across the room in a dark blue, fur-lined kaftan—legs open, fingers laced around a cup as he laughed at some joke.

Here, he wasn't Phira's servant. Here, he was someone of note.

I fiddled with the clasp of my cloak—Rosser's cloak—in the sudden heat. I loathed to take it off, particularly because Grant had insisted I wear no shawl or neckerchief tonight, dressing down the gown I'd worn to visit Phira. It wasn't that I felt exposed, but I felt false, out of my element in a world where Grant thrived. A world where tattoos crept across the throats and hands of dice-tossing patrons, where carefully displayed brands on the back of necks marked various Usti gangs, and the only punishable crime—according to Grant—was lawfulness.

As Demery had said when we told him of Mallan's proposal, "We may find our most liberal investors under the table, as it were—though if that is literal, do make sure they've enough wit to sign in a legible hand."

Demery himself was now gone, off to track down the promised Sooth and Voyager somewhere out of the city. Until the Frolick in one week, Athe was in command of *Harpy*, and Grant and I in charge of finding investors.

But when I'd volunteered for this mission, I hadn't imagined we'd start at the bottom of the barrel. My expression was cool as I surveyed the company, but inside I ached for the touch of the cold wind, the rustle of leaves and scent of woodland air.

I strode after Grant, removing my cloak with a sweep and keeping my chin high. Glances from nearby tables darted over me—my face, my high-pinned hair, the curve of my breasts and the knife at my belt.

Mallan sighted us and stood, dropping into a small bow and gesturing for the company at his table to make room. Two more chairs were produced as Mallan and Grant grasped one another's wrists in the Usti style and exchanged pleasantries.

I sat, casting a brief nod around the table. There were five men and three women present. All were well-dressed in a variety of kaftans and fine coats and bodices, but no matter how beautiful their clothing was, they were all distinctly underworldly. One woman wore lip paint as red as blood and rings on every finger. Another wore earrings all the way up the brim of one delicate ear, revealed by her finely braided crown of black hair. The old man across from her was moon-pale, with a ring of scars around his shaved scalp.

"Morgory bite." The man bowed his head towards me, showing me the top. His manner was genuine, with a smile that dared me to smile back. He spoke in Aeadine and looked Aeadine, but he had an accent I suspected was Capesh.

I'd never met anyone from Cape before, only heard their accents imitated—low and rolling and stately. My stomach fluttered with anxiety, but no one else here seemed concerned.

"You can touch the scars," the man said, "if you like."

Despite my better judgement, I reached out and touched a long mark with two fingers. It was impossibly smooth and somehow seemed to hum—some of the morgory's energy lingering in the healed flesh.

"I'm Farro," the scarred man said, sitting back and offering me his hand. It was warm and rough, enclosing mine with gentle pressure. "And you're?"

"Mary Firth," I replied.

"Daughter of Anne Firth, Fleetbreaker, and a Stormsinger in her grand line," Grant chimed in, leaning on the table. A serving boy set a goblet before him and he picked it up, giving it an absent sniff. "And we, my friends, are here to gamble."

The woman with red lips smiled at him, a sultry thing that immediately earned Grant's reciprocal gaze.

"Well, then, let's begin." The woman's Aeadine carried the same accent as Farro's. She was Capesh too. "A round of aatz?"

"I will sit out for now," I jumped in. "I know my cards, but not that one."

In truth, I did not want to be tied into the game. I wanted my attention and wits free to observe our surroundings, and Grant.

Red Lips nodded and Farro shifted his chair closer to mine with a soft scrape.

"Then sit near me, Stormsinger," he said, "and I'll teach you how to play."

"Sit near me and I'll teach you how to win," the woman with the earrings put in, and the merriment in her eyes made my nerves soften. Her accent was Sunjani, and her skin a shade darker than Athe's.

"I'll just observe," I said.

One of our other companions growled something to me in Usti, jutting their chin in Grant's direction.

"He says if you do not play, you must not help Mr. Grant," Mallan translated for me.

I nodded, cards were dealt, dice distributed, and the game began. Aatz proved to be a lively affair, earning shouts and laughter as the players traded combinations of cards for rolls of dice. The dice tumbled and the players obeyed a set of expectations attached to each number. They drank on one number, confessed a secret on another, told truth or lies, named a lover or recounted an embarrassing event—though the latter blurred together more than once. And on sixes they all drank their glasses empty, the serving boy appeared at their shoulders, and it all began again. Bets were set at the beginning of each round, wins and losses hinging on which numbers appeared the most frequently.

"Mary, my shy and sorcerous friend," Grant said after the first round ended, leaving him with significantly less money than he'd initially put down. "Join the next round, I beg you."

I glanced between him and the rest of the table, hesitated a moment longer, then nodded. "All right. Deal me in."

The night began to blur. I tried not to drink much but six appeared often, and before long I had to fold out again. Grant showed no such reserve, his frequent losses punctuated with a few large wins that kept his fingers twitching.

Finally, a general hush fell over The Drowned Prince. Musicians climbed up onto a stage in one corner. Lute and drum appeared and a woman sang in Usti as the patrons fell to more intimate discussions.

Farro laid down his last card, rolled a three, and paused to formulate a truth or a lie. I watched light glint off the scars on his head. I knew I shouldn't stare, but they were so *obvious*. What must it have looked like, having a morgory biting the top of his head? Well, something like a hat, I supposed, and that made me snort with laughter.

"Oh, think you can do better?" Mallan inquired, raising his bleached-bone eyebrows.

"Hm?" I blinked at him, startled.

"Do you think you can do better than the musicians?"

"Oh," I hurriedly paddled backwards, stuffing my wine-sodden wits into an apologetic smile. "Oh, no, no, I was just pondering what a sight it must have been for Mr. Farro to wear a morgory like a hat."

Grant choked on his wine and the rest of the table disintegrated into snickers. Farro himself let out a guffaw that shattered the peace of the room, and the music faltered.

Someone from another table scolded Mallan in Usti. Mallan replied levelly and gestured to me, saying something that earned another, collective hush.

I glanced from him to Grant and leaned closer. "What's happening?"

"We were rude, it seems, so you'll sing the next song." My companion's brow furrowed. "Is this wise? Perhaps it is. A chance to prove your quality? Or it's bad. You're rather valuable. I ought to have brought more pistols… I ought to have brought Athe. She makes me feel safe, Mary, she truly does."

The singer whose performance I'd interrupted spoke up, first in Usti, then in Aeadine when I only blinked. "Come then, Aead!"

I stood, and though the attention of the whole tavern would have normally made me want to crawl out of my skin, I strode to the stage in a haze of liquored courage. The disgruntled singer and her musicians dispersed, taking their instruments with them.

Despite the wine, I disliked the thought of standing up there without accompaniment. Singing here wasn't like singing aboard ship, where I was simply doing my job. This was for show, and my mother's rescue could ride on the impression I made.

My mother's rescue? I checked myself, blinking rapidly and biting my bottom lip to try and clear my head. That was the first time I'd thought of the prospect as fact, rather than possibility. Sometime in the crossing from Tithe, I'd come to fully believe Demery.

Well, then, I'd best make a good impression tonight.

My eyes drifted to the side of the stage, and I smiled. There, finely painted and propped open with a golden arm, was a harpsichord.

The crowd faded to the back of my mind. There had been some benefits to being the daughter of an innkeeper with enough pirate gold to pay a governess, and the instrument was one of my best.

I pulled out the bench, sat, and took a steadying breath. I let my fingers roam the keys, merging between various songs until my hands remembered how to move, how to flow. Then I cracked my neck and began to *play*.

There was only one song that, as a child, I'd battled to learn. It was a complex, highly technical piece from an opera. In that performance, two women lamented the same lover, one in dark, vengeful tones, and the other sweet and melancholy. As the piece went on, the women's lamentations turned to rage, then ended with them stabbing one another in the heart.

I sang both parts, here and there playing softly or more sparingly to let my voice rise. As I did, the air in The Drowned Prince subtly responded. When I lamented, it swirled, carrying pipe smoke in eddies about the ceiling. When I vowed bloody vengeance it stilled, trembling and brushing at the back of necks like spectral fingers. And when the protagonists of the tragedy lay dying, something like snow dusted through the air, slow and glistening and veiling me.

The last few notes faded and the tavern erupted into applause. My heart hammered but I glanced out over the room, lips twisted into a delighted grin.

"Another!" Grant bellowed.

I played another song and sang it through—fast and humorous and a little bawdy. After the third I abandoned the harpsichord altogether and simply sang, clapping and stomping the rhythm as patrons began to join in. I knew these songs like I knew how to breathe—they were the staples of my father's inn back at the Wold. But folk songs, it seemed, transcended country and language.

The rafters rang with choruses and beer sloshed from glasses. Soon I was breathless, but I decided to put in one last song.

"*Elm, she hates mankind, and waits till every gust be laid, to drop a limb on the head of him that anyway trusts her shade.*"

The company faded out, and I began to sing of the Wold. I sang of each tree, of their whispers and their personalities, the feel of their shadows, the rustle of midsummer leaves and the way they creaked and cracked in the winter chill. I could have sworn that I heard those creaks as I sang, the very wood of the floor and pillars responding to me—though that, of course, was impossible.

The company joined in again on the final chorus, carelessly overpronouncing the Aeadine words in their varied accents. Then they clapped and pounded the tables, I curtsied, and dropped from the stage with a *whump* of skirts.

Back at the table, Grant pulled out my chair and handed me a cup. The last thing I needed was more wine, but a sniff told me this was watered down enough not to put me on the floor.

"Why is a Stormsinger like you in Hesten?" Farro asked. He looked pensive, and a little unnerved. That seemed to be the most common response at the table, though Red Lips looked distrustful and Earrings had turned away to murmur to someone at another table.

"If I may," Grant interjected gently. "I am happy to discuss, but perhaps there is somewhere more private?"

Mallan nodded. "I'll arrange for a room. I can direct other curious parties there?"

Grant nodded, his satisfaction locked away behind a gracious nod. "Why, of course."

A HISTORY OF GHISTLORE AND THE BLESSED; THOSE BOUND TO THE SECOND WORLD AND THE POWER THEREIN

A ghisting may be freed if its physical form (its wood, whether tree or figurehead) is degraded beyond convenient habitation.

WHEN A GHISTEN TREE is harvested, all remaining roots and branches must be destroyed, save that in which the maker desires the being to dwell. In many cases, one may carry a ghisting within a simple shard from its previous dwelling, provided the rest of the dwelling (for example, its tree or figurehead) is destroyed. This is most useful in the salvaging of wrecked ships, where the valuable ghisting can be carried back to civilization with minimal effort. Fire, naturally, is the most affectatious means to this end. It must be noted, however, that more powerful ghistings may require a greater quantity of salvaged wood to retain them. Otherwise these may be accidentally released, their will overcoming the constraints of their depleted host substance.

If a ghisting is released, whether by accident, malice or natural means, it may soon fade back into the Other, or drift for a vast time, searching for the nearest Ghistwold and the company of its own. But all will eventually fade into the Other and be lost. It therefore remains the duty of each vessel's captain and officers to retrieve their ship's ghisting at all costs in case of wreck or capture.

TWENTY-SEVEN

Sam and Helena Make a Plan

SAMUEL

N ine bells chimed across a quiet, mild evening in Hesten. *Hart* was wrapped in twilight, punctuated by streetlamps and warmly lit windows, set in rows above the shops and warehouses of the appropriately termed Temweish—*deep docks*—where a series of locks cut the ships off from receding tides. Only the finest foreign ships were docked here, though in the winter, only the finest ships made it to Usti at all. My frequent slips into the Other told me that all the other vessels here had ghistings, and most of them had the trapped light of a Stormsinger in their bellies too.

I did not think Mary was among them, at least not the ships close to us. Her light always had a grey edge to it, and these singers were a more typical, melancholy teal.

On the rail of the ship before me, I tilted the book from the Mereish jeweler towards the moonlight. I could not risk any of the crew seeing me read a book with Mereish lettering, but there was so little light I could barely make it out myself.

Under the sun, there exists three types of magickers, and many Adjacent. First, the Magni, who control the heart and impulse of those around them. Second, the Weather Witches, whose power over wind, cloud and water is dictated by voice and impulse alike. Third are the Sooth, those who interact with that Second Plane, glimpsing the past and future. As to the Adjacent, we find many variants which may fall within the following classes: First find the Ghiseau, those bound through spirit to wood and blood. Second and likewise, the High Mariner, who captains her ship through will alone. There are the Summoners, who beckon and tame creatures of that Other World. The Mage-Healers serve both their own kind and humanity with their curative gifts. Lastly are the Variants, being those who possess two or more of the above powers and attributes.

I stopped reading and stared down at the last few sentences, baffled. I had known the Mereish had bizarre ideas regarding the Other and magic, but these *Ghiseau* and Summoners sounded like much more than cultural eccentricities—they were pure folklore.

The realization left me feeling the fool. The book had begun so well, logical and systematic. It had given me hope.

But the 'Adjacent'? Other categories of magicians, 'bound through wood and blood'? My Aeadine mind had no category to interpret those. The High Mariner, perhaps I could rationalize. Some captains did seem to have unnaturally strong relationships with their ghistings, and thus their ships. But to control a ship through will alone? If such a thing were possible, surely I would have heard of it before.

I closed the book and looked at the cover again, as if its simple embossing could explain the madness inside. Briefly I considered finding the Mereish trader again and asking for answers, but the book had already been his way of answering me.

"Mereish…" I muttered wearily. "You knew they had strange ideas."

"I thought Mr. Keo was watch captain tonight." Fisher sidled up, hands in her pockets and her collar popped. She was still healing, but she had already shed her sling. She wore boots that clicked as she walked and her hair was pulled up under her tricorn hat instead of in its usual, practical tuft. She looked… not gentler, but less official. More approachable. She still carried a cutlass and likely had more weapons hidden about her person, but I did not mind this alternate Fisher.

"He is." I slipped the book into my pocket and scrutinized her, knowing I looked wan and shadow-eyed. "I am watching the city."

"Can't sleep again?" Her question was neutral, but we both knew what it meant.

"No." I had not told her about the new coin.

"Well, this is a fine city and a fine night," she noted, settling her elbows at her sides like wings and leaning back into her heels. "Let me buy you a drink."

I scratched at my jaw, beard rasping. "Why?"

She gave me an odd look. "Because I'm not foolish enough to drink my way around a foreign port, alone in the dark with a healing wrist. And no, don't bother telling me to stay aboard ship, then. I have to go ashore or I'll lose my mind."

"So you intend to use me," I summarized, "as a bodyguard."

"As assurance against unwanted trouble," Fisher corrected and flashed one of her flat smiles. "Large, bearded companions are useful in that respect. But I value your mind too, Mr. Rosser. I don't speak Usti. You do."

"I will not help you flirt with locals," I stated, though I was already warming to the idea of finding a tavern.

"Me? Flirt?" Fisher scoffed, her grin curving up on one side. She started off down the gangplank. "I've no interest in flirting, neither with Usti nor anyone else. All I want is a night that doesn't smell like damp and tar. Are you coming?"

I joined her, boots echoing on the heavy, snowy slats. "Helena, I would hardly be a gentleman if I did not. Particularly after you asked for my protection."

Fisher's mouth quirked at my use of her first name. "Not protection," she corrected. "Think of yourself as a warning sign, one that reads 'Do not try me, I've had a very bad week.'"

I ducked my chin, unoffended. Fisher was as brave and practical as they came, though she had been quieter since her brush with death. She would not have invited me unless she genuinely wanted—or felt she needed—my company. "That, I can do."

"Good. Then let's be off."

We glanced into the windows of the first tavern we came across, only to see half the patrons were sailors from our ship. This repeated half a dozen times before it started to snow in a fine, glistening haze. Fisher frowned at the sky and crossed a bridge, into an area known as the Knocks.

"We'll head up to the Shasha," she decided. "Find a place where the coin's a bit too shiny for our rabble."

Until now she had been leading the way, I shadowing her a pace behind. But now we walked side by side through increasingly narrow streets, full of locals and sailors, whores and hawkers, and late-night vendors of everything from bottles of illicit substances to sugary pastries.

The farther we went, the less of our crew we glimpsed, and the closer together we walked. By the time we neared the bridge where I had bought the talisman earlier that day, I had already caught a dozen dubious characters giving Fisher or me the side eye. I was glad I had come.

Despite our surroundings, Fisher relaxed. We bought hot wine from a street vendor and drank it beside a canal, watching the snow fall and the water flow past its shores of ice, carrying the occasional darkened riverboat, or patrolling icebreakers with long poles. We spoke little, returned our cups to the vendor, and resumed our search.

A brief wash of lantern light swept across Fisher's face as we crossed the bridge to the Shasha. She smiled at me, her eyes crinkling.

"So, Sooth," she said. We rounded a whooping crowd and a knot of drunken dancers. "Where shall we settle in for the wee hours?"

Before I could answer, the Other snatched at me. I slowed, suddenly disoriented. The bridge beneath our boots vanished and the dark water of the canal swelled, spilling into the city. New lights appeared: a wash of ghistings in their anchored ships. Red-tinted Magni, wandering the streets or situated in buildings. Another Sooth, far distant. And a host of Stormsingers, their light a wan teal. Most of them were on ships, unmoving. But one was close and edged with grey.

Mary Firth.

I returned to my flesh and discovered I had already begun walking towards her. I stopped, suddenly discomfited at the thought of bringing Fisher anywhere near Mary. Fisher might do something rash.

And Mary might still have my coin—the real one with its three-snake stamp, the reliable one that had kept me sane since I was a boy. My hands trembled. I clenched them in my pockets, forcing myself not to grab the new, temporary talisman.

Fisher snatched at my arm and forced me to face her. "You have that look on your face. Has Demery docked?"

No sooner had the question left her lips than we heard Mary's voice. It swelled out of an opening door just down the canal, facing the Knocks and bearing a sign that read The Drowned Prince.

As it had back in Whallum, the sound of her voice quietened my mind and settled me in my bones, almost like the coin she had stolen. It was inexplicable, a product of misplaced affection and admiration I was sure, but I rested in it. I released a breath and closed my eyes for one fluttering instant—before I had to open them again, and face what came next.

"*You will hear the beat of a horse's feet, and the swish of a skirt in the dew, steadily cantering through the misty solitudes.*"

Mary's voice came low and lilting, and at the same time, the falling snow changed direction. For an instant it reversed its course, wafting back up towards the shadowed lines of roofs and chimneys.

Then the door closed behind a knot of patrons, the song dimmed, and the snow began to fall once more.

Fisher turned large eyes upon me and cracked a resigned smile. "So much for no trouble tonight. You understand what we have to do?"

I knew. It was what Slader would have insisted upon, if he were here. It was what I ought to have done long ago, but had not had the stomach for.

I stamped my reluctance and longing out and shoved cold determination in its place. Mary had robbed me, and I could not fail Slader again.

We had to abduct the Stormsinger.

"She will not be alone," I pointed out, hoping against hope that the fact would sway Fisher.

My companion was unfazed. "Then we'll just have to wait for the right moment."

One more try: "We ought to go for help."

She thought for a minute, then shook her head. "No. We cannot lose this chance. At the least, we can follow them back to Demery's ship."

That was it, then. We situated ourselves in the lee of an alleyway and began a long, frigid wait in the snow. Mary sang three songs, each one more boisterous than the next, and the peace I felt at her voice was replaced by biting cold and anxious pacing.

After the third song, Mary's voice ceased to waft when the door opened. Sometime after that, patrons began to trickle out, heading home or to other establishments, or, by the looks of them, to indulge in various felonies.

When the bells rang the single toll of the first hour of the morning, I sensed Mary approaching the door. I signaled to Fisher, who stretched her neck and slipped her left hand around the hilt of her cutlass. The right, the injured one, she held carefully out of harm's way.

I expected a flood of pirates from the tavern door, but a tired-looking Mary exited The Drowned Prince in the company of just one man. He stood an inch or two taller than her, with a build that was slim but fit, and he tucked a fold of papers into his jacket as he went.

"Isn't that Kaspin's rat?" Fisher murmured.

I nodded. Charles Grant adjusted his coat and walked backwards for a few steps, casting a laughing farewell to other tavern-goers. Mary stopped, waiting for him and glancing up at the snow. My gaze snagged on her face and my head produced a series of unhelpful observations, centering around her low bodice—which I glimpsed as she adjusted *my* cloak—and the curve of her lips.

Fisher read my expression. She shot me a hard look, followed by an elbow. "Rosser. Where are the rest of them?"

I took hold of myself and pulled my pistol from beneath my coat. Fetching a twist of powder and shot from my pocket, I shook my head. "Another tavern? They will not be far."

"Then we move now." Fisher glanced at my progress. I slid the shot home, tamped it and fit the ramrod back into place beneath the barrel with thoughtless efficiency. "Here they come."

Sure enough, Mary and Grant were almost upon us, he rambling and she half listening, her eyes sweeping the street ahead.

"We come back tomorrow," Grant was saying as they neared. "And the day after. Every day. Pity Demery is not here to witness our budding success… However, that gives us even more time to secure investors."

"Every night! I'm not doing this again," Mary protested, tired and short. They were almost to the mouth of the alley now, but Grant was slow, and Mary had to wait for him to catch up again. "Any investor we pull in at the Frolick is worth twice what that lot can offer. Watching you gamble and get drunk was not what I volunteered for."

"I'm hardly *drunk*," Grant chided, slinging an arm around her shoulders. "I'm *merry*, as were you, singing such bawdy songs. Even I blushed. Besides, that lot had deeper pockets than I expected."

Mary shrugged him off, returning to her earlier assertion. "I'm not doing this every night. You can come back alone."

"Oh, you'll come," he corrected. "As you'll come to the Frolick. Mallan is arranging for Phira's seamstress to make your gown. Isn't that nice? Why aren't you smiling? Surely you like pretty things. Mary."

Hidden by the shadows, I exchanged a glance with Fisher. Her hand hovered on her cutlass and I held my pistol at the ready, but neither of us moved. We had just overheard a great deal of information, and little of it made sense. Investments, an absent Demery, someone called Phira and a Frolick?

Mary glanced over her shoulder at the tavern. More patrons had flowed into the street, though they headed in the opposite direction. "I'll attract too much attention. I'm not putting myself at risk so you can gamble and call it work."

"Do you want to rescue your mother from Lirr?" Grant's voice became harder. "This is part of the agreement."

My breath shallowed. Lirr had Mary's mother, and Demery had offered her a deal? Was that why Mary had gone to Demery instead of *Hart*?

My determination ebbed, my eyes full of Mary's face as she frowned at Grant. "You don't get to decide that. I'm not—"

Fisher flinched forward, about to step out of the alleyway.

"You two!" A woman's accented voice reverberated down the street, making both Mary and Grant look back. A tall figure sauntered into view, followed by a knot of what my curse told me were Demery's pirates.

Fisher and I retreated deeper into the shadows.

"Athe." Grant touched his hat at the newcomer, but she barely stopped walking. Instead, she prodded him forward like an unruly child. Mary fell into step and they passed out of sight.

"What?" Grant protested, his voice echoing back towards us. "Athe—unhand me. What's the matter?"

"*Hart* is here." I caught the big woman's words just as they passed out of earshot. "Time for bed, pups."

Their voices and footsteps faded and, across the alleyway, Fisher's eyes gouged into me.

"We should have moved sooner," she hissed.

I let out a long breath, mentally bracing for the displeasure Slader would unleash upon the both of us—and the prospect of yet another night without my proper Mereish coin.

"It was not a complete loss," I pointed out. From the corner of my eye, I watched the pirates cross the bridge, illuminated by lanterns and surrounded by revelers. "Grant intends to bring her back here. We know Mary's connection to Lirr now too—he has her mother. And Mary has a bargain with Demery to rescue her."

I said all this factually, but the words felt like lead on my tongue. Lirr had Mary's mother. Mary had gone to Demery out of desperation, trusting a pirate over me. She had stolen from me in the process, yes, but understanding her situation dulled my anger.

"Perhaps we can help her," I ventured. "Strike a similar agreement and convince her to join us."

"You are not subtle, Samuel Rosser." Fisher's chin dropped so she could eye me more judgmentally. "Keep your breeches buttoned."

I shot her a flat look. "Are you jealous?"

"Always," she returned, softening her words with overdone, and entirely falsified, longing. "You stir me so, Samuel Rosser."

Before I could contemplate just how uncomfortable that made me feel, my companion stepped out of the alleyway and started to trail the pirates. Yes, we needed to follow them back to Demery's ship. I had to get my head together.

"The woman they mentioned, Phira, the one hosting the party next week," Fisher said in a low voice. We fell into step far behind our quarries. "She's sister to the Usti queen."

I leapt on that. "And Demery will be in attendance, looking for investors."

Fisher nodded, smiling that flat, steely smile again. "Slader will want to hear about this."

The Girl from the Wold

The Girl from the Wold has a spent pistol, bloody clothes, and no idea where she is. She stumbles through the forest, instinct driving her away from the body of the highwayman. His friends will come looking for him, after all, and if they find her…

She spends a night sleeping on a bed of moss between two rocky outcroppings. In the morning she feels a little better, but she also feels much worse. She is lost in a forest she does not know, a forest thick with brigands. She is hungry and aching and farther from home than she has ever been. Worse, she has no money and all her possessions are gone.

She has no choice but to start walking. Around noon she stumbles onto a road, disheveled and clutching the pistol she took from the dead highwayman.

"Saint!"

The girl turns, and there in the road is a man. He doesn't look rich, but he doesn't look poor, either—his clothing fits well and isn't outworn. He wears a brown cocked hat and looks lost, his boots slathered in mud to the knee.

The girl instinctively levels the pistol, though it's not loaded and she hasn't a clue how to use it. "Stay back!" she shouts, bracing herself for an attack.

"Do not shoot, I beg you!" The man drops his satchel and backs off, his eyes fixed on the girl's weapon. "I know who you are, madam, and I'm no fool!"

Perplexed, she shifts her grip on the weapon. "You know who I am?"

He misinterprets this question as a threat, though he looks confused as well as petrified. With one shaking hand, he digs into his pockets and throws down a coin purse with a solid, revelatory clink.

She looks from him to his bulging satchel, then back to the gun. Practicality sweeps aside her lingering surprise and hardens with the clink of discarded coins.

She tightens her grip on the pistol and darkens her voice. "I should hope you know who I am, you tallow-licking goatherd."

That night the girl settles down to sleep with enough coin in her pocket to put herself up at an inn—should she find one soon—but she is starving and her conscience aches.

Still, when she spies a peddler on the road the next day, she gathers her courage. She steps out of the brush, facing him down the barrel of her useless pistol.

The peddler promptly opens the trunk on his small hand cart. "Take whatever you like, mistress, I beg you."

The girl is hardly able to believe the ploy worked a second time, but she doesn't question it. The quiet of the wood is broken by the clink of miscellaneous items as she burrows around in the trunk, pistol pressed to her victim's sweating forehead. She wears the satchel from yesterday's take, yawning open, and proceeds to stuff it full of food and useful things.

The peddler watches her, unspeaking. A bird sings off in the trees and the wind rustles the leaves in a merry, sun-dappled rush.

"Pleasant day," the peddler croaks, clearing his throat.

"'Tis," the girl replies amicably, suppressing a stab of guilt. His hands are shaking. It really was kind of him to be so terrified of her when she'd done so little to earn it. Whoever these men thought the girl was, she must truly be intimidating. But she dares not ask.

Then her fingers brush a sheaf of paper. She's about to push past it, digging towards a clutch of candles in the bottom of the trunk, when she catches sight of her own face.

The peddler sees the direction of her gaze. "That's the latest one, madam. I'm to post them in every inn."

The girl picks up the top page and steps back, withdrawing the pistol from his forehead. It leaves a red circle on his sweating skin.

One ABETHA BONNING: HIGHWAYWOMAN OF MOST DREADFUL REPUTE stares off the page. She looks just like the girl, if a bit older and angrier. And the reward? Five hundred solem weight.

Below it, in the stack, she sees postings for various other criminals, but none of them have a bounty half as high.

The peddler gives a strained, wan smile. "Like to take that reward up myself but, you're a woman to be reckoned with. I shall leave you to the Queen's Guns and the bounty hunters."

"Bounty hunters?" she repeats, feeling ill. "You think I'm… Oh, damn."

∞

TWENTY-EIGHT

Rendezvous

MARY

The Drowned Prince applauded as I left the stage and waded through a crowd that had, over the course of the last few nights, swelled. Athe and a quarter of Demery's crew were here too, all surreptitiously armed and ready to intervene at the slightest threat to their Stormsinger.

Never mind that I was tired and longed for a quiet night in my hammock. Never mind that *Hart* was in port. The pirate hunters couldn't openly touch me in Usti territory, and Grant insisted they wouldn't dare resort to skulduggery when I was always surrounded by a regiment of unpredictable, self-satisfied pirates.

So, I sang and played cards and sat in the quiet of my thoughts as Grant teased out funds for Demery's venture.

Halfway back to the table where Grant sat with Mallan and Farro, I caught the eye of a man at the back of the room. It took me a moment to recognize him in the half-light, but when I did, my heart wedged between my ribs.

Samuel Rosser sat with his coat—his new coat—open, one hand on his thigh, the other cradling a pint of dark Usti beer on the table. He wore a cutlass and a pistol and as my eyes darted to his face, his gaze fell into mine. He looked fine that night, handsome in his guarded way.

My guilt-ridden heart started to race for an altogether different reason.

Rosser nodded to the chair across from him.

I looked at Grant, preoccupied and more than a little tipsy, then found Athe among the crowd. She was shouldering out a side door, likely making for the tavern's surprisingly well-kept water closet—the establishment's clients enjoyed the thrill that came with merrymaking on the edge of the Knocks, but not the level of sanitation that came with it.

I decided it was safe to approach Rosser's table.

"Mr. Rosser?" I said when I reached him.

"Ms. Firth. Sit for a minute." He pointed to the other chair again.

"Why?"

"Because that will attract less attention, and I do not relish the idea of ending up dead in an alleyway." He nodded to the plethora of pirates around us. "I will only take a moment of your time, I promise. I am not here to harm you or drag you back to *Hart*. This is personal."

Intrigued, I watched him for a few heartbeats, then sat on the edge of the proffered chair.

"You stole from me," he stated. He leaned forward, looming over the table and eyeing my cloak. "In my pocket—the pocket of the coat you stole along with that cloak—there was a coin. Mereish, embossed with serpents. Do you still have it?"

I sat back. He was glaring, but I saw a ghost of desperation pass behind his eyes. Or perhaps it was just fatigue. He looked as though he hadn't slept in weeks.

"I do," I replied, more perplexed than anything. It was back in my trunk aboard ship. "Pray, can you stop looming?"

"What? Looming—" Rosser looked down at himself, ruffled. He ground out, "Do you have it with you?"

"No, why would I? Sit back, please." I glanced around nervously.

He obeyed. "Ms. Firth, I do not care that you robbed me, though I do consider it a gross breach of trust. I only ask that—"

"Breach of trust?" I repeated. "What trust? Did you think I'd spend the night in a room paid for by a strange man, where you could return at any time and drag me away? Or worse?"

Suddenly he was the discomforted one. "It was cold. You required a place to stay and would not come aboard *Hart*."

"Because if I did, your captain would shackle me to the mast," I reminded him. I knew what that felt like, and I let it show in my face.

Empathy passed through his eyes, deep and real enough that I was taken aback. But instead of softening him, the fleeting expression left him harder.

"Has Demery done better by you?" He started to loom again, then caught himself and sat straight, regal and restrained. "Mary, what are you thinking, falling in with pirates? Lirr is dangerous, but so is Demery. They are connected, those two, and I fear for you caught between them."

The sound of my name silenced me. There was familiarity in his tone and words, even caring, and all of it wholly misplaced.

Over Rosser's shoulder, I saw Athe re-enter the room. Her eyes immediately fell on me, then the back of my male companion. She raised her brows in question. She hadn't recognized Rosser yet, but if she saw his face, she would.

I gave her a fleeting, casual shrug. Satisfied that I didn't need saving, she sat back down at her table and picked up her drink. But she still watched me from the corner of her eye.

The pirate hunter continued. "Surely my—our—company is preferable to that. I know your mother is involved, but—"

I stared at him. "How do you know that?"

"My commission is to capture Lirr," he reminded me. "I know many things. If your aim is to help your mother, if Demery is using her to control you—let me assure you, Ms. Firth, we will rescue her instead. You and I. Us. *Hart*."

"Stop," I hissed, cheeks suddenly flushed with unsorted emotion. "I thought all you wanted from me was a coin, Samuel Rosser. Do you even know who my mother is?"

He faltered at mention of the coin and I wondered if he might back down, but no. He plunged ahead. "She is one of Lirr's victims. Which is why Her Majesty has given *Hart* this commission. And if you would—"

"My mother is the Fleetbreaker." I leaned across the table this time. "The woman who won the Battle of Sunjai and bought the Seven Year Peace. And she did that with *me* in her belly. To buy us freedom. A safe home. A quiet life." My voice thinned as I recalled that lost security, but I told myself it was from anger. "And the queen? Her Navy dragged my mother back to sea, they lost her to Lirr, and now look where we are. Lirr has her, and I? I…"

The emotion in my voice was definitely not anger now. My eyes burned. Everything I said flowed from a dark corner of my heart, bringing with it a truth I didn't want to face.

Rosser did not say a word.

"Lirr caught me," I reminded him. "She was there. I didn't know it, but she was there. I heard her sing."

Rosser's hand started to reach across the table, but he halted it halfway. "You could not have known, nor done anything if you had."

"I *should* have known, at the least," I returned. "Somehow."

Silence fell between us for a long moment. A rebellious tear finally trickled down my cheek, destroying my attempt at dignity.

I wiped it away and met Rosser's gaze again. I expected scorn, maybe pity. But all I saw was compassion—genuine, warm, disconcerting compassion that made me want to flee, because my heart recognized that expression as safe, when I knew it couldn't be.

"I'll give you your coin back," I said, standing up. With that movement, I shoved thoughts of my mother back into the lockbox of my heart and clasped my hands before my skirts. "But this is my last night here. I doubt I'll be off the ship again until… Well, not for a few days."

"Until the Frolick," Rosser said, startling me. "I will be there."

Through a lingering cloud of emotions, a thrill that was equal parts anticipation and suspicion inched through me. I'd see him again. But: "How did you know about the Frolick?"

Rosser tried to smile, but he looked so strained by this point that I almost pushed his forgotten beer into his hand.

"Word of you is going about," he said by way of explanation. He gestured towards the stage where I'd been singing. "You have done little to hide yourself. And that man with Charles Grant is Lady Phira's footman, rumored to be the bastard son of the queen's late brother, Jarl of Koest."

I stared at the back of Mallan's pale-haired head. The man potentially had Usti royal blood? No wonder he had such sway on the lower tiers of society.

"What else do you know?" I asked, curious enough to sit back down.

He reclaimed his neglected beer and took a drink, settling himself. "I know your mother sailed with the North Fleet. My uncle was her admiral—though I know admitting that may sully your opinion of me further. When the peace ended sixteen years ago she was transferred to the East Fleet, where she sailed for years, though it is apparent she was lost during that time. I assume her disappearance was kept quiet for... understandable reasons. Pride. Reputation. Keeping the Mereish and Capesh at arm's length."

I quietly digested this.

"Now she sails with Lirr, as his Stormsinger." Rosser spoke with marked unease. "We were unaware of that, back in Whallum."

My brows drew together. "Really?"

Rosser nodded. "Mary, my deepest condolences about your mother. I can only imagine what you feel, knowing where she is. I would be desperate too."

"I'm not desperate," I said, thoughtlessly.

He looked taken aback.

"I don't know what I am," I fumbled, edging a little too close to honesty. "I'm determined, but it's complicated. I wasn't even sure she was alive until a few weeks ago."

Rosser eyed me but did not press the topic. "Are you treated well aboard Demery's ship?"

I started to shrug, then nodded. "Yes, surprisingly well."

"Then that fellow over there, the one who's been leering at you all night. He's not caused trouble?" Rosser nodded sideways. "I saw him come in with you."

I looked before I could stop myself and saw one of Demery's crew sitting a few tables off, legs spread wide beneath the table and several empty cups before him. He was looking at his drinking companions, hunched with both his elbows on the tabletop, laughing hoarsely at some joke. He wasn't looking at me now, but he was one of the crew I'd marked out as potential threats.

"No," I said, but I'd taken too long to answer and Rosser looked unconvinced. I added, "There's men like him everywhere in the world. Demery's crew are no worse than the fellows around the inn I grew up in."

I paused, catching myself too close to the truth again. But his focus was still on the leering crewman. He scrutinized the man for another moment, then finished his beer and stood.

"I ought to go," he said, looking back down at me. "I will see you at the festival?"

I stood up too, wondering what I'd done to make him decide to leave. I would have also wondered why the thought of seeing him again warmed me so much, but by then I was aware that when it came to Mr. Rosser, my feelings were not wise.

"You will," I said.

"And the coin?"

Ah. The warmth receded. "I'll bring it. Of course."

He began to button up his jacket, head bowed, not looking at me. I asked on impulse, "Why? Why is it so important?"

"It is a charm," he said simply. "To help me sleep."

"I see." I didn't entirely understand, but I noted the fatigue around his eyes again, and softened. "I'll bring it, I promise. Goodbye, Mr. Rosser."

The softness in my voice seemed to catch him by surprise. He paused over his last button, watching me until the shadow of a smile touched his lips. Then picked up his hat and planted it on his head. "Goodnight, Ms. Firth."

TWENTY-NINE

James Demery and the Harpy

MARY

Demery returned from his journey the evening before the Frolick with two Usti companions, a woman and her husband, whom I met in the main cabin. They were both muscular, their skin light brown, their hair blonde and their Aeadine accented. The husband was tall, broad and attractive enough to make all but Old Crow eye him sideways—she examined him straight on. His wife, meanwhile, was of medium stature, with a fit build that reminded me of my mother, with broad hips, and a flat chest beneath a heavy coat. Most of her hair was hidden beneath a fur-lined cap, damp with melting snow.

"This is Olsa Uknara," Demery said, gesturing to the woman, then the man, both of whom stood with him in the main cabin of *Harpy*. "And Illya Uknara. Olsa is a Sooth of the highest repute and Illya is a Voyager."

Olsa nodded and Illya raised one big hand in a finger-fluttering wave, revealing the fact that he'd lost half of his ring and pinky fingers. He was dressed similarly to his wife, though the cut of his coat was straighter and the earflaps of his cap stuck out slightly.

"Many greetings," he said, then looked to Demery. "Where will we sleep?"

"Widderow will see a cabin partitioned for you." Demery nodded to Old Crow, who eyed the pair with satisfaction.

"That I will." The old woman beamed, an expression I'd never before seen on her weathered face. "A right pleasure to have you two back aboard."

Illya gave her a salute and looked down at his wife, obviously waiting for a cue.

Olsa surveyed Widderow, then Grant and Athe, then settled on myself. Her eyes were somewhere between grey and brown. It made for an odd contrast to her pale hair, though the more I saw of the world, the more I realized such combinations were not uncommon.

"Your captain tells me you never learned how to sing the storms," Olsa said. "I can help you. I am a Sooth, as Captain Demery says. I know the Other, and your soul is tied there too. I will teach you how to use the Other to train the wind, so it will obey you more easily."

Shame turned my cheeks scarlet. Train the wind? Was that something Stormsingers did?

"Oh," I said, sounding as ashamed as I felt. "Thank you."

Widderow's glare told me I'd embarrassed her, but she wasn't surprised about it. "Follow me," she said to our guests. "I'll get you settled."

The Usti left, as did Athe and Grant, and I was alone with the captain. Demery looked around the space, reorienting himself, and fed a new log into the woodstove in the corner.

"Did Phira's gown arrive?" he asked.

"No," I replied, watching coals flicker in the belly of the stove before he closed the door again and fastened the iron latch. "I'll pick it up at the seamstress's tomorrow."

"Good. I'm sure it will be wildly impractical and quite suitable. She's sending something for me too, Saint preserve me." Demery made for his trunk on the other side of the room. He pulled a key from beneath his shirt and unlocked it. "I hear you've been singing in taverns?"

"Yes," I said. Rosser crept into the back of my mind. I hadn't told anyone about the pirate hunter's presence. This would be the time to do so, but part of me worried that if Demery knew Rosser would be at the Frolick, I wouldn't be allowed to go. Then I wouldn't be able to give him his Mereish coin. And I wouldn't see him again, but that was not the point.

Besides, the Frolick was the last place the pirate hunter would risk doing anything rash. Demery, perhaps, didn't need to know *everything*. He was still a criminal. I could keep a few cards up my sleeve.

"Grant secured the signatures of two investors just last night, and Widderow's been able to restock the magazine," I informed him.

Demery nodded, taking his hammock from the trunk and balancing it on his shoulder while he fastened one side to the beams above. "She told me. You and Grant have been doing good work. If I can secure even one large contribution tomorrow evening, we'll be set to cross the Stormwall and survive there for a goodly while. But we need to leave port as soon as we're outfitted."

Unease crept across my shoulders. "Is Lirr close?"

Demery fastened the other side of his hammock. "He can't be far off now. He won't dare sail directly into Hesten—not with half the Usti Navy a stone's throw away. If there was any chance of that, I'd never have left you here. But if we stay much longer, he'll be waiting for us in open water."

My unease turned to cold, hard fear. "How can you be so calm about that?"

"Because it's my plan," Demery informed me, unbuttoning his coat and shrugging it off. He wore a knee-length burgundy waistcoat beneath and a loose white shirt, along with a patterned bronze cravat that he pulled off and folded, with the coat, into his trunk. "With any luck, he'll give chase and we'll lead him directly into the trap I've set."

I raised my brows.

"I wasn't just tracking down the Uknaras over the past week." Demery unbuttoned his waistcoat and folded it away too, leaving him in his shirt and breeches. "Illya helped me find the perfect place to lure Lirr, where his ship will hopefully run aground, and we'll have him at our mercy."

That sounded well and good to me, but the pirate was so calm, so flippant about the whole matter.

I tried not to shiver at the memory of Lirr's laughing, blood-spattered pirates and cleared my throat. "That's it? It can't be so easy. His ship has a lot more guns, and a bigger crew."

Demery rested his hands at the top of his breeches. "No, it will not be easy. Now, are you going to stand there and watch me disrobe or may I have some privacy?"

"Oh. Of course." I sidled towards my cabin door. "Good night, then."

Demery nodded. I retreated into my quarters, realizing only once I was inside that I'd need to go back out to light my lantern and woodstove. But when I peeked back through a crack in the door, the captain was already divested of his pants. He stood in his knee-length shirt, revealing densely muscled thighs—which I examined with a respectful degree of appreciation.

He raked out his sweaty hair as he stared at the bulkhead.

Harpy, the ghisting, parted from the bulkhead like a sigh. There was already a fan in her hand and as I watched she flicked it open and lifted it to her head. A face sunk into her spectral flesh, hard-eyed and cool, and her clothing transformed into the ribbed, structured gown of a queen at war.

Brother, she said.

"Sister," he said.

All thoughts of Lirr fled in an instant. I watched the ghisting drift to Demery. She spoke again, but this time I barely understood her. The sense of them passed over me—plans, intentions, Lirr—but the words were lost, as if someone held their hands over my ears. Demery's responses, too, faded into unintelligibility.

Unnerved, I closed the door and stood in the pitch black of my cabin for a long minute, half listening, half reeling.

Brother. Sister. Ghistings spoke to Demery the same way they spoke to me. Back in Tithe he'd claimed that other people could speak to ghistings and mentioned he did too, on occasion. But I hadn't imagined their communication to be as familiar and easy as this.

I pushed the heels of my palms into my eyes. I could ask Demery about it, but that would mean admitting I'd spied on him. I wasn't sure the topic was important enough to risk that.

I fumbled my way into my hammock in the dark and fell asleep with my head full of ghistings, pirates and Samuel Rosser.

THIRTY

The Other Brother

MARY

The next day I arose to find Demery gone. I was immediately swept up in preparations for the Frolick, and by the time the fleeting winter sun ducked down behind the rooftops of Hesten, what I'd seen between Demery and Harpy had retreated to the back of my mind. I tucked Rosser's coin into my pocket to join my sewing scissors and handkerchief, combed my hair through with rose-scented oil, and set my thoughts on the party.

To my surprise, a carriage delivered us not to Phira's house, but to a grand palace at the end of the Boulevard of the Divine. *The* grand palace.

The winter residence of the Queen of Usti sprawled across a rise on Hesten's largest island. Row upon row of windows glinted down into a lavish courtyard, where carriages discharged guests in fine clothes. It was snowing lightly but every walkway was clear, and golden dragonfly lanterns spilled light over the heads of the guests as they streamed towards a pair of huge, double doors.

I let Demery help me down from the carriage and stood to the side as Grant climbed out. My skirts were widened with proper panniers tonight, cages instead of the thick pads I normally wore, and they sat heavy with the weight of my gown.

The garment was a rich ocean blue with white embroidery and a black, deeply hooded cloak. The bodice was low in the current fashion, sturdy stays and a lack of a kerchief ensuring the swell of my breasts was well on display. One curtsy too deep, one reach too far, and the rest of them would tumble merrily out.

Below this rather impractical feature, my embroidered stomacher depicted a hundred tiny ships, tangled in gusts of wind and artful waves in shades of indigo, turquoise and cerulean. My skirts were long enough to conceal the toes of my black leather shoes—or rather, my boots. They were my one victory in this ensemble, painstakingly switched in the short break between Widderow putting the final pin in my bodice and coming back to pile my hair. Whatever tonight brought, I wouldn't be tripped by my own feet.

Demery took my right arm, Grant my left, and we entered the palace. Candlelight poured from elaborate chandeliers and sconces, guiding us down a grand hallway and into a ballroom. Here, side tables overflowed with food and wine, each attended by pairs of immaculately dressed servants in burgundy who dealt out bows with each goblet of wine or plate of delicacies. The ceiling was magnificently painted, from a battle at sea to deep, evergreen wolds.

Guests swirled across the chamber, filling the air with a pleasant rumble of voices. Jewels glittered on gesticulating hands, at smooth-skinned throats and in ladies' hair, which was stacked and curled and pinned with everything from feathers to miniature ships. The clothing was equally as rich, velvets and silks turning the company into a sea of high Usti fashion.

And the scent. The room smelled of beeswax candles, pine garland, warm cinnamon, and a hundred perfumes. I took a deep breath, grateful for the bulwark of Demery and Grant on my arms, and searched the crowd for Rosser.

I spied Phira instead. The crowd parted as she came forward and extended her gloved hand to Demery.

He slipped his arm from mine and took her fingers in a gentle grip. He bowed over them, low and straight, with one hand on the gilted, basket hilt of his ornamental sword. "Madam Phira, you do me such honor."

I instinctively curtsied, and Grant bowed.

"Yes," she agreed, withdrawing her hand and scanning the three of us. "Do not cause any trouble, my son, or I shall have you thrown into the snow."

"I'd expect nothing else," Demery said with a low nod. His tone was somber, but as Phira turned away, he grinned. And I hadn't missed the way her eyes flicked over him—cursory, but familiar, and somehow... maternal?

"Son?" I murmured as Demery returned to my side.

"My godmother," he said, voice low. He didn't take my arm again, his focus entirely on the crowd. "Though she disapproves of all that I am and has made that fact clear on many occasions."

I peered at him, baffled. "But you're Aeadine."

He shrugged. "My accent is."

Before I could ask more, the room hushed. Phira moved to the center of the floor, and, on the other side of the huge chamber, another woman appeared under the escort of a dozen female soldiers.

"The Queen's Guard," Demery murmured, eyeing the women in admiration.

Their coats were long and pale blue, fitted to the waist and flaring over their hips in a way that made no attempt to mask their gender. They wore loose trousers and high boots, and each was armed with a sword, a parrying dagger and a long Usti rifle. They all wore their hair in double braids tucked tightly into their caps. The style might have looked girlish, if each guard hadn't also looked prepared to eviscerate anyone who neared their queen.

Queen Inara was no less intimidating, despite her lack of armament. She wore a deceptively simple emerald gown with a cluster of real black roses instead of a stomacher. Her skin was the mild brown of many far northerners, and her eyes were a pale, nondescript blue. Her black hair, rather than being piled high, was twisted and worked into an elaborate knot at the back of her head.

The floor cleared, her guard spread out, and Queen Inara joined Phira in the center of the room. She began to speak in Usti. I couldn't understand, but her spare smile and body language communicated gravitas and greeting.

"Why is the queen hosting Phira's party?" I whispered to Demery.

"Phira," Demery leaned down to reply, his eyes still on the monarch, "is the queen's sister."

"Pardon me? Oh ..." Understanding sunk in. "That's why Mallan's in her household. He's her nephew, if the rumors are true."

Grant, on my other side, caught Mallan's name and leaned in. "What's that?"

"And you." I ignored Grant, a sudden frown stealing across my face. "Captain, the queen is your aunt."

"Not by blood." Demery waved the words away with false modesty. "All I did was return to Phira something that she'd lost, when I was young. She started feeding me, we got attached, and here I am."

"Like a stray cat," Grant observed.

Demery's smile was quick and genuine. "Like a stray cat," he affirmed.

Inara's speech ended in a chorus of trumpets, which flowed into the first waltz. Phira and the queen, arm in arm, drifted away with the Guard at their flanks.

Demery cleared his throat and surveyed the room. "Now, I'm off to waylay some very bored, very rich jarls. I suggest the two of you make polite conversation and stay out of trouble. But join me in the study at eleven bells."

With that the captain left us. Grant and I moved off to the side, making way for more guests as they entered the dance floor. A servant brought us flutes of sweet wines, thick with bubbles and fresh berries.

"Who should we talk to first?" I sipped at my wine, eyeing the crowd. I noticed a woman with a particularly large headdress, made to look like a morgory's plume. "That lady looks wealthy. And unorthodox."

"Talk to whoever you please. Aeadine will be very common in a crowd like this," Grant replied. His flute was already empty, save the berries, and he spun it dangerously between two fingers. "I'm off to find Mallan and some proper entertainment."

"You're abandoning me to gamble?" In truth, this was good—I didn't want him around when I found Rosser—but I still felt slighted.

"Well, do you want to come?"

"Not particularly, no."

"Then yes, I'm abandoning you." Grant held out his glass until I took it. "Do be careful when the dancing starts, the Usti are known for being rather free with their hands, and you look beautiful tonight."

The last caught me off guard—not because it wasn't true, I knew it was—but because of his tone when he said it, overly off-hand and hurried. But his grin was as smooth as ever as he vanished into the crowd.

"Scoundrel," I muttered under my breath. I straightened my shoulders, passed Grant's glass to a servant, and began to wander through the crowd looking for Rosser.

Eyes lingered on me. Nods, smiles and greetings came my way, but no circles of conversation opened, and the pirate hunter did not appear. My confidence began to degrade. By the time I reached the dais where the musicians played, I felt both absurd and unwelcome.

"You're looking very fine tonight."

I turned to find Rosser standing next to the carved pillars that marked the way into the salons, where more light and chatter spilled across a smooth marble hallway. To my shock, Rosser wore a full naval uniform over his broad shoulders, complete with bicorn hat, rows of pips at his collar and a saber at the hip. His cheeks were shaved too, smooth and clean over a well-formed jaw. It made him look different, leaner, younger. But it was him.

Musicians began to play a slow, swelling waltz.

"Mr. Rosser?" I stared him up and down uneasily. "I wasn't aware you were commissioned. At least, not in this way."

Rosser stared at me for the briefest of instants, then a smile crept up his right cheek. There was a dimple there, one I'd never noticed before—likely because of the beard.

He parted his lips to say something coy, but he caught himself.

"I fear you have mistaken me for my brother," he said with a grudging laugh and a low bow. "Samuel is my twin. My name is Benedict, First Lieutenant of Her Majesty's *Defiance*."

It was my turn to stare. "Samuel Rosser is your twin?"

"The very same." Benedict straightened and closed the distance between us, stopping a respectful pace away. "I gather he never mentioned me?"

"No." I peered at the man, perplexed. They looked so alike, from the shape of their lips to the slightly haunted look behind their eyes. It was uncanny.

I drained my glass and, though my cheeks were already warm, snagged another from a passing tray.

Benedict faced the ballroom as guests began to clear the dance floor and the music grew more pronounced. "That does not surprise me, given my station. And how he lost his commission."

I looked at him sideways. "Pardon?"

Benedict tapped at his collar, with its pips. "He was Her Majesty's, same as I."

Unease prickled across my shoulders. It wasn't just from the word 'was' or the implication of an unfortunate event in Samuel's past. It stemmed from the dawning understanding that the man before me was properly in Her Majesty's Royal Navy. The Navy that hung any pirates who crossed their path.

What if Benedict Rosser recognized Demery? What if he realized who, and what, I was? The Navy needed Stormsingers too.

I drained my second glass and stared at the berries at the bottom, as if they could answer my questions.

Benedict still spoke. "But there was a rather… distasteful affair, you see. When it came out, Samuel was forced to resign."

That snapped my attention back to the lieutenant. "Oh?"

Benedict cleared his throat, looking uncomfortable. "I ought not speak of it."

"Yes, you should," I protested. "Your brother's been unfortunately involved in my life, Mr. Rosser. Tell me what you know."

"Unfortunately involved?" Something opaque darted through Benedict's eyes, then cleared into a deep concern. "Whatever do you mean by that? Has he been untoward with you?"

My unease compounded with a blush. "Untoward? No."

Benedict's eyes flicked to the dance floor, where couples were gathering for another slow waltz. "Come, dance with me."

I started to protest, but he'd already plucked my glass from my hands and set it on the pillar's square base. With a gentle touch to my back and a self-assured smile, he swept me out onto the dance floor.

My heart rose into my throat, but there was no instinct to pull back, no true displeasure at his insistence. That should have struck me as odd, but I was too distracted by his words and the handsomeness of his face. I let him take my hand and my waist, and we joined the waltz.

Music. Whirling skirts. I momentarily lost myself in them and the task of remembering my feet—the wine did not help—but I soon settled into the rhythm. I'd spoken the truth when I told Demery my father had wanted me to marry up, and my governess had been a serviceable dancing instructor.

"My brother," Benedict began, "was always a troubled boy. Prone to outbursts, no matter how he battled them. We went to the Naval Academy together and served as midshipmen side by side. But when we took our lieutenant's exams, we parted ways. It was hard for the both of us. We had never been apart before, you see. Twins. Brothers. But we were men by then, with our own paths."

Benedict's hand tightened on my side, guiding me deeper into the dancers. He'd gotten closer now too—instinctive, perhaps, given he shared such personal history. His chest pressed into mine and I felt each movement of his strong legs against my skirts as we turned, stepped, turned. There was danger to that closeness, but I couldn't convince myself to pull away, even though I knew I should. So why didn't I? My lack of willpower felt like inebriation, but I hadn't drunk enough for that.

Benedict's gaze sharpened on my face and my ponderings fled. He smiled, curious and polite. I blushed, bemused. And we spun on.

"Without me beside him, Sam... strayed." Tightness entered Benedict's voice and I thought he might not go on, then he said in a rush, "He had a child by his captain's wife."

My hands slackened. I would have stopped dancing altogether except for Benedict's oddly compelling touch. Our hips brushed closer. "He what?"

Benedict looked down at me, discomfort and regret written across his face. He had all Samuel's appeal, but I saw a depth to Benedict that Samuel didn't have—emotion, raw, and urgent to the point that I might have thought it studied, if there hadn't been such honesty in his eyes. He had a uniform too and, it was becoming increasingly clear, a good name.

"If Sam has inserted himself into your life, however that may be—and I would dearly love to know—you must understand who he is," Benedict said. He looked away, gaze passing over my shoulder. "And what he has done. Though it pains me to be the one to tell you."

"I'm sorry too." My hands, one fit into his, the other resting on his bicep, softened. His fingers responded, large and warm, wrapping a little more around me. And even though Samuel was the topic of our discussion, my thoughts dwelled more and more on Benedict. "It must have been difficult, seeing your brother fall."

Another web of emotions spun across Benedict's features and resolved into a regretful smile. "It was. But enough of me. Might I have the pleasure of knowing your name, Ms.?"

"Mary," I said, unable to resist smiling back. "Mary... Grey." My father's name, not my mother's.

Benedict's eyes traveled over my clothing with a hint of curiosity, as if trying to match my garb to my name and accent. There was a good deal of appreciation there too, though, and I was fully aware of the places his gaze lingered. "Grey. I am unfamiliar with your family. Your accent is a touch... midland?"

"Yes," I replied. I was enjoying his attention, but the way he'd marked my family's lack of notoriety gave me pause. There were a good deal of privileged men in the world who considered lowborn women easy prey. One dressed up in a fine gown and out of her element? Perhaps even more so.

That knowledge, however, was a shallow thing. My mind refused to linger on it, disappearing into Benedict's warm eyes.

"Will you walk with me? I hear Lady Phira keeps a wonderful winter garden," he said, the sound of his voice dashing aside the last of my worry. "I would like to hear about your experiences with my brother, if you are willing to share. He hasn't returned my letters in years."

"That's terrible." Perhaps I was reading too much into this man, forgetting that I'd just reminded him of what must be a difficult and painful past. "Of course."

We left the dance floor, he hooking my fingers through his own as he led the way out of the ballroom. I stared at those fingers as we walked, mystified by them. I was letting this encounter become far too familiar, far too fast. Why, then, couldn't I act against it?

"Good man!" Benedict addressed a servant posted beside a doorway. "Where might I find the Winter Garden?"

The servant glanced at me, then our hooked fingers. With Benedict's focus on the other man, I finally found the will to release his hand and pressed my knuckles into my stays, half listening as the servant gave Benedict directions.

Glancing through the doors, I saw a group of men and women gathered around a table. Cards were dealt and I spied Grant with a stack of coins and three empty glasses in front of him. He looked unsettled, speaking quickly to a woman in a simple frock coat and trousers. She didn't precisely look like a guest. A servant, perhaps?

Before I could catch Grant's eye or speculate on what he was saying, Benedict started off with a prompting, backwards look. I trailed after him, though I didn't remember deciding to do so.

Cool air wafted out into the hall as we entered a conservatory. The glass walls and ceiling rose around us, reflecting the light of a hundred free-flying dragonflies and highlighting the snow that lined each cloudy pane.

Beneath the glass, the world was green. The garden smelled of earth and growth, of forest and meadows, and my soul ached with the familiarity of it. Full-size trees reached towards the glass and myriad flowers bloomed in huge stone beds, ornate pots and hanging baskets. A fountain burbled in the center of the room and numerous other couples sat on benches around it, murmuring and holding hands. Other presences moved off through the shadows, more secretive, more intimate, and even the dragonflies avoided them.

I stifled a startled, embarrassed laugh behind one hand. I'd just walked into a trysting garden with a man I barely knew.

"We should go back to the ballroom," I said, shaking my head. Then I blinked, realizing my lips were still closed. I hadn't spoken at all, and Benedict had drawn me into a slow circuit of the outer wall.

"When was the last time you saw my brother?" he asked. We didn't touch one another now and as I passed the cool glass, my skin prickled with cold and unease. Unfortunately, it did little to clear my head.

"Tithe," I said. This time my tongue worked, but when I tried to turn it to talk of leaving, I found I'd forgotten my concerns. "I... My vessel had stopped there, on the journey here."

Benedict looked at me quizzically. "And why were you coming here?"

"I'm seeking patronage," I lied. My tongue did not want to do that, either, but I managed it. "Or employment, as a musician. Phira was kind enough to allow me to come tonight, to make connections."

"Ah, yes, connections." Benedict's eyes lit and a new smile crested his lips. "I hadn't realized you are a musician. How fine. So you met my brother in Tithe and...?"

"We were staying at the same inn and took dinner together," I replied. "It was pleasant enough."

"But you mentioned your connection was 'unfortunate?'"

I winced and scrambled to rephrase myself. "He took an interest in me. Followed me, once."

"That must have been frightening." Benedict's voice lowered. "I apologize."

Memories of that night trickled back. Samuel putting another slice of bread on my plate. The way he'd looked at me before he vanished off with the inn wife and I'd robbed him. He was presumptuous and stiff, but he'd also appeared so relieved, and seemed so kind.

But Benedict had told me of another Samuel, a side of him I had never seen. A side he must have learned to hide well to have fooled me so thoroughly.

All at once, I was glad I'd robbed him. I hadn't let him completely pull me in.

Benedict and I talked for some time, wandering the rim of the Winter Garden while I carefully spoke of Samuel. Eventually the conversation shifted, and the lieutenant told me of his ship's commission to patrol the North Sea. His voice was soft and low, as pleasurable as the sight of him in the half-light, leaning a little forward to speak to me, his hands clasped behind his back.

I wet my lips and clasped my arms across my chest. It had been a good deal of time since I'd been in the company of a man this attractive, and my instincts were not about to let me forget it.

"You are chilled," he noted. "Perhaps we should return to the ballroom?"

Yes, the ballroom. I wanted to go there. But even as I thought that, my will strayed. I was cold, yes, but the scent of greenery and earth was as intoxicating as Benedict was.

"Perhaps we could simply move away from the windows?" I suggested.

Benedict's gaze wandered off down a shadowed path. "Are you being suggestive, Ms. Grey?"

I blanched. "No! Not at all." Again, I blinked, and realized my lips had not opened. My protest remained unspoken.

"Because if you are, I am agreeable." His dimple reappeared. He ducked beneath the arch of a weeping hemlock's veil of boughs and offered me a hand. "You are beautiful, I'll admit, and it grieves me to know I'll never see you again. Perhaps you might leave me with something to remember?"

His words hit me like a splash of cold water—one which the wine in my blood made a valiant attempt to burn away.

"We just met," I protested, half disappointed, half enamored.

"And?" Benedict prompted in a tone that made my skin prickle. His hand was still extended.

"Is my conversation not enough?" I lingered by the cool glass, the boughs between us. He looked so like Samuel in that moment, my heart gave a melancholy twist. I'd genuinely begun to like Samuel, and the truth about him felt a lot like loss.

"No," Benedict replied simply. "And unless I have been misinterpreting your attentions all evening, it's not enough for you, either."

I didn't have a response to that, which was disconcerting. What was it about him that had drawn me in so fast? Was it because he looked like Samuel, and he, it seemed, was all Samuel was not?

"Come." The sound of his voice brushed all remaining confusion—and logic—from my mind. "Give me one moment, here, in the shadows. No one to see or judge. One kiss, before we return to our responsibilities."

It wasn't as though I'd never been in a situation like this before. I'd been betrothed and having an absent mother and a distracted father had given me a great deal of freedom, which I'd explored wholeheartedly. But despite the shadows there was a publicness to this moment, a rarity and a forbiddenness that was both terrifying and exhilarating.

It was perhaps that, more than desire or attraction, that made me step under the tree. Temerity gripped me, spurred by wine and injury over Rosser, the thrill of deceit and the sight of a handsome man, waiting for me.

I slid into his shadow. He took the cue, slipping his hands over my back, flat-palmed and open, holding me at the slightest distance as I plucked at the buttons of his coat for a few, bracing breaths.

Just one kiss. What harm was there in a kiss?

Planting my hands on his chest, I pressed up onto my toes. His lips were warm, a little dry but gentle, easing into mine in a heady rush. His hands moved, one cupping the back of my head as the other pressed into the small of my back, holding me close as we turned. My back met the tree, rough and familiar, and I eased into his embrace.

How many times had my fiancé and I met like this, in the Wold? How many innocent kisses turned to trysts, each joyous, forbidden moment in pledge of the life we'd spend together?

A pledge unfulfilled. A pledge lost to war and time.

What was I doing?

My lips stilled, but his did not. His hands were on my waist now, possessive and insistent. One crept up across my chest, fingers tucking under the edge of my bodice, dragging me into him.

My mind fizzled back to life, even as my body urged me to give in, to fall into a rush of instinct and desire. It would be so easy. Quick. But that was all it would be.

I turned my face away, tearing our lips apart. Benedict ignored the motion, transitioning his lips—teeth—down my throat and onto my chest, meeting the place where his fingers pulled my bodice insistently away from my skin.

"Stop." I grabbed his head and pushed it away, but he still loomed.

"Let me give you this." His voice was rougher now, edged with need.

Warning bells chimed in the back of my mind, my hands still planted on his cheeks, fingers digging into his hair. I hadn't factored what might happen if he refused to stop at a kiss—a lifetime of lessons, of warnings, shed in one foolish impulse.

Fear ignited in my stomach. I pushed at him harder, hands scrabbling on his chest. My knife. I didn't have my knife. Why hadn't I brought my knife? All I had was my sewing scissors in my pocket, and they would only irritate him.

All my thoughts slammed to a halt as Benedict grabbed my wrists, pulling them away from his head and forcing them down to my sides. "Trust me."

"Stop now," I hissed, praying my voice didn't shake. It didn't. "Or I'll scream."

One hand found the base of my throat, huge and warm and threatening. "You do not want to do that. You want this. You want me."

My clarity and determination wavered again, and my lips turned in a dizzy, listless smile. But I understood something was not right now—that knowledge had slipped past a barrier and rooted inside me, a weed that refused to be torn out.

I strained against the fog, my smile disassembling.

"Mary!" Grant's voice cut through the hush of the garden, bright and a little drunk. "Mary, Mary, my lark. I saw you off this way! It's almost eleven bells."

Benedict stilled, hand still resting on my collarbone. "Who is that?"

I managed to smile again, though I doubted he could see it in the half-light. But that meant he also couldn't see the fear in my eyes, or my horror at the situation I'd put myself in. "A friend."

A few disgruntled voices replied to Grant in Usti, and I heard more than one *tsk* of disapproval as other intimate encounters were interrupted. Footsteps came closer, wandering the edge of the garden. "Sorry— Oh, dear, *deeply sorry*, ladies. Carry on. Mary!"

Benedict's jaw flexed in frustration, but he stepped back. His hands left me, suddenly gentle again, and my head cleared like mist under the sun. "My sincerest apologies, Ms. Grey."

"I'm sorry too," I returned, stuffing my fear under a cold guise and stepping away. What had just happened? My legs felt terribly weak, my body slow to respond and my wits dull. But my tongue was tart as I added, "I see you and your brother are one and the same."

Rage snapped onto his face. He stepped after me, grabbing for my arm. "I am not—"

I darted out of reach and up against the glass of the garden wall just as Grant swept into sight.

"Mary!" he said for the dozenth time, throwing his arms out. "What were you— Oh. Hello, large man in the shadows."

Benedict, however, was already leaving. He vanished through the garden without another word, leaving me breathless beside Charles.

With every step Benedict took, my senses flooded back and my body cooled. He took every last thread of my desire with him, leaving me stunned and chilled in his wake.

That feeling. That power. I'd heard about it in stories, but this was the first time I knew I'd been influenced by a Magni.

My stomach sank and my nerves shuddered. How much of that encounter had been me, and how much a lie? Had he lied about Samuel too? Now that I was free of the man's influence, doubt flooded through me, and with it a painful twist of hope. I didn't want Samuel to be what Benedict described.

I could ask Samuel for the truth tonight, if he ever arrived, but sorcery was heavily tied to bloodlines. If Benedict, Samuel's twin, was a Magni, there was a good chance Samuel was too.

I'd be wise to stay away from both of them.

"Who was that?" Grant looked me up and down. "Are you quite well?"

"I'm fine," I answered, deciding it was true even though my shame burned on my cheeks. I slipped my arm through his, and if I held a little too tightly, he didn't comment. "Let's go find Demery."

The Girl from the Wold

The Girl from the Wold breaks another stick and feeds it into the fire, watching the flames lick hungrily at the edges of birch bark. The evening is as quiet as all the others—as each of the five nights that she has spent alone among the trees have been. She still wears Abetha Bonning's stolen name, though unwillingly now, and lives off that other woman's reputation.

But she knows the sand in the glass is running low, trickling down to its final grains. She needs a new plan, a new place to hide, and it must be soon.

She contemplates what to do as she peers into a small iron pot at the edge of the fire. A stew that promises to be bland but hot simmers inside, and she has set out a loaf of bread on a fine silver platter at her side. The platter looks incongruous, perched on the log that serves as table and chair, surrounded by fallen leaves and reflecting the flames on its glistening silver surface. But it was the most valuable thing the last traveler had, stuffed into his sack, so she had taken it.

She'll sell it at the next town, she thinks, along with the other valuables she has hidden in bags across the fire. She's not sure how to sell stolen things without attracting too much attention, but if the villages in the Lesterwold are anything like her own village, the shepherds and woodcutters will turn a blind eye. She'll trade the platter for a horse, and some shepherd's daughter will find herself with an unexpectedly fine dowry.

A stick cracks, out in the darkness. The girl looks up slowly, wary but not overly concerned. The forest is always full of sounds, if one takes the time to hear them.

But then there is another crack, and the brush of cloth against bark.

The girl draws her pistol, still spent, and makes a show of cocking it. Fear bubbles in her stomach like stew in the pot, but she's getting better at hiding it now. At pretending to be someone she's not.

Another part of her wonders if this new person, this new pragmatic girl with a powder-streaked pistol, has been there all along.

"Who goes there?" she asks.

Firelight runs up the barrel of a musket as a soldier steps into sight. An unremarkable face, mouse-brown hair swept up under a tricorn hat, two rows of matte black buttons on a deep green coat. The soldier's cloak is thrown back, musket butt resting at her shoulder.

The Girl from the Wold stands slowly, pistol leveled. The soldier aims her rifle at the same time.

"We are the Queen's Guns, and you, Abetha Bonning, are surrounded," the soldier says. Her voice does not waver, and as she speaks, the girl hears more footsteps, sees the flashes of more guns, and feels the presence of more watching eyes.

Panic flutters in her stomach. The Girl from the Wold steadies the pistol in both hands and tries to think, tries to see another way forward.

There is none. Just a dozen guns in the night, and a noose intended for another woman's throat.

Cool metal brushes the girl's neck, and a male soldier plucks the pistol from her fingers.

"I'm not Abetha Bonning," the girl says. A crack or waver in her voice would have been useful just then, any-thing to inspire pity or create doubt, but it doesn't come.

The soldier who took her pistol smirks, his eyes glistening with success. "Tell that to the hangman."

∽

THIRTY-ONE

A Most Honored Guest

SAMUEL

I followed Captain Slader through the press and laughter of the ballroom. People and voices whirled past me, obscuring my view as I searched for one face.

I glanced at woman after woman, each one more beautiful, more lavish, and more shrewd than the last. Some of them met my eyes invitingly but I did not stop, growing frustrated as Slader reached the other side of the ballroom and stepped into a quieter corridor.

"You can mingle later," the captain told me, pausing so I could catch up. He glanced over my shoulder to where a pair of Usti women watched me go, and the older man nearly smiled. "Stay focused, lad, and watch yourself."

I nodded as a servant directed us into a private room. Half a dozen others were already here, seated about a well-appointed study with glasses in their hands.

James Demery addressed the company from beside the fire. As we entered his speech slowed an iota, his eyes jumping from me to Slader. Then he recovered with grace and gestured to several free chairs.

He continued in fluent Usti, "With this in mind, can you not see the profit of such a venture?"

"Many an explorer has ventured beyond the Stormwall, looking for treasure," an old man replied, his Usti accent sliding and viscous.

He sniffed over the glass of amber liquid resting atop his round belly. "So many that I cannot begin to name them. Do you know how few have returned?"

"Very few." Demery shrugged. "But I am one of them."

"How did you manage that?" Captain Slader inquired as he took a seat.

Demery offered the other captain a nod of acknowledgement. "Before I answer that, let me remind you we stand on Usti soil, and stretching my neck would be entirely unwise."

Slader nodded. "You may be a brigand but, fortunately for you, you are not the particular brigand I am searching for. Have no fear."

Demery's smile was humorless. "In answer to your question, I crossed the North Line as a young man, and I know where the greatest riches are to be found."

"How did you cross?" Slader asked again.

"With the aid of the Fleetbreaker, prior to her recruitment into Aeadine's Fleet." Demery turned his attention back to the company. "My current Stormsinger, Mary Firth, is the Fleetbreaker's own daughter—equally as talented, and more than capable of taking us north."

Slader turned to give me a silent look, reminding me of how gravely I had failed him.

"Where is the Stormsinger?" a woman with loose blonde hair and a fitted orange gown inquired. "I'd like to see the creature."

The question alone was enough to nudge me into the Other. The walls and company vanished in a stomach-flipping jolt, leaving me on an empty plane with only myself and a handful of spectral figures. A Magni, outlined in red. Another Sooth in forest green. Two others whose talents I could not recognize. Demery himself had an odd aura about him, but before I could think too hard on that, Mary appeared.

I dragged myself back out of the Other, took a second to let my vision clear, then murmured to Slader, "She's coming."

The door opened and Mary entered on the arm of none other than Charles Grant. Grant looked well into his cups, flushed and subtly leaning on Mary for support.

Mary caught sight of me and stopped in place, staring in sudden apprehension. Grant staggered and she steadied him without breaking her gaze, her arm suspiciously easy around his back.

Baffled, I stared back. Last time we parted, she had looked at me so softly. She had even seemed—dared I think it—eager to see me again tonight. What had changed?

She pressed her lips into a cool, thin line, and broke my gaze. Unspeaking and unsmiling, she left Grant on a chaise and moved to stand next to Demery. Firelight ran up the side of her gown and angled across her chin, hiding the flush of her cheeks within a bar of shadow. But I did not miss a few red marks on her neck. *Teeth?*

I turned to study Grant. He met my gaze and offered a small smile. No guilt or gloating or possessiveness, but something else. He looked away and hiccupped surreptitiously.

Demery began to talk, introducing Mary and lauding her skills as a Stormsinger. Mary refused to look at me again but I felt the weight of her focus, and saw twitches of emotion across her face. I could not decipher them, too fast and too complex, but they felt like stones in my stomach.

Something had happened since the last time we had met. Something drastic, and it had tarnished me in her eyes.

I was so fixated on her that when I slipped into the Other again, I barely noticed. The rest of the room faded but she remained, staring at me without looking at me.

I had never seen her so close, not on this Second Plane. She wore no elaborate gown here, though her hair was still piled high. Instead, she wore her power, the soft teal of a Stormsinger. It was hedged with her signature grey and highlighted every curve of her, blurring the details but leaving little to the imagination.

Beauty. Power. The words lost meaning the longer I looked. And I knew, very clearly, why her disregard hurt me so deeply.

I cared for her. Wanted her. Deeply, painfully, and inexplicably.

So lost was I in that understanding that when another glowing figure stepped into my vision, I was slow to give it proper attention.

The red aura of a Magni surrounded Benedict. Without seeing me, he turned towards Mary and his power flared into a predatory madder.

I lunged back into my flesh and shot to my feet. Benedict's gaze snapped to me and we stared at one another over the heads of the startled company.

"What the hell are you doing here?" I growled.

"Dear brother." Benedict regained his composure and tilted his head in a condescending nod. "I appear to have wandered into the wrong room."

"Twins!" the man with a drink resting atop his paunch guffawed. He took a drink, adding into his cup, "How entertaining!"

"How rude of an interruption," the blonde-haired woman countered.

"Yes," Demery agreed. "Lads, take your dispute outside."

"No," Slader cut in, his voice cold and decisive. "Mr. Samuel Rosser, sit back down. Mr. Benedict Rosser, be on your way."

Benedict glanced from me to Mary to Slader, then proffered a short bow. "Sir."

Just like that, Benedict was gone and I remained on my feet, glaring a hole into the door.

"Sit down," Slader grated. "What is wrong with you?"

I obeyed but did not explain. Mary was staring after Benedict too, but as I sat she looked back at me. She reached a hand up to the base of her throat and refocused on Demery.

The revelation that I had a twin had not ruffled her. She had already known. And those marks on her neck? The sudden change in how she looked at me?

That was Benedict. What had he told her? What had he done to her?

What had he compelled her to do?

It took all my willpower to stay in my chair as Demery talked on, the company posed questions, and numbers began to pass between the pirate and potential investors. Mary remained next to him, the reminder of the pirate's ability to complete his proposed venture. But her attention was somewhere else.

Finally, the meeting dispersed. Those uninterested in investing left while three remained, signing a document that Demery produced. Then they too vanished, and Slader and I were alone with Demery, Grant and Mary.

"I assume you're here about Lirr," Demery said, pulling up a chair in front of Slader and offering a bottle.

Slader held out his glass, and the pirate refilled it. "Well, I am certainly not here to give you money for rum and barley."

Demery smiled at that. "Ah, well, pirate hunter, pirate—neither of our businesses are as lucrative as they once were. Not in these northern seas, at least, between the Navies and the weather."

My captain smiled wolfishly. "That depends which pirate you hunt. Your hoard, too, sounds very promising. If you survive the journey."

Demery made a contemplative noise and drank, the bottle still dangling in his other hand.

Behind him, Mary left the fireside and sat on the chaise with Grant, who leaned over and murmured something in her ear. She shook her head and did not reply.

"I'd like to propose an alliance." Slader cut right to the point. "I want Silvanus Lirr, and he wants your Stormsinger."

"Oh? How do you know that?" Demery asked, not bothering to deny it. He set the bottle at his feet and leaned back, crossing one leg over the other.

"She's the common factor in every place he has appeared in the past few months. For whatever reason, Lirr is tracking her in the Other." Slader made no mention of me and how I had been doing the exact same thing. No need to reveal our advantage.

For me, the secret was even more important. I did not need Mary distrusting me any more than she clearly already did. I needed her to give me back my coin. I wanted more than that. I wanted to explain, to assure her whatever Benedict had told her was a lie. And whatever wrong he had done to her, I needed to rectify it.

"So," Slader summarized, "since I'm quite sure you will not tell me why he's following the witch, or allow me to purchase her, join forces with me. Once Lirr is taken, you can go on your way without having to worry about him harrying your back. We both win."

Demery tapped his fingers on the arm of his chair. "I'm not interested."

"Then what will you do when Lirr comes upon you?" Slader asked, leaning forward with his glass in hand. "I've seen your ship. *Harpy* is no match for the *Nameless*. But if we put our guns together, and share your Stormsinger? We can bring him down."

"My answer is no," the pirate reaffirmed. He glanced over at Grant and Mary and lifted his chin to the door. Both got to their feet, Grant doing so with an audible sigh.

Slader and Demery rose too.

"You are making a mistake," Slader warned.

"Trusting a pirate hunter would be a far greater mistake." Demery joined Grant and Mary at the door. Mary looked back at me, her expression still closed. "Good night, Captain, Mr. Rosser."

"Mary." Her name left my lips before I could stop it. I stood, starting towards the door before the pirates reached for weapons— Grant beneath his coat and Demery to his decorative cutlass. Mary glanced between the two of them, seemingly indignant at her own lack of weaponry.

I held out empty hands. "Mary, can I speak with you for one moment? Just one."

She hesitated, looking almost grieved, then hardened herself. "No, Mr. Rosser."

With that, she slipped away. The men flanked her, and the door closed.

Silence reigned in the room for a long instant. Stricken, on the edge of bolting after her, I forced myself to still. I could not let Slader see how rattled I was, how desperate I was not only for Mary's affection, but for what she had stolen. Both were damning.

Slader considered my face as he set his glass aside. He gave a gruff, half-laugh deep in his chest. "I should have seen that coming."

I battled for dignity. "Pardon me?"

"You've fallen for the witch." Slader gave me a hard look and I braced for the tirade. But to my shock, he simply let out a breath, thumped me on the back, and started for the door. "I'll have Fisher pick her up before we leave port, then."

It took a second for his words to pry through my shock. I started after him. "Sir?"

"She's the key to Lirr," Slader said. "Demery's not leaving port with her, and you seem rather… compromised."

"This is Usti," I protested, lengthening my strides to join him at the door. "Demery evidently has the favor of the nobility. He is untouchable."

"You're a good man, Mr. Rosser." Slader stepped out into the hallway and headed back towards the light and music and chatter of the ballroom. A dance was just ending—guests stopped on the final note in swirls of skirts and waves of polite chatter.

"Go find something pretty to spend the night with and get yourself together," the captain continued. "Do not come back to the ship unless you're ready to do what needs to be done."

"Sir!" I darted after my captain, but he was already swallowed among the milling couples. "Captain, I—"

A pistol shot split the air. Laughter skewed into startled screams and guests scattered from the dance floor like rats from a dropped torch.

I ducked behind a pillar and reached for my flintlock. Female guards ushered a pair of ladies past me—Queen Inara, presumably, and Lady Phira—while others drew their swords. Then the floor was clear. Slader was nowhere to be seen and only one young man remained in the open space, staring after his fleeing partner with a look of baffled indignation.

"Vara!" he lamented in Usti, jilted. "What—" Then his eyes dragged to the other end of the ballroom, and he bolted like the rest of them.

A man in a double-breasted burgundy coat strode through the far door and a veil of drifting gun smoke. Rank upon rank of armed women and men came after him, though 'armed' was perhaps an understatement. They bristled with weapons, each in differing combination—braces of pistols, various swords, firearms, hatchets and machetes. They wore no uniforms, preferring eclectic collections of clothing from every corner of the world. I saw frock coats and kaftans, sashes and fitted breeches, their only unifying feature being functionality. Every one of them looked ready, able, and hungry for a fight.

Brigands? Certainly. Pirates? Perhaps.

I primed my pistol, movements quick and distracted. I still could not see Slader. And Mary—Saint, she and Demery and Grant had barely been ahead of us. They had to be in the crowd, but no matter how frantically I searched, I could not find them. And was Benedict still here?

The Other whispered to me, too close and too willing to help me find both the Stormsinger and my brother. But I did not dare step over the border now.

Howls and yips broke out as the newcomers—the pirates—broke rank and charged across the room. Some ran at the crowd directly, driving them back into the walls like dogs herding sheep. Guests screamed and wailed. A man hit the floor—fainted—and several women shrieked at one another as they fought to escape out a side door. Their shrieks turned to screams as more guests piled into them, overturning side tables and crushing the women into the gilt, mint and rose wallpaper.

"Enough!" An Usti soldier stepped forward. She was dressed like the guards who had escorted the queen, marking her out from the common soldiers who formed up behind her with leveled bayonets. Other soldiers waded through the crowds towards the side doors, battling to take control of the exits.

By some unspoken command, pirates grabbed guests. A new chorus of screams and wails ricocheted around the room as guests were thrust to their knees at the point of pistol and cutlass. Other pirates continued to move, their gaits turning predatory and calculated, expressions leering and shrewd.

They had a plan, and from their ease, all was proceeding exactly as they intended.

"I'm here for one woman and one man," the pirates' commander said. His voice seeped into me, and at the back of my mind, my curse suddenly roared.

Lirr. Silvanus Lirr was here, in the Usti palace, looking for Mary Firth.

"Aeadines. Foreigners. No one will be harmed if you stay calm and let me take them." Lirr spoke Usti with a gentle accent, like honey. His gaze slid around the room, and transitioned into Aeadine. "James. Mary. Come out before you get someone killed."

The hall choked into silence, every guest holding their breath and looking between one another.

"Leave, now," the queen's guard called. "This room will be surrounded in moments and you *will* be slaughtered."

Lirr glanced at her, then looked back to the crowd. "Demery!"

Slader rose from behind a toppled table, put a commandeered musket to his shoulder, and fired.

Lirr took half a step back, looking down at the bicep of his left arm. The fabric was dark and I was too far away to see how badly he'd been hit, but he shook scarlet droplets from his fingers. They fell on the glistening pale marble at his feet, bright and ominous.

I had to back up Slader. I moved on instinct, stepping out from behind the pillar. In the same movement, two of the closest pirates to Slader whipped their weapons away from the heads of their captives and fired. Both shots missed—pistols, near useless at range—but a statue near Slader exploded in a cloud of dust.

The other bullet found flesh. An older Usti man on the edge of the crowd sank to the floor with a startled, frightened exclamation.

The Usti soldiers charged the pirates. They did not dare shoot, fearing to wound more civilians, but I glimpsed flashing bayonets and swords as I sprinted across the ballroom. I darted through combatants and prone guests, pistol raised, and sighted my first target—a pirate with a saber in hand, heading for Slader.

I shot her in the chest and smashed the spent pistol into her face. She went down and I stole her sword, shoving my bloodied pistol back into my coat.

I started to move again, slashing and shouldering pirates out of the way. I saw the queen's guard off to my right, a blur of sword and dagger as she dispatched pirates and shoved guests towards safety. The pirates scattered away from the pair of us, granting me a second of reprieve.

I was just in time to see a hatchet bury itself in Slader's head. I shouted, horror and shock blurring everything except the sight of my captain crumpling beneath the rush of guests.

A cutlass stabbed at my side. My dreamer's sense foresaw it and I stepped aside without thought, parrying the blade wide, seizing my assailant's wrist and twisting my sword into his stomach. He dropped and I turned, staring again at the place Slader had been.

My breath came in short, shuddering gasps. Surely, I had seen wrong. Surely, my captain was still alive, still—

The Other rushed at me. I battled against it, fighting to remain in my own body, but shock set me adrift.

Lights flickered to life. I saw Lirr standing before me, but instead of the earthy, forest green light of a Sooth like myself, I glimpsed something opalescent, churning with every shade of green and red. It fluttered, smoke in the wind, and vacillated into a pale silver.

I had never seen anything like it. It was widely known that Lirr was a mage of multiple affinities, but this? This was beyond my knowledge.

Passages from the Mereish book of ghistlore flitted through my mind, mentions of mages and Adjacents, categories of sorcery I had never been taught. Was this what I was seeing now?

Lirr did not look at me. Instead, we both turned as Mary's light flickered into sight beyond the side door, the one where Usti soldiers were funneling guests out of danger.

Back in the physical world, something struck me. Pain jerked me back into my bones and I found myself on the floor, ribs screaming, a cudgel coming down at my head.

I kicked out, shattering the knee of my assailant, and staggered upright.

The pirates had begun to flee, snatching jewelry and candlesticks and handfuls of food as they rushed back through the yawning ballroom doors. Lirr was in their midst, pulling his people along in a wordless tide of magic. They left bodies behind, twisted corpses and bloody footprints. I saw one brigand slide through a pool of scarlet, laughing like a child on the ice, and flounce after her companions.

I picked myself up, found my balance, and charged after them.

THIRTY-TWO

Shelter

MARY

Demery led me through the shrieking guests and into a curtained alcove. The inebriated Grant carried on a few steps then hastened back to us, gritting his teeth and blinking to clear his head.

"Change of strategy," Demery said, untangling the gold-braided rope that held the curtain back. It opened with a heavy, rippling *whump*, leaving us with only a slice of light from the hallway. "Mary, stay here. Mr. Grant? You're with me."

"Stay here?" I protested. I leaned forward, trying to catch a glimpse of Demery's expression as he glanced back into the hallway. The golden rope that had held the curtain dangled at his side, fastened to a heavy bronze ring. "I'm not staying here, not with Lirr so close. You said he wouldn't even dock in Hesten!"

"I was wrong," Demery snapped. "Or near enough. He must have anchored outside the city walls."

"To the north," Grant started to say with a drunken slur, but the rest of his words were lost in a renewed fit of shrieking from the hallway. He cringed and shoved deeper into the alcove, managing to elbow me in the chest and tread on my foot at the same time.

"Sorry, so sorry," he muttered, straightening directly between Demery and me. He stank of pipe smoke and wine. "Damn, I *am* drunk."

Demery shot Grant a hard look, particularly piercing from so close, and the young man froze. "To the north? How would you know that?"

Grant appeared to battle his slow wits. "There's a smuggler's anchorage," he fumbled, then degraded into a nervous giggle as he added, "It may surprise you, good sir, but I have friends in remarkably low places."

My already hammering heart increased tenfold. If Grant was right, if Lirr *was* anchored just north of the city...

I knew where my mother was. We could rescue her, tonight.

Demery's gaze was sharp as he looked at Charles, but he pushed his questions aside. "Well, if you want to stay aboard my ship you'll come with me now. Mary, do not leave this alcove. I'm going to murder Lirr tonight, but if my bait is running free, that will be a lot harder. We'll be just down the corridor."

With that, Demery edged outside, cutlass in hand.

"Bait!" I spluttered in panic and indignation. "I'm not sitting here while Lirr comes for me! If my mother's just outside the city—you promised to rescue her, Demery. Captain!"

Demery's gaze swept back to me with the intensity of an owl. He rammed his cutlass back into its scabbard, grabbed the rope that had held back the curtain with one hand and my wrists with the other.

"We'll find her when Lirr's dead," the pirate said.

The chaos of the palace swallowed my scream. I struck out, but Grant was in the way and the alcove was a shadowed mess of limbs. I managed to free one hand and punch the captain's face before he barreled me into the wall and pinned me there, crushing the air from my lungs and filling my face with the scent of wool and salt, pipe smoke and gunpowder.

Next thing I knew, my wrists were bound to the ring in the wall. Demery pulled Grant outside, wincing at the blow I'd given him, and the curtain closed.

"Charles!" I bellowed, craning after them. "Charles Grant, you bastard, come back right now! Charles! Demery!"

All at once, the hallway quietened. The last frantic slap of running feet faded away. The last scream echoed into silence. I was alone with the candles flickering in their sconces, and the curtain, which was doing its best to smother me.

I sagged back into the alcove. I jerked at my bindings, but the rope was strong, and the ring firmly embedded in the alcove's frame. Clearly, the Usti did not take chances with their drapery.

Maybe Demery was right. Maybe I should stay here, play my part in his game and let him try to kill Lirr. But how could I do that? How could I let myself be caught and tied to a wall when my mother was so close? Yes, Demery had said we'd rescue her once Lirr was dead, but I doubted Lirr's crew would wait around for us to find them.

If Demery would not take the initiative, I had to. Lirr was already here—Demery would have to find him without me.

I twisted, trying to get a hand into my pocket, but only succeeded in making my shoulder cramp. Growling in frustration, I angled my hip into the wall. I could feel the contents of my pocket pressing into my hip. If I could somehow manage to move the pocket higher...

I proceeded to perform a clumsy, intricate dance, twisting my skirts, wrenching my shoulders and generally making a fool of myself until my fingers caught the edge of my pocket.

Scissors. Their delicate edge brushed my finger. They were small, but they'd do.

I began to snip, the valiant grind of the little blades loud in my solitude. There were other sounds in the distance—footfalls, shouted orders, gunfire and violence—but my corridor remained hushed.

The rope fell away. I shook out my wrists and tucked the scissors into my right hand, letting them poke out between my fingers as I peered into the hallway. It stretched far to the left and right, intersected in each direction by narrower, darker ways. There was no one in sight.

A long-legged shadow stretched around a corner, followed by a pair of boots.

I twitched back behind the curtain.

The boots approached, surreptitious but intent, and coming directly towards me. I could bolt right now, but whoever it was would certainly see me.

"Mary?"

The curtain pushed back and Rosser—one of the Rossers—appeared before me. I took him in, from his plum-colored coat to the beard on his cheeks. Samuel. Not Benedict. My relief was a traitorous thing.

More footsteps came, followed by unfamiliar voices. Samuel shot a sharp glance up the hallway then shoved into the alcove with me.

He was too close, too fast. I panicked and punched him in the stomach.

The man buckled with a thin wheeze, followed by a garbled curse. "Bloody— sharp?"

I gasped, remembering the scissors between my fingers. I started to apologize, but cut myself off. I didn't believe all Benedict had said about Samuel, but I needed to keep my guard up. Particularly if Samuel was a Magni too.

The thought gave me pause, and I studied Samuel's shadowed face for a few, galloping heartbeats. I searched myself for any illogical impulses, but my head felt clear. If Samuel was a Magni, I didn't think he was using his power right now.

Footsteps approached us at a jog.

"Do not move!" Grant's inebriated voice called from the opposite direction, overly loud, and no doubt completely giving away his position.

Samuel and I froze.

Another voice, familiar and low, observed, "She's there."

All I saw were the whites of Samuel's eyes in the gloom, just as round as mine.

Lirr.

"Do you trust me?" Samuel whispered, concern and urgency in his eyes.

"No." I intended to snap the word, but it came out as a rasp. I thought fast, all the while keeping a thumb on my emotions, wary of any Magni taint.

Lirr and his pirates were in the hallway. Grant was drunk, and Demery just one man. My odds of escaping this situation unscathed felt thin. Then there was the matter of my mother, trapped aboard Lirr's ship somewhere out in the night.

I needed help. But a distraction would suffice.

"Help me get away," I said to Samuel. "I'll give you your coin back."

"Give it to me now."

"After." I knew better than to take chances with a Rosser. "I promise, Samuel."

My use of his name hushed him. There was a heartbeat of silence, punctuated by boots approaching in the hallway.

"Mary Firth," Lirr's voice called. "It's over, woman. Come out."

Before I knew what was happening my legs moved forward, my will vanished into an all-too familiar haze, and I started to push the curtain aside.

Samuel threw out an arm, barring me from the mouth of the alcove and the danger beyond. He gently pushed me back towards the wall. "Mary, do not listen to him. He's a Magni. Remember what he is, hold it in your mind. It will help."

I bumped back into the wall. The cool stone jarred me and I rallied, clearing my head with a force of will. "Thank you," I breathed.

He nodded but did not lower his arm, still guarding me from the hall and Lirr's cloying influence.

"What do you want to do?" Samuel asked, and it was that question, even more than the sincerity in his eyes, that made me trust him. He was a risk, but so was every other option I had. At least with Samuel, I had his coin for leverage.

Gunshots broke the air, two, then four, followed by a shout that I knew came from Grant. Demery was making his move.

"There's a smuggler's anchorage north of the city. Lirr's ship may be there, with my mother." I added impulsively, "Help me rescue her."

"But Lirr is here," Samuel countered. He looked torn. "I have to stop him."

Disappointment made my throat thick. "Then distract him so I can escape."

"You cannot go alone," he protested.

I ducked under his arm and grabbed the curtain, letting a slice of light fall across our faces. I shrugged, knowing he was probably right, but I was unwilling to give up. "What else am I supposed to do?"

For a timeless second Samuel looked at me and through me, indecision written across his features. Then he nodded.

Before I could lose my nerve, I slipped outside and plastered myself to the wall. Lirr was tucked into another alcove on the other side of the passage, his pirates on the floor or hunkered behind benches and side tables.

Voices roared. I looked the other way and saw Demery and Grant charging towards us, Usti muskets abandoned for swords.

Lirr's eyes pinned me to the periwinkle plaster. "Stay where you are."

I felt a rush of compulsion with his words, and for the third time that night, my rationality fled. I thought I'd been prepared, but my legs locked, even as my mind screamed for me to move. I felt like an insect, impaled on a naturalist's card. I tried to do as Samuel had said, holding in my mind the truth of what Lirr was, that this compulsion was not my own, but my body responded too slow. Too slow.

Samuel stepped out of the curtain behind me, leveled a pistol, and shot Lirr. No sooner had spark met powder than he threw himself across the corridor, cutlass in hand, and attacked. Lirr fired back, missed, and flipped his own pistol across his forearm as a shield as he drew his cutlass. He deflected a thrust to the chest and stabbed at Samuel.

Blades clashed and ground. Samuel slammed into Lirr's chest and knocked his pistol flying.

Lirr's power wavered as he hit the wall, and my consciousness reared. With invisible teeth and nails I tore at his control, shredding it and grasping the last untainted thought I'd had.

Run.

My legs released. I bolted, snatching up my skirts and leaping over a dead pirate. Another's arm snaked out to grab my ankle but I dodged, nearly slipped in blood, and skittered around a corner.

I looked back, heart thundering in my throat. Samuel was obscured by half a dozen pirates, and Demery and Grant flitted through the melee.

Then, to my shock, the pirate hunter burst from the chaos and charged towards me. "Go, go!"

I took off, shouting over my shoulder as he caught up. "What about Lirr?"

Blood glistened on Samuel's cutlass. He glanced back, indecision plain in his eyes, but he forced himself to look ahead.

"He's wounded. Badly," he said as we burst through an open doorway and passed a clutch of screaming servants. "You are more important right now."

I wasn't sure what that meant, but I took it.

Hallways. Doors. Soldiers waving us in the right direction. Cold blasted my face, my lungs burned and we burst out of the palace gates onto the Boulevard of the Divine. People stared as we made

for the broad sweep of the canal and the bridge to the Knocks, feet
pounding, clothing fluttering.

The streets were packed with revelers, lit by lanterns and braziers
as the city celebrated. Light spilled from taverns and brothels, fire
dancers leapt through the streets, and musicians played raucous
tunes as we traversed the Knocks and diverted onto a road heading
north. Eventually the celebrants filtered away, and we sprinted
across a bridge into the military quarter.

Just as the masts of the harbor came into sight, Samuel tugged
me left.

"What? What is it?" I whisper-shouted, trying to find my feet in
an alleyway entirely sheeted with ice. Instead, I slipped and smashed
my knee off the slick cobblestones.

Samuel's response was a ragged curse. His boots slid, legs
locked, and for a rambling heartbeat it looked like he'd found his
balance. Then his long legs shuddered like a newborn colt's and
he hit the ice.

"Samuel!" I scrambled for the nearest snowbank, finding footing
in snow so cold it squeaked beneath my boots. I'd barely noticed
the temperature in our flight, but the night was freezing and I
only wore my gown. My cloak remained at the palace. "What are
you doing?"

"If we go that way, they are going to catch us." Rosser staggered
upright in the opposite snowbank, one hand on the wall, the other
reaching to me. There was a brightness to his eyes, an intensity that
demanded my attention. "Lirr is going to cut us off at the gate out
of the city."

"How do you know that?" I gaped at him. "I thought you injured
him!"

"I did, but he is moving again," he said, his own shock and unease
at the statement clear in his face. He snatched my hand across the ice.
"I am a Sooth, Mary. I know where you can hide. You are no use to
your mother captured."

Shouts and pounding footsteps filled the quayside, reverberating off stone and ice and wood and water. Samuel was a Sooth? A Sooth and a Magni, twins? No wonder Samuel had spoken so knowledgeably about Lirr's abilities.

Implications pestered me, but there was no time for them. "I have to try to get to her," I protested. "There must be another way."

"There will be," he said, and it sounded like a vow. "Once you are safe."

Footfalls came closer. Regret coursed through me, but he was right.

I slapped my hand into his and we fled as fast as our staggering and slipping would allow.

An alleyway. A yawning, open gate. We flickered through patches of arctic shadow and wan lantern light, Rosser turning each corner as if he'd known these streets his whole life. Only once did he hesitate, coming up short against a warehouse's huge double doors. Then he sprinted across the street, bundling me down another alley and up a flight of exterior stairs.

A bridge stretched high over the street, bracketed by buildings at either end. We flattened ourselves against the walls on our side, holding our breaths as pirates sprinted through the streets below. Usti soldiers followed them a second later, bellowing and cracking off a pair of musket shots. Pirates whooped and fired back.

Frigid wind bit at my exposed skin as we crept across the bridge and I wilted, panting, into the gloom on the other side.

"Where?" I only had breath for one word.

"The shipyards," Rosser wheezed, nodding to where the bridge passed around the building and out of sight. Sweat sheened his face despite the bitter cold, and his cheeks, above his beard, were burned red. "Right there."

"Why?"

"Ghistings." He straightened, panting. "Figureheads, for the ships. They will hide you in the Other. From Sooths, at least for a time. Lirr is so close, I fear it may not work. But there is no other hope."

Ghistings, hide me from Sooths like Lirr? Like Samuel himself? Demery had mentioned Juliette concealing me after the attack, but I hadn't understood until now the extent and uses of that power.

We hastened along the bridge, which joined the top of a wall around the back of the building. On one side, the backs of warehouses cast the shadow of winches, pulleys and ropes. On the other side, the wall dropped down into Hesten's vast shipyards, descending all the way to the frozen waters of the bay and the distant bulwark of ancient, sheltering stone walls.

Ships of various sizes slept in cradles, some nearly finished, others looking like the ribs of felled giants, topped with fresh snow. Masts cut up into the bruised sky, sailless and spiderwebbed with ropes. Masses of timber and other materials were stacked everywhere beneath canvas and numerous buildings lay dark, waiting for warmer days and a flood of hands and shipwrights.

But the ghistings? They were not asleep. My eyes flew towards a flutter of life, hidden behind the walls of a stone warehouse.

A gate barred our path. Rosser kicked it open and I ducked through, preceding him down a staircase to ground level. We joined a badly maintained path through waist-deep drifts of snow and were halfway across the yard before I wondered where the guards were. But there were gunshots in the streets—their attention wasn't in here.

The warehouse rose above us and our path ended at a heavy door. Rosser growled, jiggling the padlock and scanning for another entrance.

I ran ahead, peering around the side of the building. A smaller door sulked in the shadows.

"There!" I pointed.

Rosser passed me, eyeing the barrier. Without further deliberation he threw his shoulder into it. The impact echoed loud in the quiet, but the door didn't move.

"Together," I said, arranging myself next to him and bracing my boots in the snow.

He looked at me, a grin ghosting across his face, then he nodded.

We slammed into the barrier at the same time. It gave with a crack—loud and sudden, but that couldn't be helped. We plunged into a darkness so rife with the *otherworldly* that I choked.

We stumbled to a halt, panting and stomping. A slice of twilit night spilled around Rosser and I, along with a gust of wintery air and scudding snow.

The light half illuminated Rosser's face. He smiled between gasps. "You should be safe here. For now."

I nodded. The presences of the ghistings, still hidden in the dark, gathered around me like a heavy fog. It smothered my awareness of the outside world and dampened my fear; it felt like the Wold. It felt like home.

But as Rosser moved back to the door, apprehension nudged me. I didn't trust him or want him to stay. But the thought of being here alone was…

Sister.

The murmur sliced through my rambling thoughts. Deeper in the warehouse, I made out the speaker—a huge, anthropomorphic figurehead. The scent of wood, sap and oils hung in the air despite the cold, and shavings crunched beneath my feet.

"I am going after Lirr." Rosser's voice pried into my ears.

Sister.

"Now?"

"Yes, he lost our trail, but he is too close." There was a question in his eyes as he looked at me. "I can come back for you, once he is dead."

I knew his words should mean more to me than they did, but I was a stranger in my own head.

Sister.

"Can you hear them?" I asked.

Rosser followed the direction of my gaze, then looked back at my face, new lines of concern appearing. "No. I have to go, Mary."

I nodded without a word. Rosser followed my gaze one last time, the shadow deepening between his brows, then he stepped into the night.

"Wait." My thoughts snagged and I reached into my pocket. I held out the Mereish coin. "Take this."

His expression slackened, the dark circles beneath his eyes twitching in renewed fatigue. Then he plucked the coin from my palm. I barely felt his fingers, my skin was so cold.

"Thank you," he said. Unease flashed across his face, then he saluted with his fist closed about the coin, and retreated into the night. "I will return."

I turned back to the figureheads and closed the broken door. Darkness wrapped around me but I didn't have the presence of mind to fear it. The murmurs filled my mind.

Sister, they said.

"Siblings," I answered, because the word felt right.

I began to move through them, and as I went, specters formed of unnatural light, highlighting the curves and edges of their figureheads. The face of a nude warrior-saint looked down upon me as I trailed past, his eyes as glossy and empty as Harpy's. Another nearly identical pair of eyes surveyed me from above the carved maw of a dragon, the spectral reflection of its head ducking down to sniff me as I passed. Another saint with bare breasts and the legs of a lizard looked down her nose at me, spear and staff crossed above her head. A stylized wolf leered. A forgotten god of the sea smiled with barnacle teeth.

The voices came again, and their glossy eyes watched.

Sister. Sister. Sister.

Time slipped into irrelevance. I forgot I was cold, and my shivering ceased. The ghistings appeared fascinated by me—they asked me questions, which I answered, though I couldn't remember what we said.

Eventually, the wolf slipped out of her figurehead and began to prowl around my skirts. She considered me, opal eyes sifting through flesh and blood and bone and looking... deeper.

Free us.

Her words anchored in my mind, clear and precise and compelling. *Free us. Free us with fire.*

The door crashed open. The ghistings vanished and I spun to see newcomers, bundled in landsman's clothes. One had a dragonfly lantern in his hand, another a cudgel. Guards.

Usti words assaulted me. I stepped back, disorientation replaced with genuine misunderstanding. And their volume—Saint, they were loud. We'd certainly attract attention. If Lirr was as close as Samuel had said...

"I'm not Usti," I protested, speaking just loud enough to be heard. "Please quiet down!"

"What are you doing here?" someone demanded in accented Aeadine, fae lanternlight filling her indignant expression. "You're not allowed to be here! How did you get in?"

"What are you wearing?" another asked, more heavily accented.

Cold leapt back to my awareness, and with it, remembrance of how I was dressed—in a party ensemble, panniers wide, hair falling from its pins. I must look ridiculous, hiding in the warehouse like this.

"There were gunshots in the streets," I replied, straightening my shoulders. "I ran. Please be quiet!"

Usti scoffing and curses were the only response. I licked my lips, quickly navigating the situation. I had moments before they forced me to leave, and I couldn't let that happen.

But the situation was already far beyond my control.

Gunshots rang out. Two of the guards went down in heaps and the last turned, lantern swinging. The butt of a musket caved in his face with a nauseating crunch.

More forms flooded the doorway and surrounded me in the dark. Lirr came last, swift and brusque.

I blinked. Samuel claimed to have injured Lirr, but though there was a gash in his coat, he showed no signs of pain.

Stooping, the pirate picked up the guard's fallen dragonfly lantern and opened its door with a slow, considerate care that seemed entirely out of place. The small creatures immediately flew free, streaking off and taking their glow with them.

In the new and deeper darkness, Lirr looked from me to the figureheads.

Brother, the ghistings whispered, reverence in their voice.

"Siblings," Lirr replied.

⊸ PART THREE ⊸

AN EXCERPT FROM:

A HISTORY OF GHISTLORE AND THE BLESSED; THOSE BOUND TO THE SECOND WORLD AND THE POWER THEREIN

THE STORMWALL IS a perpetual storm which divides the Winter Sea from the eternal ice of the far north. The origins of the Wall are unknown and steeped in folklore. Various theories have been put forward in recent decades, from fault lines in the fabric of the worlds to the adverse effects of sorcery, but as traversing the Wall is improbable at best, little can be proven. However, it is generally agreed that the storm is not a natural phenomenon and has deep ties to the Other.

THIRTY-THREE

A Good Name

SAMUEL

The shipyards had burned, and Lirr was gone. After a night of futile searching and dodging musket fire, I stood in the shipyard gate as Usti soldiers flowed in and out. The yard was in ruins, all ice and char under the weak morning sun. I walked through the crumbled ghisting warehouse, now little more than blackened stone walls. Every figurehead was ash, their ghistings freed and long vanished—back into the Other, or to a Ghistwold.

Mary's corpse was not there. Blackened bones lay under a fresh dusting of snow, but they were not hers. She was a light on the horizon, fading with Lirr at the edge of my curse's sight.

Now we had been summoned to the palace—we, being the newly minted Captain Fisher and her first officer, Samuel Rosser. Slader was dead, and despite how troubled our relationship had been, I felt no relief. For all his faults he had been an experienced captain, and without him I was unsure what *Hart* would become. It was not that I doubted Fisher, but she was still young as captains went. So, for that matter, was I.

"One of *your* people, a man who you, Captain Fisher, have been commissioned to apprehend, and you, Captain Ellas, should have stopped, has orchestrated an attack on my soil." Queen Inara's voice echoed off the expanse of marble floor between her throne and our small forms, filling the vaulted ceilings and cutting through shafts of light from the high, narrow windows. Colorful tapestries of ancient Usti gods and saints hung between each window, but otherwise the space was adorned solely by the carved throne, inlaid with enough black pearls to buy Aeadine.

The queen stood before it. Her gown was blood red, her waist narrow and her panniers modest, a beautiful, middle-aged woman: regal, but not overdone. Though she addressed Benedict's scar-faced Captain Ellas, Captain Fisher and Captain Demery, her gaze included Benedict and I.

I straightened under her scrutiny, though it was not easy. My head ached, and my muscles were spent. The Mereish coin now lay safe within my pocket, but worry for Mary and guilt over my failure to stop Lirr had poisoned my sleep. Over and over again, I remembered slashing his stomach. I remembered the shock of victory, the awe and the certainty that the wound would finally stop him. The Usti would collect his body, and I would claim the credit I was due. I had known I might have to fight for that credit, that there was a chance Demery would not vouch for me—but Mary had been in danger, and I had never considered that my blow might not keep Lirr down.

Perhaps I had been wrong and I had only cut clothing, not skin. That doubt only made my shame greater. Instead of staying at the palace, instead of ensuring my commission was fulfilled, I had run off with Mary Firth, and now they were both lost.

"The death of Captain Slader is regrettable, but Silvanus Lirr will still be apprehended." Queen Inara stared down Fisher and Ellas now, her gaze unyielding. She spoke in Usti, which Benedict had never been good at. But even he startled when the queen added, "Captain Ellas, you will join Captain Fisher in this venture. It is but a small diversion from your usual cruise, as I understand it. The peace between our nations, after all, is of the utmost importance. What would these seas be without Usti force? Lawless. And her peoples? In poverty. We bring salt from Sunjai, saltpeter from our southern holdings. We bring iron from Isman."

Neither Ellas nor Fisher looked at one another, their thoughts hidden by measured expressions.

Benedict, meanwhile, shot me a glance. It was an instinct, I knew, and as soon as he did it he forced himself to look away. He would do the same when we were children—looking for cues as to how he ought to act and feel, when his own conscience could not tell him.

I ignored him.

"It will be done, Your Majesty," Ellas said with a bow that barely wrinkled her fine-pressed blue coat. From her broad tone and commanding posture, she had decided to speak for both herself and Fisher, an assumed superiority that earned her a narrow glance from my new captain. "As you say, the peace between our nations is of the highest priority."

"Good. You will also be joined by Captain James Elijah Demery," the queen added in a voice that forbade questioning. "I have issued him a Letter of Marque. On my seas, he is a chartered vassal and untouchable, is that clear?"

Neither Ellas nor Demery responded immediately, but the pirate captain watched the queen with more familiarity than I thought wise—an easy posture and a warm quirk at the corner of his mouth.

Inara filled the silence. "I understand you have a means of tracking Lirr, Captain Fisher?"

Fisher nodded without looking at me. "I do, Your Majesty."

"Very well. Captain Demery has informed me he has means to navigate the seas beyond the Stormwall." The queen paused after the last word, taking in every sharp breath and stifled murmur in the hall. "Together with Captain Ellas's Stormsinger, do you believe you can succeed in this endeavor? Or shall I rectify the matter myself and make my displeasure known to your betters?"

"It will be done, Your Majesty," Ellas assured the other woman, bowing again. "You need not trouble yourself further."

"Good." The queen turned, descended the dais in a cascade of skirts, and swept out of the room.

∽

I followed Fisher into the quiet of Slader's cabin and closed the door.
The captain himself was laid out in a shroud on the table, ready to
be dropped into the waves as soon as we reached open water. The
air smelled of tobacco and old blood.

Fisher pulled off her hat and stared at the body without seeing it.
She tucked a few stray hairs behind her ear and looked at me. "Are
you fit for this? Being my first officer?"

I pulled the coin Mary had returned to me from my pocket and
showed it to her. "I am."

She looked surprised, but pleased. "Good. However, smothering
your gift is not what I need, nor will it fix you." She laced her arms
loosely over her chest. "I still need you to track Mary Firth."

"I can track Mary." I came to stand across the table from her.
Slader's shrouded corpse lay between us, no longer judging me, and
I felt stronger for it. Fisher was right—stifling my curse with the
talisman would not fix me. But if I could sleep easily, even for one
night, it would be worth it. I would survive, as I had for the last
twenty years. I would stop Lirr, rescue Mary, and reclaim my good
name long before madness took me.

"However, I can track Lirr now too," I told her. "We will stop him,
Captain. You and I. Without Slader."

It was the first time I had addressed her as captain. She lifted her
gaze and I saw a flash of doubt there.

She immediately hardened it into a determined squint. "Very well.
Ensure we're resupplied and ready for open sea, Mr. Rosser."

∽

The next day our convoy of pirates, pirate hunters and Navy sailed
out of Hesten. As soon as we cleared the harbor, we delivered Slader

to the waves with the piping of the bosun's whistle. Then went on our way, sails full of Ellas's Stormsinger's wind.

Seeing *Defiance* off our larboard, with Benedict standing upon her decks, was something I did not grow used to in the coming days. The weather mage's songs frayed my nerves, and even when I retired to my cabin to sleep, they wheedled through the hull into my dreams. Mary sung them there, in a dark wold and a flurry of snow. I set my coin aside and reached out to her, once, but the distance between us was vast and full of monsters.

Two days out of Hesten we dropped anchor off an island, which Ellas claimed was the last solid land before the Stormwall. Ice rimmed her shores and crowned her low, rocky mountains, but there was life here, and fresh water. Crewmen rowed ashore to haul barrels to a natural spring, scattering hardy shorebirds in thundering clouds and earning indignant bellows from shaggy, rust-red sea lions.

I caught the crack and flash of muskets as I climbed aboard *Defiance* with Captain Fisher. A sea lion's dying roar echoed across the water, followed by more bays and barks as its companions fled into the sea.

I stepped up on deck and paused to watch distant forms of crewmen converge on the creature's huge body, my lips pressed into a line.

"Not a hunter, I take it?"

I looked up to see Captain Ellas watching me. Fisher stood between us, her expression dispassionately polite. Benedict stood on Ellas's other side, absently running his eyes over Fisher in a way I did not like.

He met my gaze, gave a subtle grin, and clasped one hand behind his back.

"I hunt when the need arises," I replied to Ellas, offering the captain a short bow. "Creatures or men. Captain, thank you for your invitation."

"Of course." Ellas smiled. The expression did little to soften her hard face. "Come, it would be a pity if our dinner grew cold."

Soon after, we sat down to a fine spread in the grand cabin. I expected Demery and his mate to be there, along with Ellas's other lieutenants and officers, but there were only four chairs, and four plates laid down by an aproned servant. Ornate glass lanterns were set on the table between platters of roast meat, vegetables and breads—each glass so packed with pulsating dragonflies that the creatures had no space to move.

"Captain Demery will not be joining us tonight?" Fisher inquired, the picture of decorum as she laid a napkin on her lap.

"No, no," Ellas replied, smiling benevolently. "No need to sully ourselves with the presence of pirates."

I settled in my own chair. For once, I was inclined to agree with Ellas, but my dreamer's senses prickled.

Benedict filled our cups with wine. He topped up mine last and, noticing my gaze on the nearest dragonfly lantern, reached out to flick the glass. The dragonflies took flight in a clash of wings and renewed, golden light.

"Must remind them of their purpose every so often," he murmured, then sat beside me. Across the table, he caught Fisher's gaze and added in a pleasant rumble, "Captain Fisher, what a pleasure it is to properly meet you. I do regret Captain Slader's demise, but I am reassured to see my brother serve a captain he so obviously... admires."

There was an undertone to his words, a suggestion that irked me and I knew Fisher would not miss. But we had been associates long enough to have heard it before.

"Yes," Ellas agreed, taking up her fork and knife and slicing through a fat, steaming potato. "Slader will be sorely missed. We were friends, as I'm sure you gathered."

Fisher took up her own knife and, leaning forward, carved into a thick slab of beef. Blood and juices sluiced onto the platter and the scent of the meat, rosemary and onion wafted towards me. "Yes. Did you know one another long?"

Ellas nodded. "We went to the academy together. That was some... what must it be now, thirty years ago?"

I looked up from my wine. "The Naval Academy at Ismoathe?"

The elder captain took up her own cup and smiled at me over it. "Of course. We forged a friendship, then an alliance that carried on into the war. When the Fleet disbanded and he took his honorable discharge, I was sad to see him go.

"But that is behind us." Ellas sat a little straighter in her chair. I saw the shadow of grief pass over her eyes, but she did not let it linger. "It's my hope that you, Captain Fisher, will honor his memory by maintaining our alliance."

Fisher laid down her utensils and surveyed the other woman. "What do you mean by 'alliance,' precisely?"

"Silvanus Lirr is a plague upon these seas, we all know that," Ellas said. "And he is strong, and unlikely to be brought down by a single vessel. Slader approached me, when we met at sea before Hesten, and he offered me a share in the prize in return for my assistance."

Benedict, unfazed by the tension at the table, speared potatoes and sprouts with a single-mindedness belied by his distracted eyes. He was listening.

Fisher said, "Captain Slader never spoke of this to me."

Ellas's smile was apologetic. "I am sure he intended to. He is not one to reveal his plans prematurely. But there is more. In Hesten, Slader heard the rumors Demery's crew was spreading about 'Bretton's Hoard,' this great treasure north of the Stormwall. As you can imagine, it caught our attention, and we met to discuss it."

I recalled how finely Slader had dressed in Hesten, with his pale blue frock coat and his wig. So, he'd gone to meet Ellas, and very intentionally kept Fisher and I in the dark. I had not even known *Defiance* was in port until I saw Benedict at the Frolick.

There was always the chance that Ellas was lying. But Slader had never been an amiable man, always private and calculated, so perhaps he really had been scheming behind our backs.

From the look on Fisher's face, she was as suspicious as I.

"The sea north of the Stormwall is unclaimed and Bretton was a pirate," Benedict put in, unnecessarily. "Thus, no country has a claim on the Hoard."

"Precisely." Ellas raised her wine to him in salute and took a sip before she elaborated. "The prize is more than enough for the both of us, even if Captain Demery's claims are exaggerated. However, half of *Defiance*'s share will go to Her Majesty Queen Edith. Slader's share faces no such claims. So he and I came to a new arrangement."

"He agreed to conceal a share of the prize for you," Fisher summarized, coolly. "You intend to steal from our queen."

"Our queen has a jeweled piss pot and cleans her teeth with ivory picks," Benedict replied, shucking all pretense at formality. He mirrored Fisher's icy tone, with a dash of his own scorn. "She will survive."

"The funds would go to Aeadine's defenses," I reminded him. "You would be taking money from your brothers and sisters-in-arms, not the queen herself."

Benedict gestured to the spread of fine foods before us and gave me a small, licentious grin. "We shall survive."

"Treason," Fisher stated, throwing the word on the table like a gauntlet. "You are asking us to commit treason with you."

Ellas tilted her head to one side. "Treason is a harsh word."

"A noose is harsh end," Fisher parried. "But that's what lies on the other side of your scheme."

Ellas's expression darkened. She took a long drink of wine—a hunter taking aim. "Where you see nooses and treason, I see opportunity. We will have the glory of taking down Lirr, and a proper reward for our efforts."

"We shall be heroes," Benedict put in. He did not look at me, but I knew he spoke to me all the same. "We will have done the Winter Sea a great service, and I, for one, would not turn down a laurel crown."

The image struck at me, hard and visceral—the applause, the medals, the respect and admiration. Bringing down Lirr remained my best chance to redeem myself. But to do it like this?

Furthermore, Slader's part in this did not sit right with me. He had been a cunning man, but duping the queen seemed a stretch beyond him.

Benedict picked up a loaf of bread and sat back in his chair with all the insouciance of a farmhand at a tavern. He scraped butter onto a knife and slathered it on in smooth, deft movements.

The Other tugged, and bloody red magic glistened around him. I slipped a hand into my pocket, letting my fingers linger just beside the coin, and pushed farther into that other world.

I did not go far, just enough to overlay the scene. Sure enough, Ben's scarlet magic hazed the entire table. It kept the dragonflies in a frenzy. It trickled around Fisher's nose and eyes, seeking, prying, and testing my captain's pliancy. Fisher was holding up well, evidenced by the way Ben's magic passed around her instead of through her, but this was a fragment of his power.

I cursed myself. I ought to have warned her Benedict was a Magni.

No scarlet magic lingered on Ellas. That was a surprise, but little comfort. Benedict only had two motives for anything: whim and personal gain. Just because he was not controlling her now did not mean he had not or would not. Nor did it mean he had not compelled Slader into a deadly alliance.

Naturally, Ellas would know Benedict was a Magni—he had been trained at the academy, as I had—but I doubted she knew how powerful he was. Our uncle had ensured our amplifications remained a closely guarded family secret, and even as schoolboys we had known to hide the limits of our power.

I leaned forward, catching my brother's gaze while the Other still hazed around us. "Ben, stop magicking my captain, please."

Fisher looked over sharply. In the Other, Benedict's power still dusted across her skin like ash-laden smoke.

"Benedict is a Magni," I clarified, still holding my brother's gaze. He looked back at me, inscrutable as a clouded night sky. "But he knows better than to use his power in polite company."

Resentment flared in Benedict's eyes. "Oh? What should I say of your power, dear brother?"

"Come now, enough," Ellas chided lightly. She looked between Fisher and I and fingered her cup of wine. "We are all allies here. You are a mercenary, Captain Fisher, and I know Slader would not have kept you on if you did not share his proclivities. Take my offer, and we'll all traverse the Stormwall, safe and sound."

In the Other, I saw Benedict's power retreat from Fisher. In the physical world, he lifted a piece of bloodied beef to his lips, holding my gaze as he did so. Eyes impassive, he began to chew with slow, measured movements.

"If we do not?" I asked Ellas, eyeing my brother. Despite his displeasure he had obeyed too easily. He had another, more valuable card up his sleeve. I grasped the coin and the Other fully faded.

Ellas noted Benedict's and my continued exchange. "These seas are rough, and no one truly expects all three of our vessels to return."

Color rose in Fisher's cheeks. "Threats will not help your cause."

"They are not threats." Ben surveyed her across the table, folding his hands in his lap—a satisfied fox in a bloodied henhouse. "They are facts. Even if you miraculously find your way home without our aid, there is the matter of James Demery. When he never returns to Usti, who do you think Queen Inara will blame?"

Fisher could not hide her shock this time, and neither could I.

Ellas sat back in her chair and nodded for Ben to go on.

I felt his magic flare again, not overly compelling, but dredging up emotions like long-forgotten dreams—dread, urgency, fear, submission. I steeled myself, but I saw Fisher's expression flicker under the weight of it.

"Ben," I rebuked.

He ignored me.

"Lirr is not the only pirate who will meet justice north of the Stormwall," my twin said, leaning forward. His hungry declarations about spilling the blood of pirates, when we had met before Hesten, rang through my head. "If you fight my good captain and I? James Demery's death will be laid on you, whether or not you live to see the south again. Forget Queen Edith's noose—you shall face the Usti queen's wrath, and be responsible for a diplomatic incident that could upend the balance of the world."

My brother's eyes found mine, giving his last words to me alone. "And *that* will be your legacy, my dear brother."

THIRTY-FOUR

The Fleetbreaker

MARY

My mother's voice guided us through snow so fine it hung suspended in the fog. *Her* fog. She called warm wind over the frigid, icy northern seas, and used it to shroud Lirr's warship from sight of Hesten's ice-crusted walls.

I raked in a shivering breath as Lirr's ship emerged from the miasma. *Nameless*. The vessel was huge, a proper warship with two gun decks and a ghostly figurehead. The figure had no distinct face or form, just a human shape wrapped in windblown cloth.

I drew the cloak I'd been given tighter. The night was eerie, the ship unnerving, and Lirr close enough to touch; but within moments, I'd see my mother again. That knowledge gave me strength and frightened me and dredged up a hundred emotions in between.

Pirates dipped their oars into the water and Lirr stood to grab the bottom of a rope ladder. All the while my mother's voice sang from above. *"But where are your fields and where are your lands, and where in the world does your bridal bed stand? Where in the world does your true love lie, with whom you will live and die?"*

Anne Firth waited on deck, clad in a worn brown coat over worn blue skirts, her chin buried in a scarf and her greying hair bare to the wind. The healthy, working woman's frame I remembered was almost gone, lost to leanness. But that leanness went further than narrow limbs and stark cheekbones. Her eyes, turning towards me now, were devoid of emotion. Even despair. She was a rock in a stream, an iceberg adrift in the Winter Sea.

Her song finished, and my cold and exhaustion faded to irrelevance. It was her. My mother. The woman who had swum with me in millponds and wandered through the Ghistwold on midsummer evenings, sunlight in her hair and her hand enfolding mine. The woman who had ridden away on a rainy day, never to be seen again.

She was here, living and breathing, and looking at me as though I were a stranger on the street. My heart stuttered at the blankness in her eyes, momentarily replacing it with the reactions I had expected— tears, joy, grief, regret. Her crying my name, pulling me into her arms.

She did none of those things. Her eyes lingered on my damp, impractical gown and windburned cheeks, then she turned to Lirr.

"Her cabin is ready," she said and strode away across the deck. Fog immediately obscured her.

My eyes burned as I watched the murk close between us, part of me asserting that this couldn't be my mother. My mother loved me. My mother protected me. But this woman? She had barely seen me.

Lirr's fingers took my upper arm and I squinted at him, battling for composure and control. I needed to brace for whatever was coming next.

"Give her time," he said lowly. He spoke in my ear, his voice a consoling, nearly paternal rumble. "I think in her heart she'd given up on ever seeing you again. I think, perhaps, she thinks it would have been for the better."

I swallowed tightly. "Would it have?"

The pirates began to chant, and the wood beneath my feet shuddered as the anchor started to rise. Lirr's hand left my arm, but instead of stepping away from him, I looked into his face, waiting for my answer.

"You're here for the good of us all," Lirr replied. He nodded to his crew as their voices rose in time and the rattle of the anchor chain battered the fog. "You and Tane."

Tane. The name resonated, strange and yet oddly familiar. Hadn't Harpy said that, once?

"Tane. What is that?" The question left my lips before the way he'd used the word struck me. As if it were a name. A person.

He shifted to look directly down at me. The breadth of his shoulders and his pensive expression filled my vision, blocking off the deck and the fog and the presence of my mother, somewhere on the forecastle. His lips held the hint of a frown, and his grey eyes a mild, distant intensity.

"You remember her," he said, as if testing the statement.

"Tane?" I clarified. The intensity of his gaze unsettled me, as did the revelation that Tane was a person. "No. Harpy said it, once."

"Ah." Disappointment flickered through Lirr's face. "What else did she say?"

"Lirr." My mother's voice cut through the fog. My heart fluttered and we both turned, looking up at the shadow that was the Fleetbreaker. "Not now. Leave her."

Leave her. The command in my mother's voice shocked me as much as Lirr's obedience. He gave me a look that promised our conversation was not over, then waved to a nearby pirate and passed me off. He climbed the forecastle stairs to Anne's side.

My mother sang a quick line and the wind picked up. A whistle piped, sailors began to chant and haul, and several sails opened with a thunder of canvas.

My new handler tugged me towards the open grating midship. Just as the pirate and I disappeared into the companionway, the fog lightened, revealing my mother and Lirr standing on the forecastle. They were conspiratorially close, their backs to me, he leaning down to listen to whatever she had to say.

Then the shadows and lanternlight below decks cut them off, and I was in the belly of the ship, prisoner once again.

They were allies, Lirr and my mother. I couldn't conclude anything else, standing in the quiet cabin where I'd been stowed.

My prison was a temporary thing, thin paneled walls constructed around one of the long cannons near the stern of the second gun deck. The weapon was bound in its cradle behind a locked port, with a lonely hammock swinging overhead in the light of a small, iron stove.

I sat on the gun, its metal frigid through my skirts, and wrapped my arms around myself. How could my mother and Lirr be allies? What had he done to her to break her, to bring her to the point where the presence of her own daughter hadn't drawn a second glance?

Was it his magic, overriding my mother's will as he and Benedict had done to me, back at the palace?

But it was he who'd answered to her, not the other way around.

I clawed through childhood recollections and turned over what I'd seen today, trying to rationalize the two sets of memories. I couldn't—my mother and this woman were different people.

But sixteen years had passed. I'd been a child when she left, sheltered from my parents' pasts and the Winter Sea by village life and the Wold. Maybe this was who she'd been all along.

I was not a child anymore, but I felt like one right now—small and confused, frightened and unsure. I resented that feeling, but it tormented me as the ship hit open sea, water began to roar past the hull, and my mother's frigid, ensorcelled wind pried through the cracks around the hatch.

"It's an act," I finally said. Speaking the words aloud strengthened me, pushing my fear back to a manageable level. "It's an act. She's doing this to protect me. She has a plan."

I just had to figure out what that was.

Hours crawled past. I fidgeted and paced around my little cabin, eyeing the door and hammock. I was exhausted and my muscles shook with cold and fatigue, but I didn't consider sleeping. Someone would come for me soon—likely Lirr, if I'd understood the promise in his eyes.

It was evening before the door opened. I straightened from my seat on the cannon and faced two pirates. They were both women, one younger than I and the other a few years older. Both wore trousers like everyone else aboard, though one had a posture that betrayed stays beneath her heavy clothes and the other a slouch that suggested she'd never worn them at all. They were armed too, one with a long knife and the other with a hatchet.

I stared at them, remembering the horrors aboard *Juliette* and at the Frolick. These women looked so normal, so human. How could they have participated in such atrocities?

"Come with us."

I did not move, nor speak. But leaving my cabin put me closer to my mother, so I eventually unfolded from my perch and followed them into the close, dark corridor.

They led me through a deck populated by swinging hammocks, up to the first gun deck, then back again to the stern of the ship. Small rooms, narrow passageways and multiple ladders threatened to disorient me, but I mapped every step.

We passed through a door. Heat and the scent of baking bread struck me as soon as the barrier opened, identifying the galley before I saw the rows of cupboards and barrels. There was a steep ladder-stair to one side, capped by a hatch, and another beneath it leading down. A half-barrel of steaming water stood before the stove.

I looked at my guides in confusion. "A bath?"

"Aye." The younger woman pointed to a stool piled with clothes. "Bathe and put those on. They're not so fancy as you seem used to." With that, she eyed my ruined gown with amusement. "But your tits won't freeze off."

I instinctively covered my breasts. "I… Fine."

They retreated through the galley door. Just before it closed, the older one stuck her head in. "I'd be quick about it, lass. Cook was none too pleased being evicted, but all opposites at the thought of you being naked in his kitchen."

They closed the door, sparing me the need to reply. I patted my cheeks to dispel their sudden redness and looked at the bath, tempting and hot. This felt too kind. There had to be a hitch, a trap.

I glanced at the ladder and the hatch above it. It didn't appear to be locked, so I doubted it led anywhere useful. Still, was it worth trying to slip off and find my mother, or should I take advantage of the bath and clothes?

Immediate need won out. My mother would have to see me, eventually, and the pirate had been right; I was freezing in my current gown, and I could manage my situation more efficiently once I was clean and warm, not to mention out of my wide panniers. I'd also feel considerably less exposed without my bodice's gaping neckline.

The bath was heavenly, though at any moment I expected a burly cook to saunter in, or my supposed guards to open the door and torment me in some way. Working quickly, I found a sliver of soap and scrubbed every inch of myself, from toes to scalp, then dried before the fire.

My new clothes were quite nice. There was a short shift, a clean pair of stays and a man's shirt, all of which I tucked under two layers of wool trousers and a belt. Over that I shrugged a heavy, double-breasted coat, slit at the hip, lightly embroidered and forest green. I buttoned it from waist to collar and spent my remaining moments in the galley hovering before the stove, trying to speed the drying of my hair.

It was then, with my head upside down in front of the grating, that I heard running feet. I looked at the deck above me, half blinded by damp waves of hair, and listened.

Shouts. More footsteps. My eyes dragged to the ladder just as someone ran across the hatch. They issued a desperate obscenity as they went, and their voice—a voice from a nightmare of two days tied to a mast—made the warmth flee my cheeks.

I knew that voice. My shock faded into grim need, I grabbed a fire poker and made for the ladder.

I lifted the hatch just as John Randalf hit the end of a dark passageway, clad in nothing but trousers and a dirty shirt. He kicked at a locked door with a bare, frantic foot, a candle lantern swinging madly in one hand. He swore, each word punctuated by an impact.

"Saint's. Bloody. Fucking. Crown!" One last kick and the door broke in. He vanished through, leaving me skulking in the hatchway like a suspicious groundhog.

What was Randalf doing here? Alive? It had been over a month since Lirr burned his ship. I'd seen his crew gutted, strung from the yards and roasted alive. I'd heard them. Smelled them.

Had I been mistaken? I'd never seen Randalf without a wig and this man wore none, but his face and voice…

I had to know. I peered back down into the galley, but the main door was still closed. My guards must have heard the commotion, but retrieving me evidently hadn't been their first thought.

I climbed up into the passageway and closed the hatch. With careful steps I followed the strange man, but no sooner had I reached the doorway than he reappeared.

His feral eyes fell on me and went very, very round.

I leveled the poker at his chest, claiming the space between us. "Why aren't you dead?"

He looked from me to the makeshift weapon, trying to recover himself, and slowly raised his hands. "Where have you been? Hell, it doesn't matter. Help me, woman, and I can protect you."

Protect me? I pressed the tip of the poker into his chest. "My *name* is Mary Firth, and if you haven't forgotten, you bought and tortured me. Why would I help you? Why are you here?"

Randalf's eyes flicked over my shoulder to the empty passage— footsteps and shouts drew closer with every passing moment—but at the tone of my voice his gaze dragged to me, and he looked cautious for the first time.

"I should stick this in your belly and leave you to die." I meant it. The words felt dangerous on my tongue, hot and deadly and primed with potential for violence that both satisfied and unsettled me.

He heard my sincerity too. He inched back from the poker and I followed him, keeping the point flush with his bedraggled shirt. My trained hand did not waver.

"I'm not the only prisoner," Randalf spat. I heard an echo of the man I remembered then, coldly ordering me starved and left to the wind. "I'm sure you've heard their cries? There's a hundred of us in that hold, witch. A hundred!"

"Why?" I asked. I hadn't heard anything of the sort, but I hadn't been here long. "Why would Lirr keep so many prisoners?"

Footsteps thundered closer and pirates shouted, coordinating their search.

"Saint knows!" Randalf hissed, as if that could keep us from being found. "He feeds us, even sends the surgeon to us, but he's never breathed a word of why. We haven't time for this! Help me, damn you! If you won't help me, let me go! Are we still near the Usti coast?"

I held two thoughts, one on each side of a scale, and weighed them.

One was the memory of bitter cold, and the pain of bloodied wrists. The other was a hold full of prisoners, trapped in the dark. One was vivid and real, sharp with remembered pain; the other was the babbling of a despicable man. Even if it was true—and I would find out if it was—Randalf's part in my story had ended a long time ago.

Pirates thundered past our passageway and slowed. Lanternlight swelled.

"Fleetbreaker?" someone called, deferential.

I looked over my shoulder. The pirate, a small man, startled when he realized I wasn't my mother. But when I spoke, I sounded just like her.

"Your quarry is here."

MARY

Lirr's pirates dragged Randalf into a grand cabin. A balcony stretched the length of the stern, vaguely revealed by bottle-bottom windows. The small panes, each lined with black wrought iron, diffused the dawn light over the rest of the room.

There was a long, central dining table, a writing desk, ranks of heavy chests and bulkheads laden with prizes from every corner of the world. There were swords and flintlocks, pieces of armor, small round shields painted with bright colors of Sunjai, and various eccentricities I didn't have time to identify. But it was obvious that Lirr liked his talismans, and his travels had been broad.

Despite these myriad distractions, two things demanded my focus as Randalf was shoved to his knees, surrounded by a gang of six pirates.

One was the figureheads, or rather, the fragments of them. Shattered and charred, they were arranged on the bulkheads between the trophies—half of a roaring lion's face, a reaching hand, the outline of a splintered sword, the curve of a feminine hip. But I sensed no ghistings attached to them.

The other was my mother. She stood before the windows. The light filtering through the foggy glass was pale, pastel and cool on her skin apart from a shaft of pure arctic light that cut across her face through an open pane. It bleached the darkness of her eyelashes and softened the lines around her eyes. She looked almost ethereal then: the sorceress. The Fleetbreaker.

Her eyes fell on me but she didn't move, arms laced loosely under her breasts and heavy coat open to show her worn bodice.

It's an act, I reminded myself, but her lack of emotion was a fist in my gut, and Randalf's impending punishment did little to soothe me. I drew the same blankness she wore over myself and stood off to the side.

"I offered you mercy." Lirr stood in front of his prisoner. He, too, had cleaned up since our departure from Hesten and now wore a fresh shirt, tucked into breeches. His coat and waistcoat lay over a chair and his brown hair was bound into a short braid at the nape of his neck. "I fed and kept you. This rebellion, Captain Randalf, it does not befit one with your grand destiny."

"Destiny?" Randalf choked. "Destiny! To be butchered? Dragged off like the others? I heard their screams, you bastard, there's no *mercy* here. What did you do with them? Eat them? Sacrifice them?" Randalf's voice rose into a shriek at the last words, hitching and tumbling into hysterics. "I heard them, I heard them! What did you do?"

My skin prickled in foreboding. Lips sealed and heart thumping, I glanced from Lirr to my mother, searching for any clue as to what Randalf meant.

I saw little concern in my mother's face. Only regret, and a distant preoccupation. We might as well have been somewhere else, her and I, somewhere devoid of pirates and Randalf and his looming death.

Because death, I was sure, was where this encounter would end. There was a predatory calm about Lirr, combined with a flippancy that told me how little he cared for Randalf's life. The man's supposed destiny, though? That riled our captor.

"You heard this young man's screams, perhaps?" Lirr gestured to one of the half-dozen pirates still present in the room, and they came forward.

The pirate was none other than the young sailor who'd taunted and fed me back on the deck of Randalf's ship, with his blond hair and lean smile.

He didn't look like a prisoner. His cheeks were flushed with health and his expression was easy as he observed his former captain. He was a pirate now, armed and arrayed as well as anyone else in Lirr's crew.

But I sensed more than that, as I looked at him, and somewhere in the back of my mind a key slipped into a hidden lock. I blinked, and something... changed. Was the young man's outline blurred, or was it a trick of my eyes?

My other senses shifted too. If I hadn't known better, I would have said I felt the presence of a ghisting, here in the cabin. Was Lirr's ship ghisting here, hazing the air around Randalf's former crewman?

I searched the cabin for other hints of the spectral creature. But though my sense of the creature grew stronger, I didn't see it, and when I looked back at the crewman, the haze was gone.

"Lewis!" Randalf gaped at the younger man, until his surprise transformed into rage. "You traitorous little shit, you filthy—"

"I'm no traitor," the sailor replied to Randalf, though his eyes were on Lirr. His speech was different from when I'd met him, I realized, his tone and diction subtly altered. "Captain, may I show him?"

At a nod from his new captain, the young man began to remove his outer clothes. His scarf came first, then he unbuttoned his coat and the front of his shirt. He settled his shoulders back and pulled the collar wide, revealing a scar on his chest. Right over his heart—a knot of opalescent, ruined flesh, pale as the moon.

My eyes flew to my mother. I remembered a dozen nights in a millpond, learning to swim. I remembered the very same scar, over her own heart.

Anne Firth turned back to the windows and began to sing, gentle and low. I couldn't make out her words, but the wind eased, and the tilting of the deck steadied. There was preparation in that action, and it chilled me.

"I've received a blessing, Captain Randalf," Lewis told his former captain, letting the collar of his shirt fall back into place. The scar disappeared. "I wish you hadn't sacrificed your own."

Whatever control Randalf had managed to keep so far, shattered. He tried to battle to his feet, and though most of his words were vulgarities, I shared his disbelief.

"What is he talking about?" I asked Lirr.

"Do you see them?" Lirr pointed to the pieces of figureheads on the bulkhead. "Their husks. They once housed ghistings, Mary, but not anymore."

I had no idea what connection this had to Lewis and Randalf, but I didn't let my confusion show. "Ghistings are bound to their wood. How could they leave it?"

Lewis and several of the other crew turned to watch me, and a chill ran up my spine. That sense of a ghisting's presence prickled at me again, but stronger. Diverging, perhaps. Separating.

Suspicion awoke at the back of my mind, nudging me like a thief testing locked shutters.

"Where did the ghistings go?" I asked, very carefully.

Randalf made it to his feet. "You madman, you bloody damn mad f—"

Lirr's patience with the other captain came to an end. He closed on the prisoner in a stride, grabbed his hair, and pulled a knife.

The next time Randalf screamed, Lirr shoved the knife into his mouth and held it there. Randalf's shrieks took on a fevered pitch. Blood plumed, lips split like butter, teeth jarred, and his tongue divided.

I staggered back, covering my mouth to stop from vomiting. My mother continued to stare out of the window, unaffected.

Then there was too much blood for screams. Randalf choked. The knife cut deeper as he shuddered but Lirr still held it in place with a remorseless, steady hand. I felt his Magni sorcery then, reaching towards the prisoner.

Randalf quietened. He raked in thin, wheezing breaths through his nose. Blood ran over his lips, chin, throat and clothes in a steady, scarlet trail, but he did not move again. His eyelids fluttered closed in dazed, ensorcelled contentedness.

"The most common way to free a ghisting is to destroy the wood in which it lives," Lirr told me, knife still held, Randalf still bleeding. "By fire, or great lengths of time. Most people know this. Once its wooden flesh is gone, the ghisting is set adrift, eventually to return to the Other."

Lirr's eyes ran to the wall and its array of broken figureheads. "But some do not wish to return to the Other. Some want more of this mortal world, of flesh and blood and desire. The strongest and most determined can even leave their wooden flesh before it's consumed, and pass on into other hosts, with help. These pieces here on the wall, they're remains of several such ghistings."

My skin crawled and my mind inched closer to understanding, but I walled it out. No. He couldn't mean…

Lirr continued, "The Mereish know more of these things, but the Aeadine? Our ignorance is both willful and pitiable, but I will change that. Mary, have you heard of the *ghiseau*?"

I recalled the Mereish pirate captain, throwing the word at me when Demery took her ship.

"I've heard the word," I said.

"Do you remember what it means?"

"No." I fought not to watch as Randalf had entered another choking fit, eyes still sagging with bewitched calm, but Lirr appeared unbothered. "Ghisting?"

"It's what the Mereish call the High Captains of their fleets," Lirr replied. "The ones whose flesh and blood are bound with a ghisting. The ones who share their bones." With this, he pulled the bloody knife from Randalf's mouth and used it to point to Lewis and his other crewmen. Randalf sagged forward, vomiting blood.

"And that is the blessing I give to those who please me," Lirr continued. He toed Randalf with a boot and frowned, his displeasure clear. "Whether or not they value such a gift. But this one… he's gone too far, even for my mercy."

Lirr's words were as unsettling, just as horrific, as the sight and smell of the blood. There was no lie in his eyes, nor those of his crew.

Lirr believed it. They believed it.

They believed they'd been bonded with ghistings.

I glanced at my mother. She still stared out the window, humming, but her fingers dug into her upper arms like claws.

"You're saying…" I struggled, forcing myself to look back at Lirr and his dripping knife. Blood clung to his fingers, pooling around his fingernails and in the creases of his knuckles. "That ghistings can inhabit human beings? That you… do this to people?"

Lirr smiled, but it wasn't a malevolent thing. He took a step closer to me, reaching to cup my neck in one, warm hand.

I didn't let myself flinch, even though my insides screamed to strike out and run.

"Yes," he said gently. "I do. My most favored crewmembers are *ghiseau* already, though the bulk of them have yet to be bonded. They wait for the great treasure beyond the Stormwall. But you'll remember all of that, I'm sure. Won't you, Tane?"

He was calling *me* Tane. My eyes filled with his, deep and full and rimmed with grey, and the scent of him surrounded me: cold, salt, musky soap and smoke.

"Who is Tane?" I whispered, though somewhere deep inside me, I already knew the answer.

In the center of the cabin, Randalf vomited on the deck a second time.

Irritation passed through Lirr's eyes. He shifted his grip on the knife and moved back to the prisoner.

"Get him on his feet."

The pirates complied. With perfunctory ceremony, Lirr pressed his knife low into the man's gut. "You were offered greatness, and you rejected it," he said, then drove the knife in. "Think upon that as you die."

Randalf didn't scream. Maybe that was Lirr's magic at work. Maybe he was too shocked. He only rasped bloodily as Lirr's crew dragged him from the cabin. Puddles and a smear of scarlet remained on the deck, pungent and cooling.

"Send someone to clean this up when I'm through with Ms. Firth. And tie this fool to the mast, as he tied her," Lirr told Lewis before the former smuggler closed the door. His eyes slipped back to me, adding as if his words were a gift, "Let him suffer as she did."

As much as I hated Randalf, I trembled with the violence of it all. But my question to him remained unanswered.

"Why did you call me Tane?" I pressed. "Who are they?"

The door closed. My mother, Lirr and I were left in the cabin with puddles of cooling blood and bile, and the echo of footsteps heading away through the ship.

"That is your name," Lirr told me. He moved back over to the table and set his bloodied knife on it. "Or rather, the name of the ghisting your mother left inside of you."

Anne turned from the window, letting out a long, surrendering breath as she did so. "It's true, Mary."

My thoughts fluttered through images of scars and ghistings, of Juliette in the water as Randalf's ship burned, of the reaching hand of the ghisten tree in Tithe, and Harpy watching me.

Sister.

Tane.

"The timing must be right for such a union," Lirr explained, pulling up the sleeve of his shirt to reveal a long, twisted white scar on his forearm. It glistened in the lanternlight. "Many ghistings are not like these, whose shells you see on my wall. Many do not understand, and they must be burned out. A shard of their wood is then slipped beneath the skin just before the entirety of the figurehead or ghisten tree is destroyed—thus, the spirit is forced into that single remnant. But to dwell in a shard so small? It's enough to drive a ghisting mad. Eventually they must spread. They all do—to the blood and the bones."

He held up his scarred forearm. "That is what happened to me, you see. By chance. By providence."

The fine hairs on the back of my neck rose again. I felt myself move, not towards the door, but closer to my mother. One, instinctual step. To seek her protection? To protect her? There was no divide between the two impulses.

Scarred arm still extended, Lirr held his hand forward, palm up. A ghisting materialized from his flesh, parting from him like a shadow under the waning sun and condensing into a spectral twin. For a moment, two Lirrs stood before us—one a man, one a ghisting.

The ghisting shifted, expanding into the shape of a bigger, broader individual—one with burning, heavy eyes and a face so handsome my breath caught in my throat. But like Harpy, the lines of him were subtle, more like echoes of human features than replicas.

The ghisting stood at Lirr's shoulder like a guardsman. He inclined his head towards me in respect, and there was recognition in his vague expression, even deference.

Instead of greeting me as sister, he said in a deep, oaken voice, *Hello, Tane.*

"This is Hoten," Lirr said. "Do you remember him?"

If the suspicions I'd had before were a thief tapping at the shutters, now they were a battering ram. My consciousness slipped as if I were falling asleep.

A hand closed on my wrist. I looked over at my mother— startled to realize we were of a height now—and wavered back to wakefulness.

"Stay with me, Mary," my mother ordered, her voice low and gentle.

She sleeps, Hoten observed. The ghisting hadn't moved, but I felt pinned by his attention. *She's there, but she will not stir. Perhaps if the girl herself slept…*

Around us the ship rocked and moaned, and the light cutting through the back windows dimmed.

"This is not the time." My mother's voice cut through the cabin. "We're nearly at the Line, Silvanus."

The cold air snapped me out of my shock. "It *is* the time," I stated, pulling away from her and looking to Lirr. "Tell me everything."

Lirr raised his voice over the approaching storm and my mother's glare. "Twenty-three years ago, I gifted your mother with a powerful ghisting. Tane. I took a shard from a great ghisten tree, a willing spirit, and I stabbed her in the heart. Mortal and immortal merged into one powerful creature—but I received no gratitude. Instead, your mother left me. For two decades I searched for her, ever watchful for her light on the horizon. But she hid well and when I eventually found her, Tane was gone. Where? To her daughter, to the child born of her flesh. A child hidden from my sight."

I couldn't believe him, not yet, but more questions came. "Why?" I breathed.

"To give our people freedom. To give them the world." Lirr pointed to the windows and the realm beyond. "I've been doing so since your mother left me, but the ships I take, the figureheads I burn—they're a drop in the sea. Beyond the Stormwall, a thousand of our siblings are trapped, locked in the ice, forgotten and asleep. So I have brought them new hosts. New bodies to take them south in power and liberty. My crew. My prisoners."

Cold wind was in my marrow now, freezing and cracking me from the inside out. Lirr was bringing hosts for the trapped ghistings, human beings who he intended to stab and bind to an indescribable fate. Did his crew understand what he was doing? Or was Lirr's Magni power compelling them? The prisoners in the hold certainly were not willing participants.

"More hosts will come, with the pirate hunters," Lirr continued as if he followed my thoughts, his voice all satisfaction and reverie. "Then our people will be free."

I felt truly gaunt now, weak and dizzy. He meant Demery and his crew. Samuel, and his. Athe. Widderow.

"You're going to kill them?" I hissed.

"I will free them," Lirr corrected. He smiled at me, a smile so sincere and affectionate that I recoiled. "But I cannot do it without you and Tane."

My body broke. Before I realized I was moving I tore from my mother, bolted for the cabin door and slammed into the passageway beyond.

Boots thundering on wood. A ladder. I pounded up it and threw aside a hatch, knowing there was nowhere to go and not caring. I had to put distance between myself and Lirr and the shell of my mother.

Snow blasted into my face as I scrambled up onto the deck, earning stares and shouts from a dozen nearby pirates. I took the forecastle stairs two at a time, avoided reaching hands, and skidded to a stop at the very fore of the ship.

The rail pressed into my hips and I dug my fingers into its ice-covered wood. Spray froze on my cheeks and eyelashes and the cold raked my throat with each, panting breath, but when I looked at the ocean before the ship, my breath died all together.

The Stormwall filled my eyes as far as I could see. Snow and cloud stretched from sea to heaven like carded wool, fraying here and there in tendrils of cloud. They crept south across the waves, reaching, stretching, and ominous. Already the seas were rough, choppy swells capped with white and clashing currents.

Part of me braced, knowing that at any second rough hands would haul me back below. But I couldn't take my eyes off the storm, or my mind from the gut-melting revelation of my own condition, the ship's fragility, and the fact that we were leading Demery and Samuel to certain death.

My mother drew up a pace away, on the other side of the bowsprit. She looked from me to the Stormwall, her face pale and her eyes hollower than ever.

"I'm sorry, Mary," she told me, just loud enough to be heard over the wind and the waves. "I'm so sorry."

THIRTY-SIX

The Stormwall

SAMUEL

*H*art hit the Stormwall with a groan of wood and the howl of hurricane winds. Waves clapped against the hull, chunks of ice battered us and I held fast to my line, tethered to the mizzenmast. It was hard not to lose myself in the horror of the roiling waves or the blackened sky, but I kept one eye on our two burly helmsmen and the other on *Defiance*.

Benedict's ship forged ahead of us, her weather mage barely audible. She was Aeadine, aging and thin, but her voice didn't match her frame in the slightest. It was bellowing and rich, more declaration than melody. But to all appearances, the Stormwall was not listening.

"It's not working!" one of the helmsmen shouted to Fisher, who stood at the quarterdeck rail, staring down the center of the ship with her stance wide, palms braced on the rail like a battlefield general. The helmsman's huge muscles strained as he and his fellow fought the wheel. "Cap'n!"

"Hold fast!" Fisher shouted, braced against the roll of the ship.

A wall of snow gusted across the helmsman's pleading face as he looked back at me, flakes catching on his pale eyelashes. There was a question there too, the same one that had been in the crew's eyes since we left Hesten.

Are we going to die, Sooth? Have you foreseen it?

"Hold course, Mr. Kennedy!" I called.

Kennedy still looked desperate, but he turned back to the spokes and said no more.

Harpy sailed off our larboard bow, far enough to lessen the danger of dashing into one another, but close enough to benefit from Ellas's Stormsinger. The smaller ship had her sails trimmed to nearly nothing but she still strained, relying—like the rest of us—on her ghisting to keep the ship in one piece.

Beyond her, through alternating curtains of snow and sleet, I could still glimpse clear Usti waters. There, two of the Usti queen's ships watched us vanish into the Stormwall, ready to report back to their monarch if our courage failed.

Our courage would not fail. Mine might—it was currently floating around somewhere in my watery guts—but I had not foreseen *Hart's* destruction. I had even slipped into the Other last night to check, Fisher at my side and the Mereish coin at the ready.

Now, safe waters vanished. The Stormwall completely engulfed all three ships, and we forged our way across the Line.

Minutes crept into hours. Ice thudded off the hull like an irregular heartbeat and my breath froze in my beard and eyelashes, rimming them with frost. Fisher, myself and the crew rotated frequently, attempting to thaw frozen hands in the close darkness below decks. It was too rough for fires, though, and to cook, so our only light was dragonfly lanterns and our only consolation shelter from the wind.

I rejoined Fisher on deck after one of my turns below. She grabbed my sure line and bound it to the mizzenmast next to her own, cinching the knots tight.

"Isn't so bad, now!" she shouted so close to my ear I would have been deafened in any other weather. "That Stormsinger's managing!"

I squinted in the direction of *Defiance*, but the snow was thick enough to blur them from sight. I could hear Ellas's Stormsinger a little more clearly now, though. The wind had eased. "Seems to be."

"How are the crew?"

"Vomiting and pissing themselves," I returned. "But starting to believe we'll make it."

A fresh blast of winter wind stole our breaths, so she only nodded in reply. We stood in companionable silence as the Stormwall raged, the Stormsinger sang, and Hart flickered through the snowy deck beneath our boots.

Suddenly, the Stormsinger's song went shrill. The snow around us scattered on a new, feral wind and Fisher and I snapped to attention.

Defiance came into sight directly ahead, listing to her side and far too close. She'd run aground—on a great mountain of ice, black-hearted and indigo blue.

"Brace!" Fisher roared. "Hard starboard!"

The helmsmen threw their weight into the wheel. *Hart* heeled, but it was too late.

Hart rammed *Defiance* with a deafening crunch of wood. The windows of *Defiance*'s stern shattered, she gave an ominous moan, and bodies toppled from her tilting deck into the sea.

The waves dragged the ships apart again. Fisher and I staggered and, for an instant, I thought we had slipped past. Then another wave smashed us back into *Defiance*.

This time we hit her broadside. I braced as the decks of the two ships came level and, there through the snow, I saw Benedict trying to pull a woman to her feet against the backdrop of the iceberg's bruised heart. She was the Stormsinger, limp and unresponsive.

A line gave way with a telltale crack. My eyes shot up just as *Hart*'s and *Defiance*'s masts collided—spars splintering, lines tangling and snapping. Sailors scattered while others simply vanished in a blinding whirl of snow.

"Hold fast!" Fisher shouted, and I echoed her words. Both our gazes were fixed on the masts, waiting to see if they would separate, or simply destroy both ships. There was not even time to worry about the mountain of ice.

Fresh wind gusted and another enormous wave struck. *Hart* began to pull free, but the rigging was too entangled. A groan rattled the deck, then there was water everywhere. It broke over us in a tide, knee-deep even on the quarterdeck. Midships, brave sailors held fast to their lines and one another as the sea tried to sweep them away.

"Cut us loose!" I bellowed to the crew at the same time as the bosun's whistle shrilled and Fisher shouted, "Get us free!"

The deck leveled, water poured through the scuppers, and the crew leapt to obey. They scrambled up the shrouds like squirrels, darted along yards and began to slash strategic lines, untangling others with cautious urgency.

Hart swung free just as another titanic wave hit. The world, blurred, tripped, and was swallowed by frigid water. Through that water, I felt more than heard the mizzenmast give way with a final, terrible crack.

I hunkered against the rail, totally submerged in frigid, lung-crushing water. My instincts screamed to push off and swim, but lines and sails were all around me. Up was a sideways thing, gravity skewed by the force of the waves.

I felt something hit the rail at my side and grabbed it instinctively. I felt flesh, soft and icy—Fisher? No, too big for Fisher—then the water retreated. I had just enough time to snatch a breath of air before it closed over us again.

Time lost all meaning and the Other crept close. Visions and memories assailed me, some old, some new. I recalled the day I had seen Fisher drown in another storm not so long ago. I glimpsed Mary's face, her damp hair in disarray, facing John Randalf in a darkened hallway. I saw Lirr, setting a ship aflame against a backdrop of barren rock and swirling snow.

Hart leveled out and water rushed away. Spluttering and gasping, I found myself clutching the helmsman, Kennedy, like a muscular doll in a world of unexpected, rocking calm. The sky above was still a haze of blowing snow but the waves had given way to gentle swells. The ship listed under the fallen mast; we were still afloat. For now.

Around us, low islands and dense swaths of ice spread as far as I could see. It was already dusk, though we had entered the Stormwall mid-morning.

"We made it through." I let Kennedy go, suddenly weak. I looked for Fisher, but spared the sailor a searching glance. "Mr. Kennedy, are you well?"

"Yes, sir," he panted, sitting back and staring across the ship. "Thank you, sir."

"My pleasure," I rasped. I turned salt-stung eyes across the deck and pushed myself to my feet. The other helmsman was collapsed against the wheel, holding on for his life—a situation reflected in a dozen others. Only a dozen, though. There ought to have been two dozen on deck. And Fisher.

Panic momentarily blinded me. No. Fisher could not be gone. The vision of her drowning—I had thwarted it, I had saved her. That had been another day, another time.

"Captain Fisher?" I called, hoping against hope that she would appear from a hatch or behind a web of tangled rigging. She did not.

I staggered from one rail to the other, searching the water for survivors. But there was no one in sight. Waves rippled, ice drifted, and the Stormwall raged on at our backs.

My throat thickened. "Can anyone see the captain?"

"Nay, sir!" someone called.

"She went overboard, sir," the other helmsman said with a voice raw from shouting and the cold. He coughed and met my eyes, his creased with horrible certainty. "I saw her fall, Mr. Rosser. The waves took her."

All sound faded except for the beating of my heart. One-two. One-two. Blood thundered against my temples, laborious and stilted, and my breath was gone.

Fisher was dead, and I was in command.

Part of me wanted to despair, to grieve and curse. It turned in upon itself and pulled a curtain closed. The part that remained was numb and empty, a void where only fact and action remained.

I heard my voice say, "I see a peninsula up ahead with calmer waters on her lee—get us there before this mast sinks us. Mr. Keo, get below and bring me a report. Bring me Ms. Skarrow too, if you can. Ms. Fitz! That longboat is still intact? Find and pull whoever you can from the water. If Captain Fisher is alive, we will recover her."

The Spirit in Her Bones

The Girl from the Wold can no longer stay awake. The ship rocks and the wind howls, but she slips away. Her mother's songs play at the edges of her mind—bold and demanding, assured in her control of the Stormwall's ceaseless rage.

A man—a ghisting—appears. She does not need light to see him, softly glowing as he is. Nor need she open her eyes. He passes through the wood of the wall and watches her sleep, wisps of him still licking at the wood at his back.

Tane? he asks. *He is not listening. He does not know I am here.*

I will not do it, Hoten. The voice is not the girl's, but it comes from her.

Hoten's voice hardens. *You must see it now! You see what we can be, what we can do.*

Her response is calloused, imperious. *What I see is a weak, wayward son.*

Hoten's form flickers and billows larger. *I did this for our kind. What have you done? You left them to sleep until their roots turn to dust. Trapped forever.*

Better they sleep than to become like you.

Hoten approaches the hammock, putting out one hand to stop its swaying. The girl feels the hand distantly through canvas, blankets, and the fog of slumber.

I will awaken them, Hoten vows, his voice low and deadly. *Whether or not you're willing to help. I'll burn your vessel and water your tree with her blood until you wake.*

I would wake and destroy you, she that is not the girl responds.

Hoten leans in, so close that his breath would pass across the girl's lips, if he had lungs.

Then do it, Mother.

∽

THIRTY-SEVEN

The Crossing

MARY

I awoke to the muffled roar of the Stormwall. Threads of dreams chased me and I'd no will to get up, so I lay in my swinging hammock for a long while, battling stray emotions and reliving my conversation with Lirr and my mother.

Ghistings, within human beings? That was unheard of. This wasn't even the realm of folklore or raving old men. Everyone knew ghistings were bound to wood or nothing at all.

But Hoten had appeared from Lirr, not the wood of the ship. Harpy had called me Tane. Ghistings spoke to me and I felt drawn to them.

My mind produced a dozen memories of strange, inexplicable experiences I'd had since leaving the Wold. They unsettled me, making me doubt myself all over again. I'd leapt off Lirr's ship, but hadn't drowned. I'd found Demery instead, rescued by a ghisting. The way visions that had passed between me and the tree in Tithe, my incident in the bath, and how Demery's conversation with Harpy had refused to root in my mind, as if someone covered my ears.

"Tane?" I whispered to the raging, roiling dark, dreading that I might receive an answer.

There was no response.

Hours passed. The weather worsened again, the lull that had allowed me to sleep long past. I'd no light to see by as I sat braced in a corner of my little cabin, my hammock swinging wildly and the contents of my stomach long strewn across the floor. But it was too cold to smell the bile.

Suddenly, the door opened. My mother barreled inside and clicked the barrier shut behind her, a swinging lantern in hand. Her gaze was as grim and haunted as ever, but so full of determination that my heart slammed in hope.

"We're getting off this fucking ship," my mother said. My eyes dropped to her side, where she shifted an enormous woodsman's axe into two, shaking hands. "Back away from the gunport."

I fumbled around to the other side of the room. My blanket-laden hammock smacked me in the head but I hardly cared.

"You *were* pretending," I breathed, trying not to cry, trying to be dignified. I was a grown woman, not a red-eyed child, crying for her mother to come home.

Anne turned her hollow eyes on me. There was contradiction in that look, briefly, then all was obscured in a veil of determination.

"Of course, child," she conceded.

My swelling heart twisted. I swayed towards her, desperate for the feeling of her arms around me, but sensed my touch would be unwelcome.

Anne braced against the roll of the ship and lifted the axe high, blade up, flat down.

She swung at the gunport with all the force she could muster. I cringed at the sound but the storm swallowed it—one crack in the middle of dozens of strains and pops and moans. The lock clattered to the floor and Anne adjusted her stance, eyeing the ice around the hatch. She swung again, connecting right on the frame of the hatch itself. Ice cracked, shards fell, and wind gushed around the edges.

Anne swung a third time and the gunport swung outward with a creak. Wind and storm light blasted into the cabin and I glimpsed a lurching sea, dark sky and swirling snow. And was that land? An island within the Stormwall? It was so close the ship seemed about to crash into it, skimming down an ice-rimmed shoreline as only a ghisting-possessed ship could. Hoten might live within Lirr, but he could obviously still interact with *Nameless*.

"I drove the ship as close as I could, but we'll have to swim the rest of the way!" Anne shouted over the roar. She was pulling her coat off, revealing a brace of weapons and cannisters beneath. She shoved her axe through, across her back, and bundled the coat under one arm. "You'll freeze up when you hit the water—do not let yourself panic. Breathe. Can you do this?"

I hurriedly grabbed my own, donated cloak from the strings of my hammock and bundled it under one arm. I was doubly grateful I'd changed out of my impractical gown.

Then I remembered I was not the only prisoner aboard Lirr's ship. My conscience twisted at the thought of escaping while they languished, fodder for Lirr's schemes, but I knew there was nothing we could do for them now.

This was our moment. We had to go. "Yes!" I said. "No, but yes!"

Anne paused, and for an instant, she simply looked at me—truly *looked*, seeing, sensing, taking me in. Her urgency ebbed in place of unspoken things, then a bleak smile slashed across her face. "Then swim, girl. I'll be right beside you."

I gathered every scrap of my courage and grinned back, sudden and strange and a little bit savage.

I joined my mother in front of the portal. Dark water raged, the ship rolled, and my mother's hand pressed into the small of my back.

Before she could push me, I jumped. There was no fall, no screaming drop into the waves. The ship rolled and the water was already there. It swallowed me whole.

I didn't gasp, even though my lungs should have seized. I didn't panic, though the cold was bitter and blinding, and I knew this act was beyond suicidal. I slipped silently into the water and kicked out, fighting the weight of my clothing. My mother dropped beside me, the waves retreated, and we made for the shore.

We shouldn't have made it, but the sea itself came to our aid. One swell after another bore us along until the last rushed us onto a shelf of ice. It deposited us like half-drowned flotsam on an arctic shore.

I grabbed my mother's hand. She stumbled to her feet, and together we ran.

Ice, cracked and piled like scales. Snow, lashing my face. Eyelashes, frozen. Muscles, seizing. Another crashing wave chased our boots as we hit the body of the island and stumbled into the shelter of a boulder. Curling, horizontal icicles grew from the leeward rim like claws, but we found reprieve in their embrace.

"We did it!" I grabbed my mother's arm, gasping and laughing all at once. Stray hair froze to my throat and my hands burned with the cold, but I felt wildly alive. "You're mad!"

"Just desperate, and lucky," Anne replied, holding my shoulders in return. Her face was pale and her grin was raw, and the axe over her right shoulder glistened with fresh ice. "This island stretches north, out of the Stormwall. We'll hunker down there and wait for Elijah."

Elijah? "You mean Demery?" I shouted over the wind. "How would he find us?"

"He will." Anne looked away for a long moment, breathing deeply, then pushed herself to her feet and started off, as if following an instinctual compass.

"What about Lirr?" I followed her. "He can still track us."

"He won't think to look for us for some time. And with any luck *Nameless* will sink. Even if it doesn't, I've a place to hide us. You."

"Where?"

"The same place I hid you all your life," my mother replied. "A Ghistwold."

THIRTY-EIGHT

The Second Sun

MARY

The first shelter we came across was a wrecked ship, lying on its side like a child's discarded toy. Its horizontal masts reached towards us through the storm, shredded pennants of sail snapping and ice-laden lines singing eerily in the wind.

The main hatch was jammed, so we found a crack in the hull and crawled inside. The howl of the wind muffled and I sighed in relief, settling my feet on what had once been the outer hull.

We picked our way farther into the shadows. This wasn't a warship—there were goods instead of guns piled around us and I felt no ghisting in its wood. I also spied seamen's chests, crates and bundles among the refuse, but no bodies. An unarmed merchant of this size wouldn't have had a large crew.

"Here!" I spied the pipe of a woodstove deeper in the ship and clambered stiffly over a pile of debris.

Dimly illuminated by another crack in the hull, I tossed a crate into the shadows to reveal one of the large stoves that would have kept the crew warm, back when they were alive. Its chimney was gone and it was on an angle, but it looked otherwise intact.

Twenty minutes later, thanks to flint and tinder in one of my mother's cannisters, warmth bathed us from the stove's open door. Smoke drifted up and out through cracks in the hull and we strung lines to dry our outer clothing, leaving us in our shifts and breeches.

I watched my mother as we settled in, weighing my need to know more about Lirr and ghistings with the lingering shadows around her eyes. Finally, when I saw her shoulders relax slightly, I spoke up. "I need to know if what Lirr said is true. About the ghistings."

Anne leaned forward to rest her forearms on her knees, staring into the stove. "It is."

I rubbed at my windburned cheeks and sunk onto a crate near her. "So this Tane... is inside me?"

"Yes. But it's not that simple." My mother's indecision was clear in the twist of her lips. "How much did Demery tell you of Bretton?"

"That you all sailed with him, and he had a horde of treasure beyond the Stormwall. That you killed him."

She nodded. "That's all true. But did he tell you that we actually made it beyond the Wall, and that our ship wrecked there?"

I shook my head.

My mother added another piece of broken wood to the fire and poked it about. Light flared across her features, turning her blue-grey eyes nearly translucent.

"The fires from our stoves spread and the ship was consumed," she said. "It took the magazine late, giving most of us time to escape, but Lirr was caught in the explosion. He was peppered with shards, shrapnel—including, we would later discover, a shard from the figurehead, Hoten's host. The next day Lirr's wounds were healed and he'd changed. He was more aggressive, more driven, though we didn't know to what end."

I steeled myself. "Hoten had taken him?"

Anne nodded. "Lirr claimed Hoten fled the burning ship, right into his bones. Hoten himself was too weak to appear yet, but Lirr was so different, so insistent. He tried to drown himself to prove that he was no longer 'a mere man.' He survived, unaffected by the water."

Drown himself. Unaffected by the water. Just like me.

"Samuel—Mr. Rosser, the pirate hunter—claimed that he mortally wounded Lirr at the palace," I said, wetting my lips. "Can he not be killed?"

"He can, but not easily," my mother admitted. Her upper lip twitched in a stifled sneer. "I would have put a knife in him already if it was that simple. Short of complete immolation, he and Hoten must be separate when the act is done. If Lirr is killed while Hoten is absent, Hoten will fade—not be freed, but truly die. So they rarely stray far from one another."

I pondered this for a quiet moment. "Am I the same, then? And Lirr's crew?"

Anne dropped her gaze back to the fire. "Yes. Some of them— perhaps a quarter of the crew—are already bonded. Most are waiting to take on ghistings trapped beyond the Stormwall. Lirr has presented that as a great honor." Her voice fell away for a moment and when she spoke again, her voice was softer. "I suppose this… unnatural immortality is a comfort to me, in a way. So long as Tane is within you, neither of you can come to harm."

"Short of burning alive," I pointed out.

Cavorting firelight reflected in my mother's eyes. "Yes. If too much of the host's body is lost, the bonded ghisting will be forced to separate, and then it will die. But Tane is powerful enough to have left her tree willingly, so it remains whole. If her host is… lost… she will simply be drawn back to it. Or so Lirr believes. He's counting on it."

A chill passed over me. I understood what that meant, in a cold, dull way, but could not look it in the eye just yet.

We sat for a silent moment, then I forced my thoughts back to my mother's tale. "What did Bretton do? About Lirr?"

"Bretton wouldn't believe him. Bretton was an idiot."

"What about you?" I asked. "Lirr said Tane was in you. How did that happen?"

"We found another ship, one we could repair. There are hundreds of wrecks in and beyond the Stormwall, and many, many ghistings within them. It took weeks of salvaging and working, to make it seaworthy." My mother worried at her ring finger as she spoke, touching the groove where a wedding ring had, until recently, left its mark. "I noticed Lirr often disappeared during that time, and the other pirates started to change, one by one. We would see fires at night, in the distance, but the crewmembers we sent to investigate always arrived too late. Someone was burning the figureheads of the wrecked ships.

"Elijah Demery and I discovered the truth together, one night, creeping out in the dark after Lirr. Lirr and Hoten had found themselves a purpose. They harvested shards from the other wrecks, then burned the figureheads. The shards became the last vestiges of the ghisting's host, and Lirr then buried them in the hearts of Bretton's crew while the rest of us slept. They became possessed, like him. Some willing, some not. Neither ghistings nor humans had a choice—the binding was immediate. Demery didn't escape it."

"He has a ghisting," I summarized, a little awe creeping into my voice. "Harpy?"

I saw the muscles of her throat flex. "Yes," she admitted, meeting my eyes with a gentle kind of sadness.

I thought of my father, who she'd met aboard Bretton's ship. "Father? Is he…"

"The blending didn't work for him," Anne told me. "It happened to a few of the crew. If there's a ghisting in him, it sleeps. He's just a man… more or less."

Just a man who she'd loved, but who'd given up on her and remarried. I looked at her empty ring finger again. Did she suspect my father had moved on? Had Lirr forced her to take off the ring? Now didn't feel like the right time to discuss it.

"Lirr's plot claimed us all. But there were already two souls in my body, Mary. I didn't know it yet, but I was pregnant with you. The ghisting couldn't fully wake inside of me, but when you were born, long after I escaped Lirr, I felt it go with you. It lived, in you. It was part of you, even at your quickening."

Firelight warmed my cheeks, but I hardly noticed it.

"After Lirr ran out of hosts for his ghistings, we sailed our salvaged ship south again, with Lirr as captain. I'd realized I had you in my belly by then. Your father and I escaped, first chance we got. But not two weeks into freedom, we were both picked up by a Navy press gang. They had no idea I was a Stormsinger, and I kept it quiet. The war was bad then, and the Mereish Fleet had taken the Aeadine Anchorage. After three weeks on our new ship, Mereish warships ran us down. Our Stormsinger took a cannonball right through the chest, and I stepped up."

"I thought there were fates worse than death," I murmured.

"Not when I'd you to care for," she answered in a voice like iron. The fire crackled and in her hard eyes, I glimpsed the woman I used to know. Sharp. Steady. Unbending.

Emotion clotted in my throat. I looked away.

"Our captain was a good woman—two children of her own, back on shore. When the Battle of Sunjai came, I broke the Mereish Fleet and won the Seven Year Peace. You should understand, Mary; Tane is a creature of the Other, pure and deeply connected to that world. A channel, of a sort. Even once she left me, the effect remained. With her in my bones, my Stormsinging power was enormous—as yours must be too."

I frowned, uncertain. "In time, perhaps. I've much to learn."

"In time," my mother affirmed, then resumed her tale. "I was obviously pregnant when I broke the Fleet, and I'd no desire to have you between the guns. My captain arranged for me to live ashore until the war started up again."

"Father too?"

Anne nodded. "They released many sailors after the peace—couldn't afford to pay them, anyway. But your father and I had money from our time with Bretton, so we bought the inn and settled down."

"In the Wold." I recalled what she'd said earlier, about hiding me in the ghistings' forest. I remembered Rosser, too, telling me the figureheads would make it harder for Lirr to track me in Hesten. Demery's insistence on keeping me on shore in Tithe, a city full of ghistings, suddenly made sense too.

"The ghistings hid us," I said.

Anne nodded. "Yes. And like I said, when I gave birth the ghisting, Tane, went with you."

I swallowed tightly. "What does that mean for me?"

"I don't know, not entirely." Her voice was raw with honesty. "But you were born healthy and strong and happy, so I didn't care. You are her. She's you. I never tried to figure out where you ended and she began—you're my daughter."

Everything I was tangled inside me. My mind scrambled, reliving my life in fragments as I tried to find evidence of what she said. There were strange moments, to be sure, especially in recent days, but I was still myself.

Yet I was not. I wanted to crawl out of my skin, to panic and shutter myself away. It all left me impossibly tired.

Anne read the expression on my face and pointed to a pile of sailcloth and hammocks we'd gathered earlier. "Sleep. Try to, at least. I'll keep watch."

"Not yet." I pushed stray hair back from my face. "Lirr said he needed me. And Tane. Why? Why is she so important?"

"She was a Mother Tree," my mother said, with some reluctance. "The heart of her Wold. Her tree still remains there—as I said, she was powerful enough to leave it willingly, so Lirr had no need to burn it. But when Lirr placed her shard in me, every ghisten tree within her influence fell asleep. They cannot be harvested and bonded with Lirr's crew or captives until Tane wakes them up. Then Lirr will take shards from each, and burn the Wold to ashes."

My mouth felt dry. "*Will* Tane wake them? I can't pretend to understand all this fully but… I think Hoten was right. Tane is still asleep, herself. At least, for the most part."

My mother looked into my eyes, as if she searched for someone else inside them. "Lirr intends to force the matter."

Dread turned into gooseflesh on my arms. "How will he do that?"

She looked away. "Fire. Lirr will force Tane out of you, and she will be drawn back into her tree. Then the Wold will reawaken. But we will not let that happen."

The dance of the flames in our stove was suddenly threatening, ominous, and full of portent.

For a few heartbeats I couldn't speak, then I nodded slowly. It wasn't that I'd accepted the threat against my life—it was simply too huge, too horrible and strange, for me to grasp. "I see."

"We can talk more in the morning," she said, more gently. "We've time, Mary. I'm not leaving you again. And Lirr will not harm you. You'll fight. We'll fight. But for now, you should rest."

"You should sleep too," I pointed out. I could see the fatigue about her eyes. "I can wake you in a few hours."

My mother smiled, crooked and brimming with real, calming warmth. "No. You may be grown, but I'm still your mother. You sleep first."

I opened my mouth to protest, but she held up a hand.

"Give me this, Mary. I'll wake you in a few hours."

Though I knew that was a lie, I gave up.

I curled up on our makeshift bed, turning my back to her and looking out into the cold darkness beyond the firelight. I scrubbed at my cheeks and clenched my eyes shut, warring between fatigue and worry for my mother, and the need to rationalize all I'd learned.

Tane. Ghistings. Lirr, plotting my death.

Finally, fatigue won out. My mother began to sing softly, and my world blurred.

"The storm shall not wake thee, nor shark overtake thee, asleep in the arms of the slow-swinging seas…"

The Stormwall ended in a swirl of snow, backed by twilight and the shushing of snowflakes against my hood. Pure, gentle air caressed my face and I paused, my view of the new world beyond still partially obscured.

"This is it, Mary," my mother said. We stood close, bundled not only in our own clothing but commandeered layers of coats, scarves and hats from the wreck where we'd spent the night. We had satchels too, packed with flint and tinder, bottles of meltwater, hardtack and jerky that had survived years frozen in the storm. She had her axe too, carried in mittened hands, and I had a knife I'd found among the wreckage. "From here on we move quickly, stay out of sight, and speak as little as we can."

I nodded. The last at least wouldn't be difficult—we'd hardly spoken since I woke up that morning to find her dozing at my side, axe across her knees, fire burning brightly. I still had my questions, but as far as revelations went, I'd already bitten off more than I could chew. All morning I'd imagined Lirr burning me alive.

My mother seemed grateful for my quiet. She forged north through the wind and snow, thoughts locked behind squinting eyes. She looked marginally lighter than she had aboard Lirr's ship, but her stride had the air of a forced march, and her determination was a jaded, tight-jawed thing.

Part of me still wanted to press her, to unravel the story of her last sixteen years, to bring it into the light of day and somehow… make her whole again. But what could I say? And did I truly want to know all that my mother had done and become to earn Lirr's trust?

The world expanded between one breath and the next. We stood in an endless network of islets and hulking black boulders, crowned with snow and ice. Waves took shape between shores of ice and snow and barren rock. Far distant, the sun trailed her skirts across the rim of the horizon, veiled behind a distant snowstorm.

"We called it the Second Sun," my mother said, eyeing the orb. "It never sets or rises. It only ever moves along the horizon, in a perfect circle."

"That's ridiculous," I muttered. "It's morning, that's why it's so low."

Anne eyed me. "Child, when has the sun ever risen in the north?"

I turned, reorienting myself along the line of the Stormwall. The wall ran east to west, but the sun, as my mother had said, was firmly north.

"So it is," I murmured. "But how?"

"I haven't the faintest idea."

"The Other has strange suns, doesn't it? Is this... like that?"

My mother shrugged. "Your guess is as good as mine, child."

Mystified, I led her through the last of the snow. The world filled with golden twilight, radiating from the muffled sun and reflecting off blankets of white, sheets of ice and the quiet waves between.

I shivered, but not just because of the alien sun. There was more than rock, ice and waves under the Second Sun's meager light. There were ships.

They spread as far as I could see to north, east and west, like dice tossed from a giant's cup. In and out of the water they lay in various levels of silhouette. Some were little more than ragged mastheads above the sea while others were entirely beached, sheeted with ice and piled with drifts of snow. Spiderwebs of rigging and sail fluttered, and waves slapped against long-empty hulls. It was beautiful and eerie: a graveyard of ships.

We walked for what felt like a day, though the Second Sun simply swept along the horizon at unchanging elevation. My mother hummed to the wind and I joined her, keeping the frigid wind off our skin and the snow from our path.

The farther we went, the more portentous our surroundings became. We picked our way across bridges of ice and rounded the wrecks of ships from every nation and age of sail. I began to spy vessels with burned figureheads, and my skin crawled as I realized these were Lirr's work, over twenty years ago.

The weather turned. The wind kicked up and the Second Sun passed behind the Stormwall, its light becoming even weaker, a coin glinting from the bottom of a darkened well.

"Why did you leave the Wold?" my mother suddenly asked, shifting her axe to her other shoulder. "Did someone in the village discover you're a Stormsinger? Did they turn you in?"

I avoided her gaze. I'd been putting this story off, but now seemed as good a time as any. "No, no… I was supposed to marry. A soldier, a good man. He was sent off to war before he could find us a home and broke off the engagement. So father's new wife sent me to Jurry, to Aunt Eliza, to find another match."

Anne stopped walking. She blanched with anger, and the axe at her shoulder made the expression truly intimidating. The wind began to coil around us, drawing a rush of snow over the rocks beneath our feet. "He what?"

"He waited fifteen years," I said, resolving that would be my only defense of the man. "The entire town said you were dead. The priest said you were dead."

"I don't care about that." Anne gestured sharply, slapping my words aside, though her eyes were overbright. She did care, but she was trying not to show me. "I knew you'd left the Wold for some reason—Lirr wouldn't have seen you otherwise, and we wouldn't have left the South Isles. But your father let her send you away? *You* let her?"

"Let her?" I shoved my hood back from my forehead, as if the cold air could help me put my words together. "I didn't have a choice.

And how was I to know Lirr was hunting me? Father certainly never told me."

Anne stared into the distance for a long moment, her breath misting before her. "He didn't know," she said finally. "I never told him the ghisting went to you. But I did tell him to never, ever, let you leave the Wold. That should have been enough. How did Kaspin get to you?"

I was still rankled by her implication that I'd willingly left the village, but I pushed past it. I gave a strangled, huffing laugh. "I was mistaken for a notorious highwaywoman, robbed a few travelers, was captured and sentenced to hang, then sang my way off the gallows and was sold off to Kaspin by a dandy called Charles Grant."

The swirling wind hushed, leaving us in a bubble of stillness.

"You survived all that," she said, "even though you'd never left that backwater village?"

I nodded, a kernel of pride blossoming in my chest. "I did."

Abruptly she wrapped one arm around my head and kissed me, half on the forehead, half on the brim of my hat. I froze, startled and blinded by unexpected tears.

She held there for a moment, clasping me to her and simply breathing. Tension trembled through her, as if she fought an internal war, and lost it. She started to pull away.

Before she could let go, I wrapped my arms around her and pulled her close. I heard a thump as she rested the head of her axe in the snow, one hand still limp at her side. She angled her face away from mine, leaving us temple to temple, and I felt her fight a sob. I felt the conflict in her, the shuddering grimace of emotion that could no longer be ignored.

I closed my eyes, giving her as much privacy as I could without letting her go.

"I survived," I whispered. As much as I wanted to crumble, as much as the reality of my broken mother terrified me, I managed to keep my own tears at bay. I was not a child anymore. This was her moment of consolation—not mine. "So did you. And we'll survive this too."

My mother inhaled shakily and released the breath again in a long, steady gust. Then she pulled back, cupping my cheek in one hand, and looked into my eyes. Hers were red-rimmed, her cheeks streaked with tears, but she smiled. I smiled back, small and sad.

"We will," she vowed.

The next day—or rather, when the Second Sun emerged from the Stormwall in the southeast—an island came into sight. It sat at the heart of the ruined fleet, blurring the edge of the endless grey-gold sky.

I reached into my satchel and pulled out a salvaged spyglass. Then, placing its cold sight to my eye, I held my breath.

The island held a Ghistwold. A sleeping winter forest grew from and between the bodies of beached ships, rooting in their figureheads and erupting from man-made shells into leafless ash and elm, oak and birch and poplar. Some of the ships were little more than piles of snow-caked, bleached wood, while others were more recent, their hulls intact and threadbare sails snapping in the wind. The trees were huge, grown to unnatural size despite the arctic world, the lack of daylight and the impossibility of growing seasons.

As we drew closer, I began to sense the ghistings within those trees. By the time we entered their meager shade I could hear them murmuring in wordless slumber, drawing my attention here and there. But none of them spoke to me, deep in their rest.

Shadows stretched towards us across the snow at unpredictable angles, branches like claws and trunks like pillars of night. I slowed, my heart trammeling against my ribs. I'd the sense of a traveler coming home in the dead of night; a stranger in her own home, her family asleep and unaware of her presence. This ash. That elm. I knew each one distantly, intrinsically, but they were oblivious to me.

I wanted them to wake up. I wanted their leaves to unfurl and their roots to creep across the ground. I wanted to see their spirits flit through the cold light of the Second Sun and hear their voices speak.

The golden larch grew on an outcropping of rock in the center of the sleeping Wold. Thick roots reached from beneath the snow, latticing the rock and plunging into the earth below. High above, her vivid boughs were encased in ice.

"This is her tree," my mother murmured, setting down her axe. "Tane's tree."

I lowered my satchel and looked up into the branches. Golden boughs drooped under a windblown sheath of ice and snow, and I felt the tree's emptiness. There was no ghisting here.

My fingers began to tingle, my consciousness tugged as if I were falling asleep, and then, I remembered.

The Spirit in Her Bones

They cut her from the heart of her mountainside Wold. They found her unclaimed, unprotected, those ravenous humans, and fashioned her body into the figurehead of their ship. Her mother wept as they bore her away. Her sisters cursed, and her brothers raged. And she herself wept as they changed her, carving and hacking, smoothing and reshaping, until she was no longer Tane, but a human figure of wood and paint. A forgotten saint, a spear in one hand, and a distaff in the other.

She bore them across seas and through storms. But where other ghistings grew complacent to their captivity, she who was once Tane did not. She was other, and she would not rest.

She was a Mother Tree, heiress to the Wold in which she was grown, destined to stretch from the shade of her own Mother into the light of the sun. Her roots would sustain the Wold, when the first Mother fell and returned to the Dark Water. Her energy would bind it. Her rule soothe it.

When she heard her kin lament from beyond the wall of storms, she led her ill-fated crew astray. She whispered of riches beyond the tempest and her captain, blinded by greed, believed. They braved the Stormwall, emerging into an arctic world where so, so many ships had perished.

There, she who had been Tane drove her ship onto the rocks and refused to move again. Her crew cursed and raged, but then they starved and died, and Tane's world quietened. Over the decades she reached roots into frozen earth and stretched branches to the dusky sky. And where her roots reached her kin, trapped in their own prisons, they, too, began to sprout.

A new Ghistwold grew, with Tane as their Mother. Her roots sustained them. Her energy bound them. Her rule soothed them. The cold and the wind did not bother them—their life and sustenance came from another world altogether, their roots reaching into the Other. They brought summer with them. Ash and elm unfurled leaves that the arctic winds could not tear. Snow melted beneath birches in their paper shrouds, and fiddleheads emerged from blankets of moss.

New ships arrived and wrecked, some which Tane's forest and their network of roots could not reach. But they would one day, Tane soothed them. Time, after all, meant little to immortal ghistings.

Sleep, she sang to those distant ships. *Sleep until the time is right.*

Then he came. Tane sensed Hoten's ship as it passed through the Stormwall. Her roots stretched and her fine leaves rustled, watching, waiting.

The ship wrecked, as they all eventually did. Far from her reach the vessel became a torch in the night, and she sensed the new ghisting's pain as his prison burned. Then that pain was gone, and there was silence instead.

Soon after, a man wandered into the Wold. She sensed a ghisting with him. Within him.

Horror. Disgust. The feelings overwhelmed her and spread through the forest, but the ghisting in the man exalted.

"See my freedom," Hoten said with the man's mouth. "See all I can do. Come, my siblings, good Mother. I will take you to see the world, and it will be ours."

Tane rejected the offer, as did all the other trees of the Wold. But many of the ghistings beyond her reach, the ones her roots had not yet saved, took Hoten's proposal.

Others rejected it but had no power to stop the ghisten man. He burned their wooden flesh and drove their final shards into his screaming crewmates.

Some of these creations lived. Their souls complemented one another and they grew strong. Others went mad. Some slept and did not wake. Some simply did not change. The remainder died, both human and ghisting vanishing into nothingness.

Death. Ghistings did not know death, not until that day. But by Hoten's hands, they learned.

When they entered human flesh, they became mortal.

Tane tried to stop Hoten, to stop the death and the suffering of her children, and even the humans—for she learned compassion for them. But this new creature Hoten, this hybrid, could not be harmed by her spectral hands or reaching roots. He was more than man, more than ghisting, and death would not come to him easily.

Finally, when every human in his possession was spent, Hoten returned to Tane. He brought with him two dozen of his surviving creations, and one last human woman.

The woman smelled of the Other. A Stormsinger. She was bloodied and beaten, barely conscious as he shoved her to her knees in the shade of the Mother Tree.

"I have saved the best for you." This time when the man spoke, it was no longer Hoten. He and this host had mingled now, and together they were someone new. "A powerful mage, Mother. Please. Come with me."

The prisoner turned glazed eyes up to Tane, palms braced on the earth, battling not to collapse. But she did not look away. She stared at the tree and as she did, challenge edged into her eyes.

That challenge, that strength, was something Tane knew well. It was the same strength that had driven her through the Stormwall, stretched her roots across the frozen world and founded a new Wold. Tane and this woman—they were alike.

"We will return south," the Hoten-man said, turning to address all the trees in the Wold. "And I will bring another crew back. I will bring them and slaughter them, until every one of you has a host. Until every one of you is free from your wooden prisons and the Dark Water."

Horror gripped Tane, and she realized what she must do. She could not stop Hoten as she was. She had no legs to give chase, no hands to kill with. But with the woman's hands and a weapon, she could find a way to end this. She could protect her Wold.

Again, she looked into the woman's eyes, and saw her own stubbornness there. Their souls, she thought to herself, were not so different. The melding would succeed.

It had to.

Tane willed herself from the shell of her tree into a single shard. It was a struggle, a feat of will even for her, but she succeeded. And as she went, the Wold quietened. Leaves began to change from green to brown, red, yellow and burgundy. They fell, drifting on the wind. Ghistings still lived within the trees, but they slept. The snow and the cold swept in as the summer died, and winter swallowed the Wold.

The Stormsinger did not scream or beg as Hoten took the shard of the Mother Tree and prepared to strike. Her chest shuddered and her hands shook, but she faced him.

Hoten stabbed the shard into her chest, and Tane's world changed. Blood, rushing. Heart, beating. Lungs, shuddering. Tears, streaming. Then, blackness.

Sleep. Tane slept and dreamed, within the woman's body. She slipped between the Other and the human world, unable to root on either side. There were moments of clarity, but though Tane could remember she had a purpose, she could not recall what.

Time passed. Untold, unmarked time. Then, Tane noticed another presence. It was small and fragile, a tiny light in the Other and a new, fluttering heartbeat in the human world. But it was not strong. It was fading.

A child. Tane recognized the life for what it was, and instinct pulled her towards it. She wrapped around it, strengthened and sustained it. She bound herself to that new life and soothed her.

As the girl grew within her mother's womb, Tane awoke a little more. There were moments of blazing power, of fear and fight and storms. In those moments Tane would stir, and she and the Stormsinger broke fleets upon the water.

When the child was born, Tane went with her. The child's mind filled her own and she grew with her, living and breathing, feeling and thinking and learning. Part of Tane remained dormant, listless and absent, but she was near a Wold, and both she and the girl found solace there.

Tane belonged among the ghisten trees, and so the girl did too. They were the Girl from the Wold.

It was not until they left the Wold that Tane began to strain against her rest. The girl needed her then, and Tane felt her fear.

Then, on a night of fire and death, Tane fully awoke, for a time. She saw Hoten again, and she knew only to flee to the water, dark and familiar. To another ghisting, with wide eyes and a fan of spectral hair. Juliette.

Sister.

Together, they found the bonded soul of one of her daughters. Harpy. Then, with the girl safely in the hands of Harpy and her host, Juliette slipped away again, and Tane slumbered once more.

Other ghistings came and went, each tugging her along the path towards permanent awareness. Tane did not force the change—she knew Mary could not endure the shock. So she took her time, slipping to the forefront only when Mary slept or drifted, or would have greatly suffered without her intervention.

Now, with the arctic wind on her cheeks and her own Wold before her, Tane finally, fully awoke.

∽

THIRTY-NINE

Captain Fisher

SAMUEL

Harpy emerged from the Stormwall into the twilight of a foreign sunset. I watched her limp across the water through Fisher's spyglass, retrieved from her chest in the captain's cabin. Mine had been lost in the storm, and Fisher herself still had not been found. Nor had *Defiance* emerged from that wall of death.

I could not say which absence affected me more greatly—Fisher, or Benedict. They and the hundreds of other lives we had lost were something I could not permit myself to feel, not when I was commanding officer aboard a nearly derelict *Hart*.

As to the dozens of other wrecked ships, scattered across the ice and rock and slow-moving channels all around us? They were another weight entirely, eerie and foreboding as tombstones in the perpetual twilight—a warning that unless we were able to rig a new mizzenmast, we were already one of them.

Harpy slid into the shelter of our peninsula. She was battered and low in the water but intact, her deck positively crowded with pirates in the light of two lanterns. Conversation and shouts drifted to my ears across the twilit, glassy water, interspersed with creaking lines and rustling canvas.

No, they were not all pirates. The Navy's striped trousers among them and... Benedict, Ellas and Fisher clustered on the quarterdeck.

Relief hit me like a boulder, colliding with my exhaustion and leaving me weak in the legs. I braced against the rail, battling to stay composed as they climbed into a longboat and struck out for *Hart* with James Demery.

My twin lived. Fisher had not died.

I was not alone.

We met in the main cabin. I drew curtains over the windows and lit a lantern, bathing the company in warm, welcome illumination.

Demery sank into a chair beside two Usti, a woman in pale blue and a man with a thick beard. Captain Ellas sat while Benedict took up station at her shoulder, straight-backed and casting me glances I had no time to interpret. He looked well, though, aside from a bruise on his cheek.

Fisher sidled up to me as our guests found their chairs. I watched her come, overtaken with the irrational urge to snatch her up and crush her to my chest. Her captain's hat was gone and her short salt-caked black hair was a mess around her narrow, windburned face. But she was not dead.

"I thought you'd gone down," the woman murmured. I felt her hand on my arm, light and surreptitious. "I'm glad I was wrong."

My lips twitched as I suppressed an idiotic, wild grin. "Same to you. You went overboard?"

"Nearly." Her hand left my arm. "I hit the water, grabbed a line and climbed until I was aboard *Defiance*. Demery came alongside and rescued as many as he could, but with those swells and the iceberg…"

We both lapsed into silence. At the table, the Usti woman with Demery had begun to explain her people's lore about the shipwrecks north of the Stormwall.

Fisher and I held back for another moment. I opened my mouth to say something more, but what? *I am just so glad you are alive, Fisher? I cannot face this without you, Fisher?*

"Ellas's Stormsinger is dead too," Fisher said, cutting off my thoughts. She started to step towards the table, then murmured to

382 H. M. LONG

me, "You'd better find Mary Firth, or else we're never getting home."

Mary's name came with a haze of power. I slipped my hand into my pocket and closed my fingers around the Mereish coin for long enough to extinguish the pull, then let go. "I will."

She nodded and we joined the council.

"*Defiance* has been destroyed and *Hart* is down a mast, with other damage besides. It seems clear—my ship is the only one fit to sail," Demery declared. "I'll do some minor repairs and depart as quickly as possible, likely tomorrow."

"To do what?" Ellas wanted to know, eyeing the pirate skeptically. "Pillage those wrecks, no doubt."

Demery gave her a highbrowed look. "How presumptuous you are. I will find Lirr, whereupon I shall return and we can devise a strategy to bring him down. There will be no pillaging until matters with Lirr are well in hand."

"Well." The Navy captain *tsk*ed and looked at Fisher, including the other woman as she said, "Captain Fisher and I have come to a similar conclusion. However, we will be joining you in your cruise, Captain Demery."

On one side of Demery, the Usti woman cleared her throat. On the other, her big male companion decided now was a good time to pick at his fingernails—except for the last two fingers on his right hand, which were missing at the knuckle.

"You don't agree?" Fisher asked the Usti.

"Small crews are best to scout," the Usti woman said, her accent smooth. "There are many ships here, yes, but one moving? It will be obvious. Also the water is very dangerous, with many shallow areas, and many ways will be blocked with ice. It would take much time to navigate."

"Which is why you're here," Demery pointed out, measuring the woman. "To predict our path."

Predict? I looked at the Usti woman more closely. Was she a Sooth?

She smiled wanly. All eyes had turned to her and she introduced herself. "I am Olsa Uknara, Sooth. The beard is my husband, Illya. Voyager."

The beard left off picking at his nails and smiled at the assembly.

Sooth. I must have stared at her a bit too long, for she caught my eye and delivered me a subtle, *what-do-you-want-boy*, expression.

"We only have one longboat," Demery pointed out.

"We go with feet," the bearded Usti man spoke up now, lacing his fingers across his belly and leaning back in his chair. His accent was stronger than the woman's. "And use a small boat like ferry, portage on land. We can bring bigger force this way."

"We will sail with the *Harpy*," Demery said flatly, glancing between the two. "That's my decision. Will you be with me?"

Olsa relented with a shrug and Demery started to speak again. But as she sat back, Olsa caught my eye a second time.

The Other tugged at me. I slipped just over the threshold and glimpsed her there—outlined in teal just as I was. Her glow was stronger than mine, though, outlined in grey and strong enough to illuminate Demery and her husband with a same pale light. Benedict was a brooding red off to one side.

Fisher dug her nails into my wrist beneath the table. Pain snapped me back to the physical world.

"I propose a joint venture," Ellas was saying. "I and my Lieutenant Rosser will sail with Demery, along with a detachment of my armsmen and marines. Captain Fisher, you may come if you please, however I understand if you wish to remain with your Mr. Rosser to oversee repairs of your ship and ensure that we've a seaworthy vessel when we return. Though, given that Lirr's own ship will be our prize—"

Fisher released my wrist, leaving indentations from her nails. "This is my ship, Captain Ellas, and I do not appreciate any assumptions about my conduct, especially ones that are badly veiled commands. I would remind you that, at this point, you have the fewest guns to contribute to our cause."

The hair on the back of my neck prickled. Fisher had as good as threatened Ellas. Admiration—along with a healthy dose of trepidation—made me sit back in my chair. I took my wrist into my lap, surreptitiously brushing away the indentations from Fisher's nails.

Fisher threw her gaze around the table, meeting everyone's eyes with the same challenge, including Benedict. "I agree with Captain Demery. *Harpy* should go out to scout. I will send a contingent of my best armsmen and *my* Mr. Rosser to lead them. Meanwhile I will remain with my ship and my wounded, as is fitting."

My brother glanced at me, his brows rising a fraction. We might be grown men, but our childhood knack for wordless communication was still intact.

You and I, then, brother?

He and I aboard a pirate's ship. How long would he and Ellas wait to start their butchery? What would I have to do to stop them? Saint, I stood between my own brother and pirates, lawless men and women I'd sworn to bring to the gallows.

Ellas decided, "I'll remain with Captain Fisher. I trust Mr. Rosser to see to our interests."

Fisher smiled around the table, and I was not the only one who caught the satisfied twist of her lips. It reminded me of Slader.

"Then," she declared, "we are agreed."

The meeting dispersed. I stood by as the pirates exited the cabin, nodding to Demery as he passed. He held my gaze, a question hidden in his eyes, and I wondered if he suspected Ellas. No, I was certain he suspected Ellas. I'd have to speak to him soon.

Finally, Fisher and I stood alone on the quarterdeck of our ruined ship, staring towards the shattered stump of the mizzenmast.

Fisher murmured, "Ellas will try to take *Hart* from me once you leave, of that I'm sure. Have you foreseen anything?"

I glanced towards the companionway, where Ellas and her people milled about, making themselves at home. "No. But I agree." I looked at her sideways and found her eyes already on me, quiet and assessing. "I do not like the idea of leaving you to handle her alone."

"And I'm reluctant to leave you with your brother and a ship full of pirates, but this is the situation we have." Fisher looked away and laced her arms over her chest. "You must warn Demery."

I pressed my lips closed. My ideals still strained at the thought of siding with pirates against the Navy, but our choices were few.

Fisher went on, her voice low, but determined. "We cannot fight on two fronts, and Ellas has made it clear that if we do not help her, she'll dispose of us or ruin us. We need Demery. He's not just a newly commissioned privateer for the Usti. He's effectively nephew to Queen Inara, and if we sail back into Usti waters without him? You heard her threat. If the Usti are displeased with us, they may just shift the tide of the war—and not in our favor."

Harpy nosed through the dusky hush of the ruined fleet. Soon after our departure from *Hart*, grey cloud had descended to obscure our surroundings. Fires now speckled the gloom here and there, but Demery did not investigate them.

"Lirr sets fires," he said by way of explanation. "He's burning any ships that we might use for salvage. It only means he's close."

My Sooth's sense turned at that, but he would say no more.

As to our Usti companions, they stood sentry at the prow of the ship. Olsa hovered on the edge of the Other and guided us through the landscape by premonition alone, while her husband watched for other threats.

Envy smoldered in my chest. This was one service Sooths could give to their ships, but I'd rarely been able to perform it. Next to Olsa Uknara I was all misplaced instincts and clumsy tumbles into the Other. If Slader had still been alive, I might as well have jumped off the ship and started walking home.

"She's making you look terrible," Benedict voiced my own thoughts, leaning against the ship's rail like a gambler on a bar. "At the very least you could find Mary."

The familiar way he said her name made my anger flare, but we were on deck in sight of dozens of eyes. Given what Fisher and I suspected about Ellas's plans and the dark look on Demery's face when I warned him of them, I should not cause any undue conflict. Particularly with my volatile brother.

I swallowed my temper and closed on him, stopping just close enough for him to feel my displeasure.

"I looked for Ms. Firth before we left *Hart*," I reminded him, clearly pronouncing her name. "There are too many ghistings here to pick her or Lirr out, not unless I am very close."

Benedict maintained his lackadaisical posture. "Ah yes, when you vanished into your cabin for a solid twenty minutes with your young captain. She's not precisely pretty, but I can see the appeal."

"Ben. I am broken. She knows, and she was there to ensure I did not become trapped in the Other."

He straightened and shoved his hands into his pockets, his jaded eyes narrowed against the wind. "I thought the coin solved that."

"It did. It does. But using it weakens me even more." I instinctively lowered my voice. It was doubtless unwise to admit vulnerability to my twin, but he already knew I was not whole. "I cannot use it all the time. And if I go too deep in the Other, a day will come when I cannot return. Or something will follow me back and eat me alive."

"Both splendid options." Benedict's expression was opaque.

"Hold!" The whispered word shushed across the deck of the ship, passing from one person to the next, bow to stern.

My twin and I turned. Up at the fore Olsa remained in place but Illya and Demery conferred in low, rapid tones. One wave of the captain's hand and the crew scurried to trim our sails, slowing *Harpy* to the pace of the current.

Benedict and I crossed the ship and joined the Usti and Demery. An old woman in black and grey came too, along with Athe, Demery's second-in-command.

"There's another ship—a living ship." Demery pointed northeast into the gloom, between us and the darkest part of the twilight sky.

Benedict drew his spyglass and surveyed the new vessel as Demery and Olsa conferred in Usti, too quick for me to follow. Finally, Ben passed the glass to me. I took it without thanks and looked through.

A huge, three-masted shadow slipped through an open section of sea to the northeast. I touched the Other, and sure enough, Lirr's strange opalescent light appeared between the blue glow of numerous ghistings, hazed in grey. I could not pick out Mary, though.

"Lirr is there." I lowered the glass. I nearly asked Olsa what the grey haze meant, but stopped short when I noticed that her eyes also had a grey hedge to them too, trickling into brown irises like smoke. They reminded me of… Mary's.

I looked at Demery, then Athe, and even the old woman. They all looked at me now, and in their eyes I saw the same grey infiltration.

Grey-tainted lights in the Other. Pirates and a Stormsinger with smoke-edged eyes. I did not need my Sooth's senses to realize there was more to these two phenomena than I understood.

Benedict stepped in, though I could not decide whether he had sensed my sudden tension or was just impatient. "Now we retreat to Ellas and prepare an assault."

Demery scratched his short beard and looked at the old woman. "Crow?"

"We're ready," she said.

Athe nodded, and I saw her hand drop to a pistol at her belt.

"Good." Demery turned on Benedict at the same time as Athe drew her pistol and leveled it at my brother's head. "Let's get you secured in the hold, young man. Then we're off to find the Fleetbreaker."

A HISTORY OF GHISTLORE AND THE BLESSED; THOSE BOUND TO THE SECOND WORLD AND THE POWER THEREIN

GHISÉAU AND HIGH MARINERS may be identified by two means, other than the direct manifestation of their ghisting counterparts. Firstly, a pale halo about the iris, often so subtle as to be disregarded. Secondly, a Sooth may perceive an aura about their bodies within the Other or from the edge of that Other realm. Sooths studied in Adjacent identification may also note other visible alterations around the various mages and mage-adjacent of our world—corruptions, mutations and blessings detailed in this work's companion volume, *A DEFINITIVE STUDY OF THE BLESSED; MAGES AND MAGE-CRAFT OF THE MEREISH ISLES.*

FORTY

Plots and Pardons

MARY

I stood in the shelter of a ghisten oak as *Harpy*'s longboat ground ashore at the foot of a gentle rise, from arctic sea to sleeping Wold. I was subdued, my mind still heavy with the revelations I'd had under the larch.

I was still myself. I felt the same—flexing fingers, breathing lungs—yet I knew everything had irrevocably changed. It was as if I'd woken from a dream in which I'd been convinced I was already awake. My eyes were open. The shackles unlocked.

My mother waited closer to the water, some dozen paces between us. Hair escaped her fraying braid below her cap, grey-streaked locks fluttering in the wind. Her cheeks, perpetually red with cold, curved with a welcoming smile as she saluted.

Pirates leapt out to secure the little vessel on the icy rocks and a group of seven individuals broke away, trudging through the snow to where my mother waited.

Samuel looked up at me as he went. He was bundled in eclectic cold-weather gear and looked his usual sleep-deprived self, but as our gazes met, the corner of his lips tugged in relief.

Despite myself, mine did too. I might have lingering doubts as to Samuel's qualities, but I was glad he'd survived the Stormwall. Not only that, but the way he smiled at me now, relieved and hesitant, thawed me to the tips of my toes.

Grinning so wide I thought his face might crack, Demery cupped my mother's head in a hand and bumped his forehead into hers, a gesture so familiar that I gaped.

"Sister." His voice drifted towards me. "We haven't much time, but it's good to see you."

My mother transformed as she grinned back, eyes brimming with happiness, and she folded into his arms. Over her head Demery caught my eye and his smile became a little grimmer, his gaze one of shared understanding and solidarity. Did he see the changes in her too, despite her smile?

"Brother," Anne said when they parted again. "Where's Lirr?"

"Close, but Olsa says he'll have to come on foot from his position," Demery answered.

Olsa and Illya, the Usti Sooth and Voyager I'd met back in Hesten, had settled in behind the captain. My mother broke away and nodded to the Uknaras with familiarity. They knew one another. Other members of Bretton's surviving crew?

Demery, meanwhile, called to me. "Hello, Mary."

"Captain," I returned with a heavily mittened salute.

The final member of the company was Charles Grant. He joined me beneath the oak as the others began to confer. Samuel cast us a lingering look, but was soon wrapped up in planning.

"I feel as though I should apologize." Grant glanced warily at the branches above us and settled in at my shoulder. "Though honestly, you are the one who ran away at the palace."

"You're a terrible bodyguard, Charles," I replied, but my eyes crinkled. With Lirr closing in, the vestiges of Grant's and my enmity seemed particularly irrelevant. "You practically told Lirr where you were, shouting like you did."

"I'd hardly have drunk so much if I'd known there would be fighting," Charles grumbled.

I smiled. "Well, I'm glad you're here."

"As am I." Charles squinted down at the rest of the company, currently listening to my mother. "Though I'm most interested to know how you two escaped Lirr. I assumed you would still be locked in the belly of his ship."

I remembered just how many people *were* locked in the hold of Lirr's ship, and suppressed a shiver.

"We walked," I said with intentional lightness, and was rewarded by his stunned expression.

"Walked?" the former highwayman flustered. "How?"

"Magic," I replied with a wink.

Grant gave me a flat look, but before he could press further, Demery's voice interrupted.

"Now," the captain said, looking at the assembled company before resting his eyes on Anne. "We plot."

Our council transitioned to Demery's cabin, where I settled in gratefully beside the stove as the captain, my mother, Samuel, Athe and Olsa Uknara fell to business. Grant sat on the other side of the stove from me, one leg hooked his knee and a cup of steaming, rum-spiked tea in his hands. I balanced my own cup on my lap, watching as Widderow shouldered into the room with her ledgers.

She shoved in beside Samuel and set the books down with a solid thump. "Mines. I can give you mines, James. Enough mines and grenades to turn Lirr's folk into spittle and toothpicks."

Samuel startled, either at the old woman's sudden proximity or her talk of munitions. I concealed a smile.

Grant, blowing at his cup of tea, frowned at me.

"That would be helpful, Old Crow," Demery replied. He braced on the table, palms flat, fingers splayed. "Simply put, we need to lay a trap. Mary will be the bait, at the heart of the Wold. Without her, Lirr can't finish this, so even if he realizes we're waiting for him— which he may—he'll still have to make a play."

Samuel's lips thinned to a line.

My mother spoke up. "Mary and I will wait. We escaped Lirr together—he may sense if we separate, and be suspicious."

"Lirr can track you as well, Ms. Anne Firth," Samuel said, more of a clarification than a question. He surveyed the group and I noticed an odd distance behind his eyes, as if he wasn't quite here. He chose his words carefully. "The lot of you have a… light, in the Other. Except Mr. Grant. Olsa is a Sooth, both our Ms. Firths are Stormsingers, so that's to be expected. But are you a mage, Captain Demery? Or you two?" At the last, his eyes skimmed Athe and Widderow.

It took me a moment to understand what Samuel was saying. Demery, Athe and Widderow all had reflections in the Other, even though they were not mages. But Demery, I knew, was *ghiseau*. So were Athe and Widderow too?

I nearly spilled my tea, but only Grant appeared to notice. He offered me a handkerchief, plain but obviously stolen—the initials on the corner were not his.

"Don't look at me too long in the Other, lad," Widderow chided Samuel, back at the table. "This mortal frame is not so lovely as it once was."

Samuel cleared his throat, his hand contracted in his pocket, and the distant look in his eyes vanished. "I saw only your light, Ms. Widderow. I assure you."

"Sure you did." Athe *tsk*ed, trying very hard not to laugh.

Samuel's neck flushed red, Widderow cackled, and my mother cracked a smile. She nearly glowed now, her eyes filled with grim good humor and determination. She was at home here, with these people, and my heart warmed to see it. I suspected she was more herself now than she'd been in a very long time.

"Leave the boy, Crow," Olsa chided from her spot, leaning against the wall with her ankles crossed. "He does not realize what company he's in."

"We're *ghiseau*, Mr. Rosser." Demery faced the other man across the table and offered a resigned, half-smile. "Do you know what that means?"

"Those bound through spirit to wood and blood," Samuel said with a tone of recitation. He pulled a slim red book from his pocket, its front gilded with Mereish lettering, and held it up. "I have done my research."

Athe nodded, eyeing the book with something between wariness and curiosity. "Myself, the Old Crow, James, Olsa and her husband are all *ghiseau*. Anne was, but she's passed the creature on to her get, far as we can tell."

"She did," I said. I disliked Samuel learning of my nature like this, so off-hand and communal, when I'd barely had time to understand it myself.

But more than that, I was taken aback by the affirmation that almost everyone in the cabin was more than human. Like me. *We* were something other, and we were united in that difference.

My heart swelled. *We*.

"It seems I'm the only one unaffiliated," Grant said loud enough for everyone to hear, gesturing with his cup. "What's a man got to do to get himself possessed by a ghisting?"

"That's no joke." My mother cowed him with a look.

Grant hid his affront behind a sip of tea and a haze of steam.

"Lirr is *ghiseau* as well?" Samuel inquired, slipping the book back into his pocket.

Demery nodded. As he did, Harpy appeared from the bulkhead. Other ghistings materialized too, some more vague than others, but all in the vicinity of their hosts. Harpy stood behind Demery, her face maskless and blank, skirts rippling in an unseen wind. A shadow loomed behind Athe, huge and shaggy—a bear? An indistinct shape flitted behind Olsa and on Widderow's shoulder, a spectral crow rustled its feathers. It was the pale crow I'd once seen, flying over her head in Tithe.

I glanced down at my hands, half fearing and half hoping to see them haze with a ghisten glow, but Tane did not show herself.

"Lirr's connection with his ghisting, Hoten, was accidental," Demery went on. "But they took it in their head that we should all become like them. Thus, here on these shores, twenty years ago, Lirr murdered us all with shards of ghisten wood. We intend to stop him before he does the same to you, our crews, and many others besides."

"He has a hundred people locked in his hold," I put in soberly. "Waiting to be... merged with the ghistings in the Wold and the other wrecked ships."

Demery nodded. "I'm not surprised. Many of his own crew will meet the same fate—whether they want to or not. As a Magni, his sway over them is strong."

Samuel surveyed the other occupants of the room for a stretch of long, stunned silence. Then he said, "I see. Will your ghistings aid our cause?"

"Yes, yes they will." Widderow suddenly grinned. On her shoulder the ghisten crow cawed with a voice only I, and the other *ghiseau*, could hear, and pecked at the old woman's carnelian hair pin. Its spectral flesh went right through the substance, and it cocked its head in consternation.

Demery said, "So, this is our plan. Mary and Anne will wait, in the heart of the Wold. Lirr will struggle to find you, with the presence of so many ghistings, but this will also conceal us from his sight. We'll station ourselves around the perimeter, until Lirr and his people are within our noose. Then, Mary, you'll run for the shore we met you on today. Draw Lirr's folk with you. We'll pick them off along the way—he has many *ghiseau*, but even they can be slowed—and when the rest of them reach the beach..."

Behind him, Harpy selected a mask from her array and flicked it out to reveal the face of a hungry, sly fox.

On the other side of the fire, Grant shifted, looking into his mug with a face that looked a touch too pale. I furrowed my brows at him, but Demery's next words distracted me.

"*Harpy*'s guns will be waiting to blast them to pieces. So take shelter quickly, Ms. Firth. You'd survive a belly full of shrapnel, but I'd obviously prefer you didn't have to. The same applies to Lirr— the blast will not kill him, but once he's wounded, we can dispose of both him and Hoten."

"This 'Hoten' can die?" Samuel clarified. He trailed a finger across the outline of the book, in his pocket. "I was not aware ghistings could be killed."

Olsa was the one who replied. "That's part of the reason why Lirr must be stopped. Only when a ghisting is bound to a mortal body does it become mortal. Lirr thinks he's bringing freedom to ghistings. Instead, he brings them death. We must catch Lirr when Hoten is manifesting outside his body, then we kill him, and they will both fade."

Over the next hour, the finer details of the pirates' plot were laid out. Widderow left to oversee the arming of the crew. Grant departed in Athe's shadow, expression distracted and eyes distant as the two of them went to organize the Wold's defenses. Olsa murmured something in Samuel's ear that I didn't catch, then she, too, left. My mother followed her.

Finally, I was left with Samuel Rosser, Captain Demery and Harpy, who paced back and forth across the stern windows, still wearing the face of a fox, skirts swishing about her hips.

Samuel seemed more conscious of my presence than the ghisting's, but kept his focus respectfully on Demery as he said, "Captain, I'd like your permission to visit my brother before I head ashore."

"Benedict is here?" I asked. I'd gathered Demery had prisoners aboard, but not Samuel's twin. "Why?"

"He and his captain intended to take *Hart* and kill Demery and his crew, so they are currently locked in the hold," Samuel told me.

"But, Benedict only does what is in his best interest. He has no real loyalty, nothing by way of conscience—save what I can convince him of. If I can persuade him to turn against Ellas, he would be a powerful ally. He is a Magni."

Demery measured the younger man's gaze across the table. Harpy, still pacing before the windows, cocked her vulpine head and scrutinized the pirate hunter.

I'd a sense the two were communicating, but heard nothing at all.

"Fine," Demery decided. He took up his jacket from the back of a chair and made for the door. Harpy darted after him, vanishing into his frame in one graceful, barefooted leap and a ripple of ethereal skirts. Demery did not flinch. "Speak to him and report back to me before you go ashore. I'll be on deck."

The door closed, then Samuel and I were alone in Demery's cabin. Silence bloomed between us, punctuated with the crew preparing for conflict—clatters, shouts, thuds, rolls and the tramping of feet.

"I've much to say," Samuel finally began. "But little idea how to say it, and even less time to say it in."

I felt my gaze soften. "Me too. But I can say... I am sorry I took your coat, and your coin."

His smile was wry. "I had nearly forgotten about that."

"Oh." I nearly smiled back. "Then don't let me remind you."

Samuel's grin deepened before a weight returned to his eyes. "I cannot apologize enough for my part in Kaspin's auction. I had no desire to be there... but that is no excuse. I was there, and I understand if you resent me for that."

I looked at him more closely. I remembered the way he'd looked at the auction, how uncomfortable and sour he'd been. I knew he hadn't wanted to be there, but I appreciated the apology all the same.

"And for the way I pushed you to join Hart, in Tithe," the man continued. "I had no idea the pressures upon you, or other... factors, at play."

"You did what you thought was right," I conceded. "Perhaps you *were* right. If I'd gone with you, perhaps matters would have been simpler. Perhaps I'd have been safer. Or not."

"I am glad you did not come." Samuel shoved his hands deep into his pockets, and I saw the movement of his fingers as he worried something there. The coin? "My former captain, Slader... He could not have been trusted, not with you. I was wrong."

There was genuine regret in his tone, along with a protective edge that warmed me, overturning memories of Benedict's words and Samuel's rumored past.

"Then for these things we're forgiven, you and I," I summarized, settling my shoulders. I glanced at the door of my own cabin, closed in the far wall, and felt a sudden urge to be alone. My thoughts and feelings were a tangle, not least of them due to my role in tonight's events.

But the thought of Samuel's pending visit to Benedict, and all that they might say, tempted me.

"You should go see to your brother," I reminded him. "I need to prepare."

Samuel nodded, though I didn't miss the flicker of disappointment in his eyes. "Of course. I will see you when this is over, Ms. Firth. And I hope we can start afresh."

I let myself smile at that. He returned the expression and moved to the door, opening it and stepping into the passageway.

"Farewell, Ms. Firth," he said, lingering.

"Farewell," I echoed.

I listened to his footsteps fade. I counted each step, and calculated how many he would need to take to cross the deck and descend to where the prisoners were held in the forward hold.

Then I slipped out of the door, and quietly followed him.

FORTY-ONE

Honor, Dishonor and Benedict Rosser

SAMUEL

I managed to still my shaking hands by the time I faced Benedict, but only just. Mary's forgiveness impacted me more deeply than I expected, and everything I had learned tonight was an urgent jangling at the back of my mind.

But now I had to focus on my brother.

Benedict peeled from the shadows as I approached the forward hold with a hooded lantern. Bars and barriers had been erected over the space, cutting it off from the crates and barrels and bundles that packed the rest of the hold. Demery had obviously been prepared, and the prison was sound.

"Sam." My twin leaned against the bars. Beyond him, the thirty or so crewmembers who had accompanied him languished, glaring and muttering in the shadows. "Did she tell you about us?"

"Who—" Immediately off-footed, I closed my mouth and fought to regroup. He was trying to take the upper hand, and I could not let him. "I am here to help you, Ben."

"She enjoyed it, there is little doubt of that," Benedict went on. His tone was flippant, but his stare was as fixed as a hunting wolf. And like a wolf, his eyes glistened in the light of my lantern. "Tasted like wine, and smelled of winter wind and sweat. Sweet, is a woman's sweat. On her cheeks. Her throat. Her breasts."

Rage hit me like a rogue wave. For an instant, all I could see was a vision of smashing my brother into the bars.

When the impulse passed, I still stood a pace away from the prison, but the slim handle of the lantern had bent in my grasp.

"Do not speak of Alice like that," I hissed, trying to speak quietly enough that his crew—or any pirates in the myriad shadows around the hold—would not overhear. "I am here to help you. Do you want to die?"

"Alice?" Benedict laughed, but when he continued, his voice was as low as mine. "No, *she* tasted like… what did she call it? Rosewater. Rosewater, and the lavender tucked under her pillow. So clean. So proper. I doubt Mary's ever touched rosewater in her life, no matter what they dressed her in for that party. Now Mary, she's much different than Alice. Except for how badly she wanted me."

Before I knew I was moving, I had Ben by the collar. I hauled him into the bars with a clatter and reached both hands through, grinding him into the rough iron.

"Continue acting like a dog, and you'll soon die like one," I spat in his ear. "There is only one person here who gives a shit what happens to you."

I saw the whites of Ben's eyes as he craned to look up at me. He panted in pain, but grinned all the same. "You want to kill me right now."

"I do," I growled, then shoved him, hard. He stumbled backwards and nearly tripped, but caught himself. "However, you remain my brother."

Benedict clutched his crushed face for a moment, then muttered, "Uncle's not here to whip us, Sam. You can stop being my savior."

I snorted, overwhelmed by scorn and loathing. I raked hair back from my eyes and forced my breath out in a steady, measured rhythm.

"I am not doing this because of him," I said, speaking each word intentionally. "I am doing this for myself. I do not want my brother to die. I do not want to be the one who kills him. I want you to be a better man so that I can look you in the eye and not despise you. So shut up and listen to me."

Silence fell between us. I heard a brush of fabric against wood, somewhere in the shadows, but attributed it to Ben's gaping crew, witness to everything I said.

Benedict watched me with an expression so intense, yet so opaque, I could not read it.

"Help Demery defeat Lirr. Fisher has taken care of Ellas—she is of no use to you anymore. You have few cards left to play, so play them right. Otherwise these pirates may kill you, and I will not stop them. You would have hung them all."

Ben rolled his eyes, ignoring the bit about Ellas. "Sympathizing with pirates, Sam? *You* are a traitor."

"They are the ones in power now," I countered. "You of all people ought to realize that being a pirate—a murderer, *adulterer*—does not guarantee justice. Besides, I would rather fight beside a pirate with a just cause than a 'lawful' captain like Ellas."

Consideration flickered behind his eyes.

"I ought to despise you for siding with him and locking me in here," Ben admitted, eyeing me up and down. "But I never thought I would hear you say something like that. You have always been so…"

"Do not say 'honorable,'" I growled. "I am not."

"I was going to say bull-headed and dull." My brother smirked. He considered me for another minute, then decided, "Fine. I will help the pirates, but only against Lirr. I want my prize, and I want my commission intact—help me get that. I have my eye on a captaincy."

His grin was more than a little cruel as he added, "Uncle has to be proud of one of us."

My throat thickened. I nearly abandoned him then, and left him to Demery's justice.

But in the back of my mind lingered two young boys, one's hands bloodied from a lash. I remembered a night of pain and suffering that I could have prevented.

I heard my uncle's voice too. But, no… perhaps it was no longer the voice of an admiral behind his desk. It was my own.

He is my responsibility.

"I will do what I can for you," I vowed. I considered telling him of what the Mereish merchant had said, of possibilities of healing, but the glint in his eyes told me that only blood would sate him today. "You will sail home in glory."

"And the prize?" Ben prompted.

"I will ensure you are given your fair share."

"Fine, then." My brother laced his arms over his chest and looked back at his crewmembers. I did not need to slip into the Other to sense he was using his Magni's power when he said, "Right, sailors, we are going to help the pirates kill Lirr. Any objections?"

I left him before their cheers filled the hold. I wove through the ship, passing pirates preparing for battle. They barely glanced at me, clearing for action and readying the guns. There were no insults or threats, no brawling or drunkenness. They were just men and women with tasks, some pale with nerves, others grim, and yet others laughing and encouraging one another on.

They were people, criminals, but people all the same. People who would fight and die beside me tonight.

I found Athe in the melee and told her of Ben's decision.

"He is a Magni," I warned. "Be cautious of anything you think or feel when he is about."

"I am familiar with the sort," she returned, surveying a pair of young crewfolk as they clattered cannonballs into cradles between the guns. "Demery and I will discuss it. If I'm not convinced, I will not let that man free, understood? I would sooner put him down than jeopardize this crew."

"That is all I ask."

It was not until I was up on deck, in sight of the Wold and the icy sea, that I offered a quiet prayer—for Benedict's cooperation, for my own conscience, and for Mary's safety.

Triggered by the thought of Mary, the world slipped. I blinked as the edge of the Other enfolded me, igniting the Ghistwold into a sky of soft, glowing stars. I glimpsed the ghisting Harpy, drifting along the rail of the ship like an acrobat across a wire, her expression distant. Below me in the belly of the ship, Mary's light moved.

Olsa Uknara stopped in front of me. Grey-green in the Other, she peered into my face with a distracted intensity I recognized.

"What do you see?" I asked, still half submerged in that second world.

"I see flickering light, and Dark Water licking your heels," the woman replied. There was no disdain in her practical tone, but there were hints of concern and curiosity. "Someone tried to amplify you?"

I shoved my hand into my pocket and grasped the coin, recalling myself to my flesh. "Yes. Though I have heard there is a cure in Mere."

"Oh?" The tanned skin about the Usti's eyes wrinkled as she considered this, intrigued. "Well, that may be. Or it may not. Either way, when this is over, you and I must speak. I can train you. To see, to banish and to summon."

"I was trained at Ismoathe..." I started to say, but trailed off at her last words. Summon?

"Wife!" the other big Usti, Illya, called across the deck.

"Stay alive, Samuel," Olsa instructed me. Her familiarity was surprising, but somehow, it felt right. "And I will make a proper Sooth of you."

FORTY-TWO

Harmony

MARY

Demery's and Rosser's crews spread out through the Wold, trudging through the snow to various defensive positions. Meanwhile, *Harpy* slipped along a thick ice shelf on the western shore and tucked herself behind the wreck of a huge, triple-decked Capesh warship with shredded, sun-bleached red sails.

The pirates' deck was a flurry of action as it slipped from sight. Gun crews swarmed the cannons and marksmen lined up under Bailey's command, the barrels of their long Usti rifles catching the Second Sun's waxing light.

"*Harpy* will be there to deal with Lirr's ship if he comes into play, and provide a retreat for us," Demery explained as a small army gathered on the edge of the Wold. "If you hear two cannon shots, right after one another, that's the signal all has gone to hell. Retreat to the ship and don't look back. She'll be right along the edge of the ice shelf to pick us up."

Soon after, marksmen ascended the trees of the Wold, bundled to the eyes, with rifles slung across their backs. They ran across branches like yard arms, their boots secured by ice teeth, and hid themselves in the shadowed lattice of the canopy.

Among them, I sighted Grant. He held back as his comrades started off through the icy forest.

"See, I knew my experience as a highwayman would come in

handy. Here I am, back in a forest, orchestrating an ambush." Grant grinned at me, but it didn't reach his eyes.

"Well, this is my first proper ambush," I remarked, trying to pick up the lightness of his tone. "Abetha's reputation did all the work last time."

Grant's eyes lingered on my face—my eyes, my lips—and my levity turned hollow. I'd caught this look in his eyes before, but it was clearer now, more brazen. Samuel had looked at me the same way and I'd no doubt as to what it meant, though I couldn't contemplate addressing it right now.

"You've your own reputation now," Grant said.

"As a middling Stormsinger who keeps managing not to die?" I quipped.

"You are that, yes." He cocked a grin. "But you are also brave and persistent. Saint, you put up with me. That is a heroic act."

I smiled, but he must have seen the hesitation in my eyes.

"Well," Grant cleared his throat and saluted, "I'll see you when the dust settles, Mary."

I nodded and he vanished into the trees. I stared after him for a long moment, discontent, sympathy and confusion turning my already unhappy stomach. Then I fortified myself and set off.

My mother, Demery, Olsa and Illya waited beneath the larch. I listened as Anne reiterated the plan for the dozenth time and watched Olsa and Illya leave to scout. Finally, Rosser appeared with two sailors and Demery moved to confer with him.

Samuel Rosser glanced at me as if he had something he wished to say, but unlike Grant, he kept focused on his task.

For my part, I hesitated, recalling all I'd overheard in the hold just a few hours before. I wanted to tell him I knew the truth about him and Benedict now. I wanted to tell him that I thought him a good man. I sensed what those words would mean to him, but with Lirr, the coming battle and my own condition weighing upon me, I already felt vulnerable. I couldn't summon the strength to expose myself any further.

So I smiled at him, if a little sadly. His expression gentled and he offered a nod in return, then he was gone into the snow and the shadows.

Finally, my mother and I lit a small fire, sheltered by the rock where the larch grew, and settled in. Trees moaned in the frigid wind, branches squeaking, bare limbs rattling. Loose snow raced across the crusted surface and I burrowed my chin in my scarf. I thought of the marksmen in the treetops, and Grant and Rosser at their posts. I wouldn't be surprised if, come tomorrow, half the casualties were from cold.

Anne sat beside me and started to sing softly. The wind eased and the half-night quietened around us. Even the murmur of sleeping ghistings seemed to hush. If I hadn't known this strange forest sheltered our small army, I would never have guessed it.

Their footprints in the snow, however, would betray them right away.

Anne kept singing, and as she did, words welled up in my throat too. I brushed my bottom lip across the frosty edge of my scarf for an indecisive moment, then pulled the scarf down and joined in.

The song was a common one, the kind Demery's sailors sung to pass the time, but my mother made it into a gentler thing, with sweet minors and a subtle warning behind each word. I matched her tone and took on a natural harmony, hedging her words and echoing them.

As we did, the wind faded and it began to snow.

"Oh, now the storm is raging
and we are far from shore;
The poor old ship she's sinking fast
and the riggings they are tore."

Thick snowflakes drifted down from the sky above, thickening until I could barely see Tane's larch, lording above us.

"*The night is dark and dreary,*
we can scarcely see the moon,
But still I live in hope to see
the Holy Ground once more."

The snow thickened. Our song filled the Wold until every footprint, every trace of our forces was gone.

Snow continued to fall long after Anne and I stopped singing, piling up around us and clinging to our clothes. It hissed and evaporated in our fire, the only sound other than the rush of my blood and the whisper of my breath.

Finally, Tane spoke. She felt like memory or a fragmented dream, but truer and more familiar than either could ever be.

Sister, she hummed through my chest. *They're coming.*

Gunshots erupted through the Wold.

FORTY-THREE

Black Tide Son

SAMUEL

I unfolded from the shelter of a boulder and fired. My target fell like a sack of grain and I ducked to reload. On either side of me, my companions cracked off shots, the mist of their breaths mingling with gun smoke and snow in the north's infinite dusk.

I fired again. This time an enemy musket ball clipped my forearm and I cursed, dropping back behind the boulder. Another shot slammed into the rock with a spattering of dust.

I flexed my hand against a backdrop of white snow, trying to make out the damage in the weak light. There were two tears around the elbow of my coat where the shot had passed through and I felt trickling blood, but I could still move my hand. The pain of it was distant, blurred by my racing heart and the bitter cold.

More muskets cracked and I looked left, following their sound deeper into the Wold. Our targets were following the path we had planned for them through the heart of the forest to Mary, then to the western shore—where they would be trapped between *Harpy*'s guns and our advance.

"Get ready to move," I grunted to my companions, reloading my musket as quickly as I could manage. "We push."

Word passed down the line and, clutching my wounded arm to my side, musket angled towards the snow, I crouched.

"Ready?" I whispered. "Move."

We broke cover, our boots punching through fresh powder in a low, steady jog. Flakes still drifted from the sky above, though the unnaturally fat clusters summoned by Mary and Anne's song had given way to something closer to hail, hard and fine and shushing off our clothing.

We ducked into the cover of a wrecked ship, masts lying horizontal across the forest floor. A low-spreading, immense hawthorn burst from its equine figurehead and arched over us as we ducked under the masts and around the far side of the ship.

"Hold," I called.

We fell into a line in the shadow of the hawthorn, shoulder to shoulder with muskets leveled and breath drifting. I nudged my sweaty cap back from my forehead and watched the night for any sign of movement, but the world seemed impossibly still. No bloodshed, no pirates. Just blankets of white and shadowed trees in the perpetual dusk.

Two cannon shots rang out, one after another.

Disbelief ricocheted up my spine. That was *Harpy*'s signal for retreat, but our assault had barely begun.

"Somethin's gone wrong," Penn, his own cap slid up into its usual impish point, muttered beside me. "Run for the ship, boss?"

Dread cloyed at me—I could think of several reasons why Demery would signal the retreat, and none of them were good. Perhaps Lirr's ship had arrived unexpectedly, *Harpy* was about to be taken, or Mary had…

No, I could not think of her. I had to keep focused on my task and trust her to do hers.

"To the shore!" I called in the wake of the cannons.

I barely spoke loudly enough to be heard by my companions, but it was enough to give us away.

Muskets and pistols cracked all around, pops and flashes in the night. A hawthorn branch over my head exploded and ghisten light burst in the gloom, swirling and churning over the tree.

I lunged into a run. "To the shore!"

Pirates and pirate hunters answered my call. We stumbled and leapt, bolted and jogged as, in the murk, the muzzles of Lirr's muskets went dark. Reloading.

"Go, go, go!" I roared, grabbing a nearby man—boy, big eyes, bloody cheeks—and shoving him into motion. "Move!"

We were a dozen paces on before the muskets cracked again. The boy, a pace away from me in the night, lost the back of his skull in a mist of blood and hit the snow with a wordless tumble.

There was blood in my eyes, panic in my mouth, but I could not cry out—or at least, if I did, I could not feel it. My mind snared on the boy's last moments, the fear in his young face. But my body did not stop moving. It could not, even when the Other reared.

Instead of punching through snow, my feet splashed through the shallow waters of the Wold's Other side. I kept on, straining against that second world and praying I would sprint right back into my own flesh. I was not too deep, not yet, and I sensed I was still moving in the human world. But not for much longer.

I had to get back. I strained, willed and fought. I reached for the coin but my wounded arm would not work.

The Dark Water became clearer. Blue lights ignited around me. Roots of ghisten trees arched above my head, twisted and tangled. Fae dragonflies swirled in a roar of wings and darting light, and in the water beneath me the white glow of morgories converged on my boots.

I cursed and ran for the nearest tree, a huge birch with roots that reared out of the water into a small island.

My feet barely left the water in time. I threw myself at the birch, scattering a hundred dragonflies from its rolls of bark as I pressed into them.

Morgories reared out of the water at my heels. There were dozens of them, snapping at the water that dripped from my boots. The heinous mingling of feline and equine, they bared layers of serrated teeth and unfurled their plumes in waves of fine, feathery fins. The fins shook like leaves, misting about their heads, and their blazing white eyes already tore the flesh from my bones.

I tried to return to my body. I strained and I pulled, I reached for the coin, but I was too deep in the Other.

Horror crashed over me. I was a child again, six years old and trapped inside my nightmares. Trapped by a cup of milk I had trustingly taken from my mother's hands, even though it tasted like rotted fruit and sour wine. Trapped by the foul magic the Black Tide had told her would make me more powerful, even while Benedict lay in the bed beside me, bandaged and healing from his own ordeal—the one that had shattered his mind and made him what he was. The ordeal I had failed to stop.

The morgories shrieked. The sound clawed at me like a physical force. I felt a shapeless sound tear from my throat.

In my ears, I heard a boy's shrill, sobbing scream. But I was not screaming. I was roaring, a furious, final bellow of horror and rage and a hundred other fragmented emotions.

The morgories fled. I was left standing on my root island, spine to the birch, as the creatures scattered into the Dark Water. Dragonflies escaped too, and I stood alone for a ragged, panting instant.

Passages from the Mereish book of ghistlore flickered through my head. I had devoured as much as I could of the tome in the final hours before the battle, and now my mind tried to etch out the significance to what I had just done. But my blood was too high to think clearly.

Somewhere distant, my fingers closed around the coin. I snapped back into my limbs to find someone trying to haul me upright beneath a sleeping, winter birch. Snow melted on my skin and filled every crevice of my clothing, susurrating into my eyes.

I blinked like a man reborn. Beyond my companion, the canopy of the Wold had thinned. The edge was in sight. I was back, I was alive, and we were almost to the shore.

"Sir!" Penn saw my eyes open and staggered back. "Thought I'd lost you! Are you injured? Got to move, now, sir, now!"

My breath hitched in my throat and emerged as a chaotic laugh. I sounded like Ben, but I did not care. The monsters had fled from me. I had fallen into the Dark Water, the worst had happened, and I had emerged unscathed.

Penn's eyes rounded in unease. "Boss?"

"Run, Mr. Penn!" I shouted, finding my feet. Gunshots cracked in the frigid dusk but I felt immortal, my muscles fluid, my blood hot and my will like iron. The pain in my arm was nothing, a mere flicker on the edge of my consciousness.

Together, we ran until a ship's lanterns glistened in the gloom. *Harpy*. Ahead of us, the rest of our crew burst out of the Wold onto the open shoreline.

More cannons boomed. I had half a heartbeat to see their muzzles flash, half to realize they were firing *at us*, then shrapnel blasted the beach. My elation flickered, burned, and turned to ash on my tongue.

Men and women fell. Penn screamed and buckled into me, just in time to save us from certain death. We hit the ground in the shelter of a huge ghisten yew as bullets and shards of metal peppered into the other side.

I landed on my wounded arm. Pain burned all the way into my skull and I gasped a breathless curse. The last of my elation fled, boiling down to a hard, clean focus—and a bright, searing pain.

"Saint, what is this?" Penn cried, half growl of agony, half terrified plea. "Why's she firin' on us?"

Something was horribly, terribly wrong. I forced myself to move past the pain and peered out from under the branches.

The long guns were quiet now, but the twilight was not. Men and women screamed all down the shoreline, dying and bloodied and broken. The lanterns I had seen still floated on the water, but they were too high, and too far apart for *Harpy*'s.

There, in the spot where Demery's ship should have been, was Lirr's great warship.

We had run right into our own trap. How had they known? How had they taken control so quickly?

"Guns down and hands up."

I looked up the barrel of a musket. Blood thudded in my ears as I stared up into a pirate's face, and raised my hands in surrender.

FORTY-FOUR

Lirr's Rat

MARY

The forest around the larch filled with Lirr's pirates, shadows coalescing into men and women, guns and machetes.

There was no sign of Lirr himself, but fear made me want to claw out of my own skin. I battled it, standing beside my mother as pirates formed a half-circle around our fire, and I was proud when my hands did not shake. I was both terrified and in control.

"Surrender now, Fleetbreaker," someone called. "Cap'n wants you two alive, but he don't need you whole."

I raised a hand in signal, and muskets cracked from the treetops. Pirates dropped and staggered, crying out and cursing. Others scattered for shelter, throwing themselves behind ghisten trees or the hulls of wrecked ships. One even fled for Tane's larch, scrambling up her rocky perch before a shot picked him off. He hit the ground with a sickening crack.

But half a dozen pirates still charged. They rounded the fire and threw themselves at my mother and I with reckless, howling determination.

I held steady until the pirates were within four paces, chin lowered, pulse fluttering. Then I reached beneath my layers of clothes.

Four pistols leveled at the oncoming threat—two in my mother's hands, two in mine. We fired in unison. The pistols bucked, muzzles flashed, and three pirates went down.

Anne immediately shoved one pistol back through her brace and drew her cutlass. The other pistol she flipped, holding it back along her forearm as a shield. Then she threw herself into the fray.

She met our attackers with a witch's feral scream and a flurry of deft slashes. The wind came with her, an extension of her own flesh— throwing icy snow into the faces of our enemies as she blocked, cut and thrust with tight, rapid movements.

I had no time for awe, no time to watch her and the wind and their uncanny union or envy her skill. I had my own part in this plan.

It took all my strength to turn my back on her—on the mother I'd lost and found and might lose again. But I did, turning with purpose towards the distant *Harpy*, and I ran.

The Ghistwold folded in around me, snow crunching and cold burning. My breath rasped as I pelted in the direction of the western shore, leading any pursuers straight through the heart of the Wold and a corridor of death.

A muzzle flashed behind me. I instinctively plunged sideways into a snowbank, only to find my foot snared on the icy crust beneath the powder.

I crawled free with a curse, but I'd lost time. Pirates closed in. Lirr stalked out of the trees in the midst of them, illuminated by the horizontal light of the Second Sun. He wasn't alone—three people fled before him, Demery's or Samuel's crews, I couldn't tell.

Whoever they were, they weren't *ghiseau*. They fell so easily. Lirr shot one in the belly, and I was close enough to see the horror in her eyes. The second buckled under his companion's weight, and Lirr kicked them both down. He left them on the ground as he stabbed the third, slashing their knees with brutal efficiency.

I felt a moment of baffled dread. He wasn't killing them, though he easily could. Yes, the belly shot was a mortal wound, but not one that would kill with any speed. Why?

My thoughts fled as a pistol flared. The second victim pointed his smoking pistol towards Lirr's head, elation in his eyes. There was no way the shot could have missed, not at that range, but Lirr barely flinched. Instead, he rested his sword below the shooter's eye, and twisted its tip into his skull. His scream rang loud through the trees, rising and falling in unfettered horror.

It still echoed as Demery's folk loosed another volley from the treetops. Lirr's oncoming pirates scattered, plunging into the shelter of trees.

Lirr left his dying victims and advanced on me just as I freed my foot. I took off in a stumbling run, but the snow was so deep. I hit a drift and sank in again, cursing and panting in my panic.

Lirr grabbed the back of my coat and hauled me around. There was blood in his hair, smeared across his face, but he seemed unaware of it.

"Mary," he grunted in a perfunctory greeting and started to drag me back the way I'd come. I shrieked like a feral cat and beat at him until he shook me so hard my neck cracked and my vision blackened. Magni power flooded into me at the same time—dizzying and stifling.

"Stop. Fighting," he growled.

A musket cracked. I blinked blearily, and Lirr jerked as the shot buried itself in his collarbone—joining the bloody blossoms of more than one other lead ball. He didn't fall, but his power wavered.

I slammed my elbow into his and knocked his grasping arm wide. His attention snapped back to me and his cutlass flashed in his free hand, aiming for my legs, but I'd already pulled my knife.

Charles Grant would have been proud. We hadn't often fought knife against cutlass, but I was already inside Lirr's guard, driving the blade through his heavy coat into his thigh—once, twice, three times. Then I moved to his arm, slashing it open as I jerked free. He roared and I felt Magni power lance after me again—but it shuddered, weakened by his pain.

I fled into the trees, sprinting in the direction that felt like the shore, struggling through drifts, my breath ragged in my lungs. Sweat caked my face and cold seared every inch of my exposed skin.

Two cannon shots rang out, one on the heels of the other. They echoed all around me, distorted by trees and ice and muffling snow, but I recognized the signal to retreat.

I almost stopped running, shock coursing through me and muscles quaking with urgency. Something must have gone wrong at the beach, but what? I was the crux of the plan and here I was, waylaid but still heading towards my goal, Lirr in close pursuit.

Unless something had happened to *Harpy*.

I forced myself to start running again. Get to the shore. Get to the ship—that's where my mother would be headed. Even if everything *had* gone to hell, Athe must still have our retreat and I could escape Lirr.

I glanced over my shoulder. I couldn't see the pirate—the forest was still, the only movement distant and fleeting—but that was no comfort. My skin crawled.

"Mary? Mary!"

I spun at the sound of Grant's voice, slipped, and hit the ground with a painful thud. I wheezed and tried to stand up, but I'd wandered onto a frozen river, hidden beneath the fresh snow. I went back down.

Grant skidded into sight. He poised for an instant on the ice to find his balance, arms outstretched, then gave a hoarse laugh and skated towards me.

Relief made me wobbly. I shifted onto my knees and, finding a knot of roots on the riverbank, managed to pull myself upright.

"There you are! You're going the wrong way." He spoke with forced cheer. His face was deathly pale, making his scarred cheeks stand out even more amid his blond stubble. His cutlass was still at his belt but he'd lost his gun.

His crew of makeshift highwayfolk were nowhere in sight, but I didn't let myself think of what had happened to them, or my mother, or Rosser, or Demery or anyone else. If I did I'd lose all nerve, and we had to get to *Harpy*.

"Lirr's behind me. Not wrong way." I coughed, still trying to find my breath. I glanced in the direction I'd been running. Still no sign of Lirr. I was sure I'd been heading the right direction. I hadn't really thought about it; I was relying on Tane's senses and memory of the Wold.

He's lying, the ghisting whispered.

Lying. Not wrong, lying. My relationship with Grant may have started badly, but he'd proven himself since. And I hadn't forgotten the way he looked at me earlier. Whether or not I reciprocated his feelings, they should protect me. For the most part.

"No, this is the way." I nodded in the direction I'd been heading. "Follow me."

At that moment, more cannon fire echoed through the Wold. I flinched and Grant threw his arms over his head, shouting some profanity that was drowned by the guns.

"What the hell was that?" I asked, overloud in the silence.

"Lirr's ship." Grant grabbed my hand, and even through layers of wool and leather, I felt him shaking. "Please, Mary, follow me."

"How…" I drew back, though his fingers remained fast around mine. The situation pulled me back to the gallows, when I'd grasped his hand in the maelstrom and trusted him to lead me out of danger.

But he hadn't, had he?

"Charles, how do you know that's Lirr's ship?" I asked, very carefully.

"The guns sound too deep," Grant tried, but there was a weakness in his voice. He stared at me for a round-eyed, frustrated instant, dropped my hand. "Saint's blood… Mary…" He stepped back, pushing his hat off his forehead.

"Grant," I snapped, his name an accusation and a demand. "What's wrong with you? We don't have time—"

"It was because of him, Mary."

"What?"

"Kaspin. My debt was paid, but I would never have been free of him. I needed a way out of Aeadine, so I tried to join Lirr's crew in Whallum. Kaspin sent me to invite him to the auction and when I saw the ship…" Grant shakily brushed at a scarred cheek. "I thought it was my way out. But Lirr laughed at me, Mary. Laughed and said I'd no idea what I was asking. He said he'd only take me if I proved myself worthy, and my pride was up and… I agreed without even knowing what I'd have to do. Stealing, I thought, or maybe a murder. How could I have known he'd ask me to spy on Demery?"

I knew distantly that we should be running, but I was momentarily blinded by rage and shock. "What?"

"I think he meant it as a joke," Grant mumbled, flinching under my stare. "A foolish gamble, a way to drive me off or get me killed by my own stupidity. But I was so angry by then, so determined to prove myself. I thought, hell, why not be the best damn spy the murderous bastard has ever had?"

"What have you done, Charles?" I demanded. The wind began to move around us at the sound of my voice, whisking snow across the ice under our feet.

"Too much. Not enough." Grant's eyes softened, near pleading. "I'd no idea what he was, Mary, you must believe that! And I warned Randalf, to protect you in Whallum."

"Did you do this?" I stabbed a finger in the direction of Lirr's waiting ship, beyond the Wold. My heart hammered in my throat. "Did you betray Demery? You've killed them all!"

"Mary, please—"

"Are you going to hand me over to him? To be butchered?"

"No!" He shouted the word, his voice breaking halfway through into an agonized whisper. "I warned Lirr, yes. His… That creature of his found me last night, Mary, the ghisting, and I told him about *Harpy*. But I'm not taking you to him. I'm saving you."

"Saving me?" It took all my strength not to scream the words back. "How?"

Sister, run, Tane warned.

"You said you walked through the Stormwall." Grant stepped towards me, his expression, his posture—all of it sincerity and guilt and urgency. "You're a Stormsinger. You can get us back south. We can walk away from all this, leave them to kill one another. You and me."

I couldn't move. My muscles had turned to stone and my head felt as though it were underwater.

Sister! Tane hissed.

Hoten stepped around the trunk of the nearest tree. I'd barely registered the long shard of wood in his hand before he drove it into Grant's neck.

I did scream then. I lunged forward, tried to save Grant despite what he'd admitted, but strong arms locked around me. Grant fell to his knees, clutching the wooden dagger in his flesh in terror and confusion and hopelessness, and all I could do was scream.

The wind shuddered and branches clattered overhead.

"There now, Tane," Lirr whispered into my ear, his voice thick with sorcery and his breath the only warm thing in my icy, terrible world. "It's time to go home."

AN EXCERPT FROM:

A HISTORY OF GHISTLORE AND THE BLESSED; THOSE BOUND TO THE SECOND WORLD AND THE POWER THEREIN

THE SUMMONER ADJACENT remains one of the rarest abilities associated with the Sooth. As an overflow of their preternatural connection to the Other and their ability to traverse its waters, Summoners may attract the attention of Other-born beasts such as morgories, dittama and huden, which can do them grave physical harm. The dittama remain the most dangerous of these, encompassing a larger subcategory of beasts which are too numerous, and too difficult to study, to be effectively rendered here.

The more these beasts are attracted to a Sooth in the Other, the greater the likelihood that the Sooth is, indeed, a Summoner; one who may command the loyalty and favor of such beasts, though at great peril.

FORTY-FIVE

The Summoner Adjacent

SAMUEL

A pirate thrust me to my knees beside a bonfire. The small flame Mary and her mother used to lure Lirr's pirates was gone, built into a hellish blaze at the foot of the larch's rock. It filled the Wold with light and heat and roaring flames, and turned everything beyond its reach into pure, impenetrable darkness.

Penn huddled beside me. The tops of his ears were white with frostbite but he was oblivious, long past pain. "They're bringin' in more prisoners, sir."

I followed his gaze, each shallow breath fogging from my lips. My crew and Demery's pirates, many of whom had suffered in the carnage on shore, were hauled into sight. Clots of other prisoners came with them, men and women I did not recognize, haggard and stumbling and linked by long chains—the captives from Lirr's hold, I imagined.

Charles Grant was among those Lirr's loyalists dragged into sight. His glassy eyes stared out at the forest as they set him down against a boulder and left him there, slumped and silent. He was pale as sun-bleached canvas, a shard of wood embedded in his throat.

He ought to be dead, judging from that wound and the amount of blood on his clothes. So should dozens of the other wounded around him. But their chests rose and fell, and Grant's glazed eyes blinked every so often.

Fear clawed up my spine. Had Lirr already bonded them? Had that shard held a ghisting?

The pirate himself emerged from the forest after his subordinates who had borne Grant. He had Mary by the back of the head, her arms bound before her. He barely glanced over the assembly before he jerked her towards the larch's great rock and shoved her upwards. She'd been divested of most of her outer clothing, leaving her in her trousers and a thick wool shirt.

Run, I willed to Mary, but her movements were lethargic. One blink into the Other told me why. There, on the edge of worlds, I saw Lirr's eyes hedged with red—full, bloody, violent red.

His influence spread as I watched. The whimpering of the injured faded and his loyalists tracked his progress up the rock with worshipful eyes.

Lirr was in the height of his power, here, at the end.

"Lirr!" Anne's voice called from the other side of the fire.

It took all my strength to look away from Lirr and find the older woman. She was here. Mary was here. Lirr was here. So where were Demery and the Usti and Athe? Had anyone escaped *Harpy*?

Benedict. I tried not to think of him, locked in *Harpy*'s hold as the ship went down, or as Lirr's pirates tore through her hatches.

"Lirr!" the Fleetbreaker shouted again, her voice rife with hatred. "I'll kill you, I'll—"

Her cry broke off as several pirates grabbed her and wrestled a Stormsinger's mask over her face. She screamed into it and the air around us shuddered. Snow kicked up, swirling into the fire with a shushing hiss.

Lirr ignored Anne, dragging Mary to a stop at the foot of the larch. Firelight filled their faces and cast their shadows onto the broad tree trunk at their backs.

A second figure stepped from Lirr's frame. A ghisting, tall and broad and looming.

Beside me, Penn started to curse then slipped into a prayer instead.

I had known this was coming, but I felt the same instinct to pray. As Demery had said, Lirr was *ghiseau* too. But knowing the truth and seeing it were two vastly different things.

"Some of you have waited decades for this day," Lirr began, raising his voice above the roar of the bonfire.

His ghisting, Hoten, slipped to Mary's other side and watched the pirate with an intense gaze.

"Some of you have yet to understand the blessing you will receive," Lirr went on. "I've many siblings to be freed once this forest awakens and burns, and it's you who will have the honor of joining with them. I give you this prize without cost—save your trust, and gratitude."

Lirr's pirates cheered, the raucous, blood-hungry cry of revelers at a hanging. My mouth was dry, the pain in my arm forgotten as Lirr's influence wafted over the heads of the assembly. A lifetime with Benedict had hardened me to Magni power, but even so I barely resisted it. My heart thundered, and desire pulled at me—desire to please him, to be like him.

Ghiseau.

My skin crawled.

Mary had retained enough of herself to glare at him and say something I could not hear. He grabbed her bound wrists and prodded her to the edge of the larch's rocky perch, right over the roaring bonfire. Firelight played across Mary's face and her shadow grew taller on the trunk of the great larch. Then Lirr's shadow passed over it, swallowing it, and he laid heavy hands on her shoulders from behind.

"Return to your tree and your children, Tane," Lirr said, expression cool and intent. "Or let the fire free you from this world."

I needed no vision to foretell what would happen next.

Lirr's hands softened on Mary's shoulders, and he pushed.

The drop into the bonfire was short. Mary hit the blaze in a burst of dancing sparks and the dozen gut-melting cracks of—wood? Bone?

I heard Anne howl into her gag, but could not see her anymore. I lunged to my feet, only to be kicked back down by a pirate. A boot connected with my skull and the world momentarily faded.

The Dark Water sensed my distraction and erupted all around me, shallow and cool. The light of the fire faded but ghistings lit up the night like torches, sapphire ghistings, indigo ghistings, ghistings edged with grey and attached to human flesh. Lirr's loyalists. Lirr.

Mary. She struggled to her knees, here in the Dark Water—or rather, her reflection did, teal and grey and swirling. There was no fire here, no blazing heat. But she burned brighter than the fire ever could, and as she did, a new visage overlaid her.

Another being manifested in Mary's flesh. At first, the ghisting was a mirror image of Mary herself, as perfect a replica as Benedict was of me. Then she began to change. She aged and hardened—into Anne, into someone else, someone with angular features, lithe limbs and a drape of captured moonlight.

I could still see Mary through her, and she screamed. She fought towards the edge of the fire but something pushed her back— swords? Rifles?

"Mary!" I shouted. I tried to thrust myself back into the human world, but I was stuck. I could not reach the coin in my pocket, not with my hands bound.

My eyes filled with Mary and her ghisting, and the memory of the flames. How long would she survive? How long before the flames took her?

I was helpless. Again.

No, not helpless. Passages from the Mereish book welled again in my mind, and this time their meaning was clear—uniting with the memory of the morgories I had banished.

I staggered upright in the Dark Water and began to shout, still straining at my ropes. Lights flickered beyond the Wold as Mary burned, oranges and umbers appearing between sapphire and grey all around us, until the Wold had as many lights as the night sky.

The ghistings turned to me, first. Then the fae dragonflies converged, the murmur of their wings turning to a howl as they closed around me like a sea spout and cut Mary from my sight. I felt a momentary panic as she vanished, but I had one last hope—a wild, reckless hope—and I intended to use it.

"Come!" I demanded of the Dark Water. "I am here, come to me!"

A new light appeared through the trees, bloody orange and dreadfully swift. Elation swelled in my chest and crashed into panic; I had seconds before they arrived.

Back in the human world, one of my straining hands broke free from my bonds. I seized the coin in my pocket.

I lurched back into full consciousness, gasping and sweating. Pirates and prisoners watched in rapture as Lirr faced the larch tree. The fire still blazed, too high and dense to see Mary through.

There was no way she still lived. I knew that, but rejected it, and as I did, I heard the voices.

They were thin and distant, whispers that grew in strength. The ghisting who stood with Lirr raised his head, looking up to the treetops as they swayed—not in the wind, but of their own accord.

There was a crackling, a rustling rush. Leaves began to take shape on arching branches, hazing and shuddering. The snow and ice beneath my knees melted to mist and steam. Moss blossomed, carpets of green creeping across earth and root and rock and tree. Fiddleheads and mushrooms burst up from the soil and, above, firelight filled a sudden, lush canopy. The cold vanished, and the ghistings of the sleeping Wold awoke into a warm, midsummer dusk.

Nearby, Penn gave an awed, baffled sound.

The serenity was short-lived. Just as sweet, warm air filled my lungs, the bonfire died. Darkness clapped down around us, smoke filled the air, and a monster tore out of the Other.

Enormous tentacles wrapped around straining trees, leaves fell and the trees moaned. The beast solidified into a bloody orange nightmare, suspended between the trees above our heads—the fang-ridden, ravening union of octopus and hunting spider, easily the size of *Harpy*.

Smoke wafted across my face as I gaped up at the monster I'd summoned, horror crashing over me like waves. I had wanted a distraction but this... What had I done?

Where was Mary?

"Run!" I shouted to Penn, to my crew, to anyone else who could hear and respond. At the same time, I lunged for the extinguished bonfire, free hands pushing off warm summer earth.

People took flight, captor and captive fleeing the beast. Others still watched Lirr in rapture, surrounded by thick, cloying smoke, oblivious to the danger. Lirr turned. Irritation transformed into shock as he watched the creature crawl out of the fabric of the world and settle in the trees right above our heads.

"Mary!" I coughed and covered my nose against the smoke, eyes burning as I tried to make her out in the remnants of the fire. But it was too dark, the smoke too thick, and heat still billowed up from blackened coals. I could not see her—dead or alive.

"Mary!" I shouted. "Mary!"

Above me, the larch shuddered. Lirr continued to stare at it, but his ghisting stalked down to the fireside, his form as otherworldly as the smoke all around us. Like me, the ghisting did not seem to find what he was looking for. Had Mary escaped in the chaos?

As if sensing my question, the ghisting looked up at me for the briefest moment. He had no face but he looked like Lirr, just then. He *was* Lirr.

The monster I had summoned gave a chattering, gut-melting snarl.

It descended. Bloody orange light washed over us as it came with impossible speed, becoming more and more substantial with every passing moment. Finally, its light waned as it seeped fully through the boundaries between worlds and settled into the arctic Ghistwold.

Even Lirr's Magni power could not combat his crew's fear. What remained of his crew broke. But the beast did not give chase. Instead it fixed its eyes on Lirr's ghisting, and charged.

The ghisting vanished and, up on the ridge, Lirr disappeared into the murk. The beast roared in vexation and turned, limb by limb, to regard me. It spoke no words, but I *knew* what it wanted.

A command.

I wanted to laugh and wretch. Tempting a creature to chase me into the physical world was one thing. But controlling it? The book had spoken of this, but could I truly do it?

"Cause chaos," I said, willing all shock and uncertainty from my voice. "But do not kill."

The monster shrieked and scuttled off into the trees after a pair of Lirr's pirates. I was not completely sure it would obey, but it was no longer an immediate threat.

I sagged, shock and awe momentarily overcoming me. Then the screams rose to my ears, I saw Penn struggling to his feet, and I remembered who I was.

A pirate bolted past me in a swirl of displaced smoke. Without thinking I struck out with my left hand, landing a fist squarely on the man's jaw. He went down and I stole the knife and cutlass from his belt. My injured arm was not strong, but the knife was not for me.

In a moment I was back at Penn's side. I cut him free with quick movements and handed him the shorter blade.

"Regroup and hold fast," I instructed the sailor. "Find Mr. Keo and Ms. Skarrow, if you can."

"Aye, sir!" Penn's bloodied leg barely took his weight on the loamy forest floor, but that did not stop him from starting to bellow a stream of orders. What remained of our crew and Demery's pirates began to rally. Lirr's crew would not be far behind, but with their leader vanished and their number scattered, we had a moment of reprieve.

On the edge of the chaos, a new specter separated from the shadows. I twisted and raised my cutlass into a long guard, only to see my own face staring back at me.

"Ben?" I breathed, half shedding my stance.

"Athe decided to trust me," Benedict returned, flicking sweaty hair from his eyes. He was sodden and barely dressed for the cold, but then again, the cold was gone now. "I can be very persuasive. Was that monster your doing?"

Before I could answer, three pirates burst from the forest and attacked. Benedict and I parted instinctively. He parried a slash and drove his cutlass into an opponent's chest. I opened another's belly and faced the last just as Ben ran her through.

"Right, what is going on?" my twin shouted. "Give me an objective, man!"

"Where's Lirr?" The voice came from Athe, who cracked off her pistol at a fleeing enemy and turned grey eyes on us. A ghisting appeared from her flesh—a ghisting in the shape of a bear—and bolted off into the forest. It passed a shadow as it went, a shadow I swore was James Demery and a woman in a long, ethereal dress. But they were gone before I could be sure.

"What are you doing?" I asked Athe, staring after the ghisting. "If you're killed now, separate from your ghisting—"

"A risk I will take. The ghistings will find and corner Lirr faster alone," the woman cut me off. "Did you see where that bastard went?"

I turned to sweep the ridge. It was still hard to see, but Lirr was nowhere to be seen.

"He's gone," I said. My thoughts came more rapidly now. "Benedict, secure the clearing and gather our forces. Mr. Penn will assist you."

"We'll take care of Lirr," Athe stated, unfaltering, and set off after her ghisting.

Benedict eyed Penn, who had already freed a good number of our folk and armed them. He nodded. "Very well. I assume you will find the Stormsinger?"

I hesitated. Benedict was here, Athe was unharmed, but could I trust him?

My brother's eyes were expressionless, but as I examined him, he cracked a smile.

"I know where my interests are best served, brother," he chided, flicking blood from the end of his cutlass. "Go find your witch."

I had no time to linger on his use of 'your.' I returned to the remains of the bonfire at the same time as Anne Firth. She threw her mask aside, along with a glittering key, and stood panting over the empty coals, searching for any sign of her daughter.

I forced myself to do the same. The smoke had cleared and my eyes had readjusted to the darkness by now, and I feared I would finally make out her charred, shriveled form.

But instead of death, I saw life. There, where Mary had fallen, a sapling uncoiled from the earth. It was barely knee-high, but as I watched it shook and stretched, extending new branches. Another larch. A new ghisten tree.

And beyond it, footprints in ash. There were only two, and then they vanished in the midst of a stride—as surely as if Mary had stepped from one world, into the Other.

Gooseflesh prickled up my arms.

"She'll have gone after Lirr. Give me that. Are you with me, Mr. Rosser?" Anne raked frozen hands over eyes red with exhaustion and cold. She held out her hand, and I realized she wanted my cutlass.

I handed it over and she took it in a sure, steady grip.

"I am, Ms. Firth. Lead the way."

FORTY-SIX

The Woman in the Wold

MARY

My world was fire and heat, pain and terror. My thoughts skipped and jumped, every thought fragmented, every feeling a spark in the maelstrom.

In that blazing moment, I saw Tane separate from my skin. Still tethered to me by the touch of one hand, she reformed into my reflection, then someone else. She touched my face and poured over my flesh like fog on a sea breeze.

Then my world was cool water and a forest with its roots in the sky. I—Tane and I—ran through ankle-deep pools with a vanguard of a thousand dragonflies, gold and purple. Morgories stuck their heads from the water and unfurled their deadly plumes, rattling as we passed. A creature with the head of a horse and the body of a mangy dog crept through the shadows, head lowered and twisted body radiating pale orange light. A huden.

And though I had never been in this place before, I knew the feel of it in my bones, and understood what it was with a dreamer's certainty.

The Dark Water. I had stepped bodily out of the fire into the Dark Water.

Before the awe and panic and impossibility of that thought could take root, my world shifted a third time.

I stumbled into a summer Wold of soft wind and cool moss.

I knew what had happened with the same surety as I'd recognized the Dark Water.

Tane had awoken the arctic Wold.

"Tane." I coughed her name, clutching at my seared clothes. They were mostly intact but my boots were burned through, and I nearly twisted an ankle as I tried to find my balance. "Tane!"

I'm here, her voice returned. She manifested before me, taking on the same form she'd worn in the fire—a mixture of me, my mother, and someone else. Her expression was calm but urgent, and she kept one tendril of her spectral flesh tied between us, chest-to-chest.

My mother's voice rang in my head, distant with memory. *So long as Tane is within you, neither of you can come to harm.*

That's what this tether was. Tane, ensuring our connection remained, protecting me from death—and in doing so, guarding herself.

Tane spoke again. *We've passed through the Dark Water, Mary. We're safe.*

"How?" I wheezed.

"We're one flesh, you and I," Tane said. "Entwined from the womb, in a way that Lirr and the others can never be. And I am a Mother Tree. Much is possible for us, but now is not the time for such things. Lirr is on the move."

I straightened, terror still fluttering through me with every beat of my heart. The heat. The flames. The scent of smoke that still clung to me, so thickly that I felt I couldn't breathe. I remembered Lirr's hands on my back and the force of his power, driving me up the ridge to the larch and my certain death.

I shouldn't be alive. I shouldn't have been able to flee through the Dark Water, body and soul. But I already existed in a world of impossibilities.

I myself was one of them.

"He won't escape," I said, strengthening myself with the words. With that strength came a little more clarity, and with that clarity, anger. Lirr had tried to burn me alive. He had ensorcelled me and submerged me in a terror so fierce, so smothering, I still could not find its edges.

I did not take well to being terrified.

Lirr intended to maim and murder every creature in this strange, misplaced Wold, human and ghisting. He had stolen my mother and left her a shadow of herself. He had killed Grant—or transformed him. He had destroyed uncountable lives, tortured and tormented for decades.

No longer.

Yes. The force of Tane's power and determination roared through me. She slipped closer, more tendrils of her spectral flesh drawing towards me like smoke towards an open window.

"Where is he?" I asked, though I already knew the answer. Lirr was still in the Wold, regrouping, skulking, plotting, hunting. But Tane was the Wold. I doubted I could kill him alone, but I could slow him down until my mother and Demery caught up.

Follow me.

My senses flowed together with the ghistings as I kicked off my destroyed boots and ran. I knew each tree, each root, each step I needed to take to find Lirr. My bare feet carried me there, and somewhere along the way, Tane slipped fully back into my flesh. There was no strangeness, in the joining. She was simply a drink of water on a hot day, and I welcomed her.

We ran. We hunted. We slipped through the shadows and ran across the decks of derelict, moss-covered ships. Other ghistings emerged, varied forms and shapes joining us until we passed the reaches of their roots, and they stopped, watching us go. They spoke to us, whispers and welcomes and encouragements and warnings.

Only three ghistings kept pace. One was a mighty bear, flanking me. The second and third flitted through the canopy above on silent wings: a white crow, and a winged harpy.

Demery's, Athe's and Widderow's ghistings. I felt a moment of elation, encouraged by their presence, then a swell of dread.

"They've left themselves vulnerable," I panted to Tane as we topped a ridge that proved to be a forgotten hull, latticed with ivy.

They do as they must, Tane replied.

The bear roared. Tane understood it a fraction before I did. I felt her face turn, separating from my skin so that I saw, for an instant, in two directions.

My eyes still took in the summer Wold ahead and a spattering of pointing, clamoring ghistings, all straining at their tethers. I glimpsed the panic in their eyes, and heard their warnings from a distance.

Tane's eyes saw Hoten part from the vine-choked wood beneath us and drive a wooden dagger towards my chest.

I diverted on light feet, ducking around him and half leaping, half tumbling off the shipwreck. The dagger flashed past my shoulder and I hit the moss in a roll, twigs cracking and ferns rustling.

I lunged back to my feet just as Lirr stepped from the shadows of the wreck, leveling a pistol.

"I gave you freedom!" he roared.

I did not stop moving—if I did, I'd freeze.

Tane separated partially, just in time to block another downward stab of Hoten's knife. She knocked it from his grasp, snatched it from the air, and slipped back into my frame in the same breath.

Impossibly, the knife appeared in my hand—just as the shard had when I faced the Mereish captain.

The pistol went off. I felt something bite into my side but momentum carried me forward into a low twist, knife punching out.

The pirate, rather than turn away from my blade, threw out his hand. The knife stabbed right through his palm and he discarded his pistol, grabbed my wrist and jerked me off-balance.

I hit the moss again. The knife tore free in a crack and splatter of blood but Lirr didn't care. He grabbed my throat and slammed me into the earth. I stabbed again, this time taking him in the chest. My vision clouded but I bucked my hips and twisted the knife deeper. He grunted in pain, slipped, and I shoved him aside.

Tane attacked at the same time, and Hoten half parted from Lirr to stop her from embedding a shard of wood in his host's spine.

The Mother Ghisting seized Hoten and hauled. Hoten nearly separated from Lirr but a tether remained, thick and binding. Just as Tane remained tethered to me. But how far would it stretch?

Then Hoten leapt fully from Lirr's flesh and tackled Tane to the ground. Both tethers snapped.

I lunged for Tane, trying to restore our connection. A hand seized my ankle and hauled me back.

I twisted to see Lirr, cursing at me with blood-lined teeth and eyes full of malice. For a fraction of a heartbeat, he held my gaze. Just him. Just me. No Hoten, no Tane.

Athe's ghisting bear attacked Hoten, massive claws seizing his shoulders and jaws closing about his head. A white crow plunged from the trees and darted at Lirr, making him flinch, but Harpy was nowhere to be seen.

Using the corvid's distraction, I kicked Lirr in the face. He seemed to sense it coming, dodged and grabbed my other foot, shoulders hunched against the crow's repeated assaults.

The bear roared and a musket cracked. I struck out and struggled, my world a blur of dirt, deadfall and striking limbs. I sighted Olsa Uknara sprinting from the forest, musket smoking, and Demery and Illya behind. Harpy separated from Demery in her human form, flicking a mask onto her face. She changed from indistinct woman to an armored goddess of war, spinning a spear into position as she charged towards Hoten, Tane and the bear.

More ghistings came, gathering close—a feline the size of a hound, coiling around Olsa's legs, an eldritch oaken god detaching from the wreck, a lithe stream of smoke from Illya's parted lips and glaring eyes.

From all around, from flesh and bark, ghistings emerged. I knew each of them as Tane's children. They joined with Tane and the ghistings of my companions, trapping Hoten outside of Lirr's flesh.

Bellowing a wordless cry of rage, Lirr grabbed me around the throat with a forearm and forced me backwards, wooden knife in hand. I twisted and bit down on his hand like a feral dog, thoughtless in my need to survive. I felt warm skin and fine hair, tense muscle—then spurting blood and raw flesh on my tongue.

Lirr staggered away from me with a disgusted, pained howl. Another pistol cracked. Lirr moved just before it, but it still struck. There was a wet crackle of bone and Lirr's knee buckled.

Our enemy roared, rage and agony combined. I spat blood and bile and swayed upright, as he too clawed, punishingly, to his feet. His shattered leg sagged but he grasped a nearby tree with his mangled hand and reached to pull a steel knife from his boot.

Demery closed in. Anne, Samuel Rosser and Athe materialized from the twilight at his back, joining the Uknaras. My mother had reclaimed her axe, and now she hefted it in both hands as the others surrounded them—the ghistings trapping Hoten, the humans Lirr.

I could feel Lirr's blood on my face, more blood seeping down my side, but I smiled at my mother and gave a short nod. I'd survive.

Rosser slipped up to my side, breathing heavily. "Are you all right?" He spared me a glance, his eyes drawn to the hole in my side, seeping a steady scarlet bloom. "You've been shot!"

I nodded, though I could no longer find the will to speak. Samuel moved closer, as if his shadow could shelter me from further harm, and I did not protest. I'd done all I could, and my debt of vengeance was not the greatest here tonight.

Lirr hissed as Demery and Athe advanced, and the sorcery in the sound was enough to make even the ghistings waver. But Demery, Athe and my mother resisted. They closed in.

Lirr's eyes darted to his ghisting, who watched him with a similar, dire gaze through the restraining horde of his kin. Harpy herself held his arms behind his back.

"Don't be a fool, Tane," Lirr called. Demery and Athe moved to flank him, and my mother passed Samuel and me by as she came to face Lirr directly, axe in hand. "I did this for our people. For us."

We want freedom. Tane's voice was warm deadfall under a summer sun. She came through the crowd to stand at my side, and our tether re-formed. The thundering of my heart began to calm. *But not this. Not suffering and death.*

Lirr laughed. "Death? Look at you! You're perfect, Mother. Unified, with that girl. I *made* you."

No. Tane looked to my mother, her sea-glass eyes reflecting my own. *She did. And together, we are more than you ever imagined. We are more than you can stop.*

"That is very nice," Olsa commented dryly, resting one hand on the head of the feline ghisting at her side. A lynx, I realized. Its tufted ears flicked to and fro. "I also have many feelings. But we need to kill them now."

Anne hefted her axe and gave Demery a meaningful look. He nodded.

The axe took Lirr right in the throat at the same time as the ghistings erupted. Ethereal screams and howls tore through the Wold in a keening cacophony of joy or lament or something in between.

One strike, two. I closed my eyes on the third and felt Tane slip back into my skin. The blood seeping from my side slowed and my pain retreated.

I exhaled and started to open my eyes again, but hesitated. When I looked at the world once more, Lirr would be dead, Hoten extinguished and the battle over. I'd be standing in a summer Wold on the Winter Sea, with pirates and Samuel Rosser, my mother and a swarm of ghistings.

Whoever I'd been when I stood on the gallows in Fort Almsworth would be truly gone. And what I'd become, the life I'd choose and the people I'd spend it with? They were nothing like the Girl from the Wold had ever imagined.

I opened my eyes. The first thing I saw was not Lirr's headless corpse. It was not Hoten fading from existence, crumpling like ash, and the ghistings that cavorted or stood solemnly by to mark his passing. It was not even the shape of a monstrous spider, lingering among the trees like a hound awaiting its master.

I saw my mother, pulling me into an embrace.

And Samuel Rosser, smiling down at us.

FORTY-SEVEN

A Doorway in the Birches

SAMUEL

Through a veil of fine snow and the eternal dusk, I watched *Hart* drop anchor in the channel beyond the Wold. I stood at the edge of the forest, its gentle heat at my back and the north's bitter cold on my face. Around my boots, mist curled from bare earth and moss. It prickled at the exposed skin of my forearms, where I had pushed my sleeves back and my bandages clung. The scent of the forest was easy in my lungs, earthen, deep and cool—the bridge between unnatural summer and endless winter.

Hart was battered and crippled, but he lived. His stovepipes released plumes of grey into the drifting snow as he settled in, his crew moved with calm efficiency, and Captain Fisher stood tall on the quarterdeck.

As the crew furled patched sails above her cocked hat, Fisher saluted me. I raised my good hand in return and started to pick my way down to the water, over the snowline and onto a blood-soaked beach that had, a few hours before, been covered with dying and wounded. Most of them were aboard *Harpy* now, moored off an ice shelf to the south next to *Nameless*, or housed in tents inside the summer Wold. We would mourn the dead tonight.

My relief at seeing Fisher was sweet, but exhausted. I had been run off my feet since the conflict ended, organizing a search for missing allies and lurking enemies. I had dismissed my Other-born spider under Olsa's guidance too, and it had faded back into its own world. But not before I looked it in the eyes and dispelled any last threads of fear.

"This is the beginning," Olsa had told me as the creature faded. She patted my back and smiled with an amused, maternal glint to her eye. "You may be broken, boy, but you also have power you have not begun to understand."

I had taken her promise to heart, tired and aching as I was. Beneath my weariness, there was deep, visceral satisfaction. Lirr was dead, and justice served. When we returned to Usti and the world learned who had brought Lirr down, my name would be beside Fisher's, Benedict's and Demery's. It was the closest thing to redemption I could hope for, while Benedict's lies remained intact.

I had done what I set out to do, and that knowledge was iron in my spine. But what came next?

When Fisher's longboat drove onto the beach, I grabbed the bow with my good hand and hauled with the rowers. They had leapt out with a splash of water and crunch of rock and snow, and now their eyes strayed towards the mist-wrapped forest.

"Who survived?" Fisher dropped from the boat and took my forearm, her brusque comradery belied by the happiness around her eyes and the gentleness of her fingers. Half of her face was scraped raw, as if it had been scoured with sand. It oddly reminded me of Ellas's scars.

She noted my bandaged arm with a wince.

"Everyone save Lirr, and many good sailors," I replied. I held her forearm a moment longer, gave it a small squeeze and nodded up the beach as I let go. "The pirates have set up camp in the Wold."

"The Wold…" Fisher eyed the summer forest, running her gaze from broad, wind-rustled leaves to the hedge of snowmelt surrounding it. "I have many questions."

"So do I." We started back up the rise, the crew from her boat falling in behind. "What happened to Ellas?"

"She's dead," Fisher admitted. She ran her tongue over the inside of her ruined cheek, then continued, "It was exactly as we feared. She and her crew waited until the ship was back in working order, then they tried to take it. She was shot."

The fact that she did not identify *who* had done the killing worried me. I met my captain's eyes, a question in them, but Fisher only gave a resigned smile.

"There will be questions, when we go home," I murmured lowly. "Ellas was a decorated captain."

"I know," Fisher returned, without dropping her voice. The crew from her longboat, following us, watched her carefully. "I did what I did to protect my ship."

"There's not one among us who'd say different," one of the crew commented. "Beggin' your pardon, Cap'n."

Fisher cast the woman a small, thankful nod.

The Other pulled at me, sending half a dozen images of battle and blood through my mind. Some I knew were from the battle aboard *Hart*, while others remained obscure. I glimpsed Fisher, wrapped in snow, her pistol sparking. Men and women screaming. A stag bellowing. Ellas, toppled into the sea.

I touched the coin in my pocket and the visions abated, though the feel of them remained—the tension, the shock and the pain.

But I felt no regret over Ellas. In truth, I wished I cared that she was dead. I ought to have borne some compassion; I had no idea how far Ben had pushed her, and how much of her betrayal was his influence.

But one look at Fisher's battered face made that unease harden. However Ben had swayed Ellas, it did not change what she had done once he was out of sight.

"Did she do that to your face?" I asked my captain.

"The deck did this." She looked at me with an amused crinkle in the corner of her eyes. It transformed into a grimace. "Though I suppose you could blame Ellas for dragging me across it. I'm quite all right, Mr. Rosser. Now, we're all eager to know… Has Demery revealed Bretton's Hoard yet?"

My boots crunched over the rim of ice and melt at the edge of the Wold. The temperature immediately rose and mist eddied about us, doubling the eeriness of the place. The crewfolk murmured among themselves, shoving back hats and tugging down scarves with wide eyes.

I pushed a branch out of the way and stood aside for Fisher to precede me into the trees. "No, but there's a great deal of muttering about it. I wouldn't be surprised if the pirates set out first thing tomorrow."

Fisher looked at the canopy over our heads and turned in place, taking the forest in with one, long sweep. She raised her brows in something between admiration and pleasure.

"This is… uncanny," she decided. "As to the pirates, good. We'll go with them. Now, brief me on as much as you can, Mr. Rosser, and then I want to see James Demery."

The following morning, when the sun slipped from behind the Stormwall and the gloom lightened a fraction, James Demery and Anne Firth led a small party through the Wold.

Our boots sank into ankle-deep moss and skirted freshwater springs. A few ghistings watched us pass, lingering about their trees and taking the forms of forests beasts, or imitating various members of the party—Olsa, Widderow, myself, Benedict. Some even followed us as far as the reach of their roots would allow—a phantom wolf, a running little boy. Then they faded, and others took their place.

To my ears they were silent, but I saw Mary acknowledge them. She strode with her mother, clad in a man's shirt and women's petticoats. Tane was nowhere to be seen, hidden beneath her skin, but if I touched the Other, I saw her telltale grey haze about her skin.

Only once throughout the journey, through happenstance—or cunningly contrived circumstances—did we end up striding next to one another.

"Does Tane know how much farther the hoard is?" I asked her.

Mary's expression became more distant. I wondered if that was how I looked when I slipped into the Other.

"Another half hour or so," Mary replied.

I looked at her askance. "Is it difficult for you?"

"Having Tane?" Startled by the question, she glanced around to make sure no one was listening. Anne and the pirates were ahead while Fisher and Benedict trailed behind.

I nodded.

"I'm growing used to her," Mary admitted. "It's not as though she suddenly came to me, not like it is for Charles and the rest. She has always been part of me, even if her consciousness slept. There is no me without her."

Something in Mary's tone made me consider her more directly. I met her eyes, prompting her to go on.

"I… I can see why you'd find it perturbing, though," she admitted. She looked away again, but not before I saw a deeper truth behind her words. "Knowing what I am."

"I do not find it perturbing," I said honestly. "Does it bother you that I am a broken Sooth who summons monsters from the Other?"

A smile tugged at the corner of her lips. "Did you really intend to do that?"

I almost grinned in return, but this was the closest conversation Mary and I had had since our reunion, and my palms had begun to sweat. I cleared my throat. "Yes. We needed a distraction."

"We did." Mary frowned at the path ahead, then shrugged the memory away. "Well, it's odd, but nothing to be ashamed of. Olsa says it's a rare side effect for amplified Sooths. The Mereish are aware of it and the Usti suspect, but the Aeadine…"

"The Aeadine disregard much that the Mereish or even the Usti say about spiritual matters. You have been discussing Sooths with Olsa?" The last surprised me—and more than a little intrigued me. Had I been the topic of conversation?

Suddenly, Mary put a great deal more attention into where she placed her feet on the forest floor. "Magic and creatures have been a popular topic aboard *Harpy*."

"Ah." I nodded. "Mary…"

At the sound of her name, she looked back up at me, and my thoughts scattered like chaff. The Other leapt into the breach and for the space of a few heartbeats, that world wrapped around us—its forest with roots in the sky, Mary wreathed in blue and grey, and I in soft green, dark water about our ankles. Then it was gone.

"Your bond with Tane does not bother me," I reiterated, hoping she heard the sincerity in my words. "You are the same woman who scolded me in an alleyway in Tithe and brought winter down on Whallum… and has been in my dreams ever since."

I spoke the last before I thought it through, and only realized what I had said when Mary's cheeks reddened.

I waited, desperately hoping she would make a joke and discard the comment, but she did not.

"I've thought about you a great deal too," she admitted. She lifted her eyes and glanced behind us at Benedict. "But your brother… He said a great deal about your past, Samuel."

"He told you," I stated. Every spark of hope fled me with those three small words.

I could tell her the truth. I could tell her that Benedict had lied, but would she believe me? And even if she did, what would she do with that knowledge? She had no affection for Benedict. She could tear him down, expose him to the world, and then all my sacrifices would be for nothing.

A small part of me railed that Benedict deserved to face the truth. But I could not turn my back on Benedict now, not when we had been finally reunited, and whispers of a cure in Mere itched at the back of my mind. If I wanted it—for now, I was not so sure.

Lost in my own reasoning, it took me a second to register Mary was speaking again.

"He told me many things," she said simply. "But I know they're lies. He's the worst of men, Samuel Rosser. I know that now. And despite all that's happened, despite your faults—and mine—I know now that you're the very best."

She met my gaze for one long, purposeful moment. Then she left me, jogging to rejoin her mother.

I stared after her, her words still ringing through my ears.

Fisher's hand suddenly thumped into my back, pushing me back into movement. A piece beyond her, Benedict strode with one hand on his cutlass. He too watched me, close enough that I wondered if he had overheard Mary, but he did not speak.

"What was that about?" Fisher wanted to know.

I collected myself. "Nothing."

"Did you speak with her last night?" My captain nodded to where Mary now walked with her mother and Demery. "Like I told you to?"

"No. She was with Mr. Grant," I admitted, turning my attention back to the forest. The reminder cooled my elation but did not dispel it. "I decided not to interrupt."

Fisher nodded in consideration. "He'll survive?"

"It seems so. But if he does, he'll be *ghiseau*." I stepped long over a knot of rocky roots and glanced back at Fisher, offering a hand to help her over the obstacle. She accepted it lightly and dropped down beside me.

I added, unnerved by the thought of another bond between Mary and the highwayman, "He will be like her."

"And here you are, you a mere first officer, a petty Sooth who leashes monsters," Fisher said in false lament, and for a moment, she was not my captain anymore. We were back in our cabin, she wearing my stolen socks and I glowering over a bowl of porridge. "Chin up, Mr. Rosser. Just because she's friends with Mr. Grant does not mean there is anything more between them. Look at you and I."

He's the worst of men, Samuel Rosser. You're the very best.

Hope wove back through me. I wanted to revel in it, to ponder it and rationalize it and decide my next steps, but Fisher's words required a response.

"Are you saying we are friends?" I asked coyly.

Fisher shrugged and pushed a branch out of our way. "Perhaps."

"Is it appropriate to be friends with one's captain?" I asked, philosophical.

"No. I could not be friends with my first officer," Fisher said, catching my eye. Her smile was gone now, replaced by calculation. "But I could be friends with *Hart*'s new captain, if I was to, say, take a new ship."

Stunned, I nearly stopped walking. "Pardon me?"

"We're here!" Anne's voice echoed through the forest overhead.

I burned to interrogate Fisher, but when I saw what lay before us, every thought in my mind quietened—even the ones of Mary.

Fisher, too, trailed into silence.

Three enormous ships lay within the Wold, toppled like a child's forgotten toys. Their figureheads had rooted into three lording birches, decorated with curls of papery bark and round, dancing leaves. The ships themselves were layered with moss and blanketed in ivy, the latter of which choked masts and yards all the way up into the forest canopy.

The central ghisten tree was so large it had split down the middle, right across the prow. There, what looked like a doorway led into the blackness of its ship's hold. But as we came closer, I saw that the way was too small for anyone to pass through.

Benedict, Fisher and I stopped beside Demery, Anne, Mary and Olsa. Widderow joined us, her corvid ghisting visible on her shoulder. The ghistings who had trailed us through the forest spread out to observe in an eerie, watchful half-moon.

Tane appeared. She slipped from Mary's skin like a sigh and formed into a reflection of the woman herself, though her features were a little older, a little harder. She wore a simple dress, like Mary, and her long, loose hair moved in a non-existent wind as she strode towards the birch door.

I drew a deep breath, looking from her to Mary, who watched her ghisting without a word. But I heard her voice in my mind, her words shifting and settling into a truth that made my heart ache.

You're the best of men, Samuel Rosser.

Tane spoke to the door, though I could not hear what she said. The birch tree groaned. The divide in its trunk yawned larger and larger, until Widderow's crow swooped through with a raucous caw.

The old woman followed it with a perfunctory glance at the rest of us. "I've waited twenty years for this," she complained, raising her lantern. "If we stand about gawping, I'll be dead before I can spend my share."

With that, she vanished into the cleft.

Demery smiled wanly, then gestured for Anne, Mary and Olsa to proceed him. Mary and Tane then vanished through the door together.

Benedict shouldered ahead of me into the shadows. "I hope this was worth it," he muttered.

Beyond the doorway, thin lanternlight illuminated a staircase down into the dark. I carefully descended, each step accompanied by a forbidding creak and a rustle of hanging roots and falling dirt.

Finally the lantern stopped moving, the shadows settled and I joined Benedict on a dark, crooked deck. Ahead, Widderow tugged up the slats of her lantern and held the light high.

Golden light spilled across a treasury fit for queens. No, not queens. Gods.

There were chests of gold, barrels of gems, and sacks of gilded weapons. Urns spilled coins across the lichen-covered decking.

Trunks yawned, packed with so much wealth they could not be closed. There were figurines of humans, animals and Other-born beasts in every precious substance. There were goblets of silver, horse tack marked with emeralds, and a hundred other items I was too stunned to identify. Everywhere I tried to look, a new marvel dragged my attention elsewhere.

Widderow made a gleeful sound and picked up a long, slim box. She opened it to reveal an array of hairpins exactly the same as her signature carnelian pin, but these carved in other semiprecious stones. She ran her fingers over them lightly, and cast Demery a beaming grin. The man smiled back.

Behind me, Benedict picked up a silver plate and rubbed it with his sleeve, then stared at his own reflection.

"Bretton's original hoard was farther north," Anne said, watching as Mary picked up a jade disc and held it in her palm. The older woman had a new steadiness about her, though I still perceived a shadow behind her eyes. I had seen shadows like that before, in my own eyes, in the eyes of veterans and widows, and I suspected it would never fade.

She continued, "Lirr moved it here before we sailed back across the Stormwall. These three ships house the bulk of it, but there are more caches throughout the forest."

"There's …" Mary seemed at a loss, turning the jade piece over. She surveyed the hoard. "There's so much."

"There's enough." Olsa Uknara swiveled a satchel from the small of her back to her hip and opened it, then started selecting small, cut gems from a chest.

"Well, you can retire now," Anne said to the captain. She scuffed meaningfully at a spilled sack of coins with a scrape and a jingle. "Still have your eye on Sunjai?"

"Mereish South Isles," Demery said, picking up the half-moon headdress of some ancient priestess. Silver glittered and a fringe of dangling jewels clinked as he held it to Anne's forehead, as if checking how it would look on the woman. "Lirr had the right of it, lying low down there. I'll buy myself an island and live out my days as an eccentric lord. Maybe I'll even marry? I'll visit Hesten every so often, though, of course. Phira would have my head if I did not."

Lowering the headdress, he narrowed his eyes at it. "I should bring her something, shouldn't I? And the queen… Damn it."

Anne smiled. It was the first time I had seen the expression on her face and it caught me off guard. She looked younger, less harrowed. More like Mary.

"You're welcome to come," Demery added, tucking the headdress under one arm. From his tone, I sensed that this was not the first time he had extended the invitation. "To the Isles."

Anne's smile faded a little and she glanced at her daughter. "We'll see."

"Will the ghisting remain here?" Fisher asked.

In perfect unison, Anne, Mary and Tane looked at her.

Fisher cleared her throat. "Will you remain here, Tane?"

"Wherever we go, we go together," Mary said. "The new Mother Tree is already growing in her stead, and a new Mother Spirit within it. Tane is not bound here."

Tane herself nodded silently, and I remembered the sapling growing where the bonfire had been. Where Mary ought to have died. The horror and the uncertainty of that memory turned my stomach and made my fingers clench. But it was over. Mary was safe and quite properly rich.

"Tane, do you not want to be free?" This question, to my shock, came from Benedict. He had lowered the silver plate, though it was still in his hand, and he looked directly at the ghisting.

The ghisting's mouth curled up in a smile.

"Whatever circumstances brought us together, we're one now. Freedom is a relative thing," Mary concluded, closing her fingers around the jade disc. I saw the regret in her eyes, but she kept it from her voice. "As to where we'll go… We can't go home. Even if

Mother and I weren't both known Stormsingers, I fled the gallows. Maybe I can prove I'm not Abetha Bonning, but I'm not willing to risk it."

Fisher settled in at my side and laced her arms across her chest. "The new captain of *Hart* will need a Stormsinger," she whispered to me.

I looked at her sharply, reminded of what she had started to say outside.

"What are you saying?" I hissed back.

Fisher ignored me and looked at Demery. "Sir, you and I need to discuss the division of prizes."

Demery gestured to the riches all around us. "Take your pick, Captain Fisher. What do you desire?"

Fisher smiled, sly and vulpine. "Well, I have my eye on a new ship."

FORTY-EIGHT

The Woman with Two Souls

MARY

Shoulder to shoulder with my mother, I sang. The waterfall of cloud and snow that was the Stormwall parted before us, swirling and rushing over dark waves and drifting ice floes. Cold burned my cheeks and my eyes watered, but I sang with all the power in my bones.

Magic thrummed through me, Tane whispered in my blood, and high above us *Harpy*'s sails filled with ensorcelled wind.

Behind us came *Hart* and *Nameless*, wrapped in the shelter of our power. The waves buffeted us and chunks of ice thudded against our ghisting-strengthened hulls, but our course was steady. Under the Fleetbreaker's care we'd be across the Wall in a matter of hours, and to Hesten in a day.

Despite weeks of rest and contemplation, the thought of reaching Hesten brought a wash of uncertainty. I faced so many decisions, though they all hinged upon the greatest, and most daunting choice of them all.

My mother intended to go south with Demery. He needed a singer, after all, and the decades of weariness behind my mother's smile told me she needed rest. Like the rest of Lirr's former prisoners, she might be free of her chains, but they had left their mark. I wanted that rest for her, that security away from the eyes of the Navy.

Grant would go with them, so Demery could guide him through his transition into *ghiseau*. In the weeks since his betrayal and near death, our relationship had gone from strained to reconciled. I'd nearly told Demery that the highwayman was a traitor several times, but seeing Grant so broken, so pale and close to death had softened me. His guilt and suffering were recompense enough.

For his part, the hope behind Grant's eyes when he looked at me was gone, replaced with the knowledge that, after what he had done, little more than friendship could survive between us.

So, I would go south with *Harpy* too, wouldn't I? I'd developed an affection for Demery and Athe and Old Crow. Grant was—or could be—a friend again, and I'd finally found my mother. Of course I would go with her. I would find a quiet life away from the constant threat and dangers of the Winter Sea, from people like Kaspin and Slader and Ellas, who would use my power for their own gain. And then...

What? I felt as though I'd only just left my village, just stepped foot into places like Tithe and Usti. Would I now close my eyes to the world and retire before my life had even begun?

My concentration wavered, and Tane's voice brushed at the back of my mind.

We can make our own path, Mary.

A path to where? I asked. Our silent conversation came second nature now, flowing as easily as my own thoughts, one into the other.

Of their own accord, my eyes dragged back to *Hart*. I couldn't see him from here, but I knew that the vessel's newly christened Captain Rosser stood on his quarterdeck, just as Captain Fisher would pace the deck of her newly claimed *Nameless*.

Wherever we choose, Tane replied.

FORTY-NINE

The Queen's Favor

SAMUEL

Bells rang out over Hesten as I made my way down the dock towards *Harpy*. Unlike our last visit to the port, this time we were housed in the royal docks, and dragonfly lanterns glowed against a deep winter night.

I brushed my fingers across the Mereish coin in my pocket and grasped the folded paper next to it. My heart started to hammer at the feel of the parchment, at the potential of it—both for gladness and devastation—but I suppressed it all and waved to Widderow, who smoked a pipe at the top of *Harpy*'s gangplank.

"Boy." The pipe remained pinched between her teeth as she asked, "What do you want?"

"I'm here to see Mary," I said politely.

"Oh, are you now?" She withdrew the pipe fully and raised her eyebrows. Smoke drifted from her lips into the night sky. "Fine. She's in the great cabin."

I nodded my thanks and found my own way through the quarterdeck doors, then down the short passage to Demery's cabin.

Mary opened it at my knock. The captain and her mother sat at a table behind her, drinking companionably as the remains of their dinner cooled on platters.

"Samuel." Mary smiled in greeting, but as she took me in a furrow creased her brow. "Join us?"

I glanced past her to Demery and Anne. "Captain, Ms. Firth, pardon me." Looking back to Mary I said, "May I speak to you privately?"

She glanced back at the other two, her expression thoughtful, but nodded and stepped out into the hall. The passageway was not wide—few spaces aboard ship were—and I found myself aware of how little space was between us.

I decided brevity and honesty were my best tactics.

"*Hart* is mine," I said, shoving my hands into my pockets. "Captain Fisher will sail back to Aeadine and officially take on Slader's Letter of Marque."

"Will you need to petition for your own letter?" Mary asked.

I started to nod, then shook my head. "Yes, but... I already have one, you see."

Mary looked at me curiously.

"The Usti queen has given me a commission and intends to dispatch me to the free channels." I drew a deep breath before I continued, "It seems strange, I know, to work for the Usti, but the queen has her reasons, I am told. And this gave me the opportunity to make an unusual request."

Mary leaned against the bulkhead, increasing the space between us a fraction and lacing her arms under her breasts. "Oh?"

"I will need a Stormsinger."

The woman's face darkened, so much so that I felt a stab of dread.

I hastily pulled the letter from my pocket. "I would never ask this of you, Mary, not without guarantees."

Mary took the parchment from me and unfolded it. She moved closer to the light leaking from the galley, and I hovered as she read.

"This is a contract," Mary said, lifting her eyes to mine. "Verified by Queen Inara."

"A contract for a Stormsinger aboard my ship, *Hart*." I nodded, quickly pointing to the stipulations in question. "Stormsingers used to have a guild to protect them, and I have based it off their papers. You may sign on for as short or as long a term as you choose, and there is this clause that allows you to leave if circumstances do not suit you—I left that language very broad."

Mary was silent for a long, long moment. I heard footsteps pass across the deck above and the clink of glasses from Demery's cabin, but the hammering of my heart almost drowned them both.

"And the Usti will enforce this?" Mary clarified. "What about other Stormsingers?"

"This is an exemption for you alone," I admitted. "However… It is a place to start. The beginning of change. We can be an example to the world, you and I."

Another stretch of silence. My nerves were in tatters by now, but I kept my back straight. I saw more questions behind her eyes and braced myself.

But when Mary spoke again, her inquiry was simple. "Why?"

I had an answer for this, I reminded myself. "Because I admire you, I can think of none better to guide my ship. And I cannot bear the thought of not seeing you again, Mary."

She eyed me in a way that made my mouth dry—amused, guarded, softening, with a blush creeping across her cheeks.

"Say something," I pleaded. "If Benedict and the rumors make you reluctant to associate with me, I understand, but please give me the opportunity to—"

"They're rumors." She looked down at the contract again. "I know the truth. That's not why I'm hesitating. This contract will do nothing to protect me from those who don't care for the Usti crown."

"I'll do that," I said before I could stop myself.

She smirked. "You're sweet, Samuel Rosser."

"And," I added pointedly, "you are a daughter of the Fleetbreaker, the Wold and the Dark Water. After a few seasons of experience, I doubt there will be anyone in this world that could threaten you or the ship you choose as your home."

That last word seemed to catch her, and the smile on her lips faltered. "I've much to learn," she warned.

"As do I," I returned. "Olsa has barely given me a moment's peace. But we will learn, and together? Your power and mine, and Tane and Hart?"

There were more possibilities for me, in Mere, but I did not mention those yet.

I went on, "Together, Mary? We will be a force to be reckoned with. We will fight for peace and protect our shores, and ensure those like Lirr never regain power on the Winter Sea."

Her smile returned in a rush, crooked and a little shy. "You seem quite taken by the thought of us being together."

I swallowed a lump in my throat. "I am."

She folded the contract slowly, then faced me in the close quarters of the passage. Absently, she rested her fingers on the buttons across my chest and looked up into my face. I could tell she was enjoying her power over this moment, and I might have hated her for it, if I had not loved the expression on her face—soft, coy and quizzical.

"Well, then, Samuel," she said, pushing up onto her toes. She put her lips to my cheek in the gentlest, most excruciating kiss I had ever been subjected to, and whispered in my ear, "You have a deal."

MARY

I sang softly to the brisk, salty air. The tines of the great figurehead clad the fore of *Hart* as he divided the Winter Sea, and the violet-gold of late afternoon hung in the west. To the east, the rocky northern shores of Aeadine could just be seen. I'd glimpsed them several times since I signed aboard *Hart*, but the sight still awoke a quiet ache in my chest.

Beyond that coast, beyond the craggy, sheep-strewn hills of the north, lay the Ghistwold and home. I would return to them some day, to the inn and the sunlight on the moss, and the shelter of the yew. But the Winter Sea was before me now, the wind rushed across my cheeks, and a good man stood at my shoulder in a cocked hat and a long coat.

In my bones, Tane rested content.

"They are due north," Sam murmured. He had the distant expression he wore when he was half in the Dark Water and half in the mortal world, a look I'd come to recognize well. I slipped my hand into his, keeping him rooted with me. "Past the border into Mereish waters."

"Then that's where we go." I squeezed his hand, released it, and began to sing low and steady.

The wind curled up from the south, bringing with it pale clouds of fog. It crept across the waves and slipped into my lungs—heady and sweet, bold and bracing. It tickled my cheeks and reminded me of how the leaves of the ghisten yew once rustled in a lilting, child's song.

SONGS REFERENCED

"The Female Smuggler," a traditional English ballad

"One for Sorrow," a traditional English nursery rhyme

"A Tree Song" by Rudyard Kipling

"Seal Lullaby" by Rudyard Kipling

"The Way through the Woods" by Rudyard Kipling

"The Holy Ground," a traditional Irish song

ACKNOWLEDGEMENTS

Dark Water Daughter and I have a long history. It was conceived long before my debut—in fact, it was one of the first novels I wrote, as a child. It has had many names and plots and settings, various versions that have come and gone over some twenty years. In total, I believe I rewrote this book five times before I found the right tone, shape, and structure.

Dark Water Daughter is the story I could not give up on, even though I shelved it for years at a time. Very little remains of those original versions—a nautical setting, a lost fleet, and the core cast of characters (Mary, Sam, Demery, Grant, Anne and Lirr). But I still see those other versions when I look at this book, and there's something so powerful about finally getting Mary and Sam's story out in the world.

Given how long this book's journey has been, acknowledging all those who've played a role in this story is no easy thing. But I will try!

A heartfelt thank you to my agent Naomi Davis for championing me and my stories. To my wonderful editors George Sandison and Elora Hartway, thank you so much for working on my books with me, teaching me so much, and helping me make these stories the very best they can be.

Thank you so much to Katharine Carroll, Lydia Gittins and Kabriya Coghlan for getting my books out into the world, and to

Julia Lloyd, for creating *Dark Water Daughter's* lush, watery cover.

Thank you to my Mum, who read *Dark Water Daughter* at every stage, gently critiqued, and pointed me in the right direction, who helped me write query letters at fifteen, took me to writing conferences, and giggled with me over endless typos. To my Dad, who drove me to South Carolina so I could explore the setting of the original *Dark Water Daughter* (back when it was a historical fiction), who arranged for American stamps for my SASE, and encouraged his teenage daughter to fight toward her goals. To my Grama Janet, who has shared her love for this story for so many long years, and for whose support I'm endlessly grateful for. To my brother, Eric, and my favorite human Marco—thank you for always pushing me not to give up.

To my beta readers Loie, Jean, Cheryl, Stephanie, Jenny, Gabby, Robyn, and Susanna—I hope you can see the influence you had on this this book, and know how incredibly valuable your feedback, patience, care and creativity have been! Cheryl Bowman, thank you so much for your extra work on the gorgeous map!

Thank you to my debut buddies and my agent-siblings of the SFF Powerhouse for your endless encouragement, listening ears, and wisdom. You take the loneliness out of this author life, and I'm so grateful for you.

Finally, a sincere thanks to all my readers. YOU make this possible, and worth it. Know that I see your likes, your shares, your comments and your messages, and they mean the world to me. Thank you for giving my books your time, for treasuring them, for sharing them and supporting me. I sincerely hope you've loved *Dark Water Daughter*, and that we'll share many, many more stories to come.

ABOUT THE AUTHOR

H. M. Long is a Canadian fantasy writer, author of *Hall of Smoke*, *Temple of No God, Barrow of Winter,* and *Pillar of Ash,* who loves history, hiking, and exploring the world. She lives in Ontario, but can often be spotted snooping about European museums or wandering the Alps with her husband.

For more fantastic fiction, author events,
exclusive excerpts, competitions, limited editions and more

VISIT OUR WEBSITE
titanbooks.com

LIKE US ON FACEBOOK
facebook.com/titanbooks

FOLLOW US ON TWITTER AND INSTAGRAM
@TitanBooks

EMAIL US
readerfeedback@titanemail.com